THE
UNDISCOVERED
COUNTRY

A NOVEL

MIKE NEMETH

NEW YORK

LONDON • NASHVILLE • MELBOURNE • VANCOUVER

THE UNDISCOVERED COUNTRY

A Novel

Published in New York, New York, by Morgan James Publishing. Morgan James is a trademark of Morgan James, LLC. www.MorganJamesPublishing.com

The Morgan James Speakers Group can bring authors to your live event. For more information or to book an event visit The Morgan James Speakers Group at www.TheMorganJamesSpeakersGroup.com.

Publisher's Note: This novel is a work of fiction. Names, characters, places, and incidents are either products of the author's imagination or used fictitiously. All characters are fictional, and any similarity to people living or dead is purely coincidental.

ISBN 9781683506973 paperback
ISBN 9781683506980 eBook
Library of Congress Control Number: 2017911896

Cover and Interior Design by:
Chris Treccani
www.3dogcreative.net

In an effort to support local communities, raise awareness and funds, Morgan James Publishing donates a percentage of all book sales for the life of each book to Habitat for Humanity Peninsula and Greater Williamsburg.

Get involved today! Visit
www.MorganJamesBuilds.com

For my mother
She taught me that age does not diminish value.

"...*The undiscovered country from whose bourn*
No traveler returns, puzzles the will
And makes us rather bear those ills we have
Than fly to others that we know not of?"
—**William Shakespeare,** *Hamlet*

ACKNOWLEDGMENTS

My wife, Angie, believed in this novel so I wrote it.

Thanks once again to the team at The Editorial Attic—Angie and Cheryl— for making my humble manuscript a thing of beauty.

And my gratitude to the team at Morgan James Publishing for making a man's dreams come true.

Chapter One

Although the handwritten nameplate on the door read "Elaine Marks," the woman in the bed did not look like my mother. One low-wattage light in the cold room leaked only enough illumination to reveal the woman's undignified state. Her face, obscured by an oxygen mask, was gray as the worn pillowcase beneath her bony skull, and her steel-gray hair lay in sweaty disarray, unlike the perfectly coifed, jet-black hair of the mother I embraced the day before I went to prison. This woman was smaller. Much smaller. I could have switched on the bright overhead lights, but I didn't want to alert the staff to my presence. I wasn't prepared to see this scene any more clearly either.

I took the woman's hand and recoiled at its coolness. In a panic, I leaned closer until I detected the weak flow of breath through the mask and the slight rise and fall of her shell-like chest. Then I checked the monitor on the wall above her bed. Heart rate: slow; blood pressure: low; respiratory rate: slow; blood oxygenation level: low. Slow, low, slow, low. Barely alive. Why weren't the doctors and nurses crowding around her bed? A crucifix, half-hidden by the monitor, hung above the bed, a reminder that doctors didn't have total control of this situation.

The insistent hum of pumps and monitors signaled technology's effort to keep my mother alive. The smell of illness assaulted me. I retched. Out of duty, I bent to kiss her forehead. She shuddered, whether from an involuntary response or recognition that I was with her, I didn't know. As a test, I whispered that I loved her. She did not react.

With a tired sigh, I sank into the clumsy overstuffed chair beside her bed. I remembered my promise to call Glenda, my daughter's mother, but rather than wake her at this hour, I texted her: *Made it safely. I'm fine.* A lie. I was never "fine" in Augusta.

Overnight, I had driven from my home in Dolphin Beach, Florida, through Ocala, diagonally across the state to Jacksonville, then northward to Savannah, where I exited I-95 and transitioned from the "New South" to the "Old South." Using secondary roads paralleling the Savannah River, I drove through small towns razed by General Sherman during the Civil War and past shotgun houses, plantation manors, and oak trees as tall as a house and magnolia trees as wide. Through shadows so dense my headlights could not penetrate them, I passed mile after mile of cotton fields where I imagined slaves had once toiled.

As the false dawn lit the horizon, I transitioned from "Randle," the adult persona I had invented, to "Jack," the child and the past I couldn't seem to escape. Today was just the fourth day since I had been paroled, and already I had been forced to exchange one nightmare for another. For only a moment, I closed my eyes to erase the vision of my mother in a hospital bed from the video screen in my brain.

***

A firm hand shook my shoulder. "Sir? Sir?"

With two hands, I wiped sleep from my eyes, but I couldn't touch the fatigue. A round face encircled by short blonde hair above medium-blue scrubs leaned to within inches of my face. "Are you family?"

I rocked my shoulders, stretched my legs. "I'm her son."

The nurse backed up and smiled. "Another son. Good. Can you give us a few minutes with her? We need to clean her up and get her ready for tests."

A dark-haired nurse swept into the room, went straight to Mom's bedside without acknowledging me, and stuck a needle in her arm to take blood. With both hands I pushed myself out of the chair and noted that the clock on the far wall read 6:35 a.m. I had only been asleep for an hour. I looked down at my mother. Her eyes were open. I bent over her and said, "Hello, Mom. It's Jackie."

Her eyelids fluttered, closed and opened again, but she stared straight ahead. I thought her lips moved behind her mask. Draping myself over her bed, I said, "It's Jackie, Mom. I'm here to help you."

She nodded, but her eyes didn't seem to focus. I waved a hand in front of her, but her eyes didn't track. To the blonde nurse, working at a cart covered in needles and vials, I said, "What the hell?"

She stopped her tasks and said, "She's blind."

"Blind! Blind?"

Hands on her hips, she said, "Not like Ray Charles or Stevie Wonder. I should have said, 'She can't see.' Happens sometimes with strokes."

Good God. A stroke too? When Beth, my sister-in-law, had called the night before, she told me that Mom had suffered a heart attack.

"Can she hear?"

"We think so. We need to prep her now, sir. Her doctor will be here soon."

"Okay. I'll go find a cup of coffee." I grabbed Mom's hand and gave it a gentle pat. I walked around the bed, under the TV mounted high on the wall opposite Mom's pillow, past the white board that listed nurses' and doctors' names and my brother's cell phone number. On the opposite side of the room, a sink and a counter on which a small computer screen displayed the hospital logo filled the space between the bed and the private bathroom. There wasn't a closet or a bedside table.

As I wound my way between the rolling medical carts, I asked where they had stored Mom's things, her purse and clothes. The nurse pointed to a plastic bag on a shelf under the rolling bed. "She was just wearing a nightgown when she was admitted. She didn't have a purse."

* * *

Fifteen minutes later, I returned from the cafeteria with a large black coffee to find Mom's room overflowing with medical staff. Two males in lab coats and a male nurse had joined the blonde and the brunette. Fearing the worst, I barged through the crowd to my mother's bedside and found her staring at the ceiling but still breathing. Relieved, I turned to the surprised medical staff.

The blonde nurse—I noticed now that her nametag read "Shelby"—announced, "He's another son."

The medical team relaxed. Shelby pointed to a heavyset man with rimless glasses and black lacquered hair streaked with a white stripe like a skunk. She said, "This is the cardiac surgeon, Dr. Metzger."

I stuck out my hand to shake his. That seemed to surprise him as it took him an awkward moment to accept my hand with a reluctant grip.

The other doctor, less than average height and slender, proactively reached for my hand and introduced himself as Dr. Kaplan, the hospitalist. He smiled warmly beneath soft brown curls, soft brown eyes, and a long straight nose.

As though it was intuitively obvious, Metzger said, "She's emitting the enzymes that indicate a heart attack, but that's not her only problem." He gestured toward Kaplan to add his comments.

Kaplan cleared his throat. "Our first challenge when she was admitted was her arrhythmia. Fortunately, injections directly into her heart restored a normal rhythm. We don't know what caused the arrhythmia, but we do know the arrhythmia caused her heart attack. She's retaining fluid in her lower extremities, typical of heart attack victims, so we're pushing Lasix to dry it up. The fluid did not get there overnight. It should have been a warning sign that her heart was failing."

He emphatically delivered a recap of service as though I were an intern on morning rounds. His hands moved constantly, sometimes pointing to my mother, sometimes chopping air. "She has a serious case of stasis dermatitis on her legs, and for that we've applied a topical antibiotic. It doesn't appear that was being treated either. We also suspect she suffered a stroke. Tests today will confirm it, but her loss of vision is a strong indicator. And she's getting warfarin to prevent clotting and another heart attack or another stroke." He took a breath and spread his hands like the Jesus statue above the beach in Rio de Janeiro.

I sifted through his summation to find a silver lining. "So, her heart is stable, we'll find out today what caused her heart attack so we can fix it, and then you can figure out how to restore her vision. Is that about it?"

Kaplan and Metzger traded warning looks. Metzger decided to play the bad cop. "Your mother isn't likely to survive all these problems, Mr. Marks. We don't know how much damage her heart sustained. It could stop pumping at any moment. We have no evidence that she can speak or even think following her stroke."

"She can think! She acknowledged me."

The doctors traded dark looks again. Kaplan volunteered, "She has sores on her heels and her bottom that indicate she's been bedridden for some time. She's old and weak and malnourished." He gave me sad brown eyes and pursed lips.

Malnourished? What the hell? When I called her with the news that I would soon be released from prison, she had said she was "fine." She had urged me to come see her as soon as possible, but not because of her health. All the air escaped my balloon. "What are you going to do for her?"

"We'll do an EKG to determine her heart condition, and we'll do an MRI to survey the brain damage," Metzger said. "Don't get your hopes up."

"She'll be out of the room till late afternoon," Kaplan said. Noting my red-rimmed eyes and slumped posture, he added, "You should get some sleep."

"Put your mother's affairs in order." Metzger glanced at his sympathetic colleague. "Go to the chapel and say a prayer."

We had to step aside then as attendants rolled my mother's bed out of the room. Metzger turned away and followed the patient without further ado, but Kaplan squeezed my shoulder before he left.

I wiped a tear from my right eye as I wondered if I'd ever see Mom again. Many times I had taken a knife to the ties that bound me to my parents, but I had always stopped short of slicing them all the way through. Whether I could admit it, their lives had been mooring lines lashing my little boat to origins I could neither embrace nor discard. When my father passed away, my little boat, tethered only by Mom's lifeline, swung in an aimless circle, but it soon stabilized. Losing my mother wouldn't be as easy a blow to absorb. Without her, my little boat would have no past— only an uncertain future.

Without Mom and her bed and the incessant hum of the machines that had been switched off, the room was barren, chilled, and deathly quiet. It was as gruesomely suitable for dying as for healing. I didn't have a key to Mom's house and no money for a hotel room, so I had nowhere to go. The chapel was an option, but God would recognize the hypocrisy. He knew I had a low regard for people who suddenly turn to Him when they are desperate and a low regard for institutionalized worship. My relationship with Him was consistent and continuous, but informal and private. Presumably, my brother and his wife would arrive soon, so I dropped into the ugly orange easy chair to wait for them.

Chapter Two

For the second time in less than two hours, a strange hand shook me awake.

"Where's Mom?" my sister-in-law asked.

I looked around the empty room as though Mom could be hiding in a corner. "Tests," I croaked through the cotton growing on my tongue. "They took her for tests. Won't be back till afternoon."

"Is she going to be okay?"

"I don't think so, Beth. Have you met the heart surgeon, Metzger?"

"No, just the emergency room people last night."

Sure, they expected Mom to pass during the night. Now they've had to assign specialists. "He has the bedside manner of a Nazi camp guard. He told me to put Mom's affairs in order."

With a sudden burst, Beth bawled like a child. It wasn't a good look for Mary Beth Marks. She was a plain woman of average height and build, with shapeless brown hair framing a pale complexion and pale brown eyes. As she cried, everything turned as red as a boiling lobster. I felt sorry for my sister-in-law. She was the sweetest, gentlest soul in the family, and she was married to a man exactly like my father. I levered myself out of the ugly easy chair and took her in my arms.

"There's also a hospitalist named Kaplan. He's more comforting but not a lot more optimistic."

Beth kept weeping.

"Where's Billy?" I asked.

Between sobs, she said, "Parking the car."

Good, he'd have a key to Mom's house. I wanted a hot shower and maybe another hour of sleep. "Is Katie on her way?" My sister, Katie, lived in Atlanta, less than three hours from Augusta.

"Katie can't come yet. Brad says she has work commitments."

Bradley van Kamp was my brother-in-law.

"It's Saturday, Beth. Is she working the weekend?"

"I don't know, Jack." Strident now, she leaned back in my arms but didn't try to wriggle free. "I didn't talk to Katie. I talked to Brad."

"Is he on his way?"

"Not yet."

"Does he have work commitments too?"

Exasperated, Beth blew air in my face. "Why are you giving me a hard time, Jack? I'm just delivering the message."

"Okay, Beth, but please call me Randle."

Everyone called me Jack as I grew up in Augusta, and my mother called me Jackie—an alternate form of my formal first name of John— but I symbolically erased that history when I began my professional career. My business cards and signature block read "J. Randle Marks," and I asked my colleagues to call me Randle, my mother's maiden name. Changing my name was only one of the many reasons I was the black sheep of the family. Before I left Florida for Augusta the night before, Glenda had said, "You'll always be Jack to those people. Don't waste your energy trying to change them."

"Sure," Beth said now. "I can do that."

"What about the grandkids?"

Beth slumped against me again and talked into my chest. "Joey is on his way. Brad is supposed to tell Nicki."

My siblings each had one child. Billy and Beth had a son, Joseph III, away at college. Katie and Brad had a daughter, Nicole, who was a couple of years younger than my daughter, Jamie. I had no idea what Nicole was doing with her life. I patted Beth on her back as she bathed my shirt in tears.

When William Tecumseh Marks marched through the door, Beth sensed his presence, pulled out of my embrace, and crossed her arms over her modest bosom. She did not go to her husband for comfort.

"What's going on?" Billy said in a tone that implied he was worried more about his wife in my arms than he was about his mother's status. Billy and I are opposites in every way. I'm an optimistic dreamer, while Billy is pugnacious and contemptuous. I have dark hair and brown eyes like our mother, while Billy has sandy hair—thinning—and steel-blue eyes like our father. I'm tall and lithe. Billy is short and square. I played college basketball. Billy was a power hitter in baseball and a running back in football. Unfortunately for Billy, he was one of those sad people for whom high school was the high point of a life that ran downhill after graduation.

"Mom's undergoing tests—heart and brain—and won't be back till late afternoon."

Billy moved a few steps into the room. "I didn't expect to find you here."

I glanced at Beth and saw fear on her face. When she had called the previous night, she asked that I not disclose how I had learned of Mom's hospitalization. I hadn't seen Billy or Katie since my father's funeral nearly three years ago, and neither of them had called me since my incarceration. "The hospital called me. I'm on the next-of-kin list."

Billy looked doubtful; Beth looked relieved.

"Still wearing my father's watch?" He pointed to the gold Rolex President on my wrist, my father's retirement gift from the Savannah River Plant. He didn't want to wear the symbol of his desultory career, so he presented it to me as we exited his ceremony. It was the only keepsake he had ever given me. My siblings had plundered his other possessions when he passed.

"Yes, it's *my* father's watch. The metal band wore out, so I changed to a leather strap."

Billy sneered. "Never understood why he gave it to you. He thought you were an idiot."

"The feeling was mutual."

"Then why wear it?"

"To remind myself to prove him wrong."

Billy shook his head and edged closer to us, creating a conversation circle. "What have the doctors told you?"

Ignoring Billy, I spoke directly to Beth. "What happened? I talked to Mom a week ago. She said she was fine."

"She told us you called, but she wasn't really fine, Randle. You know how she sugarcoats everything."

I did know. Mom never wanted anyone to worry about her.

"Tell me about yesterday," I said. "How did you find out? How did she get here?"

Beth flushed. Without asking Billy for permission, she said, "It started Thursday night. Mom had pain in her legs and couldn't sleep. Could hardly walk."

"The fluid buildup," Billy said.

"The symptoms of a heart attack are different for women than for men," I said. "It was about to happen, and she didn't know it."

Beth nodded. "Friday around lunchtime, she used the bathroom but then she couldn't stand up. She was paralyzed. She had to crawl to the bedroom to get to a phone."

"Took her four hours," Billy added.

"She called me at home," Beth continued. "Billy was at work, so I called 9-1-1 and met the first responders at her house. It was terrible, Randle. Her panties were still around her ankles. She was so embarrassed."

I could imagine the scene: the prim Southern Belle in shocking disarray. It made me very sad to think this might be the messy end of my mother's neat and proper life. "Could she see?"

"I guess so. She crawled to the phone, dialed my number."

That implied she had the stroke while she was in the hospital, under a doctor's care. That puzzled me. I paused to think about the ramifications.

"So they transported her, but then they didn't do anything for her."

"They gave her shots that saved her life, Randle. They put her on oxygen."

True, but they didn't assign a cardiologist and hospitalist until she proved she could survive the night.

"We were here all night," Billy said.

I knew that wasn't precisely true, but I didn't challenge him. "Is she still paralyzed? They never mentioned it to me."

"No," Beth said. "She regained movement after they treated her in the emergency room."

That's a relief. Now that I had the background, I recapped for Billy and Beth what Metzger and Kaplan had told me. They were shocked to hear that Mom couldn't see. I had more pressing matters to pursue.

"Why is she malnourished?"

Billy constructed an innocent expression. "She's not. She gained weight, ballooned to a hundred sixty pounds at one point."

"She's a skeleton now. Do you guys check on her?"

Billy's nostrils flared like a wounded bull in a fighting ring. "We live in Martinez, not around the corner. Why didn't *you* check on her?"

"I've been occupied."

"With that hocus pocus you call science? How's that worked out for you?"

"You know where I've been."

"Yeah, making license plates." He snorted in derision.

I had to change the subject before I strangled my baby brother. "When was the last time she's been to the doctor?"

Billy shrugged. "Not long ago."

"Was she being treated for water retention?"

"Sure, she has pills."

"What about the infection on her legs?"

"She takes steroids. We took care of her while you were 'occupied.'"

"I'm here now. I'll look after her."

Billy shook his head. "Too late, Jack. You can go back to your ex-wives and your boats and your houses—all the things that have been more important to you than family."

"Randle."

"Huh?"

"You need to call me Randle."

Billy waved a dismissive hand. "Go home, Jack. Leave the dirty work to us, as always."

"I'm staying until Mom is well. She doesn't need you," I said.

Billy's fists curled into tight balls, and his sinewy arms flexed over and over. He wanted to hit me in the worst way, and that's what I wanted too.

Beth broke the tension, asking me, "Where are you staying?"

Billy and I relaxed and moved slightly apart. The routine logistics for family visits, established decades ago for no explainable reason, were that Katie and her family had first dibs on Mom's house while my family and I stayed in hotels. Of course, that protocol assumed Mom was in her home as well. But right now, I had no money for a hotel.

"Since Mom is in the hospital and Katie's not here, there's room at Mom's," I said.

"You always stay in a hotel. *Our* house was never good enough for you," Billy said.

"Give me the keys." I stuck my hand in front of Billy.

Like a kid who won't share his candy, Billy smirked and shook his head. "You're not welcome in our house."

Beth gave me a sad look. Reluctant to reveal my penury and give Billy a reason to feel superior, I made a show of hugging my brother's wife before moving to the doorway. I pointed at Billy and said, "See if you can keep Mom alive until I get back."

Chapter Three

Since Billy didn't want me to stay at Mom's house, I was determined to do exactly that. Two months ago, while I was still in prison, Mom had written me a letter in which she requested my advice about a family estate issue. She hadn't elaborated on the matter but asked me to visit her after my release. She also asked me not to discuss her request with my siblings. I assumed my brother wasn't managing her finances effectively, but I hadn't considered it an urgent matter. I had intended to enjoy my new freedom for a while before braving a trip back "home," but now I feared she wouldn't be able to communicate her concerns. I wanted to see if she had left me any clues. Then there was the pragmatic matter of money—I had none.

Mom's house—our childhood home—stood on Lumpkin Road, just five miles from the hospital. The two-story white colonial sat one hundred feet back from the roadway and ten or fifteen feet above it. The property, five acres of lush lawn with a border of mature trees, was zoned commercial because the original owner had had a row of small cottages for rent at the back of it. My father bulldozed those cottages when he bought the place for the princely sum of thirty-five thousand dollars. Today the property was easily worth ten times that much and had long been clear of any liens.

As I looked around the yard, two memories came to mind. In the first, I was an adolescent watching my attractive mother cut the back lawn with a riding mower while wearing a bikini. She only did that while my father was at work. In the other memory, I was a preteen hiding Easter eggs for Katie and Billy to find. I always cheated so Katie would find more eggs than Billy.

We had joked that our home was the "Church of Marks," as it was situated beside the Cliffwood Presbyterian Church and across the street from the Lumpkin Road Baptist Church. Whenever we returned to the house, we would say we were "going to church." Of course, our church was a rare phenomenon in Augusta—a Catholic church.

On the small back porch, I searched the usual places for a spare key—under a planter, the underside of the railing, the ledge above the door—but couldn't find one, so I moved around the far side of the house. Opposite the driveway and sheltered from the street, I found myself staring at the windows to Mom's master bedroom. The first one I leaned into and pushed up on didn't budge. Neither did the second. For as long as I had lived in this house, Mom had cracked a window at night for fresh air, but now the windows were sealed as though it were a mausoleum. At my feet lay a row of decorative rocks bordering the flower bed. I picked up a large one and, without hesitation, hurled it through the window. I had learned an abiding lesson in prison: I had a license to be disinhibited. I could do most anything to survive. Everyone in prison learned the same lesson.

After picking glass shards out of the sill, I levered myself through the opening and dropped into Mom's bedroom. It was the first time in my life that I had entered my parents' room unaccompanied and without permission. Mom's bed was unmade, and a telephone handset lay on the floor. I tossed the rock out the window, replaced the phone in its cradle, and walked through the country kitchen to the back door. Beside the door, an alarm keypad flashed the word "unsecure" in iridescent green letters that would be visible in the dark. I had never known the house to have an alarm. I wasn't sure Mom would know how to operate one. Thankfully, it had not been set. Below the alarm, a rack held about a dozen keys of various shapes. I tried each of them in the kitchen door, but none worked. Once upon a time, Mom had kept a spare on that key rack, but things change.

I didn't relish the idea of coming and going through a broken window, so I walked through the house, looking for her purse. I spotted it on a side chair in her bedroom and unzipped one of its pockets, which revealed a keyring holding two keys. A silver key, its fingerhold wrapped in dirty white tape, unlocked the back door. Smudged black numbers, 0125, could barely be distinguished on the tape. I had heard about dementia patients who pin their addresses to their shirts or blouses so they can remember their address when they are away from home. Mom's house number was 1927, so that wasn't the significance of 0125. I figured the numbers were the passcode for the alarm system.

I carried my bags into the kitchen and began a quick inspection. There were no dishes in the sink. The pantry contained a couple of lonely cans of soup and stale bread. The refrigerator had only butter, eggs, and milk. My mother had not been eating regularly.

The living room—Mom called it a drawing room because she received guests there—looked like a furniture showroom that no shoppers ever entered. The hardwood floor was waxed and covered by the same Oriental rugs I had seen three years ago, when my father passed. My father had used the drawing room as a family court to hold his wayward children to account. Although he had died three years ago, his spirit permeated the large space. He hadn't believed in corporal punishment, yet he had effectively communicated his displeasure with neglect, disappointment, shame, and ridicule. For me, in particular, he set unattainable expectations to crush my spirit and erode my confidence. Although I had attended Georgia Tech as he wished, I chose not to become the nuclear engineer he had hoped I'd become. Instead I became a data scientist, a profession he neither understood nor respected. I had made the basketball team as a "walk on," but I never played enough minutes to earn a scholarship.

Although I had always eked out a living, I had never held a job for more than three or four years because the groundbreaking companies I helped launch collapsed like a row of domino bones. Although my father never warmed toward Glenda, my first wife, for him our divorce confirmed I would never be the kind of man who sustained a marriage and provided for a family over a lifetime. Although he hadn't been alive to witness it, my felony conviction would have confirmed for him his judgment of me as a failure. Although I wouldn't have to confront his physical being, the butterflies that hatched in my stomach whenever I stepped into my boyhood home were back.

The parlor, at the front of the house, was more welcoming, carpeted, and somewhat lived in. My parents had reserved it as their private sanctuary. A lap blanket draped a rocking chair that must have been Mom's favorite place to rest. A magazine lay open on a table beside the chair.

Back in the master bedroom, I threw glass shards out the broken window and closed the drapes. Then I made the bed before surveying the master bath. On the vanity, a cluster of pill bottles indicated that my mother was indeed under a doctor's care. All the prescriptions had been written by a Dr. Fowler.

Upstairs I deposited my bags in the large room Billy and I had shared as kids. Two double beds flanked a bedside table that had been uneasily contested territory. On the common wall with Katie's room, my father had constructed two built-in desks, sitting side by side, and in between, a built-in bookcase still held model airplanes and long-forgotten children's books. Neither Billy nor I had had enough privacy or enough distance from one another to be comfortable. He was eight years younger than me, so we had no shared experiences, no shared secrets, no common friends, no reason to bond. As adults, we had lived hundreds of miles apart and had rare encounters at family events. I hardly knew the man.

Katie's private bedroom and the one Jack-and-Jill-style bath we had shared with her completed the second floor. Six years younger than me, Katie hadn't yet become a makeup- and fashion-crazed teenager when I escaped to Georgia Tech, but later she became a daily obstacle for Billy. Like Billy, Katie inherited our father's dishwater blond hair, blue eyes, and lack of stature. Like Billy, she also inherited our father's Catholic devotion and "Yankee" sympathies. While I had attended a public high school, our father insisted that Katie and Billy attend Aquinas Catholic High School.

I sat on "my" bed, lumpy and worn out, and rang Katie. Her voice mail message informed me in a superior tone that Ms. Van Kamp was not available to take phone calls. I left a message urging her to call me ASAP.

Next I called Glenda at her store in Oldsmar. As I brought my ex-wife up to date, I closed my eyes and composed a picture of her. She was of medium height but appeared taller because of her slim build, ballerina-like posture, and unruly pile of fiery-red hair that matched her personality. I imagined her standing in her shop, a little store that attracted "earth muffins"—aging hippies and beatniks and New Age spiritualists—to whom she sold an eclectic combination of candles, scents, books, figurines, and even clothing. I thought of it as the Florida version of a New Orleans voodoo shop. While we were married, she had devoted all her energy to it, to the detriment of our marriage. Of course, that hadn't been the only reason for our divorce.

"The prognosis is poor, Glenda. Can you come up here?"

Glenda made a tortured sound. In her lyrical Southern drawl, she said, "Oh, Randle, if you need me, I'll come. But you know I'd rather kiss a snake than sit in a waiting room with those people. They don't like me, and I don't like them."

She considered my family to be rigid, self-righteous, secretive, and rude. They had no kinder assessment of Glenda. They found her to be flighty, free-spirited, and imbued with odd beliefs. Had we all lived in seventeenth-century Salem, Billy would have accused her of being a witch. It didn't help that Glenda had been raised a Southern Baptist.

"Will you be okay down there by yourself?"

She snickered. "Sure. Carrie's in prison, and I can handle the Beretta."

Carrie was my second wife and the biggest mistake I had ever made. Glenda was only half-joking about having to protect herself with a gun.

"What about the wedding?"

"It's all set for a week from today."

Glenda and I had been divorced for more than eight years, but we had never stopped caring about one another, never stopped wondering if we shouldn't get back together. When I was divorcing Carrie, two years ago, Glenda and I had rekindled our romance. She had been a willing and enthusiastic partner in our conspiracy to send Carrie to jail. While I was in prison, she had visited regularly and we had decided to remarry, much to the consternation of those who cared about both of us.

"Shouldn't we reschedule?"

Agitated and strident now, she said, "We can't do that. The arrangements have been made."

"We haven't told Jamie." We had planned to disclose our plans to Jamie the night before, at a backyard family barbeque and welcome-home party, but I had packed a bag, jumped in my Bronco, and rushed off to Augusta as soon as Beth gave me the news about Mom.

After a moment, Glenda calmly said, "Let me worry about Jamie. If worse comes to worse, Jamie and I will fly up to join you. Otherwise, get your mother on the path to recovery and come back to your real family." To avoid a confrontation, I agreed. Satisfied, Glenda said she had customers to tend to, so we hung up. I stretched out on the bed, closed my eyes, and tried to sleep, but too many thoughts raced through my cluttered mind. After rolling around for thirty minutes, I got up to take a shower and prepare to head back to the hospital. But then my cell phone rang and stopped me in midstep.

A tired female voice said, "Hey, Jack, I didn't recognize your number."

"Randle."

"Hunh?"

"My name is Randle."

"Whatever." I heard a sniffle, as though she had a cold. "I'll call you Captain America, you want me to."

"Why aren't you here in Augusta?"

"I'll get there. I just can't come yet."

"Is work that important?" Katie was a successful commercial realtor and her husband, Brad, was an independent financial advisor. They had a flashy lifestyle that my father both abhorred and threw in my face whenever we argued about careers.

"There's a lot going on."

Katie sounded half-asleep or drugged. I had to shake her out of her lethargy. "Mom's going to die, and you're going to miss saying goodbye to her."

"Oh, Jack." She sniffled again. "Sorry, *Randle*. Billy cries wolf every few weeks. While you were away, he had me over there five or six times and they were all false alarms."

"It's serious this time, Katie. The doctors think this is the end."

After thirty seconds of silence, Katie said, "I'll get there as soon as I can."

I asked whether she planned to stay at Mom's and so forth, but there was no response. Apparently, she had fallen asleep and dropped the phone without hanging up.

I gave up and hung up and stripped and showered using soap and shampoo that had been left behind by a woman. While I toweled off, I peeked into Katie's old room. Dirty sheets lay in a ball on the stripped bed. The comforter lay in a heap on the floor. The wastebasket overflowed. Katie had indeed been here recently, but Mom had not climbed the stairs to clean up after her.

Dressed in shorts, Top-Siders, and a Polo shirt, I drove to a grocery and bought beer, bread and cold cuts. That was all I could afford. It felt eerie to be in the house alone, in this place filled with painful memories, so I drove back to safe ground—the hospital.

Chapter Four

St. Thomas Aquinas Hospital squatted on the southern end of the Bobby Jones Expressway. In the years since Billy had been born here, an addition of glass and steal for emergency care had been sewn onto one end of the red brick main building, and a two-story stucco appendage, housing an outpatient clinic and offices for doctors' visits, had been tacked onto the back. In the main lobby, little had changed. The interior was clean but worn; the paint was fresh but dull beige and pale green; the air was redolent with a musty-cum-medicinal smell.

An elevator took me to the cardiac ward on the fourth floor, where I emerged onto one long institutional corridor, more oppressive in its lack of light and air than any prison block. A faint but pervasive electronic hum accompanied me as I limped down the linoleum hallway. Every twenty paces or so, a grotto had been carved into the wall to hold a statuette of the Virgin Mary or Saint Thomas Aquinas. They reminded those who passed by that death is rebirth and that good Catholic souls join the saints in a better life. Or perhaps they reminded a patient's family that if they prayed hard enough, the patient might escape this dungeon.

Mom hadn't returned from her tests, so I wandered around until I found Billy and Beth in the waiting room. Beth sat silently in a side chair, while Billy stared out a window with his back to me. Another family huddled at the far end of the room, whispering urgently to one another. When Beth saw me, she gasped. I had been wearing jeans when I arrived, and now she saw my leg for the first time.

"My God, Randle, are you in pain?"

Billy turned around and gave his wife a dirty look. It pleased me that she called me Randle over her husband's objections. "No pain, just scars. Now the leg is three-eighths shorter than the right, so I wear a riser in my shoe to level my hips."

Beth cupped her hands over her mouth. Frowning, and pointing to my mangled left leg, visible below my shorts, she asked, "Are you going to get it fixed?"

I glanced at my "war" wound. The steel rod that had replaced my tibia was canted at an odd angle, and where a bulging calf muscle should have given the leg a humanoid shape, a bundle of fleshy nodules like the knuckles on your fist were fastened to the leg by zipperlike incision scars. More scars bisected my knee, and my kneecap protruded in the shape of an inverted triangle. More ruined leg hid beneath my shorts. The wounds were reminders of the gunfight with Carrie and her ex-Green Beret ex-husband aboard my boat, the *Wahine II*. I was more concerned about getting the boat fixed—it had absorbed multiple shotgun blasts and pistol shots—than I was about my leg. The leg was an eyesore but didn't hurt anymore.

"It is 'fixed,'" I said. "Just needs a little dressing up once I find health insurance. Do you think Obamacare covers cosmetic surgery?"

Beth chuckled dismissively, while Billy moved closer to have a look. "Shotgun?" he asked.

"Twelve gauge."

Billy smirked. "How come they didn't finish you off?"

The cops had asked the same question. "I had a pistol and I used it."

Beth gasped again. Billy said, "And you went to prison for shooting people."

Shooting people didn't put me behind bars, but it kept me safe while there. Most of the prisoners shied away from the crazy guy who tried to kill his wife. I didn't feel obligated to explain the story to my brother. "I wasn't the only one who went to prison. Carrie's still wearing pinstripes."

"Carrie was always good to me," Billy said. "Good to Mom too. You were her problem."

"You have no idea who she is."

"Well, we all know the other one. I hear you're shacking up with 'the witch' again."

He meant Glenda. Mom must have told him about my living arrangements. I let Billy's remark pass and sat on a couch. That left Billy the option to sit next to me or stand. He stood.

Wanting to shift the conversation to a more congenial subject, Beth said, "Where did you find a room?"

"Mom's house," I said innocently.

"What?" Billy said, agitated. He turned to Beth and said, "Didn't you set the alarm?"

Beth appeared ready to cry. Her face scrunched into a small ball like Kleenex ready for the wastebasket. "We were in a hurry to get Mom to the hospital," she whined.

Hoping to defuse the squabble, I said cheerily, "I realized I had an old key from years ago, and I'll be darned if it doesn't still work."

"That can't be," Billy said suspiciously. "We changed the locks a couple of months ago."

I threw up my hands and shrugged. "Maybe you didn't change the kitchen door."

His lips quivered nervously, but he didn't speak. Then, as though it had suddenly occurred to him, he said, "When Katie gets here, you'll have to move."

Having just spoken to Katie, I said, "She's in no hurry, says you've had her over here for too many of your wild goose chases and will wait this one out."

Billy appeared genuinely confused. "I haven't asked her to come over here. She sneaks over here so she can be with Mom without us around."

That confused me. Why would Katie lie? To mollify Billy, I said, "When she gets here, I'll move. No problem."

Billy exhaled loudly. Then he pointed a finger at me, just like my father once did. "Don't mess with Mom's things. She doesn't like that. And clean up after yourself."

"Sure." To Beth, I said, "Will Joey and Nicole show up today?"

Billy and Beth traded cautionary looks. Beth answered me. "Joey will be here tomorrow. I don't know about Nicki."

"Joey is at Georgia College in Milledgeville, right?"

"Yes, he's a junior now. He doesn't like to be called Joey anymore, sounds childish. His friends call him Trey, for Joseph Marks the third. But he still lets me call him Joey."

And his mom is proud of him. Joseph III, named after our father and grandfather, had now progressed a year in school further than his father and his aunt, both of whom had dropped out of college after two lackluster years. Beth hadn't attended college. In defense of Katie, she had dropped out of Vanderbilt to marry Brad and start a family. But Billy had not been up to the academic rigor at the University of Georgia in Athens.

"Where's Nicki?"

Billy shot another warning look at his wife.

In a falsely cheery voice, Beth said, "She's working in Florida. She'll have to drive all the way up here."

I nodded. For some reason, they didn't want to talk about Nicki, so I was about to change the subject when a petite woman in civilian clothes poked her head in the room. "Are you the Marks family?"

My heart sank. Billy choked out, "Yes."

"I'm Karen Schmidt, the patient advocate."

I was pretty sure real doctors announced deaths, so I relaxed. Ms. Schmidt, who looked like a maiden aunt, held out a hand. No one seemed to know what to do, so I shook it. Billy and Beth gathered themselves and did likewise. In her other hand, Ms. Schmidt carried a sheaf of papers. She waved them at us.

"Your mother doesn't have a living will, so it's standard procedure in cases like hers to get a DNR."

Before I could respond, Beth asked, "What's a DNR?"

"A Do Not Resuscitate order. You don't want her on life support, do you?"

Billy and Beth shook their heads no.

"What do you mean by 'cases like' our mother's?" I made air quotes with my fingers.

Ms. Schmidt seemed taken aback. She stumbled a bit before saying, "I've been told we don't expect her to be with us much longer."

Got it. Ms. Schmidt is a vulture. "You're way premature," I said. "No one expected her to live through the night, but she did. She's undergoing tests now. We'll wait for the results."

Ms. Schmidt was flustered. "This will apply in any case. No matter how long she survives." She extended the papers and a pen toward us, and Billy took them. He sat on the couch, ready to sign.

I couldn't let that happen. I couldn't let Mom pass without a fight. I grabbed the pen and threw it, startling the other family at the back of the room.

"Hey!" Billy yelled. "I have her power of attorney."

"That doesn't give you the right to decide her medical treatment. The only people who can do that are Mom, a legal guardian, or a Georgia Advance Directive for Healthcare—in other words, a living will. Tell him I'm right, Ms. Schmidt."

Ms. Schmidt looked scared. "He's right," she said to Billy. "But with your POA, you can sign the DNR if she's unable to communicate her wishes."

Billy hesitated. In that moment, I grabbed the DNR and ripped it in half. Like the pen, I threw it, but it didn't fly very well. It fluttered to the floor in pieces. "We're going to give Mom a chance—a chance to live, a chance to express her wishes." *And a chance to tell me why she was worried about the estate.*

Fear blanched Ms. Schmidt's face. She moved away from me while Billy sat motionless, his mouth open. Beth regarded me with something like respect. She'd love to defy Billy as I had done.

"I'll have to report this," Ms. Schmidt said as she backed farther away.

"Be sure to tell your superiors that Mom's family is in charge of her health, not some social worker," I said.

She huffed and puffed, turned on her heel, and left.

"Why are you making Mom suffer?" Billy said.

"Why are you letting her die?"

Billy stood and grabbed his wife's hand. "Come on, Beth. I don't want to be around the crazy man. Let's go to the cafeteria." He dragged Beth out the door.

The other family rose and followed my brother and his wife out. As they passed, they gave me plenty of space and dirty looks. They weren't gone long when doctors Kaplan and Metzger shuffled into the waiting room. Behind them, attendants pushed Mom and her bed down the hallway toward her room. Kaplan and Metzger marched to a stop in front of me like grammar school kids reporting to the principal. Simultaneously, they noticed my leg. Metzger tilted his head, curious, like a neophyte in an abstract art museum. Kaplan grimaced.

"It's not as bad as it looks," I said. "Have to find the time to have some cosmetic surgery."

The doctors did not comment. They did a bit of Alphonse and Gaston before Metzger found his tongue. "We've identified your mother's problem. She has a faulty mitral valve. It caused an atrial fibrillation, which triggered the heart attack."

When Metzger stopped suddenly, Kaplan felt obliged to explain. "The mitral valve sits between the upper and lower chambers of the heart. The upper chamber fills with returning blood, and when the chamber is full, the valve opens so the blood can flow into the lower chamber to be pumped around the body. Then the valve closes so that blood can fill the upper chamber while blood is pumped out of the lower chamber. It's an asynchronous process. Your mother's valve doesn't close properly, so when the lower chamber pumps and squeezes, blood flows back into the upper chamber, interrupting the incoming flow and disrupting the rhythm of the process. When the backwash becomes extreme, it's like your car engine has lost one cylinder and the rest aren't firing in the right sequence. The engine seizes up and parts break."

Metzger looked at Kaplan as though that were the least apt analogy he had ever heard, but I understood it.

"That can be fixed, can't it?"

"If your mother was young, strong, and healthy," Metzger said, "I could fix it. But she is old, weak, and sick, so I can't fix it."

I turned to Kaplan. He gave me puppy dog eyes. "Your mother can't endure that kind of surgery."

I looked back at Metzger to see his self-satisfied smirk. I suspected he would rather be right about her impending doom than save her life and prove himself wrong.

"We're not giving up on my mother. We'll nurse her back to strength so she can endure the surgery."

They looked at each other and then looked away. After an uncomfortable moment, Metzger delivered the *coup de grâce*. "Look, Mr. Marks, the valve is malfunctioning. Your mother's heart will go into A-fib again long before she becomes strong and healthy. You need to accept the truth." He punctuated his statement with a crisp, short nod. Like an actor who had just delivered his last lines, he then left the stage.

Kaplan took my arm above the elbow and led me back to the couch. Gently, he sat me down. "Your mother's heart is weak, but it's functioning. If she doesn't experience another A-fib episode, she *will* grow stronger. I've ordered that she be fed intravenously."

"Thanks. I'm grateful."

"I'm also adding an ophthalmologist to the team. Your mother's loss of vision isn't due to a stroke."

That got my attention. "Then what?"

"We don't know. That's why the ophthalmologist." He smiled. "Tomorrow you'll meet the neurologist, Dr. Rosenberg, as well. He says your mother suffered three ministrokes, but they weren't in the area that controls vision. Better yet, they weren't caused by blood clots."

He waited for me to digest that information. "Then what?"

"It's a bit of a mystery. We'll ask Rosenberg tomorrow. Till then, go tell your mother goodnight. We've given her a sedative so she will sleep deeply and calmly. No need for you to stay here."

Kaplan left to take care of other business, and I walked down the hallway to my mother's room. She was alone, but she wasn't asleep. The monitor above her head showed that her blood pressure had slightly improved and her oxygenation rate was nearly normal. Progress.

I took her hand and kissed it. Then close to her ear, I whispered that we were going to make her well, get her out of the hospital, and get her back home. I guaranteed it. Behind her mask, she smiled.

Before I left, I erased Billy's cell phone number on the whiteboard and substituted my own. Then I drove downtown to my favorite restaurant, the Frog Hollow Tavern on Broad Street. On the way, I called my literary agent, Tim Rosenthal. Time in prison had passed quickly because I used it to write a book, *Medical Predestination: The Relationship between Genetics and Disease.* Now I had speaking and consulting assignments waiting for me. I looked forward to the coming weeks, to my book launch and interviews, and to making some money to support my family. Right now, however, I needed to clear my calendar so I could spend an entire week with my mother before returning to Florida to get married.

"Randle? What's up, buddy?"

"I'm in Augusta. My mother's in the hospital. We don't know if she's going to make it."

"I'm really sorry to hear that, Randle, but this couldn't come at a worse time. When will you be back?"

"I have no idea. Depends on her progress."

"You have to be back by Thursday. That's your book launch party, then you've got a speech to the Chamber of Commerce on Friday and a book signing on Saturday. That's all in Tampa, but the following week we're on the road: Stanford, San Francisco, Los Angeles—"

I cut him off. "Stop, Tim. When are the events in Augusta and Atlanta?"

"I'm working on Atlanta. Tampa and California are more important."

"Understood, but now we have to make Georgia a priority. I'll call you when I know more, but I'm sure we'll have to push Tampa and California into the future."

"Randle, there's no 'pushing' these events. We'll have to cancel and hope we can reschedule."

"That's what you're good at, Tim. I'll call you with news before Monday so you'll know what to do when you get to the office."

I ate shrimp and grits and the chef's unique version of mac and cheese, made with lasagna noodles and smoked gouda. I imagined Billy and Beth eating pudding at the hospital cafeteria. That cheered me up.

Chapter Five

When I bounced into Mom's room at seven a.m. on Sunday, I was rested, albeit tattooed with the imprints of angry bedsprings. I was also confident—I had not received a call from the hospital overnight.

"Morning, Shelby. How's she doing?"

Shelby was already at work, swabbing Mom's face with a wet towel. She turned toward me and pointed to the counter by the sink. There, a doctor I didn't recognize was typing into the computer.

I waited for him to finish and then said, "Hi, I'm her son, Randle."

He stuffed his hands into the pockets of his lab coat and said, "Harrison. Immunology."

Young, with long, carelessly swept blond hair, Harrison looked more like a model for the cover of a trashy novel than a doctor.

"What's going on?" I asked.

"Your mother has a B strep infection. We found it in the overnight blood sample."

"B strep? Is it serious?"

"B streptococcus. It's common in women, so she probably brought it in with her. Not serious for healthy women, but your mother's immune system is weak, so it's a threat. We can't let it spread to other patients, so we have to stop it in its tracks."

"Can you?"

"I've started a course of antibiotics, and we'll keep an eye on her." Harrison gave me a tight smile and walked out of the room.

I moved to Mom's bedside, where Shelby was swabbing Mom's arms and hands. "Got to keep her clean to fight the bacteria," Shelby said. Then she looked at me with compassion. "If you want some good news, she won't have to wear the oxygen mask. Her saturation level is good, and her respiratory rate is decent. Blood pressure and heart rate are still a concern, but she's hanging in there."

"Still blind?"

"Yes, the ophthalmologist, Dr. Nieman, is due any time now. And the patient advocate wants another word with you."

Shelby moved to the computer and began scrolling through the pages. The computer had apparently replaced the old-fashioned chart at the foot of the bed.

Mom grinned into space. In a hoarse voice, she said, "Will you get me out of here, Jackie?"

Her once peaches-and-cream complexion, still beautiful and unlined at eighty years of age, was now a sickly gray. With her bright brown eyes and shiny black hair, Mom normally looked cute and doll-like. In his more gracious moments, my father had referred to her as "Doll" or "Doll Face."

I took her hand and kissed her dry lips. "We'll get you out of here soon, Mom. Till then, you have to rest and follow doctor's orders."

She frowned. Like me, she wasn't good at taking orders.

I asked Shelby to bring some water for Mom. As she ran tap water into a glass, brought it to Mom, and helped her drink, I did two Google searches. In the first, I found a quote from the Hippocratic Oath that I wanted to use on Ms. Schmidt. In the second search, I found background information on B strep in Wikipedia.

As Shelby wiped a drop of water from Mom's chin and I read the Wikipedia entry, an army of medical practitioners crowded into the room. Metzger led the invasion followed by Ms. Schmidt, who peeled off and leaned against the wall next to the door. Kaplan, looking sheepish, entered with a tall bespectacled doctor I assumed to be Nieman, the ophthalmologist. Trailing behind was a fortyish doctor with patchy black hair. That had to be Rosenberg, the neurologist. At the last moment, Harrison ducked in the door, completing the team.

So, Ms. Schmidt has brought reinforcements.

Ms. Schmidt crossed her arms and adopted a haughty expression like that teacher you hated in fourth grade. Metzger spoke for the group, which was uniformly tense. "We don't think you understand your mother's prognosis, Mr. Marks. We're all here to answer your questions, but I'll summarize for you: the heart attack damaged her heart, and it's barely pumping. She has a faulty mitral valve that will undoubtedly trigger another attack, and she won't survive it. She's blind, and that's a very scary situation for her. She's had several strokes, and they were likely connected to the heart attack."

I glanced at Rosenberg, and he cocked his head as though to say, "Maybe." Everyone turned toward the door then as Billy shouldered his way into the room. Beth was left standing in the hallway. Billy had the good sense to listen before speaking.

Metzger resumed his summation. "The fluid that had built up in her legs has now found its way to her lungs. If that isn't reversed, we won't have to wait for another A-fib episode—the pneumonia will end her life. And we've just discovered she has a strep infection that could be fatal."

I glanced at Harrison. He shrugged.

Metzger was going to continue, but I cut him off. "I know she's sick, doctor."

"She's very, very sick, Mr. Marks, and we can't operate. The best thing would be to move her to a hospice where she can be cared for, a place where the family can make her last days comfortable."

Metzger was fortunate I wasn't holding a weapon. He saw my fury and held up a hand. "Sign the DNR, Mr. Marks. Save yourself the agony of life support and decisions about pulling the plug." He gestured to Ms. Schmidt, who nodded. She had obviously organized this lynch party.

I waited for my body to return to a normal temperature. The group probably thought I was considering Metzger's recommendation. I was not. As the tallest person in the room, I had a perch from which to deliver my response.

"That is a living, breathing, thinking, and feeling human being," I said, pointing to my mother. "Assuming God has a plan, we're all tools for His purposes. Your role as skilled tools is to heal that human being until His will overrides your skill. It's not your prerogative to make decisions for Him, and it's sure as hell not my job either."

I heard intakes of breath and shuffling. Ms. Schmidt's face contorted into an angry mask. Billy looked scared. "Let me remind you," I continued, "that you all took the Hippocratic Oath and spoke aloud the words, 'Above all, I must not play at God.' I looked it up."

Now the doctors gave one another embarrassed looks. I had them on the run. "I also looked up B streptococcus in the Wiki." I waved my cell phone at them. "I learned that most people contract it in hospitals. Since my mother's case wasn't discovered until she had been here for thirty hours, I'd guess she contracted the infection right here in your hospital."

Harrison turned scarlet. The other doctors avoided eye contact.

"If she dies of the infection, you can expect a lawsuit."

Ms. Schmidt's mouth formed a large "O." Metzger inched toward me, invading my space. "See here, Marks, there's no need to threaten us. We're all trying to do what's best."

"Good." I turned directly to Metzger. "If we can clear up the peripheral problems—infections and blindness—my mother can gain strength so you can fix her heart. I am not going to let her die for lack of attention, and neither are you."

Metzger shook his head. "Believe me, Marks, there's nothing I can do." He muscled his way through the crowd toward the door. Before exiting, he said, "The rest of you can do what you want."

Ms. Schmidt elbowed Harrison out of the way and traipsed after her ally. Harrison slipped out behind her. Kaplan grabbed Nieman by the arm and walked up to me. Rosenberg, left standing alone, said, "Call me later, Dr. Kaplan." Then he left as well.

Kaplan smiled and shook his head in wonderment. "You made a few enemies, but every patient should have an advocate like you, Mr. Marks."

"Call me Randle."

"Okay, call me Daniel. This is Dr. Nieman, the ophthalmologist. Let's give him some space so he can have a look at your mother."

I turned back to Mom and saw that her eyes sparkled. I bent to kiss her forehead and heard her say, "You gave 'em hell, Jackie."

I patted her cheek then pulled Billy with me out of the room. Billy pushed Beth ahead of him, and together we walked to the waiting room. On this Sunday morning, families crowded the space. Beth sat in the one empty seat, and Billy and I stood on either side of her.

Between clenched teeth, Billy hissed at me, "There's nothing they can do. Why piss them off?"

I scoffed at him. "There's plenty they can do. They just need motivation."

Billy growled and found a different line of attack. "It's not right to use Mom's house when she's not there. I moved you to the budget motel on the Bobby Jones Expressway. For a man used to a prison cell, it will seem like a palace."

What? "Okay, Billy, you want a war, you'll get a war."

He gave me a self-satisfied grin. I stared straight ahead, making no eye contact. Synchronously, we rocked from side to side uncomfortably and silently far longer than we had anticipated. After nearly forty-five minutes, Kaplan stuck his head through the door, assessed the crowd, and waved at us to join him in the hallway. Nieman stood beside him.

"I've added another drug to your mother's regimen for the fluid buildup in her lungs," Kaplan said without preamble and without emotion. "We'll feed her by mouth today so she gains strength faster."

"Thanks," I said, but Kaplan ignored me and turned the conversation over to Nieman.

"I found mucus and white cells in the patient's eyes," Nieman began. "She has an infection. Her vision loss could be due to a wall of floaters—infectious material in her eyes. If that's the case, I can prescribe an antibiotic and restore her vision."

"That's fabulous," I said.

"I've taken a culture and sent it to the lab. Once they identify the bacteria, I can prescribe the correct antibiotic."

"It can't be the B strep," I said. "She was blind before she got that infection."

Nieman regarded me as though I were a poisonous spider crawling up his leg. Kaplan gave me a dirty look. I had made a mistake.

"I should have a lab report before the end of the day," Nieman said. He and Kaplan traded nods, and Nieman walked away.

Trying to recover, I said, "We really appreciate this, Daniel. You're giving Mom a fighting chance."

Kaplan didn't answer immediately. He hesitated as though he were considering how to jump off a cliff.

I saved him by saying to Billy and Beth, "Let's sit with Mom. The waiting room is overcrowded."

Kaplan grabbed my arm before I could walk toward her room. With a pained expression, he said, "I can't let you back in there."

"Why not?"

"The hospital administration has restricted your access to visiting hours."

"What?"

"I also have to ask that you leave the room whenever nursing staff is caring for your mother."

"That's outrageous."

"It applies to your whole family," Kaplan said, looking at Billy and Beth.

"I told you," Billy said. "You pissed them off and screwed it up."

"Well, Daniel, the hospital's sensitivity to my observations tells me that you do fear you've made mistakes. You should let me help instead of hiding in a bunker. If you don't get the prohibition lifted, I'll consult with an attorney."

"Shut up, Jack!" Billy yelled.

"Cooperate with us for a while," Kaplan urged. "We'll all relax if you just obey the rules for a while."

"Lift the ban, Daniel."

For the first time, Kaplan exhibited anger. "I don't know what you do for a living, Randle, but your bullying techniques won't work here. Use some finesse and you'll get better results."

"He doesn't have any finesse," Billy said.

"Keep me informed, Dr. Kaplan. I'll be here all day."

Kaplan shook his head and walked away.

Billy grabbed his wife's hand. "We have to get away from you. We'll be back for visiting hours."

Beth gave me a sad look as they walked away.

CHAPTER SIX

I raced to Mom's house, afraid Billy might show up to guard the fort. His insistence that I stay at a motel convinced me that he was hiding something.

I opened the kitchen door, and the alarm system chirped like a wounded bird. The green letters on the display panel beside the door now read "Secure." Holding my breath, and hoping I wouldn't be arrested so soon after my release from prison, I keyed the numbers 0125 into the alarm keypad. That silenced the alarm, and I exhaled. The green word "Unsecure" flashed on the display screen. *Two can play this game, Billy.* I pushed the menu button and selected "Change Password" from the list. It required the old passcode and then a new entry to reset the code. I entered 0926, Glenda's birthday.

Billy probably thought the premises were secure, but I didn't want him to interrupt my search, so I hurried through the kitchen to the small room that my father had used as an office. When a child passes away, parents often cling to their memory by leaving the child's room untouched. It appeared that nostalgia had compelled Mom to take the same approach with Dad's office. Papers, books, and pens still lay on the desktop. Unopened envelopes stuck out of the mail slots on the shelf above the desk. A thick layer of dust coated surfaces. Upon my father's death three years ago, time had stopped in this small room.

Joseph Marks Jr.—"Father" to all of us, including Mom—was born in Wisconsin and had earned a mechanical engineering degree from the Milwaukee School of Engineering. Upon graduating, he took a job at the Savannah River Plant, a nuclear energy facility just across the South Carolina border. He toiled there his entire working career.

In the desk drawers, I found the implements commonly used by an engineer: a slide rule, a compass, a T square, a sophisticated HP calculator, and pads of paper pre-lined with square boxes. In the shallow middle drawer lay a checkbook, but the checkbook was not used as a record of checks written and deposits made. Above the desk, Father had constructed a honeycomb of built-in cubbyholes of various dimensions to hold mail, papers, pens, and so forth. I emptied one cubbyhole after another and finally discovered something of value—a safe deposit key in a small red envelope and a signature card for access to the box, held by the Georgia Atlantic Savings Bank. Father, Mom, Katie, and Billy were all named on the signature card. Whether anything of value was stored in the box or whether anyone had accessed the box since my father's passing I couldn't know, but I took the key and card with me as I searched the rest of the house.

I looked in closets and kitchen drawers and bookshelves but did not uncover any secrets. Upstairs, I rifled my bedroom, the drawers in what had been Billy's desk, and our shared bathroom, but I found nothing of interest. Then I went into Katie's room and looked around with fresh eyes. I dumped the wastebasket on the bed and sifted through the refuse. Among the soiled Kleenex and ear swabs lay three empty prescription bags with stapled receipts for prescriptions written by a Dr. Burton.

The prescriptions, one for Vicodin and two for OxyContin, had been written for Mom. Katie had apparently filled the prescriptions for her.

I took the bags with me downstairs, and for the second time in my life I entered Mom's bedroom unaccompanied and without permission. This time I opened dresser drawers (just clothing), looked under the bed (house slippers), and swept my hand along shelves (dust). In her bathroom, I opened vanity drawers and pushed towels and sheets around in the linen closet. Nothing suspicious.

On her vanity I found no painkillers that matched the prescription receipts I had uncovered in Katie's room. There were no prescriptions written by a Dr. Burton either. I found that odd, so I made a copy of the prescription bags using Father's antique copier in his office. Then I grabbed a brown sandwich bag from a drawer in the kitchen and put the three copies in it. Back in the bathroom, I swept Mom's pill bottles into the bag and stuffed it and the original receipts into my briefcase.

Last, I searched Mom's closet, which was connected to the bedroom by the bathroom. It pleased me that my father's clothing had been removed and that her clothes were neatly organized. The closet smelled as though my mother had just walked past me after a long soak in a tub of bath oils. On the shelves above her racks of hanging clothes, rows of boxes were lined up like soldiers at reveille. Most were shoe boxes, but there was also a banker's box in which files normally would be stored, and a smaller, feminine box bound with a ribbon. I reached up to shake each shoe box in turn and convinced myself that they all contained shoes. I eased the heavy banker's box off the shelf and set it on the floor. I had to jump to reach the smaller box, but I snared it like a rebound off a basketball backboard.

Intrigued, and just a bit ashamed of myself, I untied the bow and opened Mom's pretty box. In it were approximately twenty slim envelopes addressed to Elaine Marks, in care of her brother, my uncle Frank Randle, in Columbia, South Carolina. The postmarks were decades old. Using the postmarks and the dates of my and my siblings' birthdays, I deduced that the earliest letter was written about two years after Billy had been born and the last less than three years later. That meant I had been ten, eleven, and twelve at the time. Very difficult years for me in the Church of Marks.

I sank to the floor and, sitting cross-legged, ordered the letters chronologically and began to read them in order. Each was a single page of good stationery, no letterheads, just a couple of paragraphs of sweet devotion. From the first, I realized the letters had been from a lover named Albert. Sometimes he signed them "Al," and sometimes just "Me." It was also obvious that my mother had responded, sometimes by mail, more often in person. My uncle Frank had been the enabler.

What do you tell yourself when you discover that your eighty-year-old mother was once another's man mistress? I said, *I'll be damned. My sweet mother was an adulteress.* Then I thought, *Can't blame her.* And then, *Why didn't she divorce him? My life would have been so much better.*

While I had played Little League Baseball and my father acted as if I didn't exist, my mother had carried on with another man! Recalling those days, an incident at the ballpark forty-seven years ago erupted on the big screen in my mind like a movie trailer.

* * *

At the crack of the bat, I turned and ran. Over my left shoulder, I watched the ball climb over the sun and hesitate at its apex before hurtling toward the warning track far ahead of me. In desperation, I pumped my arms and dug my spikes into the soft field, but there wasn't time to run. After three long strides, I pivoted to face home plate and located the ball falling from the sky like a meteor crashing through earth's atmosphere. Fear froze the blood in my veins. I stretched my glove hand over my head and jumped as high as my eleven-year-old legs could propel me, but I caught only a handful of spring air. The ball collided with the outfield wall ten feet behind me, bounced once on the warning track, and caromed off my leg.

Scuttling on hands and knees to retrieve the ball, I watched the batter round second base and head for third. There was still a chance. In one fluid motion, I rose and fired the ball toward the infield. The ball sailed over the cutoff man, landed on the pitcher's mound, and skittered toward home plate. Afraid the ball might get past him, the catcher smothered it on the infield grass as the opposing player slid across the plate behind him.

Game over. We had lost. I rested on my haunches, holding my breath to stave off the tears that would betray my shame. After several minutes, I spotted my father waving for me to get off the field, so I shuffled toward the dugout. My teammates, their faces long and sad, congratulated the ebullient winners as we had been taught by our coach. When one of the winning players gave a high-five to the kid who had hit the home run, our pitcher yelled, "It was just a stupid fly ball."

My teammates think I lost the game. A scuffle ensued, but the adults quickly separated the teams, and the players dispersed. Slowly, I walked toward my father and my coach, who waited for me on the third base line with their arms folded across their chests. When I was within earshot, my father said, "You run too long in one place."

I wondered if that was a professional opinion. After all, he was an engineer.

"He shouldn't have looked back," the coach said. "It slowed him down. We teach 'em to run to the spot then pick up the ball, 'cause you run faster looking straight ahead."

"He was playing too shallow."

I was playing where the coach told me to play.

"He doesn't have the speed to cover center field no matter where I position him."

I stopped on the infield grass, not sure if I should join the adult conversation or catch up to the kids. I wasn't sure I wanted to hear what my father had to say either. All I ever wanted to be was a center fielder because Mickey Mantle was my father's favorite player, and he was a center fielder. I asked my teammates to call me "Jackie" because it sounded like a center fielder's name.

"Are you going to cut him? He can't hit a lick. His baby brother hits it farther in T-ball."

"No way. Did you see that throw? Your kid's got a cannon."

Surprised, but suddenly optimistic, my father said, "You think he could be a pitcher?"

The coach spat out his chewing tobacco. "Nah, but I need a catcher, and I'd like to have a catcher with a gun." The coach looked at me before he finished. "If he ain't afraid of the ball, that is."

Catcher! The position reserved for kids who can't run and can't hit but are willing to demean themselves by chasing wild pitches around the backstop. Suddenly, pleasing my father was less important than avoiding the embarrassment of not making the team.

I was pretty sure I could speak now. "I'm not afraid of the ball, sir."

"Then I guess you're a damn catcher, Jack." My father shook his head and walked away.

The coach shrugged and said, "Let's get you some equipment."

I followed him to the dugout, where he filled a canvas bag with shin guards, a chest protector, a face mask, and a padded catcher's mitt. Then I walked home alone with the "tools of ignorance" slung over my shoulder.

As I had feared, my father didn't waste his time watching a "damn catcher" play Little League Baseball, so he never knew that I became the best catcher in the league. I wasn't afraid of the ball, or the bat, or foul tips, or runners sliding into home base. No wild pitches got past me, and no runner ever stole a base.

My father was right about my hitting, however. I rarely got a clean hit, but I learned how to coax a walk and I was on base often enough to earn the respect of my teammates.

As the season came to a close, we played for the championship against the team that had beaten us in the opening game. Leading by two runs in the bottom of the last inning, with two outs and a runner on second base, we gathered on the mound with our coach to get final instructions. The next batter would be the kid who hit the ball over my head to win the opening game of the season.

"We're not going to walk him, not going to let them think we're afraid of him. Let's end this right here," the coach said. His finger probing the pitcher's chest, he said, "Give him somethin' to hit, make him put the ball in play. Y'all do your jobs, and we'll be champions."

As I trotted back to my place behind home plate, the batter took vicious practice swings and sneered at me. "Gonna be just like last time," he said with a laugh.

Fearing he would be right, I squatted behind him and nodded to the pitcher that I was ready. He did as he was told and laid a "fat" pitch down the middle of the plate. The batter swung so violently his helmet flew off, and he fell to one knee in the batter's box. The ball was struck hard, but the batter had overswung and topped it. Like a laser beam, it streaked along the ground to the left of second base as the batter got to his feet and stumbled toward first base.

The shortstop, our best fielder, nearly made the play. The ball kicked off the heel of his glove and ricocheted back toward the left field foul line. The runner from second base scored easily, cutting our margin to a single run, as our fielders chased the fleeing ball like cops chasing a purse snatcher. The shortstop finally smothered the ball in foul territory as the batter neared third base. I tossed my mask aside and planted one foot on either side of the plate. The throw was strong and true but a few feet short of the plate, nearly striking the runner as he began his slide.

I caught the ball with two hands and dropped to my knees as the big batter crashed into me, spikes first. The impact flipped me onto my back as the crowd groaned and murmured oohs and ahs. Time stood still as the batter and I waited for the umpire's call. When the dust cleared, the umpire reached down and turned my glove over to reveal the ball resting on my chest protector.

Punching the sky with his right fist, the umpire shrieked, "Out!"

Before I could stand up, my teammates mobbed me. Later I realized that my uniform had been ripped and my thigh had been sliced by the batter's spikes. I refused treatment and walked home with my badge of honor plainly visible.

When Mom saw the gash, she was horrified and hastened to clean and bandage it. As she applied Mercurochrome and murmured sweet nothings, my father said, "Stop babying him. You'll turn him into a bigger pansy than he already is."

Mom paused but didn't argue, so I related my heroics to my father. He didn't believe me. "Looks more like you've been in a fight."

No, I insisted. I won the championship for my team.

All he said was, "Will we have to pay for the uniform?"

***

Al would have come to see my Little League games. After daydreaming for a while, I realized how selfish my thoughts were. Mom had endangered our family by having an affair.

I shuffled the letters into a random sequence, replaced them in the pretty box, and retied the bow best as I could. Obviously, the letters held great sentimental value for her or she wouldn't have kept them. Idly, I wondered where she had hidden them while Father was alive. I guessed that Uncle Frank had been the repository. Had Billy tried to preserve Mom's dignity? *Don't worry, Mom, your secret is safe with me.*

Worried that Billy could walk in at any moment, I turned my attention to the banker's box. I removed the lid and found statements and bills and manila folders piled haphazardly.

I carried it to my father's office and cleared a space on his musty desktop. I organized the papers until the pattern became clear: half of them were routine utility and repair bills, the other half were financial statements. Within a short time, I had four piles of statements representing four accounts: a checking account, of course, and a money market account, a brokerage account, and an annuity.

Mom received a monthly income from the annuity, which had a value of about eighty thousand dollars. I could cross-reference the payments to deposits in her checking account.

The latest statement for the brokerage account listed a value of one hundred fifty thousand dollars invested primarily in dividend-paying stocks. Once again, I cross-referenced the dividend payments to deposits in Mom's checking account.

The first whiff of a problem raised its smelly head when I read the money market account statements. The account, essentially a liquid savings account, had once held fifty thousand dollars. Now it was empty. Over the course of a year, six relatively large withdrawals, all less than the reportable limit of ten thousand dollars, had been withdrawn. When I tried to cross-reference the withdrawals with the checking account, I could find no corresponding deposits. *Is that why Mom wrote to me in prison?*

Mentally, I combined my father's pension check, her Social Security check, the stock dividends, and the annuity payments and came up with a number that represented a substantial income for an elderly lady with limited needs. And yet the checking account balance was always near zero.

When Father passed, Katie and I agreed that Billy should manage Mom's financial affairs because he lived nearby. Carrie, my wife at the time, had objected, saying, "You'll never see a penny of inheritance if you don't take charge. Billy will steal it." I had scoffed at her cynicism and in rebellion never involved myself in any of Billy's financial decisions. Now I wondered if that had been wise. Either he couldn't control Mom's spending habits or he was stealing her money.

In either case, I needed to preserve the evidence in case Billy found a way to keep me out of the house. I stuffed all the papers back into the banker's box and grabbed a flashlight from the kitchen junk drawer. I bounded out the kitchen door and down the steps into the fenced portion of the backyard. There was one place Billy wasn't likely to search, a place I had used as a child to hide my secrets from him: the crawl space under the house.

Around the side of the house, as cicadas serenaded me, I found the wooden door to the crawl space. The door was latched but not padlocked, a signal that it no longer harbored anything secret. Crouched in the entranceway, I swept the entire expanse with the weak yellow beam of the flashlight. Under the house, a foreboding space straight out of a horror flick, replete with black widow spiders and scorpion nests, waited. Along the far wall, a feral cat cowered and hissed at me. On my belly, I used my undamaged right leg to crawl fifteen feet to a supporting pillar. I dragged the banker's box in one hand as I swept the flashlight beam left and right with the other. I placed the financial records on the blind side of the pillar and laughed hysterically. Billy had never found my hiding place when we were kids, and he lacked the ingenuity to find it now.

I replaced Mom's pretty box where I had found it, on the shelf in her closet. As I left the house, I set the alarm and locked the back door. It was my fort now.

I drove to the motel, got a room key from the front desk, and told the clerk to leave the charge on Billy's credit card. After changing out of my soiled clothes, I repacked my bags and put them into the Bronco. Then I left without checking out so that Billy would continue to pay for the empty room.

CHAPTER SEVEN

At the hospital, I took the elevator to the cafeteria in the basement, bought a chocolate milk, and found an empty table in a corner. I spotted no signs of Billy or Beth. After two hours of watching sad families come and go, nurses grab salads, and doctors opt for coffee and sweets, I took the elevator back to Mom's floor. The hallway was deserted. Only a couple of people sat in the waiting area. As though I were sneaking up on the enemy on a battlefield, I tiptoed toward Mom's room. If I were discovered, I would say that I was simply getting some exercise.

Mom was alone and awake. When I identified myself, she gave me a sad smile, so I tried to make her more comfortable. I fluffed her pillow, brought her some water, and made sure she knew how to use the panic button to summon a nurse. She asked that I find her favorite TV channel. Although she couldn't see, she could listen to her daytime shows. She was grateful and she relaxed, then she nodded off before

I could ask her any questions about the letter she wrote me and her missing money.

I was about to sneak away when the computer on the counter caught my attention. The temptation was too strong to resist. I touched the mousepad, and the screen came alive with a listing of today's activities: doctors' visits, medications, vital signs. Scrolling backward, I realized I was looking at a record of Mom's entire hospital stay. I wanted to transcribe it into my iPad but had the feeling I had already been in the room too long to get it done before getting caught.

I was right. As I walked to the door, Shelby came flying through, halted with a hand to her mouth, and said, "You can't be in here."

"I just gave her some water and turned on the TV to keep her company."

"You can't be here," she said again as she backed around me and toward the bed.

"I'm no threat to you, Shelby. I know you're helping her."

"I have a license to protect. Kids to feed." She said this with her head jutting toward me, emphasizing her urgent fear.

I raised two hands in front of me and backed toward the door. "You have nothing to fear, Shelby." I hurried away.

Shelby had no reason to fear me, but I had reason to fear her. If she reported me to the administration, I might never be allowed back into the hospital. With that in mind, I decided not to leave the building. I also decided not to be where hospital authorities might find me. I went to the chapel to pray.

***

My conversation with God had dissolved into daydreaming long before Kaplan slipped into the pew beside me.

"Does your god permit talking in his house?" he asked.

I took a quick look around. We were the only supplicants in the chapel. "My God is very tolerant of talkative Jews," I said. "He once was one."

Kaplan smiled, and his chest rose and fell with a stifled laugh. Then, like a professor revealing an astonishing and rare fact, he said, "You were right, it wasn't the B strep. It's the dermatitis."

"It moved from her legs to her eyes?"

"More accurately, infectious material broke away from her legs, swam through the bloodstream, and landed in her eyes, where it's blocking her vision. Means the dermatitis bacteria had been allowed to fester and grow for a long time."

I stopped myself from castigating Mom's personal physician, or my brother, for their incompetence and neglect, but it wasn't easy. Kaplan seemed to be making peace, so this wasn't the time to start a new war.

"How do you remove infectious material from her eyes?"

"Antibiotics. Nieman knows exactly what to prescribe now. Your mother should begin to see as soon as tomorrow."

"That's amazing, wonderful!"

"There is a danger, however, that the dead bacteria will break away and travel to places it shouldn't go."

Kaplan stopped and watched me to see if I could intuit the implications. I had no medical rationale for the guess I made, but it was logical that the two organs that had presented symptoms were the two organs Kaplan was worried about.

"Her heart and brain?"

"Correct. You could add lungs if you were paranoid about it. Nieman has a theory. If you promise not to use it against us, I'll let you in on it."

"Ah, bribery. Like the Pharisees at the Temple."

"I want to come out of the bunker."

"Okay, Daniel, I'll be a good boy."

"Nieman thinks the vegetation has indeed traveled to her heart and brain. The easy guess is that small bits of the material caused the three ministrokes that we know weren't induced by clotting."

I nodded.

"We'll have Rosenberg confirm tomorrow. If the vegetation traveled to the eyes and the brain, it's a very small leap to believe it is in the heart." His eyes twinkled. "Have you ever seen barnacles on a ship's hull?"

"I have."

"Think of the infectious material as barnacles and think of your mother's mitral valve as the ship's hull." He smiled broadly.

I got it, of course. The implications were enormous. "There's nothing wrong with Mom's mitral valve except that it's clogged with material from a damned leg infection."

"I didn't say that, but it's possible. It's also possible that Dr. Metzger is right and the mitral valve is faulty. The infectious material may simply have exacerbated the malfunction."

"So, what do we do now?"

"Tomorrow we'll perform a transesophageal echocardiogram—we refer to it as a TEE test—and that will tell us whether the vegetation is in the heart. Then we'll clear the material and retest the heart to see if the mitral valve works properly."

"I'll keep my fingers crossed."

"That's what you're doing in here, isn't it?" He swept his hand to indicate the chapel.

It was my turn to chuckle. I opened my briefcase on my lap. "Can you do me a favor, Daniel?" I handed him the paper sandwich bag containing Mom's medication bottles and copies of the OxyContin and Vicodin prescribed by Dr. Burton. "These are all the meds Mom had been prescribed before her admittance. I figured you should include them in her treatment here, but can you tell me what they are and why she's taking them?"

Kaplan glanced around as though he were a spy being handed the secrets of the realm. Sensing no immediate danger, he took the bottles, read the labels, and thumbed the painkiller prescriptions.

"I don't recognize all of them," he said, but his eyebrows danced across his forehead.

"Can you ask other doctors?"

He dropped his eyes to think about it and expelled a deep sigh through his nose. "I'll ask the pharmacist."

Slick move. Avoids being questioned by your colleagues. "Thanks. If I don't see you tonight, I'll find you tomorrow for an update on Mom's condition."

Kaplan nodded, slid out of the pew, and left me alone with my god.

***

As Sunday evening visiting hour approached, I returned to Mom's room. Shelby was delivering dinner on a tray, so I stopped in the threshold. She gave me a conciliatory smile. "You can come in."

I shook my head. "I'll wait."

I backed out of sight in the corridor as my brother and his family approached. Joey—Trey—was barely recognizable. I had last seen him at my father's funeral. He had been a high school senior with longish, unkempt hair, a wispy chin beard, and a cavalier nonchalance about his clothing. Now he sported short hair with a neat part on the left side. His face was clean-shaven, and a small gold ring pierced his left earlobe. He wore skinny jeans, sandals, and a pale pink and white shirt, untucked, with the sleeves rolled above a multicolored bead bracelet. Gone too was the baby fat; he was rail thin.

I had relished the role of the "cool uncle" and had sometimes been mistaken for the "rich uncle." I had always been a nonjudgmental friend to my niece and nephew.

"Hello, Trey." We hugged and traded how-are-yous as Billy frowned at us.

Shelby emerged from Mom's room and said, "Go on in. See if you can get her to eat."

Mom was propped up on pillows, and a tray of hospital food sat untouched in front of her. She turned toward the noise as we approached and smiled as she identified voices. Beth walked around the far side of the bed to spoon-feed Mom while Billy and Trey blocked the near side. Patiently, I watched the family tableau. The scene was certainly preferable to a funeral.

Beth had no luck with the food. "It doesn't taste good," Mom said over and over.

"No one can cook like you do, Mom," Beth said. "But you have to eat to regain your strength."

"Medications can affect her taste buds," I said.

Billy bristled. "You just know everything, don't you?"

I let it slide. If Billy and his gang didn't leave soon, I would miss another chance to ask Mom about her letter. I walked to the door and looked up and down the hallway. Families milled about; most patient doors were closed to give visitors some privacy. No doctors or nurses were in evidence. I pushed Mom's door shut.

While Billy and Beth cajoled Mom, I moved to the computer. Once again it came alive at the touch of the mousepad. I tapped the page-up key, which backed the record to Mom's admittance form. Then I began transcribing information into my iPad Mini.

"What are you doing, Jack?" Billy asked.

"Copying her records so we'll know what the doctors know."

"That's private."

"Exactly. It's Mom's info, not the hospital's."

"You're going to get caught."

"I've been caught before."

Trey broke away from the bed and walked to the door. Leaning on it, he said, "I'll stand guard."

I gave him a thank-you smile. Billy threw his arms up in disgust. I tapped information into my tablet as fast as I could but had only gotten through Saturday when a knock rattled the door. I had no idea how to make the computer sleep. I pushed the page-down key and held it to make the record advance to the present time, then nodded to Trey. He opened the door a bit and a nurse I didn't recognize stuck her head in.

"I have meds," she said.

Trey hesitated and looked at me, but I couldn't think of a reasonable way to bar her from the room. Trey drew the door open, and I leaned against the counter with my back to the screen. This blocked the nurse's view of the computer as she moved to Mom's side with two small white paper cups containing pills.

"Let's get some water to wash this down," she said.

"I'll get it," Trey said. He took a glass from Mom's tray and walked over to the sink to run tap water. He winked at me as he filled the glass, then handed it to the nurse. Mom had difficulty swallowing the pills, but after multiple attempts, the drugs coursed through her system.

The nurse came to the counter and said, "Excuse me."

I had no choice but to move aside and allow her access to the computer. When I glanced back, I was relieved to see the hospital logo on the screen.

She updated Mom's record, then said, "Visiting hour ends in five minutes. One of those pills was a sedative, so she'll be asleep soon." With that, she left.

Billy and Beth hadn't bothered to ask if I had learned anything while waiting for visitors' hour, so I decided to leave them in the dark. I said my goodbyes and moved toward the door.

"Enjoy that motel bed now, ya hear?" Billy said.

I laughed and laughed and walked out the door.

***

I left the Bronco idling in the driveway at Mom's house as I considered how to hide it from view. I wasn't sure the detached garage would hold two vehicles along with the usual things stored in a garage, but, on foot, I traced my headlights to the wooden structure and heaved the manual door upward. In the headlights' glare, I could see that it was barren. Not only was Mom's car not parked inside, all of Father's tools and yard equipment had been spirited away. I wondered if Mom knew. I pulled the Bronco into the cavernous space and closed the big door.

In the kitchen, I made a peanut butter and jelly sandwich and poured a glass of milk. Then I turned out the light. I sat at the Formica-topped table in the dark and made my phone calls. The first was to Glenda.

"It's about time," she said. "I didn't want to disturb you, but I was getting scared."

For ten solid minutes, I recounted my two days in Augusta. I told her everything about Mom's condition, the missing money, and Mom's missing car. I even included my missteps and half-baked theories. Along the way, Glenda made tiny sounds at descriptions of Mom's maladies and of Billy's behavior, but she didn't interject.

When I finished, she said, "Have you had a chance to ask her what the big secret is?"

"It's got to be the money, but Billy and Beth and the nurses and doctors are always around. And now I can only see her during visiting hours."

"Maybe you should get back in the doctors' good graces. It wouldn't actually hurt to sign the DNR, would it?"

"I'm not going to give up on her, Glenda. I think her personal physician screwed up, and then the hospital bungled her case. I can't let that happen again. If we sign the DNR, we give them permission to let her die, and the doctors will get away with her murder."

"You're being a little dramatic, aren't you? I know you have trust issues caused by your relationship with your father, but, damn, Randle, it's time to get over it. Let the professionals do what's best, and stay out of the way."

"The doctors will do a better job if they know I'm watching their every move."

Glenda didn't respond immediately, but I could hear heavy breathing, as though she were recovering from a sprint. When she spoke, her voice was calm but firm. "I miss you. I need you to be home Thursday night so you can help me with the wedding prep on Friday."

"We'll get the test results tomorrow, and then I'll give you an update."

"You need to make it happen, Randle."

"Have you told Jamie?"

"Yes, she's fine." We said our I-love-yous and disconnected.

What I had thought would be a week with my mother had now shrunk to only three days. My little boat was being swamped by waves that threatened to capsize it.

I had to create some maneuvering space, so I called my agent. Tim received an abridged version of events.

"I need to know when I can schedule shows and interviews," he whined.

"Just cancel everything in Florida and California until I can leave Georgia. Set something up here in Augusta or over in Atlanta. I could do NPR or Georgia Public Broadcasting."

"Those aren't the most important markets."

"Connect with Emory in Atlanta. They hold one of my patents."

"The publisher is going to bounce off the walls, Randle. Books are in distribution; they've spent a ton of money promoting the book."

"Libraries and universities don't have timetables. It's not going to fly off the shelves at Barnes & Noble."

"You could be wrong. Regular people are very interested in the role of genetics on their future health. A lot of people think genome research is the first step toward immortality."

Holy crap! "That's the way you're promoting the book?"

"Sure. You're the pioneer that gets the wagon train rolling."

And you're the agent who will collect the commissions. I had written an academic tome for the research community, but the business guys hoped my book would cross from academia to mainstream. They hoped I was the next Bill Bryson, explaining technical complexities in a way that fascinated the masses. I was flattered *and* horrified. Anyone who bought the book to read at the beach or on an airplane was going to be very disappointed with its impenetrable mathematics and lack of Hollywood drama.

"Doesn't matter, Tim. I have to stay here until my mother's future is clear. I'll call you in a day or two."

I placed my third call to Katie. My sister sounded more lucid than she had yesterday. The version of events I gave her fell somewhere between the superficial version I gave Tim and the unabridged version I had shared with Glenda.

"I had no idea it was this serious, Randle. Billy makes everything sound like the end of the world. But you have it under control."

She's lying again. "When are you going to join us?"

Katie didn't respond immediately. After a long pause, she said, "Why don't we take turns? You take the first shift since you're already there, know all the doctors and the details. I'll come over in a couple of weeks, and Mom will always have one of us until she's better."

Her proposal *was* logical, assuming Mom continued to improve. One of us would always be present to ride herd on Billy and the medical staff, and eventually I could leave and resume my writing career. *Oh*, I thought, *don't forget that you'll be able to get married.* But the paranoid little man who lives in my brain also wondered if Katie was avoiding me.

"Weren't you just here? Your bedroom is still unmade."

Another hesitation. "That was a while ago, Randle. I should have changed the bed."

"Yeah, maybe Mom forgot or couldn't climb the stairs."

We hung up after that, but my stomach felt queasy. I grabbed a beer and climbed the stairs to my bedroom.

I got into bed with my iPad and my beer and read Mom's hospital records by the light of the little computer screen. The emergency room doctors made no mention of paralysis or a loss of eyesight. When she was moved to the cardiac ward, the attending physician had noted "Prognosis negative." Nurses took her vitals at four a.m. Saturday morning and discovered she couldn't see. Kaplan was assigned as hospitalist at four-thirty a.m., but he didn't arrive at the hospital until five a.m., shortly before me. He added Metzger to the team thirty minutes later. Hours after she had suffered her strokes, Metzger prescribed warfarin for the first time. Around lunchtime, Kaplan had entered "No DNR" in the record.

Although Mom hadn't yet suffered her strokes, the emergency room staff had triaged her case and assumed she would die before morning. When she didn't pass, the cardiac team predicted it would happen soon. But my tough little mother had beaten the odds. I put the iPad aside and fought for sleep. Each time a car passed on the street, I lurched awake and waited to see if it would turn into the driveway. Each time I sank back under the covers.

I would have slept better at the motel.

Chapter Eight

Thinking I could get the jump on doctors and family, I arrived at the hospital at six-thirty a.m. on Monday. I wanted to ask Mom questions in private, and I wanted to transcribe the rest of her records into my iPad. I was too late. When I eased her door open, I found Shelby and Nieman on the near side of her bed while Kaplan and Harrison stood on the far side. They gazed at Mom as though she were the dearly departed in her casket and spoke over each other in excited tones. Mom lay between them, at once the focus of attention and yet disconnected from the conversation.

My heart rate accelerated and adrenaline pumped through my veins as though a dam had burst. Without asking permission, I raced to Mom's bedside and squeezed between Shelby and Nieman. They allowed me to take in the scene: Mom's face appeared red as a stoplight and grotesquely swollen; through closed eyes, tears still streamed down her cheeks; her hands and lower arms reflected the same color as her face; her body tensed against pain.

THE UNDISCOVERED COUNTRY | 63

"It hurts," Mom gasped.

"What the hell?" I said to no one in particular.

From Kaplan again I got the puppy dog eyes. "She's had a bad reaction to medication. She has pain in her eyes, so we think it was the antibiotic we injected into them to clear up the floaters."

"It wasn't anything I prescribed," Harrison said.

Everyone looked at him for a moment. He responded with a one-shouldered shrug. When no one challenged him, he left us.

"Go check the chart," Nieman said to Shelby.

She walked over to the computer, found the overnight record of prescribed drugs, and read it to the doctors.

Without thinking, Nieman said, "We've overdosed her with antibiotic."

"My God! You people are killing her," I said before I could suppress my anger. I worried that I had given them another reason to kick me out of the room, but Daniel kept his cool. He gave me a "stop sign" with one hand and continued his consultation with his colleague.

"Antidote or wait it out?" Kaplan said.

"It's not dangerous to wait it out, but it's uncomfortable for her," Nieman said.

I wanted to yell at them to stop her pain, dammit, but bit my tongue. I took Mom's hand and caressed it.

"Would the antidote preclude the tests we have scheduled?" Kaplan asked.

"No," Nieman said.

Kaplan considered me, then said to Nieman, "Let's relieve the symptoms."

"Okay," Nieman said. He walked to the computer and entered a new order for the antidote.

I doubt they'd have taken that step had I not been in the room. After entering the order, Nieman said he'd check on her later to see if the antibiotic was working.

When he left, Kaplan came around to my side of the bed, took my arm, and walked me toward the door. "She'll be going down for the TEE test this morning, and Dr. Rosenberg will have another look at the MRI to see if bacteria caused the strokes. She'll be out of the room all morning, Randle. Go see your family."

Kaplan had no idea how incongruous that thought was.

"Sure. I'll find something to do."

"Don't hang around here. You make people nervous. Make yourself scarce, and I'll see if I can get the ban lifted."

***

I considered hiding until everyone had left Mom's room but decided to wait for a decision on my ban. I'd be less likely to get caught at the computer if I had permission to be in the room. As I walked down the hallway, I peeked into the waiting room, and the sight of Beth, Trey, and a young woman who had to be Nicole caught me by surprise. Visiting time was still hours away. Curious, I joined them. Trey popped up to shake my hand, but Nicki just smiled and kept her seat. Beth hugged me.

"I hoped to see Nana before I have to go back to school," Trey said.

"His roommate is giving him a ride," Beth said.

"I'll have to get back to work," Nicki said, "if Nana's okay."

"She has a long way to drive," Beth explained.

My head swiveled from one person to another, but my eyes rested the longest on Nicki. She was a striking woman with hair bleached yellow by the sun, suntanned skin the color of milk chocolate, and provocative clothing. She wore a beige lacey top that stopped short of her midriff. It exposed a navel piercing and flared open at the top to reveal an impressive bosom. *Where did she get those?* She wore cutoff jeans that drew my attention to an intricately inked tattoo encircling her meaty left thigh. A fleur-de-lis tattoo graced her outer right calf and a third tattoo on the top of her right foot appeared to be a Chinese or Japanese character.

"They don't expect her to get back to her room until afternoon."

"I'll have to tell Raymond," Trey said. "He's waiting."

"Can he leave, Randle?" Beth asked. "He saw his grandmother yesterday."

Trey and I locked eyes. His were pleading. "Trey's not so far away that he can't come back if necessary."

Trey nodded a thank you and hugged his mother before walking away.

Nicki caught me staring at her. "Long time no see," she said.

I broke my stare. "Yeah, you're all grown up."

Smiling coquettishly, she said, "So, how does it feel to be out of prison?"

Beth chided her niece, but I said, "It's okay. Reasonable question to ask."

In truth, prison had not been a difficult experience. I found it easier to do the time knowing I was innocent than if I had been guilty of the charges brought against me. While in prison, I was comforted knowing that Glenda awaited my release. It had been an easy time because Carrie was in prison for a crime she *had* committed.

To Nicki, I said, "It feels like I'm adrift in a small boat at sea. There's only room for me in the boat, and only I can decide where to paddle it. That sensation should be exhilarating, but the sea is vast, so right now it's daunting."

Nicki looked sympathetic but nonplussed. She hadn't expected a philosophical answer. She stood and declared, "I need a bathroom break."

After Nicki left, Beth dropped her head onto her chest and shielded her eyes with one hand as though she were facing sunlight. She was quietly sobbing. I joined her on the couch and put my arm around her.

"Where's Billy?"

Without looking up, she said, "He went to work. He disapproves of his son and his niece."

"Trey seems to be on the straight and narrow."

She gave me a funny look and searched my face for hidden meaning. She cocked her head and raised an eyebrow but didn't say anything.

"Why don't you and Nicki go shopping or something until visiting hour? Too much stress here at the hospital."

She looked at me with relief. "Thanks. We'll get some breakfast when Nicki comes back from the bathroom."

I had nowhere to spend time except Mom's house, so I took the elevator to the lobby and walked out the front doors into the rising heat of a summer day. I noticed Nicki at the far end of the building beside a standing ashtray. Her bathroom break was actually a smoking break. As I approached, she stubbed her cigarette out and constructed an insolent expression.

"Going to give me a lecture?"

"Not my job."

"But you disapprove?"

I shrugged. "Of what?"

She shot me a look that said "Don't play dumb" and shook a fresh cigarette from her pack. With the cigarette dangling from her lipsticked mouth, she fumbled in her cloth purse. She found a red book of paper matches and, as she lifted them from her purse, I took them, struck one, and offered the light.

I turned the matchbook over and read the advertising. The matches were complimentary from the "Princess Gentleman's Club, Orlando."

"My boyfriend went there once," she said.

Uh-huh. "Have a pen?"

She gave me a questioning look but dug one out of her purse. I wrote my cell number on the inside cover and handed the book to her. "Call me if you get into trouble. I'm not far away in Dolphin Beach. I'll help if I can."

An amazed look spread across her face. Before it could morph into anything else, I hugged her. She was limp in my arms. I let her go and headed for the parking lot and my car.

As I walked between the rows of parked cars, I saw Trey and a young black man I surmised to be Raymond, the roommate. I angled toward them to say a final goodbye, but they didn't see me coming until I emerged into their walking lane. They were holding hands as they walked. When he saw me, Trey dropped his roommate's hand and yanked his own away as though he had unintentionally touched a poisonous snake. He blushed.

I walked up to them with a smile and extended a hand to the roommate. "You must be Raymond."

He kept his cool and shook my hand. "Raymond Morris."

"Uncle Randle—" Trey began, but I held up a hand, stopping him.

I started laughing. They were perplexed. "I told your mother you were on the '*straight* and narrow,'" I said as I tried unsuccessfully to stifle my laughter. "She knows, right?"

Trey and Raymond laughed with me. "Yes, she knows," Trey said. "She likes Raymond, but of course Dad is oblivious, and there's no way we can tell him."

"Don't worry, that's not my job. You guys will find a way, eventually." Trey hugged me again and whispered, "Thank you."

***

As I approached Mom's house, I noticed a green SUV in the driveway. I had an idea who it belonged to, but I didn't want the intruder to know I had discovered him. I pulled into the church parking lot across the street and slid into a space between two other cars. After only ten minutes, Billy appeared from around back and got into his car emptyhanded.

After he left, I replaced him in the driveway. When I unlocked the back door, the alarm remained silent. I imagined that Billy had tripped the alarm when his passcode didn't work and the security company had called him. Billy knew the secret password, so the alarm company turned off the siren and didn't notify the police. But Billy wouldn't have been able to reset the passcode because he didn't know the current code. Billy hadn't armed the system when he left in case he wanted to reenter the house. That was my reasoning.

Before I did anything else, I checked my room and confirmed that my bags and clothes had not been disturbed. Billy would know by now that his credit card was being charged for the motel room. My things weren't what he wanted.

I had two tasks to complete at Mom's house. First, I used Father's computer to surf legal self-help websites until I found one from which I could download a generic, durable power of attorney. I printed the form on Father's computer.

Second, I called Mom's bank and, masquerading as Billy, asked them to fax copies of the past year's withdrawal slips to the fax machine at Mom's house. I identified myself by giving them the last four digits of Billy's and Mom's Social Security numbers, both of which I had known for decades. Then I poured a glass of orange juice and waited. Twenty minutes later, a cover sheet and six photostats of withdrawal slips for Mom's savings account chugged out of Father's printer like a locomotive straining to haul a long line of railroad cars out of the loading yard. As I sipped the juice, I paged through the fax. All six slips bore Mom's signature but not in Mom's distinctive, flamboyant handwriting. Mom hadn't thrown the money away on swamp land in Florida. Someone had forged the withdrawals.

I intended to drive back to the hospital for afternoon visiting hour, but my phone rang before I could leave the house.

"What are you guys doing to me, Dad?" Jamie said.

I could have played dumb, but I knew what she referred to. Glenda was wrong: Jamie wasn't "fine."

"I'm sorry, Jamie. We meant to discuss it with you Friday night, but then I got the call about Nana."

"I should have known that living together wouldn't be enough for you guys. I made Mom promise not to give up her place. Now you're back on the merry-go-round."

I blamed my daughter's tendency to violate social etiquette on a combination of my genes—I come from a family of socially awkward people—and her profession as a cop. To elicit facts efficiently, she was often blunt. As an only child, she also felt at liberty to criticize me, and her mother, for making a mess of our lives. She had not visited me during my fifteen months in prison—she said it was unthinkable for an officer of the law to have a felon for a father—and that had been part of my punishment. I accepted my penance and gave my daughter a pass on her behavior because she had saved my life during the gunfight on the *Wahine II*.

"We've never stopped loving each other, Jamie. Our divorce was our mistake, not our marriage."

"You are reckless people. You split up, you get back together, you split up again, and then you get back together again. After each breakup, you move on with your lives, get married to someone new, but I'm left twisting in the breeze."

"We've learned from those experiences," I said. "We know what we want now."

"Do you have to rush into it?

"Your mom has already made all the arrangements." I hoped that didn't sound like I was throwing Glenda under the bus.

"Take care of Nana, Dad, and I'll take care of Mom. The damn wedding can wait."

"As long as you're there when we do get married, we'll be happy."

"Don't worry. Every kid wants to be present for her parents' marriage. The guys at the station will get a kick out of this when I ask for time off."

I returned to the hospital then, my little boat rocked by another rogue wave.

Chapter Nine

Beth, Nicki, and I sat in the waiting room, traded trivial gossip, and watched the hallway for Mom's return from her tests. Nicki and Beth relaxed, and the time passed easily until Beth started relating stories from our childhood. We chuckled and slapped knees and teared-up over the melancholy stories. Beth encouraged me to add to the nostalgia by telling Nicki the story about me driving the family car when I was a teenager. I did not want to relive the episode, but Beth harangued me until I relented.

While I was in high school, we owned only one automobile, and although I worked summers as a caddy at a country club, I could not afford a car of my own. I borrowed the family car, Father's car, for dates or weekend nights with my friends. Father charged me for the pleasure at fifty-one cents per mile, plus gas, which he claimed was the cost of owning the car. I was offended by this arrangement—it was the *family* car and I was a member of the family, wasn't I?—but he was adamant that it was good training for my life as an adult. As revenge, I would drive ten or twelve miles and then disconnect the odometer—you could do that in those days. Before returning the car, I would reconnect the odometer so that a night on the town only cost five or six bucks.

This arrangement remained in place for two years until I graduated from high school. As a graduation gift, and in front of our extended family and all my friends at my graduation party, Father presented me with a savings account passbook containing the money I had paid for use of the car. He said, "Would have been a lot more if you hadn't cheated me on mileage." Everyone laughed except me. I was mortified. Had he made his point in private, I might have accepted it as a valuable life lesson. Instead, I wanted to kill the son of a bitch.

Beth laughed, but Nicki didn't find it humorous. She said, "That was cruel. He didn't do that out of love; he did it to show he was in charge."

"He taught you a valuable lesson," Beth said. "And it stuck."

Nicki and I traded disbelieving looks, but I let it drop and the conversation waned. Shortly after lunch, attendants pushed Mom's bed past the door. She was propped up into a nearly sitting position, which I thought was a good sign. Although it wasn't yet time for afternoon visitors, we leapt to our feet and moved into the hallway. If we thought we could follow Mom into her room, we were wrong. Kaplan brought up the rear of the entourage and blocked our path.

"I have some good news and some bad news."

Generally, I like the bad news first, softened by the good news second, but Beth spoke before I did. "We need some good news, doctor."

Kaplan nodded his assent. "We'll do a culture later today to confirm that the dermatitis is gone, but we think that problem is solved. The B strep is responding, and your mother's condition is no longer critical in that regard. The fluid is gone from her lungs—another immediate threat averted—but we're still battling what remains in her legs." He paused as though remembering everything he wanted to impart. "Her eyesight is slowly returning. She sees shapes and motion. It appears she'll regain full vision as the antibiotic kills the infectious floaters."

"That's great, doctor," Beth exclaimed. "Thank you so much."

"We're just treating all the peripheral issues," Kaplan said modestly, "as Randle asked us to do." He glanced at me. I interpreted the look to mean that the peripheral issues were insignificant compared to news he had yet to give us.

"Go on, Daniel," I said.

"Dr. Rosenberg conducted a series of tests to determine if there was any brain damage from the ministrokes. The good news is that her mental faculties are intact and functioning normally."

Again Beth squealed in delight, but I knew the bad news had to be next. "So, what's the bad news, Daniel?" *Come on! Get to it.*

"The TEE test shows that the dermatitis infected her mitral valve. We call a heart infection endocarditis. We can say definitively that infectious material traveled to her brain and caused the ministrokes."

He hesitated, so I said, "Isn't that good news? The dermatitis caused the heart attack and the strokes and now the infection has been healed."

"The dermatitis may have *triggered* the heart attack—there's not very much material on her valve now, but there may have been more at the time of the myocardial infarction—but it was going to happen sooner or later. Her mitral valve is defective."

Beth put a hand to her mouth; Nicki shifted nervously.

I said, "Is the mitral valve problem serious enough to cause another attack if it isn't covered in barnacles?"

"I'm afraid so," Kaplan said. "To make matters worse, the infarction damaged her heart muscle, which is why it isn't strong enough now to resist the fluid buildup."

"What do we do now?"

"Her only chance is to grow strong enough for surgery. It's a long shot, Randle. You've got to make her eat."

"I can do that," I said. All three of them looked at me with questions on their faces, but I wasn't ready to share my idea. "Can we see her now?"

Kaplan hesitated, as though considering the bounds of his authority. "Give them a chance to set her up in the room. Don't abuse the privilege."

I squeezed his shoulder and said, "Thanks."

Kaplan turned to leave, but I had one more question. "What about her prescriptions?"

He looked at Beth and Nicki and said to me, "Walk with me. I've got another place to be."

Kaplan and I left the women in the hallway and walked toward the elevators at the far end of the corridor. He said, "The prescription bottles are for the typical issues of an aging woman: high blood pressure, high cholesterol, elevated sugar level, a mild case of arthritis. The curious thing is that there isn't a diuretic for the fluid in her legs or a steroid for the dermatitis."

I gave Kaplan a sharp look. Billy said Mom had just been to the doctor for both problems. I thought of one more thing Billy had told me. "My brother said Mom couldn't have been malnourished; she had gained weight immediately before her episode."

Kaplan didn't take offense; he had an easy explanation. "Water weight, about thirty pounds of it."

Warning signs that were missed! "Now don't get upset, Daniel, I'm just trying to understand." I paused to gather my thoughts. "To me, it sounds like there was an obvious indication of impending heart trouble, but it wasn't taken seriously enough. Then the dermatitis was allowed to grow, travel through the bloodstream, and trigger the event for which there had been warnings."

"I wouldn't testify to that," he said.

"You won't have to. What about the other drugs?"

"A puzzle. There were no traces of either OxyContin or Vicodin in her bloodstream, and she has no symptoms that would warrant strong painkillers."

"Do you know these guys, Fowler and Burton?"

"No. I'm not allowed in their clubs."

We traded rueful smiles. I thanked Kaplan and watched him board the elevator.

Why would Katie fill prescriptions that Mom neither had nor took? I googled Dr. Burton. Sebastian Burton was a dentist, not a medical doctor, with offices in Augusta, Georgia. *Maybe Mom had oral surgery and took the pills long ago?* I checked the dates on the prescriptions and found that they had been filled once a month for the past three months. They hadn't been prescribed for a single occurrence of a dental problem; they had been filled on a recurring basis to satisfy a more sinister need.

I rushed to judgment: the painkillers weren't for Mom. They were missing because Katie had taken them with her to Atlanta. My sister was in trouble. That's why she couldn't come to Augusta.

My end of the corridor was quiet, so I dialed Katie's cell number. Brad answered. "Katie can't come to the phone right now."

"I know what's going on, Brad. Let me talk to her."

"You don't know anything, Randle. We'll call you when she can speak."

Before he could disconnect, I shouted, "I know enough to put Burton behind bars!"

Silence. Heavy breathing. I waited. "He's a friend, Randle. We did undergrad together at Vanderbilt. He did us a favor."

"Supplying drugs illegally? That's a favor?"

Another silence. He sobbed. "She was buying on the street, Randle. Places in Atlanta you wouldn't want your sister to go."

"What were you doing? Driving her around?"

"Yes!" An explosive, crying, gasping outpouring of grief came through the phone. "You have no idea what she's like without the pills."

Unbelievable! "Don't you know what happens next? She resorts to heroin, which is cheaper and more readily available. At that point, she's over the cliff and stuck with a life of hard drug addiction. Your buddy Burton won't be able to do you any favors then."

A long, heavy sigh. "That's why she can't talk to you. She's in detox, at the Freedom's Path Rehab Center here in Atlanta. Your mother's situation convinced her to clean herself up so she can join the family."

So that's the silver lining: my mother's death prompts my sister to clean herself up. "Okay, Brad, I'm glad to hear that. When will she get out?"

"It's a six-week program, but sometimes patients move into outpatient care after two weeks. The physiological withdrawal from opioids takes three to five days, but the psychological dependency is a continuing challenge."

I consoled him then—nothing to be gained by beating him up— and asked him to keep me up to date on Katie's recovery. As I walked down the corridor toward Mom's room, I wondered if Billy had wanted to find the prescription receipts to cover for his sister.

In the three years since I had last been around my family, since my father's passing, the family had unraveled and morphed into something unrecognizable. My eighty-year-old mother, who had once carried on a three-years-long affair, hovered near death. My unreasonably antagonistic brother struggled to accept a gay son while extorting my mother, and my sister had raised a pole-dancing daughter. Now my sister was in rehab to cure a prescription pill addiction. Add me to the list of failures: I had gone through another divorce and had been to prison. Maybe Father *had* been the glue that held us together. Wouldn't that be ironic?

***

Beth and Nicki sat at Mom's bedside, and Beth was again trying in vain to get Mom to eat hospital food.

"She's never going to eat hospital food," I said. Pulling my last twenty-dollar bill from my wallet, I instructed Nicki to go to the Red Robin Diner and order Mom a Whiskey River BBQ Burger and onion rings. "That's her favorite. Text us to see if the coast is clear before you bring it in here."

Nicki chuckled. She relished her role in a small conspiracy. After she left, I told Beth to stand outside the door and tell anyone who wanted to come in that I was having a private conversation with Mom about her disposition. I figured the staff would encourage that conversation and not interrupt. Beth complied. I imagined she was accustomed to being told what to do.

Mom reached a hand toward me and smiled, as though she wanted to chat, but I told her I had one thing to do first. "Then we'll talk, Mom."

I walked over to the computer and woke it, backed up the record to the overnight hours on Sunday, and began transcribing information as fast as I could type. I took special care to get drug names and doses correct. In less than fifteen minutes, Mom's entire medical record lived in my iPad. As I walked away from the computer, the door opened. I froze. *Thank God. It's only Beth.* She reported that Nicki was downstairs with the food.

Nicki hadn't yet arrived when the door opened again, and Shelby swept into the room. "I just need her vitals, and I have one med for her."

Before I could block her path, she was at Mom's bedside. "Can that wait? We're in the middle of a discussion about her final wishes. I'm not sure we'll get a better chance." I gave her a pleading look.

Shelby hesitated and grew sad. "Of course," she said. "Let me know when you're done." She turned to leave and saw that the computer was not asleep; the day's entries were displayed on the screen. A question clouded her face, but she didn't ask. She walked to the machine, shook the mouse, and ran up and down the timeline to confirm that the machine was working. With a shrug, she walked toward the door, then glanced back at me with an odd look.

I said, "Thank you," as though I had no idea what she was thinking.

Shelby left, and before the door could snuggle up to the doorjamb, Nicki swept into the room grinning broadly. Beth unwrapped the food and handed Mom half of the burger. Ferociously hungry, she wolfed it down, belched, and grinned. Bemused by the idea, she said, "I'm full."

Beth packed the remains back in the bag and laid them on a chair. She remarked that there must be a microwave nearby to reheat the food later. If anyone asked about the bag, Nicki would say it had been her lunch.

Beth stood on the window side of the bed, and I positioned myself on the near side. Nicki moved to the foot of the bed, and we all stared at Mom wordlessly, unsure how to carry on a conversation. I certainly couldn't broach the subjects on my mind.

Mom broke the silence. She waved at Nicki and said, "Move to the side, honey. That's where Jesus stands."

Nicki looked at Mom as though she were delirious, but she shuttled obediently to Beth's side of the bed.

"You see Jesus?" I asked.

"Don't you see Him?" Mom said. "He's watching over me."

Beth and I traded looks. I wondered if Mom had been overdosed again.

"Does He want you to go with Him?" Nicki asked.

Mom smiled benignly. "He's not sure yet."

Wondering what Mom could see, I asked Nicki to hand me a magazine from the window sill. I showed Mom a page and asked her to tell us what she could see. She distinguished people in pictures, though not fine detail, and she could read headlines but not small print.

Although she constantly wiped away tears and said her eyes still hurt, her eyesight had improved dramatically. If her eyesight wasn't the source of her hallucinations, perhaps it was her mind.

"Do you see anyone else in the room now?" I said.

Mom glanced around. "No, not right now. They come and go. Once there were Chinese performers in beautiful gowns. Angels, I think. They sang and danced for me and offered me beautiful jewels. When the performance ended, a bright star appeared and people in heaven reached out to help me."

Oh boy. "Did you fly through a tunnel?" I asked.

As though I had jogged her memory, she nodded assertively. "I was pushed toward a warm loving light at the end."

To Beth and Nicki, I said, "That's a very typical description given by people who are clinically dead and then revived. I'll see if there's a mention in the record."

To Mom, I said, "Was that the first night you were here?"

"No. Yesterday, I think."

"More likely it was the night she was admitted," I said to Beth and Nicki.

I couldn't recall any mention in her record of a code blue or a crash cart, but I resolved to read her entire record over dinner. Although I was pleased by Beth's and Nicki's willingness to keep a bedside vigil, I also resolved to trick them into leaving so I could speak to Mom in private.

Before I could concoct something rational, Kaplan pushed through the door and asked if he was interrupting. Shelby stood next to him. I assured him they were welcome and moved out of the way, next to the sink and computer terminal.

"We're going to take a culture of the dermatitis bacteria to confirm that they're dead. If they are, we'll stop the antibiotic. One less pill for her to take."

Kaplan seemed artificially sociable. My antennae went up. They took their samples, then Kaplan walked over to the computer to leave a note in the record. As he typed, and as Shelby talked to Mom, I moved behind Kaplan and just to one side of him so I could see what he was writing. It's an old golfer's trick. When your playing partner is putting from a greater distance but on the same line as your ball, you stand behind him so you can watch his ball zig and zag toward the hole. Then your put becomes easier because you know the turns the ball will make.

Kaplan finished typing, then hit the escape key to close the file. The hospital logo appeared. He then pushed ctrl–alt–del simultaneously to put the machine to sleep. *Nice to know!*

After Kaplan and Shelby left the room, we reassembled in our appointed places around Mom's bed like infielders poised to snare the next batted ball. No one had anything to say until Mom blurted, "They're back." She seemed pleased.

"They're gone," Beth said.

"Not the doctors," Mom said with a hint of impatience. "The fishermen."

Despite myself, I looked around the room and found nothing out of order. The TV was off.

"Do you know them, Nana?" Nicki said.

Mom gave Nicki the look mothers give to slow children. "Of course. The Apostles. They're pulling in their nets, full of fish."

CHAPTER TEN

escaped at that point, leaving the ladies to watch TV, or the Apostles as the case might be. Maybe they could ask the nurses to fry Mom some fish for dinner. I took the elevator to the basement cafeteria and marveled at how surreal this situation had become. Mom's general condition, which had been neglected prior to her hospitalization, had improved, but her seminal issue—the ticking time bomb in her chest—could not be treated. Mom often seemed lucid, able to communicate rationally, and then she would shock us with a religious hallucination out of character for the Elaine Marks I knew.

Raised a Southern Baptist, Mom had converted to Catholicism when she married Father, but she had never been observant or devotional. When we were children, Mom herded us to Mass each Sunday to please Father, but after we had grown, Father attended alone. Other than for Father's funeral, I doubted Mom had been inside a church of any denomination for decades. Neither had I. So why the biblical hallucinations? Had to be her medications.

I ordered a cup of coffee and sat at a small table unlikely to attract a tablemate. Slowly and carefully, I read through Mom's medical record on my iPad. Again, I began with her admittance. In the emergency room, doctors had used amiodarone to restore "sinus rhythm." The record did not mention a resuscitation that may have precipitated Mom's near-death experience. It did not mention paralysis or blindness, and yet she awoke "blind" on Saturday morning. Only then did staff administer her Coumadin, a blood thinner, to ward off repeated strokes or heart attacks. So the ministrokes, caused by migrating infectious vegetation, occurred in the hospital.

Overnight, Saturday to Sunday, a routine blood test revealed the B strep infection, obviously contracted in the hospital, and Harrison had prescribed an antibiotic when he arrived Sunday morning.

Sunday, an atropine injection dilated Mom's eyes so a culture of her eye matter could be taken. Nieman prescribed an antibiotic. Kaplan also prescribed a drug to counteract the fluid buildup in Mom's lungs. That was all they had done for her over the weekend. Mom had poorly timed her heart attack to occur on a Friday evening. At that time, the hospital transitioned to a skeletal staff and most doctors spent their weekend playing rounds of collegial golf. She had to survive the weekend on her own before she gained access to a full staff on Monday morning. Maybe Jesus kept her alive.

As I scanned the overnight hours, Sunday to Monday, I found an entry for epinephrine. Following the application of the drug, staff typed this into the record: "Patient stable." *Bingo!* Mom had told the truth: she had had another A-fib episode last night, and no one had bothered to mention it to us.

Today, Nieman reduced the dosage for the dermatitis antibiotic they injected directly into her eyes and prescribed another drug I assumed to be the antidote for the overdose. But when I checked his original prescribed dosage against the actual application, I found them to be the same. He had implied that nurses had injected the wrong dosage when in fact Nieman had overprescribed the dosage. On the other hand, the antidote hadn't relieved her bad reaction, so maybe his antibiotic wasn't the culprit.

I also found that on Monday morning, Harrison had changed the drug he was using to fight the B strep. He had pretended to be confident that his drug wasn't causing Mom's bad reaction when in reality he hadn't been all that sure.

Now one of the cocktail of drugs was inducing Mom's hallucinations. All the doctors were hiding from a malpractice suit like cockroaches scurrying to their hiding places when the lights are switched on in the middle of the night.

I wanted another cup of coffee, but the cafeteria was too noisy for the calls I had to make. I took the steps up one floor to the lobby and found that crowded as well. With no other choice, I walked outside into the heat of an Augusta summer. The temperature had soared into the nineties, the humidity nearly as high, and there was no mitigating breeze. A pang of longing for my home in Dolphin Beach, Florida, skittered across my chest. It wasn't much, the house, just a white-washed, two-bedroom, concrete block bungalow with a rickety dock on the Intracoastal Waterway, but it was my favorite place on earth. For fifteen months, I had dreamed of standing in the backyard, next to the pool, watching the sunset. Now I was in the last place on earth I would want to be. Although the sun was more intense in coastal Florida, the humidity was lower and a compensating sea breeze blew continuously. Of course, the weather and my house weren't the only things I missed in Dolphin Beach.

Considering the fact that this was a hospital, an amazing number of staff in scrubs had congregated around the ashtray at the far end of the building, so I walked to the opposite end where no sane person would stand in the sunshine to make calls. That ensured privacy if not comfort. I first called Glenda at her store.

She was happy to hear from me but disappointed in my message. "I can't leave until Katie gets here." *And only then if she's sober.*

"Your mother is as good as she's going to get until God takes her. Leave it in His hands."

"You mean the doctor's hands. I can't do that."

Glenda shouted, "Stop it! Your mistrust of authority is a sickness, and I want you to get help when you get home. You do not have to control every aspect of everyone's life. Trust the authorities, Randle."

"Like I trusted the lawyers and judges in my court case?"

She became angry then and asked why the sudden devotion to a family I hadn't paid any attention to for decades when I had a family that needed me and cared about me in Florida. It was a valid question, and one I hadn't yet been able to answer for myself. Some unfamiliar force was driving me to save my mother and unravel the mysteries surrounding my siblings. As I stood silently sweating, I knew that explanation was a rationalization. Maybe an obfuscation. I needed to use this crisis to put my past behind me, to kill off Jack Marks forever so I would be free to live as Randle Marks.

I wasn't ready to say those words out loud, even to Glenda. To mollify her, I feigned agreement that I would come home as soon as possible. I don't think she believed me. We followed my promise with our habitual and meaningless conclusion: "Love you." "Love you too."

Too hot, too sweaty, and too perturbed to stand in the sunshine for a second call, I retreated to the noisy lobby before dialing my agent. Tim too was happy initially to hear from me. Perhaps he thought I was calling to announce I'd be back in Florida for the Thursday book launch. Once again, I disappointed him. I told him I couldn't leave until my sister arrived. Like Glenda, he became angry. So did I.

"Tell them to take my book off the summer list and put it on the fall list."

"They can sue you for violating your contract."

"Move the launch to Atlanta. Do your job, dammit."

This time Tim hung up on me. That put me in a poor mood as I traveled back to the fourth-floor looney bin. When I entered Mom's room, I found her repetitively reaching above her bed, alternating hands to grab things invisible to the rest of us to pull them down to her.

"What is she doing?"

"Helping the Apostles harvest grapes," Nicki answered. She chuckled while Beth looked horrified.

I walked to the bed and attempted to embrace Mom to divert her attention back to us. She shrugged me off and continued harvesting two-thousand-year-old grapes. We watched silently until she tired of the exercise. Done with the grapes, she looked at us, one at a time, with a fierce determination to recognize us. "My kids would never behave like this. My kids would get me out of here."

"I am your son. I'm Jackie. As soon as you're well, we'll get you out of here."

She used both hands to figuratively wave me away, as though asking us to stand back. It is the gesture old folks use to mean, "Get outta here. You're fulla shit."

"Maybe we should take a break," I said. "Give her some time alone with Jesus and the Apostles."

Relieved, Beth and Nicki came around to my side of the bed, prepared to leave. To Nicki, I said, "I don't think she'll want the leftover hamburger for dinner. Go to Sonny's BBQ and get her a quart of Brunswick stew. It's another favorite."

Nicki seemed pleased to have the assignment. Before she could get out the door, Kaplan bumped into her on his way into the room. "Good news," he announced. "The culture didn't grow bacteria. The dermatitis is dead, and we can stop the antibiotic."

"Maybe that will stop the hallucinations," I said.

Kaplan looked confused. "The antibiotic wouldn't cause hallucinations."

"Well, Daniel, something is causing it. She's delusional, been communing with biblical figures all afternoon."

He chuckled. "Catholics aren't usually Bible thumpers."

"Take this seriously, Daniel. Something you're giving her is driving her crazy."

Kaplan pulled at his chin. "Do you have a theory about that? We know you've been reading her computer chart." He pointed to the computer terminal.

The women looked scared, like the accomplices to a prank watching the school principal grill the ringleader. I decided he couldn't know for certain what I had done or what I knew. He was fishing to see if I'd confess. "I only know what you told me, and one thing that doesn't add up is that she didn't get a blood thinner until Saturday morning, well after she suffered the ministrokes. Why was that?"

He gave me a sly smile. "Because amiodarone and Coumadin counteract one another. You can't prescribe them at the same time."

A tilt of the head waiting for me to respond. *I see the trap, Daniel.* "Coumadin is a blood thinner, right? What's amiodarone?"

He took a moment to decide whether I was putting him on. He had no choice but to answer. "Amiodarone was used in the emergency room to restore your mother's natural heartbeat."

It hit me then; the proverbial ton of bricks fell on my head. Mom had not suffered another A-fib episode last night. If she had, they'd have administered amiodarone to restore sinus rhythm. Instead, they used epinephrine because Mom's heart had *stopped beating*. The episode had been buried because the entries included no alarming remarks about a crisis, a code blue, or a crash cart. But if Billy had signed the DNR, Mom would now be dead.

"Okay, so you got lucky and the strokes didn't kill her. How many other times have you been lucky?" I watched passively as a cloud formed over his face. "How many more times will you *be* lucky?" I challenged him.

Lightning flashed in Kaplan's soft brown eyes, and his shoulders shuddered as though shaken by an intense clap of thunder. He controlled himself and tempered his response. "I'll check your mother's list of meds to see if anything could be causing hallucinations, but I want you out of the hospital this evening. That's an order. The stress of the situation has turned you into a conspiracy theorist, and it doesn't become you."

"What's going on?" Billy said as he walked up on our little conclave. I hadn't seen him coming.

Kaplan tugged my left bicep, gently. "Let your brother and his family look after her tonight, Randle."

"Sure," I said, and Kaplan walked away.

I turned to Billy. "Does Mom have a lawyer?"

He gave me a suspicious look. "Why would she need a lawyer?"

"You mentioned a POA."

His expression relaxed. "My lawyer drew it up."

"But she does have a financial advisor, doesn't she?"

The suspicious look returned in an instant. "Father's account was with Gibbons and Lewis. Now it's Mom's account. Why?"

I nodded, then reminded Nicki not to forget the Brunswick stew.

Before she could leave, Billy said to her, "I thought you'd be back in Florida."

Looking at me, Nicki said, "I'm going to stay awhile."

Billy wasn't pleased with that response. To Beth he said, "I've got a question for Mom. After that let's get something to eat and then come back for an hour or so."

I couldn't leave then. I needed to know what Billy wanted to know.

Billy greeted Mom, then asked, "What's the alarm code for the house now?"

Mom gave Billy a blank stare. After a moment, the answer came to her. "It's written on the key."

"You must have changed it," Billy said. "0125 doesn't work anymore."

"I don't know how to change it," Mom said.

That confirmed what Billy must have guessed. He swiveled toward me with a fierce scowl.

I shrugged and said, "Hey, you want something from the house, let me know and I'll bring it to you."

***

I drove downtown again. The Frog Hollow Tavern was a welcome retreat, but I wasn't interested in food. After pushing pork chops around on my plate for an hour, I walked along the banks of the Savannah River and watched small boats motor slowly up and down the sluggish waterway between Georgia and South Carolina. On the far bank stood the mansions of Augusta's elite who had escaped Georgia's higher tax rates. On the near side of the river, Augusta's charming but antiquated business district, a relic of life in the 1950s, bustled with activity. A few blocks away, the University Medical Center served as a temporary home to many people who, like Mom, were fighting for their lives on this sultry evening. I sat on a park bench, contemplating the arbitrary nature of life and death, until mosquitos and gnats chased me back to Mom's house. I didn't bother to hide the Bronco. I turned on all the lights. Evening drifted into darkness without any calls from the hospital, but Nicki texted me as they left Mom for the night: *She's OK.*

CHAPTER ELEVEN

O nce again, I thought I'd be first to Mom's bedside for a private chat, and once again I was wrong. As I approached her room on the otherwise quiet fourth floor, I heard shouting and banging, incongruous sounds in the normally hushed hospital setting. Her door was propped open, and nurses crowded around the portal. "Get out!" Mom screamed at them.

I tapped the shoulder of a nurse I hadn't met and said, "I'm her son. What's going on?"

The nurse had long red hair and freckles. She reminded me of Glenda. "She's gone bonkers."

Mom threw a Kleenex box at the nurses, but it fell harmlessly to the floor. Since that had no effect, she swept her breakfast tray off her rolling table. It hit the floor with a shocking clatter and a disgusting splatter of eggs, grits, and toast like vomit in a toilet bowl. "I'm not eating this shit!"

The nurses were frozen in place by this weird spectacle, so Mom found a more dangerous projectile, her plastic cup of orange juice, and cocked her arm. The nurses ducked and shimmied toward the door as the cup sailed through the air. It struck a young brunette, and the sticky liquid climbed up her back, and into her hair.

"That woman has lost her freaking mind!" she shrieked as she pushed through the crowd and ran down the hallway.

"Get Shelby," I ordered the redhead. "And keep everyone out of here until I calm her down."

The nurses obeyed and dispersed. I edged into the room as Mom muttered a litany of curses. "Can you see me, Mom? Know who I am?"

She looked my way. "Of course I can see you, Jackie. Get me out of this place!"

Cautiously, I eased to her bedside. She had nothing more to throw. "As soon as the doctor gets here, we'll ask him when you can leave."

She frowned, disappointed that I wouldn't just whisk her away. "Tell me the real reason I'm being kept in the hospital."

"You had a heart attack. You need to stay calm. We need to be sure it doesn't happen again."

She squinted and examined my face. "You aren't working with them, are you, Jackie?"

I chuckled. "No, Mom. It's you and me against the world."

It had always been the two of us against the world. Mom was born and raised in Charleston, South Carolina—a place as old and traditionally Southern as a culture can be—and with Father she raised a divided family that proved to be a microcosm of America's Civil War turbulence. Father, Billy, and Katie were "Yankees." Mom and I were "Rebels." Mom and I were outnumbered and outgunned—how fitting—but the Yankee camp was never as tightly knit as the Rebel camp.

Mom's face softened into a proud smile, and she nodded, as though confirming a plan. She waved me closer with her fingers so she could whisper.

"They want me to die so they can steal your money." Her expression said, "Aha! I figured it out."

My money? Fearing my mother had indeed lost her mind, I said, "Somebody stole some of *your* money, but I'll make sure they don't get the rest."

She grabbed my hand and gripped it with surprising strength. "They're broke," she insisted. "Both of them."

I patted her cheek. "I have a document for you to sign so I can control the money. Will you do that for me?"

She looked confused. I pulled the POA and a pen from my briefcase and placed them on the tray in front of her. "Just sign right here, Mom," I said, pointing to the dotted line.

She still looked confused. "I fixed it," she said.

This is how it begins, I thought. Dementia, Alzheimer's, senility—whatever you want to call it. More urgently, I said, "With this I'll be in charge instead of Billy."

The confusion drained from her face, and she looked at peace. She scribbled a few pen strokes on the paper.

Just then Nicki and Beth walked through the door and stopped to consider the scene. Hurriedly, I stuffed the POA into my briefcase, hoping I didn't appear to be doing something sinister.

Before they could question me, Shelby arrived and called out "Hello." She had paused in the doorway, not wanting to disturb my efforts to quiet Mom.

To Shelby, I said, "She's calmed down, but you might want to stay out of her vision. What's the problem this morning?"

Without moving, Shelby said, "She refuses medical attention, refuses to eat. Throws things."

"Yes, but why?"

"Temporary psychosis. She's having another drug reaction."

"To what?"

"There's not much left in her system. See for yourself." She motioned toward the computer.

Another trap. "You'll have to show me."

She gave me a don't-bullshit-me look but moved toward the counter. I joined her as she woke the computer and paged back to the overnight hours. She pointed at the screen. "The B strep is gone, so Dr. Harrison stopped the antibiotic." She paged back to the prior evening. "The dermatitis culture was negative, so we stopped that antibiotic. Dr. Kaplan stopped the med for lung fluid yesterday morning. All she's getting is Lasix for leg fluid and warfarin to thin her blood."

Shelby continued to flip through pages toward the present time, but as she flipped I noticed something and stopped her. "And atropine," I said.

"Sure, they dilate her eyes each time they do a vision test. She's virtually normal now." Shelby smiled at me, then her face went slack and she closed her eyes. "Oh my God. It's the atropine. It's always been the atropine."

"Is there an antidote?"

She opened her eyes. "I'm not sure. Dr. Kaplan is on his way in to the hospital."

"Okay. Tell everyone to back off until he gets here."

Shelby hit ctrl-alt-del to put the computer to sleep and turned to leave, but Kaplan and Karen Schmidt, the family counselor, burst through the door and blocked her path. Everyone talked at once.

"It's the atropine," Shelby said.

"You're not welcome here," I said to Ms. Schmidt.

"It's not your call," Kaplan said.

"Your mother has to make her own medical decisions," Ms. Schmidt said.

"I want to go home," Mom said.

"It's just the atropine," Shelby said to Kaplan. "She'll be fine if we stop using it."

Kaplan gave Shelby a cross look, slid past me to Mom's bedside, and took her hand in his. "We're going to honor your wishes, Mrs. Marks. You'll be discharged today. You're well enough to go."

Mom's eyes sparkled as she said, "Thank you, doctor. I'm ready."

"Hold on!" I shouted. "She could have another A-fib attack at any minute."

"Millions of Americans live with A-fib," Ms. Schmidt said, "but they don't have a room here."

Kaplan composed himself. "The dermatitis is gone and so is the B strep. Her vision has been restored. We've dried up the lung fluid. She does have some fluid in her legs, but that will recede as her heart grows stronger. We've done all we can do."

"She's able to feed herself," Ms. Schmidt added.

I gave them a stern look. "But she has a bomb in her chest."

"She's had a long life," the obnoxious counselor said. "She has to learn to live with her physical condition."

I shook my head to make my jumbled thoughts fall into some sort of rational order. None of this made sense to me. "Ms. Schmidt, if your house had a fire that destroyed the kitchen and family room, and the heartless insurance company wouldn't pay for the repairs, would you learn to live in the rest of the house?"

Ms. Schmidt understood the analogy. She turned as red as an ambulance.

"Of course not," I finished.

"There's nothing to be done until she's strong enough to tolerate surgery," Kaplan said in a conciliatory tone.

"This hospital has to keep her alive so she can grow stronger," I shot back. "The epinephrine injection saved her life when her heart stopped Sunday night."

That didn't shock Kaplan. He was prepared to spar with me. "We could sue you for illegal computer access."

"They are her records, not yours."

"That's right. *Her* records. You violated HIPAA regulations."

"Sue me all day long, Daniel. It won't stop me from saving my mother's life."

With that, the argument halted and everyone took a deep breath. Like a ghostly apparition, Billy suddenly appeared in the doorway but didn't move into the room.

"Why aren't you at work?" I asked.

"I called him," Ms. Schmidt said. "We have to decide where Mrs. Marks should go."

"You were supposed to go home today," Billy said to his niece, his voice edgy.

"I'm doing things for Uncle Randle," Nicki replied defiantly.

"He doesn't have her medical power of attorney," I said to Ms. Schmidt, referring to my brother.

"The whole family should participate," Ms. Schmidt said.

"What are the choices?" Billy said, tentative.

This was the counselor's area of expertise. "She can't live alone, but she could move in with a family member."

I stared at Billy, and he blanched. "She can't live with us. Our house isn't set up for an invalid."

"She could move to a hospice," Kaplan said.

"You mean a nursing home?" Billy said.

"He means a place where she's put out of her misery and we're left to watch her die," I said. "It's the same as putting a dog to sleep."

"No, no!" Kaplan and Shelby said in shocked unison, but Ms. Schmidt kept her cool. "You could always try rehab," she said.

Relieved to have another alternative, Kaplan said, "If you think she can get strong enough for surgery, a rehab center would be the way to go. Of course, it's more expensive than hospice care."

"How much?" Billy asked.

"That's what we'll do," I said.

"How much?" Billy asked again.

"We should see what Mrs. Marks wants to do," Ms. Schmidt said.

Everyone turned toward Mom. She said, "Whatever Jackie wants."

Kaplan looked confused, so I explained that Mom called me Jackie.

"How much?" Billy asked yet again.

"I'll arrange it," Ms. Schmidt said. She left the room before anyone could change their mind.

"We'll have to prep her for transport," Kaplan said.

"I'll take care of it," Shelby said. She gave me a triumphant look before she left.

"What about the atropine?" I said.

"It will wear off," Kaplan replied. "She's just on strike. She'll be happy to get out of here."

"You'll be happy to get me out of here."

He smiled. "True enough." He clapped me on the shoulder and eased me and our family into the corridor. "A word of advice, Randle: if she doesn't respond to physical therapy, let her go. Doctors have learned to use less technology and less medicine than average citizens, and we die more peacefully."

"You don't resuscitate."

"We make it easy for our families. Desperate measures just prolong the inevitable."

"I read an article on the Internet the other day about a young man who was adjudged brain dead by his doctors. His father wouldn't let them pull the plug, held off the medical staff with a handgun. He was arrested and sent to jail, but the kid remained on life support. Years later, after the father got out of jail, the kid woke up and now father and son enjoy a life together."

"Have it your way." Without so much as a handshake, he spun on his heel and took two quick jabbing steps, like a sprinter accelerating out of the starting blocks.

"If my mother dies, I'll make you pay," I said to his back. He acknowledged me with a dismissive wave as he disappeared into another patient's room.

Chapter Twelve

Billy and Beth looked shocked as they moved toward the visitors' lounge. Nicki stayed with me. I asked her to stand guard outside Mom's closed door. I told her not to allow anyone into the room, to tell anyone who came that I was confirming that Mom wanted to go to rehab.

In truth, I wanted to see the current entries in Mom's medical record. Since they had decided to discharge her, they must have entered a discharge order. Ignoring Mom, who showered me with questions about her impending release, I woke the computer and paged forward from the spot where Shelby had put it to sleep and on to this morning's entries. As I had suspected, discharge orders had been added to the record. My first impulse was to read through the long list of instructions, but I didn't have time. Agitated, I shook the mouse, and the cursor streaked back and forth across the screen. As it moved over the area near the top of the screen, a menu line appeared. It featured an array of icons I had seen before but hadn't used out of fear that system technicians could track my activity. Now I no longer cared what they discovered. On the line, I noticed the familiar "connect the dots" icon representing the ability to send the record outside the hospital system. *Eureka!* Hospital staff would use this option to send the record to doctors or facilities outside the hospital. I pressed the icon, and a panel popped up into which I entered my own email address and hit "send." It would have been safer to send the record somewhere anonymous, but I had no time to think of an alternate destination. After receiving an "email sent" confirmation, I paged to the spot where Shelby had left the record and hit ctrl-alt-del to put the computer back to sleep.

I stood at Mom's bedside when Shelby and a platoon of nurses marched into the room like an invasion force expecting to catch me doing something wrong. As the nurses worked on Mom, I shuffled to the back of the room where Billy, Beth, and Nicki had assembled. Shelby joined us and briefed Billy and me while Beth and Nicki listened. She explained that she had found Mom a bed at the Sacred Heart Rehabilitation Center on Richmond Hill Road, midway between the hospital and Mom's house. Sacred Heart, affiliated with the Catholic Church, was one of the "good places," Shelby told us proudly.

"How do we pay for it?" Billy asked.

"Medicare," Shelby said. "Just like the hospital."

Billy accepted that answer, and I was relieved that we wouldn't have to fight over Mom's disposition.

The activity around Mom seemed frantic, as though an unspoken timetable had to be met. Shelby narrated as nurses installed a PICC line in Mom's arm. That device, Shelby told us, eliminated the need for IV changes and reduced her exposure to infection. An IV could only be used for three days while a PICC line could stay in place for three weeks or more, she said. I guessed it also simplified IV insertions for the lesser-skilled nurses at the rehab facility.

Shelby shooed us out of the room then and told us to wait at the front entrance. A nurse would bring Mom down in a wheelchair to meet her transport. I thanked Shelby for taking good care of Mom and made a feeble attempt to hug her, but she deftly dodged my embrace and pushed us through the door.

"I hope your mother never has to come back here," she said.

You hope I'll never come back here.

The four of us rode the elevator in silence and walked out the entrance into the stifling stillness of the calm before a storm. Roiling black clouds pressed down upon the earth, and ozone clogged our nostrils. Birds gathered in flocks and fled to the largest trees. We stood under the overhanging portico as a taxi skidded to a stop at the curb. The driver leapt out of the cab and rushed past us through the main entrance. Nicki ambled to the far end of the building to have a smoke. Maybe it was the pent-up tension in the air that caused me to say what was on my mind.

Pointing a finger at my brother, I said, "You didn't want me to stay at Mom's house because you didn't want me to see her financial records."

"They're none of your business," he said.

"She has plenty of income but the checking account is always empty."

"Mom buys stuff from the TV shopping networks," Beth offered.

"Everything in the house is ten years old, Beth." Looking at Billy, I said, "Why are you stealing Mom's money?"

Billy grunted in disbelief. "I'm not stealing it. I'm preserving it."

"And the sooner she dies, the more you preserve."

I expected his reaction, and I was prepared for it. He cocked his right arm, fist clenched, and telegraphed a sweeping right cross. A shift of my head, three inches to the left, was all it took to evade the blow. Beth screamed. Nicki came running. The taxi driver emerged from the entrance and stopped to watch.

We gave them a show. I danced to the left, confining his power side, and circled a frustrated Billy as he swiveled gracelessly to follow my movement. His head down, looking through his eyebrows, feinting with a left hand he didn't want to throw; my head up, standing tall, dancing around him, we reprised Ali and Frazier. Like Ali, I taunted my opponent, "Come on, little boy, you've waited forty years for this chance."

Beth tried to grab Billy's sleeve, but I was moving quickly and he tore away from her grip. Twice he landed glancing blows to my midsection before making a Joe-Frazier bull rush, but, like Ali, I reached out my left hand and placed it on the crown of his head and held him off. At six-foot-three, I was seven inches taller than my little brother, and I had an even greater advantage in reach. His punches fell short of their mark.

Nicki laughed at the comical spectacle.

"Stop it!" Beth yelled.

"I'm going to kill him," Billy growled.

"Nobody's doin' nothin'," the taxi driver said as he slid between us, one hand on each fighter's chest. Like most adults who get into a fist fight, we dropped our guard immediately once a peacemaker rescued us, unconvincingly feigning reluctance to stop fighting.

Pointing an accusatory finger at Billy, I said, "I found the empty savings account. You won't get away with it."

Billy's chest heaved a couple of times while his eyebrows walked all over his face in consternation. "I didn't do it," he muttered.

"Wish I could believe you. Somebody's been withdrawing money from the account for a year. Mom wouldn't do that."

"Mom does strange things, Randle," Beth said. "Puts her dirty dishes in the refrigerator and her leftovers in the dishwasher."

"Dementia," Billy said. "She knows I watch the checking account, but I don't pay close attention to the other accounts. They're just there."

I was about to say, "Yeah, right!" when a fiery spear of lightning struck the earth just beyond the parking lot, accompanied by a concussive explosion of thunder. We flinched in unison. Within moments, rain cascaded over the portico like a Hawaiian waterfall and formed a wall between the dry sidewalk and the taxi. Shortly, an anonymous nurse pushed Mom through the front doors and asked the driver to open the taxi's back door. We realized then that Mom wouldn't be transported in an ambulance or shuttle van. She was dressed in the crumpled nightgown she had worn upon admittance. She was going to be soaked by the rain.

Over the staccato roar of plump raindrops on the portico, I yelled at the nurse, "She can't go in a damned taxi. I'll take her in my car after this storm passes."

The nurse shook her head. "Can't do that, sir. Transport has to be an authorized vehicle."

"A taxi is better than my car?" Still yelling.

"It's an authorized transport, sir."

The taxi driver meekly opened his rear door.

"Is there a more protected place to load her?"

"Not really."

The nurse tried to move Mom toward the taxi, but I blocked her path. "When the rain stops."

Her name was Woodley. She was young, chubby, and nervous. With pleading eyes, she sought help from the others, but Nicki sidled up to me and strengthened the blockade. Exasperated, Ms. Woodley pulled a cell phone from her pocket and called someone. After listening for a moment, she handed her phone to me.

Before the other party could say anything, I said, "Not while it's raining. When she can leave with dignity, I'll let her go." I pushed the "end" button and handed Woodley her phone.

The standoff lasted for another thirty-five minutes. No one came to rescue Woodley. She backed Mom against the building, away from the windswept rain splatters on the pavement, and fidgeted. Mom's head lolled and her eyelids drooped. She had trouble following conversations, and her eyes didn't track motion. They had drugged my mother to ensure her cooperation during the move.

I had read somewhere that the average thunderstorm lasts fifty-five minutes. This one was average. As soon as the rain ceased, the taxi driver backed his cab away from the dripping portico and Nurse Woodley loaded Mom into the backseat. As they pulled away, we ran to our cars and formed a caravan to the Sacred Heart Rehabilitation Center. Nicki rode with me.

***

The rain stopped as the taxi led us to a single-story, red-brick rectangle with one short side fronting the street and the other overlooking a par 3 hole on the Green Meadow golf course at the rear. Only a handful of cars rested in the cramped parking lot, which didn't have to be any larger to accommodate the sparse flow of visitors to the center.

As I emerged from the Bronco, a male nurse met the taxi, levered Mom out of the backseat, and settled her into a wheelchair. He pushed a round metal button on a steel pillar beside the walkway, and an oversized set of double doors swung open automatically. The main entrance was constructed for easy access by wheelchairs. Or rolling beds. Or stretchers.

I joined up with my haggard family, and we followed our patient into the muted lighting and sudden chill of the interior. An overweight man in his mid-forties, with hair too black to be natural and matching horn-rimmed glasses, greeted us.

He stuck out a meaty paw and said, "I'm Luke Ponchalk, the general manager."

We took our turns shaking his hand as the nurse pushed Mom farther into the bowels of the building. "Rodney will take Mrs. Marks to her room and get her settled in. She'll need toiletries, some everyday clothes, and clothes suitable for exercise. The residents don't wear hospital gowns here, so that should be your first priority."

He waited for us to get the hint, and we assigned the task to Beth and Nicki. As they walked away, I realized Beth would trip the house alarm if she entered 0125. I yelled at Nicki to wait and ran up to her. I whispered the passcode in my niece's ear as Billy and Beth looked on in stunned silence. There was no hiding it now—we were at war. I would have to reset the code again when I got to the house. Ponchalk then invited Billy and me to his office to discuss "business."

The heavy man squeezed behind a small wooden desk that sagged under piles of paperwork, and Billy and I sat in armless metal chairs. He explained that Sacred Heart was a rehab facility, not a nursing home. A rehab facility, he said, is a waypoint and not a destination. He grinned. "Patients do not live out their years here; no one comes here to die. We're an extension of the hospital system. We treat patients with physical and psychological therapy so they can resume active lives. As a result, morale is higher than at nursing homes. Our patients aren't depressed; they're optimistic about their futures."

That sounded to me like an advertising slogan. He paused, obviously waiting for acknowledgment, so Billy said, "We understand. What does it cost?"

"Your mother is a Medicare patient—most of our residents are—so the government will fund her treatment if she complies with government rules. Medicare pays all costs for the first twenty days, but you pay coinsurance for the next eighty days after that."

Billy shook his head. "How much is the coinsurance?"

"One hundred sixty-one dollars per day," Ponchalk said.

"Good God," Billy said as he considered what I quickly calculated to be nearly five thousand dollars per month.

Ponchalk held up a hand to signify he hadn't finished explaining all the numbers. "Under the law, Medicare will fund a maximum of one hundred days of therapy, but only if she makes progress toward recovery and is released from our facility within the one-hundred-day window."

Billy and I traded confused looks.

"Sacred Heart is a waypoint," he reiterated. "The goal is to restore your mother's ability to care for herself—walk, bathe, feed herself. So long as she's on a path to achieve that within a one-hundred-day window, Medicare will fund most of her treatment."

"Who makes that call? That she's making appropriate progress?" I said.

"My staff."

"And what happens if she doesn't make enough progress?"

"We bill your mother directly, seventy-five hundred dollars per month, prorated, of course." He grinned again.

"You know she's a heart patient, right? She may not make progress at the same rate as someone with a strong heart."

"We'll take that into consideration. Initially." He grinned again, and I realized that his hair was an unnatural color because it wasn't real—it was a toupee and not an expensive one. I guessed that when he was promoted, he'd become a funeral director.

"What if she makes some progress but not enough to get out of here in one hundred days?"

My phrasing did not offend him. "Then you'll have choices. She can stay here at her own expense and continue to receive treatment, or she can move to an assisted-living facility, or she can move in with a relative and receive in-home nursing care." He didn't grin. Neither did Billy, who was mentally calculating the relative costs of the three options.

Being a conspiracy theorist, I wondered if Ponchalk made more money from self-funded patients or Medicare patients. If families were poor, Ponchalk would milk Medicare for the maximum and then kick the patient out the door. If self-funding was more profitable, he would convince families that their loved ones were making progress and should stay at the facility but were not progressing enough to be funded by the government. In that case, he would want the patient to stay for an extended period so he could reap the profits. That left the door open for an insidious form of fraud. We had walked into a bear trap. We would have to hide Mom's financial resources.

"Okay," I said. "We'll ensure that Mom takes her therapy seriously and makes good progress."

He gave me a thin smile. He knew he was in complete control. "We won't count today toward her Medicare timeline. It's already afternoon. Her therapy will start in the morning."

Thanks for nothing. Only the wealthy can afford to stay healthy. The rest of us die when our money runs out.

He ushered us out of his office and introduced us to his business manager, a tall, slender but rock-hard woman with severe features. Her name was Bonnie Mueller. Mueller wanted to get Mom registered, collect her personal information, Medicare insurance details, and so forth.

I pushed Billy ahead of me and said, "This is the man who knows the details." Then I slipped out of the administrative area to look for Mom.

A broad linoleum corridor ran the entire length of this long side of the building. Straight ahead, an opening led to the cafeteria. I walked in to have a look and found a large room filled with round tables seating six each. Small gatherings of patients played cards or board games. At a couple of tables, patients visited with younger family members. At the rear of the room, cafeteria-style counters stood stacked with dispensers of coffee, tea, and soft drinks. It didn't seem to be a bad environment, and I momentarily felt guilty about my conspiracy theories.

Back in the hallway, I remembered that Rodney had turned to the right when he entered the building, so I started in that direction. Patient rooms were semiprivate, two beds to a room, with built-in shelves and wardrobes around each bed. Each room had a private bath. Each patient had a landline telephone with a direct-dial number. The rooms had been constructed along the outer wall of the building so each room had a window and sunlight. As I walked down the hallway, I passed patients in wheelchairs and patients on crutches, getting some exercise or traveling to a friend's room. I reached the end of the hallway without locating Mom.

The short side of the building that faced the street housed a sizeable nurses' station where practitioners huddled for conversations, picked up vials of pills to deliver to patients, or crouched over computer terminals. Nurses nodded as I made my way to the other long side of the building. The construction on the far side mirrored that of the near side—semiprivate rooms erected on the exterior wall. In the middle of the hallway, another opening on the interior wall revealed a TV/sitting room half the size of the cafeteria. Bookshelves and magazine racks lined the walls. Widescreen TVs mounted back to back divided the room in half. In each half of the room, empty couches and easy chairs faced the TVs, and the afternoon dramas played to a nonexistent audience. The old folks knew better than to waste their last days watching the soaps.

I had nearly reached the back of the building before I found Mom, sitting on her bed, talking to a nurse with short red hair and freckles. The nurse seemed to be calming her down.

"Everything okay here?" I said.

The nurse wore a nametag emblazoned with a long string of consonants interrupted by one vowel plus a couple of "Y's." "I'm Carol," she said.

"Why can't I have a private room?" Mom said.

I sat next to her and put an arm around her shoulders. "There aren't any, Mom. Medicare only pays for semiprivate rooms. But these are nice." A plastic curtain hung from a slide rail affixed to the ceiling so that the room could be divided for privacy. "When you want privacy, we pull the curtain."

She looked doubtfully at the curtain. "Don't leave me here, Jackie. I don't want to die here."

Carol gave me a sympathetic look. I was sure she had heard this conversation many times.

"You won't die here, Mom. They're going to help you back on your feet so you can go home."

"When?"

A shiver of shame coursed through me for lying to my mother, but I had to boost her morale. "As soon as you can walk and bathe yourself."

"Will you stay with me, Jackie?"

"I'll be here every day."

Mom laid her head on my shoulder, and Carol gave me a smile of thanks.

"What's her name?" It was the woman in the other bed, a raw-boned, red-faced creature who looked like she had just climbed off a tractor in a Nebraska cornfield.

"Elaine. What's yours?"

"Maureen. Why's she here? She looks okay."

Mom hardly looked okay, but I surmised she meant that her disability wasn't visible. "Had a heart attack. Last Friday. Did you break your leg?" A cast traveled from Maureen's knee to her waist.

"Naw, my hip. They say I'm lucky to be alive."

I was no longer sure I knew the meaning of that phrase in the context of the disabled elderly. Was it lucky to be confined to a rehab center? "Are you able to rehab with a broken hip?"

"Upper body. They say it will help after my hip heals."

"Won't that take a long time, before you can actually rehab the hip?"

"Yep. I'll be here awhile, but it's better than my son's house. Little kids, a screaming wife. This is better."

"Sure, but expensive. Medicare only pays so much, right?"

She cackled like a movie character witch. "Medicare will pay whatever Bonnie tells 'em to pay."

Oh, I'll remember that. "Mom's a little shy, but she'll come around and you guys will be good friends before you know it."

Mom raised her head off my shoulder and gave me a scolding look. She was far from shy, but she was an elitist. Although she never joined either organization, she was qualified to be a member of the Daughters of the American Revolution and the Daughters of the Confederacy. In her estimation, she had a pedigree. Father had no such pedigree. The son of German and Polish immigrants, he had been second-generation American. From Mom's perspective, he was still a foreigner on the day he passed away.

Mom burrowed into my shoulder again, as though the room would disappear if she just didn't look at it, and I struggled to think of more soothing words to allay her fears. Beth, Nicki, and Billy's arrival rescued me. The women carried bags of clothing and personal effects, while Billy held a sheaf of paperwork.

"Oh good," Carol said. "We'll bathe her and change her clothes. That will make her feel better."

Beth hung clothes in the small closet, and Nicki set family pictures, magazines, and books on the shelves next to Mom's bed. Carol asked us to wait in the cafeteria until she brought Mom in for dinner, so we retreated and camped around the last unoccupied table in the quickly filling dining hall.

We engaged in a stilted and desultory conversation. Secretly, we all prayed we wouldn't end up here in our own final days.

Then I dropped my bombshell. "I have proof that you've been stealing Mom's money," I said to Billy. He stood to leave, but Beth clung to his arm. I slid my copies of the withdrawal slips toward him. That stopped him, but he didn't reach for the copies. Beth gave him a questioning look and picked up the papers.

After she had looked at each withdrawal, Beth said, "We didn't write these slips. Billy has a POA, so he doesn't have to forge Mom's signature."

That was no longer the case, but it wasn't time to disclose my new POA. "Do you recognize the handwriting?" I asked. "Is it Katie's?"

Beth paged through the documents again and shook her head. "I don't think so."

Billy jabbed a finger in my direction. "Never again, Jack. Do not accuse me of mishandling Mom's money."

I gathered up the copies and put them back into my briefcase. Like a pendulum, I swung from one wild conclusion to another. Now I concluded that Brad had stolen Mom's money. Probably for Katie. Probably to fund Katie's habit.

As waiters and waitresses delivered meals to other tables, we remained silent. Suddenly, my cell phone rang. My daughter, Jamie. *Please don't lecture me about marrying your mother*, I thought. I asked her to hold on while I left the table to find a quiet place to talk. Residents filled the TV room, so I walked through it and into Mom's hallway. Mom's door was still shut, so I continued out the back door to a concrete patio overlooking the golf course. I watched a threesome of golfers tee off on the short downhill par 3 hole directly behind the rehab center.

When I could hear Jamie, she said, "Carrie is scheduled for a parole board meeting."

"No one gets paroled their first time in front of the board."

"The jury acquitted her of burglary, Dad. She's only doing time for a gun violation."

"The parole board knows she drove her accomplice to my house in her boat and broke the bathroom window for him. She'll be punished for a crime they couldn't prove by keeping her in jail for a crime they did prove. That's the way it works in your business."

"Whatever you say, Dad. You're the expert on the criminal justice system." Jamie sounded exasperated. As always.

A golfer teed off behind the center and his ball flew long, landed on the back edge of the green, and caromed into a bunker. "Have you told your mother?"

"No, I'll leave that to you. You need to come home, Dad."

Jamie's concern over Carrie's possible release seemed unwarranted. I had won my battle with Carrie—a Pyrrhic victory to be sure, but a victory—and that episode was behind me.

"Carrie is history, Jamie. That chapter is over."

"She's psychotic, Dad. She'll want revenge, and if she can't find you, she'll find Mom."

A second golfer hit a tee shot into the trees to the right of the green. I wasn't thinking clearly, but I doubted that Carrie knew Glenda's role in her conviction. "If Carrie gets out, can your mother stay with you, or can you go stay with her for a while?"

"Your mother has other family to care for her. If you are committed to *my* mother, get your ass down here."

Jamie hung up. I found it ironic that although she wasn't pleased I was going to remarry her mother, she did want me to protect her.

The third golfer came up short in the bunker fronting the green. Such a short, easy hole, yet none of the golfers managed to hit the green. Sometimes the seemingly easy tasks in life are the most daunting.

I watched the threesome play out the hole as I built my courage to call Glenda. Despite their poor tee shots, all three of the players managed to score a bogey.

I reached Glenda at her store. She was closing for the day and wanted me to call her later at home.

"This can't wait." I related to Glenda what Jamie had told me.

"Then she did do it. She killed Rudy."

"What!?" "Rudy" was a white heron who frequented my backyard to sip from my pool and beg for food. I considered him—or her—to be a pet.

"I found him in the pool. His neck was broken."

"She's still in jail, sweetie. It had to be an accident."

"It's creepy here without you. Come take care of me."

I explained the situation in Augusta. Glenda listened without comment. "Can you stay with Jamie or your mother for a while?" I said.

"This isn't a temporary situation, Randle. We have to find a way to live normally in spite of your baggage. Let the rehab nurses look after your mother. Let Billy clean up his own mess."

"Billy is part of the problem!" *And I promised Mom I'd stay with her.*

Glenda's fiery nature got the best of her. "If you had reached a divorce settlement with Carrie, instead of trapping her in a crime, she wouldn't be in jail and she wouldn't be out for revenge. Oh, by the way, we'd also have money from your stock options. But no, you wanted to impose your own twisted view of justice, so you both went to jail and now we all have to live with the consequences."

I could have argued that I had settled my divorce in a way that was fair, but Glenda already knew the story. I said, "We've got some time. I'll take care of it."

Glenda took a moment to compose her response. She sounded calm but resolute. "Fine, Randle. Come home this weekend, and we'll face Carrie together. I'll reschedule the wedding for a week from Saturday."

To end the conversation on a high note, I thanked her and agreed. We hung up after exchanging the usual "I love yous," but hers didn't sound genuine.

I sat on a lawn chair and watched as the next group of golfers arrived on the tee box. The paved patio faced the setting sun, but the tall oak trees on the golf course shaded it. It was a pleasant spot to think or chat with a friend. It inspired me to weigh the pros and cons of my dilemma. On the one hand, the rehab center wasn't a terrible place. Mom's only chance to extend her life was to gain enough strength to endure surgery. The rehab staff would look after her. I didn't think Billy had stolen the money market funds, and now he'd watch her money more closely. Even without the savings account, she had enough money to pay for her treatment. If I returned to Florida, Beth and Billy could console Mom until Katie and Brad could replace me.

On the other side of the coin, I doubted Carrie would be released in anything less than a month given the pace at which courts and prisons operate. And when she was released, she'd have nowhere to live, no money, and no job. I guessed she would move in with her parents in New Port Richey or try to rekindle her romance with the lover she took before our divorce. That man had divorced his wife to be with Carrie, but that was before she was incarcerated. I doubted he would want his mistress back.

I had some time. And I had made Mom a promise. That meant I could use the three days that Glenda had allowed me to get Mom's rehab off to a good start, and then I would return to my life in Florida and Mom would be in God's hands.

I paged through my phone contacts and found a number I hadn't called in well over a year—the number for my once and former attorney, and erstwhile best friend, Tony Zambrano. Melissa, his paralegal, answered the call and behaved as though I were a vile bill collector interrupting family dinner. She put me on hold. Familiar Muzak serenaded me.

After less than a minute, she said, "He says he's busy."

To be expected. I had deceived him during my divorce proceeding. "Ask him if he'll help me get a restraining order against my ex-wife. She may be released from prison soon, and my fiancée is alone in our beach house."

Melissa blew air in my ear and put me on hold again. In thirty seconds, she was back. "He says you have no grounds; she hasn't done anything to you or your fiancée. He says there are plenty of attorneys with lower standards who might help you."

I was nice to her. I thanked her for helping and hung up. As usual, the law protected the rights of the potential criminal before protecting the rights of potential victims. The criminal has to assault you before you can receive protection against a second assault.

I re-entered the building, and as I passed Mom's room I noticed that the occupancy indicator slide was set to red for "Privacy, Please." I crossed from one side of the building to the other by cutting through the cafeteria, which was abuzz with activity, most tables crowded with vociferous seniors drinking after-dinner coffee or eating desserts. No one sat at the table we had occupied, however. I wound my way through the cafeteria tables and emerged in the main lobby, where a restless Billy, a bored Nicki, and a concerned Beth waited for me.

"Is everything okay in Florida?" Beth said.

Before I could respond, Billy said, "Mom's down for the night. We're going to grab some dinner and go home." He took half a step and leaned toward the door, hoping to start a stampede, but the women weren't ready to leave. Beth had made him do the courtesy of waiting for me.

"Nana wouldn't eat the cafeteria food, so I picked up some lasagna and she took it to her room," Nicki said.

Mom had come and gone in the short time I'd been on the phone.

"Can you be here for Mom's therapy at eight a.m.?" Beth said. "Nicki's driving back to Orlando tomorrow, and I want to have breakfast with her before she leaves."

I assured them I would be with Mom all day. Nicki and I stepped into an instinctive embrace, and I whispered that she should save the matchbook with my number. She gave me a conspiratorial smile and said, "Come to dinner with us."

Billy wobbled from side to side like a kid's punching dummy, then looked to Beth for rescue. She nodded slightly. He was trapped temporarily by decorum, but Nicki's impending departure would soon release him from her pressure to be nice to me, so he relented. "Let's get it over with."

Chapter Thirteen

We drove to Frank and Pat's Pizzeria, where I ate a meatball sub, drank two bottles of Peroni, and contributed little to a contrived conversation that detoured around sensitive subjects until Billy admonished his niece to lay off the marijuana.

"Don't get caught like your uncle did."

Nicki squealed with delight and grasped my arm. "You got caught with pot?"

"When he was in college. Got thrown in jail," Billy said.

"It wasn't mine," I said.

Beth gave me a stern look, but Nicki wouldn't let it pass. "Come on, Uncle Randle. Tell us the story," she said gleefully.

Had I wanted to tell her the unvarnished truth, it would have gone like this . . .

My roommate and I lived in half of a duplex, west of downtown Atlanta and just beyond the boundaries of the Georgia Tech campus. The neighborhood abounded with drugs and crime, but the duplex was affordable for penurious students, and Terry and I were oblivious to the safety risks. The three students in the other half of the duplex supplied Terry and me with pot when we had the spare cash to buy it, which wasn't often.

On the Friday night of the overly dramatic police raid—three cruisers and a paddy wagon—two of the neighbors and three other friends crowded into our small apartment to drink cheap wine and celebrate the coming weekend. When the cops banged on our front door, I shouted that the door was broken and they'd have to come around the back. Through the small window in the door, I watched one cop write on a clipboard while the other considered his options. I'm sure he thought I was resisting and delaying his entrance so that evidence could be destroyed, but after several moments he directed his raiding party around the back of the unit and stationed one uniformed cop at the front door to prevent our escape.

I walked through the living room and the kitchen to open the back door, telling my guests to remain calm and behave themselves. As I waited for the cops to make their way through the alley and the bushes separating our duplex from the house next door, I saw the third neighbor, the one who hadn't come to our party, on his back porch, throwing things into the backyard. He laughed at me and swiftly retreated into his apartment.

Once the cops were inside our unit, they shepherded all of us into the living room while they searched the rest of the apartment. As they did, the toilet in the neighbor's unit flushed continuously, and the two neighbors who were with us snickered. Fifteen minutes later, the searchers joined the guards in the living room and reported nothing found. It appeared they were ready to call it a failure when one cop reminded the others that they hadn't searched individuals or the living room. They frisked us one at a time and stored us in the kitchen before searching the vacated living room.

By this time, our guests were laughing at the cops, and the cops were frustrated by their fruitless raid. But, just as everyone relaxed, the cops tore the cushions off the old green leather couch to expose a silver wad of tinfoil. Inside the foil rested a residue of marijuana seeds and stems. The cops rejoiced; they had found something.

"Who lives here?" the lead cop asked the group.

Terry and I admitted that we were the tenants.

"You're under arrest for possession of a controlled substance," the lead cop announced.

Our guests gasped, and Terry and I said in unison, "It's not mine."

"You live here, so it's yours," the cop said.

Terry turned to our guests and angrily asked who owned the pot. No one volunteered to be arrested, so the police handcuffed us and led us to the paddy wagon. The cops told our guests to leave the premises and go home.

The cops locked up Terry and me in a cramped cell in the city jail. That night terrified me like no other experience. The noise level precluded sleep as prisoners shouted, cried, and argued. All night, guards herded fresh prisoners, protesting their innocence, to their cells. In the wee hours of the morning, the guards dragged a drunken white man wearing a pink blazer past our cell. He struggled against his captors and shouted over and over, "I'm a big nigger in Atlanta!"

"Just what we need in a predominantly black population is a jackass inciting a race riot," I said to Terry.

He was despondent. Continuously, he hypothesized how fate had landed us in this predicament. His favorite theory: one of the neighbors had dumped the tinfoil in the couch while we were being searched. "Who was sitting on the couch?"

I shrugged and told him I didn't remember.

His companion theory: the cops had planned to raid the neighbors' half of the duplex, but at the last minute changed that plan when they realized our half had the rowdy crowd. "Just a coincidence."

At daylight, all the cells were emptied and the prisoners moved into a large bullpen while trustees mopped and cleaned the cells. We gravitated toward the few other students who had been incarcerated overnight and formed a defensive perimeter against what we perceived to be a menacing criminal population. Our fearful group included the subdued man in the pink jacket. He introduced himself as the owner of a popular student hangout. There had been fights the previous night, and he had tried to protect a couple of boisterous students. He had gotten himself arrested for the effort.

"Police harassment," he said. "I'll bail out this morning, and I'll be fined again. They want to close me down, but they'll never run me out of town."

No incidents occurred while we were in the bullpen. With their alcohol-induced hangovers fogging their brains, the prisoners were docile. Each clique kept its distance from every other clique. After the trustees mopped the floors, the guards led us back to our cells and we were safe with our troubling thoughts.

Around lunchtime, we learned we had a visitor. A haggard man in a cheap, checkered sport coat and loose tie informed us that he was our court-appointed attorney. He explained that we would be arraigned on Monday morning. If we couldn't make bail, he said, we'd be moved to the Fulton County Jail. "You don't want to go there."

He also explained that we had been arrested lawfully given prevailing statutes and that the "substance" in the tinfoil had tested positive for .31 grams of marijuana. The penalty for possession, even for such a small amount, was two years on a Georgia chain gang.

"Like in *Cool Hand Luke*?" I exclaimed.

"Like *Cool Hand Luke*," he said. "You should prepare yourselves and your families for that."

Saturday night reprised Friday night. We learned to sleep during the quieter daytime hours. Midafternoon on Sunday, our three neighbors came to visit. They were sheepish, and Terry asked them directly if the tinfoil was theirs. No, they said, only amateurs stored pot in tinfoil. They promised to bail us out after we were arraigned the next morning—tapping their stash of drug profits—and that confirmed for Terry that they were trying to assuage their guilt.

On Monday we were arraigned, bail was set, and a trial was scheduled two months into the future. Minutes before we were to be bused to the county lockup, the neighbors bailed us out.

Our friends no longer talked to us, and no one would come to our apartment. We were pariahs. The days passed swiftly, like calendar pages flipped by some invisible hand in the movies. Disaster loomed, but I couldn't bring myself to inform my parents that I would soon wear pinstripes in some god-awful South Georgia prison. Less than a month away from the trial, one of my professors—a "cool dude"—took me aside after class and advised me to hire a father/daughter legal team called Solocov and Solocov. "They've gotten a lot of my students off," he said.

I called them and learned that we would have to pay five hundred dollars for a consultation. I didn't have even half of that and neither did Terry, who was in school on a hardship scholarship. That led to the most difficult phone call I've ever made—a call to Father to admit my plight and beg for money.

He didn't believe I was innocent. "You've made your bed, and now you have to lie in it."

I cried. Mom got on the phone to hear my story, and then they held a conversation with the receiver covered. Father took over again and gave me the verdict: he would give me the money. "It's a *loan*, not a gift."

I camped at the Western Union office until the funds came through. That same afternoon, Terry and I met with Morris and Rebecca Solocov.

Morris was a craggy-faced septuagenarian with wisps of gray hair. Rebecca was an attractive blonde in her late forties. In a pine-paneled conference room, we described the raid, the search, and the arrest, but the lawyers were more interested in our families, our grades, our behavioral histories. Old Morris's eyes lit up when I revealed I was a member of the basketball team and that my status as a player was in doubt as a result of the arrest. After the interrogation, Morris said, "Okay, we'll get you off." We had questions about the trial, but the consultation was over and they ushered us out of the office without further ado.

We walked across the downtown connector overpass heading to the campus, and Terry said, "You just lost five hundred dollars."

As I waited nervously, and as Terry insisted repeatedly that our doom was a fait accompli, a week slipped by before we heard from Rebecca Solocov. "The investigation will cost another five hundred dollars," she said. Later, Terry would tell me that I was a fool to give the "shysters" more money, but I called Father again and borrowed it. This time he insisted on a quid pro quo: if I was acquitted, I would move into a dorm my senior year. That would be an embarrassment, but I agreed to the terms of the loan.

During the next two weeks, I didn't sleep but I didn't get out of bed either. I didn't attend classes—what was the point?—and therefore I was in the apartment when Rebecca called and said we could come to the office and pick up our court order. Just days before our trial, our case had been dismissed!

The court order explained why: "The search warrant is insufficient on its face, having no city or state listed in the address of the premises to be searched. The Park Avenue address on the warrant could as easily have been an address in New York City as an address in Atlanta, Georgia."

"They bribed a cop to swap search warrants," Terry said. "That's why they asked all those questions about our character. They bribe cops to get 'good kids' out of trouble."

"I saw the cop writing on the warrant on our doorstep, Terry. He just didn't finish the address. It's what you said all along: they were supposed to raid our neighbors, but all the people were at our place."

Terry snickered. "We got off because you're on the basketball team. If that happened to someone else, I'd be outraged, but since it happened to me, I'm okay with it."

Our friendship waned, and I lost touch with Terry during my senior year. It wasn't because I had moved into the dorm; it was because I knew who the amateur was who slipped the tinfoil between the cushions of the green couch. I was that amateur. Would I have allowed my innocent roommate to endure the horrors of a chain gang for a crime I had committed? I'd like to think that if our case had gone to trial, I'd have admitted my guilt, but I'm not certain. I wrestle with that sometimes when I'm alone on a sleepless night. My insides feel like they are liquefying, and I blush with cowardice and shame. I hope I'm a better man now, but the unwelcome memory still makes me question my character.

The state didn't find justice for my crime of pot possession, but I felt the punishments fit the crime of moral bankruptcy. Although all charges had been dropped, the coach dismissed me from the basketball team—there were plenty of walk-on candidates with no arrest records—so I spent my senior year in a dorm occupied by freshmen. As Terry said, if this had happened to someone else, I'd have been outraged, but since it happened to me, I was okay with it.

***

"There's no story to tell," I said to Nicki. "The cops messed up, and the case was dismissed."

"On a technicality," Billy said to his niece, then turned to me. "Did you ever repay Father for the attorney fees?"

Father hounded me for the money like a dog digging for a bone, and I repaid the "loan" to get him off my back. He didn't believe in helping children over the age of eighteen—we were supposed to be independent adults. But he had helped Billy find employment when he dropped out of college.

Billy was a civilian supervisor in the base maintenance operation at Fort Gordon, just west of Augusta. If your lights burned out or your bathroom sprang a leak, you called Billy and he'd assign someone, usually a civilian contractor, to fix it. Father's priorities for good employment were a clean environment, little pressure to perform, and a reliable paycheck for life.

The irony is that Father held such a position—mechanical engineer at a nuclear power plant—and yet he was never happy with his station in life. The nuclear engineers at the plant looked down their noses at him. Yet Billy pleased him with his government job. That dichotomy had always puzzled me.

"Yes, I did."

"Served you right. He knew you were guilty."

Before my punishments, I would not have considered attending a dorm social with snooty, entitled coeds from Emory University, but after the punishments, I had no life outside of classes. When my dorm arranged a dinner party with a women's dorm at Emory, I gladly attended. And that's where I met Glenda, a woman Father never found a way to like. Served him right.

Gently, Beth said, "No one is guilty until they're convicted, Billy."

"Well, he was convicted this last time, wasn't he?" Billy said in a superior tone, so I changed the subject.

"Have you talked to your parents?" I asked Nicki, who had followed our exchange with more than casual interest.

"Yeah, they're not coming until you go back to Florida, so I won't get to see them. They said this will be a long haul, so we should all take turns in Augusta."

I interpreted her response to mean she was unaware of her mother's pill problems, but talk of taking shifts prompted Billy and Beth to suggest we also take shifts visiting Mom here at the rehab facility. If I would take the days, they would relieve me in the evenings. I had nothing better to do with my evenings than visit with Mom, but I agreed. The plan would keep Billy and me apart.

As Billy hustled Beth to their car, Nicki hung back to walk with me.

"Did you do it?" she asked.

"The crime in Florida?"

She nodded her head, eyes twinkling in anticipation of a scandalous response.

"Carrie outsmarted me. She set me up for stealing $100,000 worth of her jewelry."

"Didn't the cops know you were innocent?"

"The prosecutor thought I had lured Carrie into the gunfight, but conspiracy is hard to prove. They were happy enough to send me away for something else."

"Oh," was all she said. And with that, we climbed into our cars and went our separate ways.

At Mom's house, I reset the alarm passcode to Jamie's birthday. Then I drank a couple of beers—maybe three—and forgot about the medical records I had pilfered. I fell asleep in her rocker in the parlor. It smelled like lilacs.

Chapter Fourteen

Rodney rolled Mom, comically garbed in sneakers and sweats, into the makeshift gym at precisely eight a.m. Mom had never worn anything but open-toed sandals and heels and wouldn't have allowed sweats to hide in her closet, much less hang on her desiccated frame. She grinned when she found me waiting for her with her physical therapist, Monica Howley. A buff twentysomething with a dark ponytail, Monica had been a collegiate gymnast, accustomed to stringent training regimens driven by sadistic coaches. I had briefed her on Mom's condition, and she had listened politely, but nothing I said influenced her plan for Mom's rehabilitation.

"We follow a process," she said, and she assumed that was explanation enough for a family member.

I dubbed her the Ice Maiden.

Today's objective, Monica told us, was to test Mom's capabilities and set a baseline for her progress metrics going forward. Therapeutic exercises would begin tomorrow. She asked me to stay out of the way;

Rodney would help her move Mom around and would be Mom's safety net to prevent falls.

As I watched nervously, Mom failed every test. She couldn't stand unaided in front of any exercise machines. She couldn't walk up and down wooden steps while holding onto the rails. Obviously, she couldn't use the treadmill or stationary bike. Propped up by Rodney, she could take wooden discs with her right hand and slide them across a wire to her other side, but she couldn't stand long enough to slide them back and pass the test. Sitting in her wheelchair, she could curl two-pound weights, but only twice with each arm. The moment she exerted herself, she was out of breath.

"It's her weak heart, not a problem with her lungs," the Ice Maiden decreed as she took meticulous notes on a clipboard.

After ninety minutes, Mom was a simpering, exhausted mess. "Enough already!" I said. I shoved the Ice Maiden out of the way, sat Mom in her wheelchair, and headed for the door.

"Hey, I need to establish her baseline."

"You can torture her again tomorrow."

"It's my job to follow the process and get this done."

I stopped and faced the therapist. "You're working to the wrong objective. It's not your job to mindlessly follow a process; your job is to build her strength."

I resumed my march toward the exit, but Rodney blocked my path and said, "Let me do this. Please."

I stepped away, and he pushed her back to her room to change her into everyday clothes. I asked Rodney to put her back into her wheelchair so we could move around the facility after she was dressed. Then I waited in the hallway. I was beginning to think they had forgotten me when Mom finally emerged twenty-five minutes later.

"She had to use the restroom, and she wanted to brush her hair and put on some makeup," Rodney said.

That's my mother. I thanked Rodney and pushed Mom into the cafeteria, where most tables were occupied. She said she had eaten breakfast earlier—"You can't screw up toast and fruit"—but was thirsty. I drew two glasses of orange juice and wheeled her outside onto the back patio. Facing west and shaded by tall trees, the patio was pleasantly cool, and we settled in to sip our juice and watch senior men play the par 3 hole. They were more adept at hitting the green with their tee shots than the younger men had been yesterday afternoon.

"I'll never get out of here, will I, Jackie?"

"This is day one, Mom. Your strength will return over time if you keep a good attitude."

"I'm not afraid to die, but I don't want to die here. Let me go home to die."

"You're not going to die, Mom."

"I've had a lot of time to talk to Jesus about it. He's ready for me in His home."

Oh boy. More religious hallucinations. "You're too young to die. You didn't get proper care for your infection and water retention, but we've solved those problems. I'll help you regain strength so you can get out of here."

She smiled warmly, a motherly smile for her favorite child. "You're sweet, Jackie, but I've deteriorated. I'm tired. Stop worrying about my health. Jesus will take care of me."

Her delusions about Jesus made me uneasy. I wanted to bring the conversation back to practical matters and test her about her finances. "You know the savings account has been drained, right?"

"Of course," she said irritably. "I read the statements."

All the monthly statement envelopes had been opened, but I had thought perhaps Billy had read them. Maybe he was telling the truth. If he was stealing the money, he would have hidden the statements. That meant he wasn't covering for his sister. That meant he was looking for something else in the house.

"The checkbook for the account is missing."

"Billy has all the checkbooks."

"When I was in prison, you wrote me a letter and asked for my help with a question about your estate. What was that?"

She gave me a sly look. "It's all taken care of." She patted my cheek. "I fixed it."

No, I was going to fix it with the new POA, but I wanted to know everything I needed to fix. "I'm sure you did, Mom, but what was the problem you fixed?"

"Don't worry. Katie will never find the papers." She patted my hand.

"Why are you hiding things from Katie?"

Mom looked around at the other patients, made sure no one was eavesdropping, then leaned close and whispered. "She looks for the papers every time she comes to visit, but she'll never find them." She emitted an abbreviated cackle and leaned back in her wheelchair with a satisfied look.

Katie comes to buy pills. Beth could be right: Mom may be demented. "Did you hide them in your safe deposit box? I found the key in Father's desk."

She waved a hand at me. "Those are the old papers. They don't matter anymore."

Nonetheless, since Billy and Katie had access to the box, I wanted to know what was in it. I pretended to accept Mom's dismissal of the "old papers" so she wouldn't become annoyed at my intended snooping.

We sat in the peaceful shade for a bit longer, holding hands, and then she said, "It's too warm now. Take me back to my room."

I wheeled her indoors and suggested we go to the cafeteria, but she said she wanted a nap. She sounded tired.

As we entered her room, a foul odor assailed us as though we had descended into a sewer. I stopped in the threshold and was about to back away when Mom said, "She messes her pants if the nurses don't come fast enough." She referred to her roommate, Maureen, who wasn't ambulatory.

"Let's go to the cafeteria, Mom."

"No, it's okay. They'll come soon." I gave her a questioning look, and she shooed me away. "Go on now."

I felt bad about leaving her in the stinking room, but I obeyed her. I kissed her cheek and left, confused and concerned.

Chapter Fifteen

I drove straight to Gibbons and Lewis, Mom's financial advisor's office, filed a copy of the POA, and ordered Mom's brokerage account liquidated and deposited into my checking account in Florida. Billy and Katie were now effectively blocked from further theft.

My second stop: the Georgia Atlantic Savings Bank. The female bank officer appeared skeptical when I presented Mom's safe deposit key because my name wasn't on the signature card. I explained that Mom was incapacitated and showed her the POA. After comparing my driver's license to the POA, she granted me access. She stipulated that because I wasn't listed on the signature card, I could review the stored documents but I couldn't remove any documents from the vault. She gave me a pad of paper and a pen so I could take notes.

Alone in the narrow vault with only a counter on which to prop the safe deposit box—there wasn't space for a chair—I opened the box and probed into my family's murky past.

The old power of attorney, giving Billy the right to sign documents for Mom, lay on top. No surprise. It had been executed, with everyone's concurrence, days after my father had passed.

With his authority in place, Billy had taken several actions. He had converted Mom's checking and savings accounts to joint accounts naming himself as co-owner. Not an unreasonable step to take, but it meant that upon her passing, the residual funds would be his and not subject to estate probate. He had also submitted a change of beneficiary on the annuity, naming Katie as sole beneficiary. Once again, the funds would be exempt from probate; anything left upon Mom's death would go to Katie.

All that remained to be divided by a will were her home, her possessions, and the stock brokerage account. Billy had addressed those assets as well. Three months ago, at the start of the school year, he had signed a title transfer on Mom's "land yacht," a huge four-door sedan, transferring ownership to his son, Trey. Mom couldn't drive any longer, but it was annoying to discover that the transfer had been made without any consultation within the family. I wondered if Mom knew.

Next, I removed a more complex title transfer, a transfer of the deed for the "Church of Marks"—Mom's home—to Beth, signed by Billy. That transfer had been executed three months ago as well. Did Mom know that her estate had been stolen out from under her?

Mom's life insurance policy, issued while I was in prison, completed the story of Billy's financial maneuvers. The term policy had a face value of two hundred and fifty thousand dollars, and it cost a fortune in monthly premiums to maintain. The only beneficiary listed was Billy. No mention of Katie. No mention of Jack/Jackie/Randle, the forgotten son.

My blood pressure had risen with each document I removed and read, and my dread as I lifted Mom's will out of the box reached a crescendo. The will followed a standard form for the State of Georgia—wills are individual and not joint in Georgia—so, in Mom's will, Father would have inherited the entire estate if Mom had passed first. His will would have contained the same stipulation, and thus Mom had inherited from Father upon his passing. But upon the death of the last parent, detailed bequests were specified. Shock and fury overcame me as I read the terms. Certain pieces of Mom's jewelry were bequeathed to Nicki and Beth, and the rest of the estate was to be divided equally between Katherine Annette van Kamp (*née* Marks) and William Tecumseh Marks, the children. But those weren't the only children. John Randle Marks—the eldest child—was not mentioned. Did the son of a bitch hate me so much that he cut me out of his will?

The money didn't concern me. I was hopeful that Mom would spend it all to get healthy and live many more years. However, the devious duplicity of my father and my siblings crushed my ego, my psyche, my being. I felt as though I weren't a part of this family, so why was I bothering with this crisis? The pendulum of evidence swung once again, and I concluded that Billy had wanted to remove the safe deposit box key from the house.

I should just go back to Florida where I've been hiding for most of my godforsaken life.

I stood in a daze in front of that counter so long that a clerk knocked on the door and asked if I was all right. In reply, I asked if she could make copies of the documents. She asked the officer for permission, and he granted it. The last document in the safe deposit box was my parents' marriage certificate. I added it to the others and handed the clerk the entire pack.

Within minutes, I left the bank with my trove of damning documents. A desire to immediately confront Billy overwhelmed me, but I waited in my car for my senses and intellect to overcome my emotions. After I calmed down, I decided to speak to Mom first. Did she know all of this? Was there a logical reason for this arrangement? She must know; she had asked me to come see her about an estate problem.

I drove to the home that Mom no longer owned and sat in the parlor with the documents and drank a beer. I rifled the documents but I didn't concentrate on them. When the first beer evaporated, I got another. After that, I drank yet a third. I anesthetized myself to the pain that is peculiar to family betrayals. I couldn't think of anything sadder.

Before retiring for the night, I flipped through the documents one last time, hoping the words had changed. They hadn't. The last document in the stack, to which I had paid no attention, was Mom's marriage certificate, somewhat smaller than a letter-sized sheet of paper, covered in official seals. I held it unsteadily in front of my eyes and read the inscriptions. Suddenly, my heart stopped and my life shattered like a windshield struck by a rock. The marriage certificate evidenced a conspiracy far sadder than the will.

CHAPTER SIXTEEN

went straight to the gym, expecting to find Mom receiving therapy, but Monica's victim on this Thursday morning was a toothless, grizzled old man maniacally spinning the pedals on the stationary bike while howling like a mad dog under a full moon. Rodney saw me enter and abandoned the madman to meet me. "She refuses to exercise this morning." Looking apologetic, he added, "This will count as a Medicare day even if she doesn't take a therapy session."

He told me that Mom was waiting on the patio. When I talked to her, I planned to emulate the bulldog-like prosecutors on TV dramas. I would put Mom on the euphemistic witness stand to grill her mercilessly until I had bled the last drop of truth from the secretive old woman. I had already composed a long list of questions in a logical sequence that would eliminate any possibility that Mom could beguile me with her Southern charm. In the wee hours of this morning, I had composed the questions on a yellow legal pad with space between each to record her answers. Today I would determine who the hell I was and who the hell *they* were. To get through the entire list, I would pose as a dispassionate seeker of the facts and strive to keep Mom calm and on point. To that end, I poured myself a cup of coffee in the cafeteria, constructed a disarming smile, and strode with false confidence through the door to the patio.

Mom sat at the far end with space between herself and the boisterous groupings of elderly patients happy—and surprised—to have witnessed another sunrise. She had a cup of coffee cooling in front of her on a small wrought-iron table. As I made my way around the crowd, she returned my smile with a small, nervous smile of her own.

"Morning, Mom." I kissed her cheek and took a seat. She had probably feared a scolding for not exercising, but when I placed my sheaf of copied documents and my yellow legal pad on the table, she shivered and an icy film of terror clouded her eyes.

To put her at ease, I said, "You look good today." It was true. Her cheeks blossomed with color, and although her roots needed a touch-up, her brushed hair shone in the morning sun. Her clothes were fresh and her posture erect.

"Not too shabby," she said. That was Mom's favorite way of characterizing something as having exceeded expectations. We sat in silence thick as mattress batting. She sipped her coffee, and her hand shook as she replaced the cup on the table. She sat stiff as a blindfolded prisoner in front of a firing squad, awaiting the crack of the rifle shots that would extinguish a life.

Breaking the spell, Mom said, "You looked in the box, didn't you?"

"Yes," I said easily, not wanting to raise alarms. "I have a few questions."

She gave me an imperious look. "I'll do my best to explain everything."

I crossed my legs and propped my legal pad on my knee. With a click, my pen was ready to record her answers. That was cruel. She shivered again, but I wasn't empathetic. I wanted her to feel some duress to prompt honesty.

"Do you know that Joey owns your car?"

Mom seemed relieved that I was starting with small stuff. "Yes. Billy told me I couldn't drive anymore, and Joey needed transportation."

Usually, the loss of driving privileges is psychologically traumatic for seniors, but Mom pretended it was a routine change for her. I took a note, then looked up with a serious expression. "Do you know that you don't own your home?"

She looked genuinely surprised. "Of course I own my home. We paid it off years ago."

"No." I shook my head. "Billy sold it out from under you. To Beth. They own the house."

A hand went involuntarily to her mouth. "It's mine until I pass. The will says so."

"The will just divides what's yours on the day you pass, Mom. The house is no longer yours to divide."

A fierce look erupted on her face. "I knew they were stealing from me."

I extracted from my file the form that changed the beneficiary on her annuity policy. "Katie is now the sole beneficiary of your annuity. You get payments until you pass, but what's left over isn't controlled by the will either."

"They're working together," she said, as though this information confirmed a conspiracy she had long suspected.

"Maybe. Billy took out a life insurance policy on you a few months back, and he's the sole beneficiary."

"He wants me to die."

"Billy is also co-owner of your bank accounts, so that money goes to him when you pass. He'll want to preserve as much as possible."

"He told me to be more careful with my spending."

"So you stopped eating?"

"I'm never hungry now, Jackie."

Never a good sign. "You know that one of them already emptied the savings account."

"It's like I've been butchered, and they're selecting their favorite cuts of meat. Billy couldn't wait for God to take me. Thought I might buy swamp land in Florida or something crazy."

I chuckled to relieve the stress of the moment. "I want you to use it all up by living a long life. That will screw up their plans."

She gave me a sad smile. "I don't know, Jackie. Jesus says my time is near."

Ignore it, Randle. "What I care about is the fact that you and Father didn't acknowledge me in the will at all. That hurts."

Tears welled in her eyes. She stretched across the table to hold my free hand. "Father knew you could make your own way in the world. You must remember that before Father passed, you bragged that you were about to get rich. Billy and Katie were the runts of the litter. They would need help if there was money left when I died."

A hopeful look spread across her face as she waited to see if I'd swallow that story. I didn't remember bragging that I might become rich. It was simply a possibility that didn't come true.

"He hated me, Mom."

She recoiled in her wheelchair. "You're wrong. You were the boy with potential. That's why he drove you so hard."

"Wish I could believe that, but I never felt a bit of warmth from Father."

"He wasn't a warm man, Jackie. He was first-generation American, raised in the Old Country style by Old World parents whose only purpose in life was to persevere. He was more sympathetic toward your brother and sister because they were weak, not because he liked them more."

Nice story. "It doesn't matter anymore. He's gone, and I don't want your money. I just want to teach Billy and Katie a lesson for their backstabbing."

She broke into a broad smile. "I took care of that. I fixed it."

"A new will won't do any good, Mom. All that's left is the money in your investment account and your clothes and furniture." I didn't mention that the investment account was being liquidated and transferred to my account.

"You'll get your money," she said. "Trust me."

One third of the one-hundred-fifty-thousand-dollar investment funds? So what? "I don't care about it, Mom."

I leaned back in my seat. The hardest part was yet to come. I sipped my coffee, but it had grown cold. I made a bitter face.

"Want to go inside, Jackie? Get a fresh cup in the cafeteria?"

"Not yet. I have one more question."

Once again, she looked like a prisoner with hands tied to the whipping post, unable to evade the volley of bullets. I pulled the marriage certificate from the file of documents and waved it at her so she could see what was coming.

"It says here that Joseph John Marks Jr. married Elaine May Randle at the Church of the Most Holy Trinity in downtown Augusta on July fourteenth, three years after my birth. The copy is clean; the date hasn't been smudged or altered. But that can't be right, can it?" I gave her an innocent look.

My mother turned pale. It made me think of how she would look in her casket despite the undertaker's cosmetic efforts. She repeatedly wrung her hands, and they took on a sweaty sheen. She must have known she'd face this moment, but it was a moment that couldn't be practiced for.

"I'm so embarrassed by this story, Jackie." She gave me a pleading look, but I returned a stony look. I gave her no quarter. She swallowed hard. "Your father and I fooled around when we were dating, and we made a mistake—you. You were unplanned. We were ashamed of ourselves, but I wasn't ashamed of you. You were beautiful."

She stopped, as though hoping I might let it lie. "So, my birthday is correct?"

"Of course. This was about us, not you. I told your father he was free to go his own way, but he would have none of it. We moved in together and lived as though we were married."

"But you didn't get married."

She shrugged. "We couldn't for a long time. You know your father's Catholic upbringing. The priests wouldn't condone it at first. I had to go through conversion training before I qualified to be your father's wife."

Plausible. It was a different time. "So, you finally got married, and I became legitimate?"

She flushed with embarrassment. "You were always 'legitimate,' Jackie. But your father did have to adopt you after we married."

She let out a breath as though she had passed through a gauntlet and emerged unscathed, but I wasn't done with her. "And you hid it all these years. Why?"

"We didn't want you to carry the burden of having been adopted, even by your own father. We wanted you to feel the same as your brother and sister. And we were ashamed of ourselves. How could we preach decency to you when we had made such a mistake?"

"Times change, Mom. What seemed shameful when you were young is no big deal today. You could have told me, and it wouldn't have changed how I felt about you as my parents."

"Each generation has its own standards, Jackie. We were ostracized by both of our families. That's why you never met your grandparents. Your father didn't care about his family, but losing my family was a great loss for me. I stayed in touch with my brother Frank in Columbia, but I never spoke to my parents again."

Believable. I was born when premarital sex and children out of wedlock were still serious matters. "You always told us you were married the year before my birth. That means that when we celebrated your twenty-fifth wedding anniversary, it was really your twenty-second. Awfully elaborate lie, Mom. It seems to me we were all old enough to understand by then."

"We didn't think of it as a lie." Testy now. "Things went smoothly once we were married, so we let life continue without disruption, not expecting you would ever have to deal with your beginnings. It was our mistake, not yours."

I wondered then if I should let sleeping dogs lie or if I should push my last button and finally reach the concrete truth about our family. It was growing warm on the patio and the crowd had dissipated, most patients opting for the cooler confines of the cafeteria. This was my last chance to make my mother come clean.

"You and Father pretended that things were 'smooth,' but there were problems between you and Father. You had a boyfriend—Al."

She slapped the table violently, shocking me. "You had no right to go through my things."

"I was looking for financial records. I found the love letters by mistake."

She glared at me. "You were, what, nine or ten, when I met Albert? Albert had nothing to do with you."

So she was a beautiful young woman in her prime—the sexually attractive mother I remembered cutting the lawn in her bikini—when she fell in love with Albert. She tried to propel herself away from the table, away from her past, away from me, but she couldn't figure out how to release the brake.

"Stop, Mom. Let me apologize. What you did is none of my business, but I wish you had left Father. Your life would have been better. So would mine."

She collapsed then and sobbed. She didn't recover quickly, so I moved around the table and wrapped my arms around her. "I'm not displeased with you for having an affair. I'm disappointed for you—and for us—that it didn't work out."

She turned her ruined face toward me and the tears slowly dried up, like receding floodwaters. "I asked for a divorce, but your father and his damned Church wouldn't grant it."

"And you lived in a failed marriage for the rest of your life. That's awful."

I handed her my handkerchief. She mopped her face. As she recovered from her tears, she said, "It wasn't an affair. Southern women call it a dalliance, an innocent flirtation. Most of the time we met at Frank's home in Columbia. He was Frank's friend. That's how we met. We just visited, drank iced tea, enjoyed each other's company. We never did more than neck."

Back when sex was a serious matter. The visual of my mother necking with someone other than her husband amused and repulsed me. "You were faithful, but Father didn't deserve it. What did he ever do for you?"

She gazed at my face, searching, interpreting. She decided I meant what I said, and her countenance cleared. "It was precious because it didn't happen. We could imagine for the rest of our lives what it would have been like to have been lovers. We had our dreams, and they could be anything we wanted them to be. We were happy with the memory."

"Where is he now? Still in Columbia? Can I bring him over here?"

She reached up to hug my neck. "He's gone, Jackie. He passed last year. I'll meet him in heaven."

"I believe that more than ever, Mom. You will go to heaven. You deserve it more than anyone I know."

We both cried then, all the way into the building and back to her room. Nurses and patients thought something bad had happened, but we were happier than we had ever been.

Then I convinced Mom to change into exercise clothing for a therapy session.

"Do I have to, Jackie?"

"Yes, Mom. We're not going to waste any time getting you back home."

Mom reluctantly agreed, and so did Monica, who made it clear that it wasn't her job to cater to the whims of crotchety old residents. She declared that no further schedule changes would be tolerated.

We behaved as though we had been suitably admonished for the disruption to Monica's precious schedule. Mom completed her baseline tests, and although she performed no better than the day before, she tried harder, cooperated more cordially. Monica was pleased to have satisfied the tenets of her process, and we departed with optimism about the coming therapy sessions.

Rodney and Carol ministered to Mom and got her showered and changed into fresh clothes. Mom then announced she needed a nap.

***

With nothing better to do, I retired to the cafeteria and found a seat at a table occupied only by a woman with implausibly curly, steel-gray hair. She studied me as I fired up my iPad, hoping, perhaps, I was a relative she didn't recognize. I nodded but didn't speak, didn't want to encourage a conversation while I worked, and she held her peace.

As I waited for the iPad to boot, I replayed the thrust and parry of the morning's conversation with Mom, and I became increasingly uneasy. Mom's answers had sounded rehearsed. Her story was a little too practiced, as though she had had it ready for years in the event I stumbled across some evidence of impropriety. Her slap of the table when I disclosed my knowledge of her indiscretions could have been contrived to gain the moral high ground. The only surprise I had evoked had been over the theft of her home. That hadn't been a part of the script. It was clear now that she had written me because she suspected Billy and Katie were picking the bones of her financial carcass before she was even in her grave.

But why had she insisted upon "fixing" the will? There was nothing to "fix," just a few bucks in her brokerage account that were now in my control. More importantly, why had she hidden the timing of her wedding date and the fact that I was adopted? Her emotions had distracted me, and I had lost control of the interrogation. Begrudgingly, I gave her credit for her performance; she was one crafty lady. But if I knew my mother, she had reasons for her actions. What were they?

First, I searched online for my birth records in Augusta. For the supposed year of my birth I could find no record, at any hospital, of a baby with the names John Randle Marks or John Randle, born to Elaine Randle and Joseph Marks. Just to cover the ground, I tried Columbia, South Carolina, and Charleston, South Carolina, with the same result. I wasn't born in any of the places I would have expected. *Where the hell was I born? I'm a ghost.*

For a long time I stared at the old lady and she stared back. I concluded I would have to speak to Mom's brother, Frank—if he was still alive—to confirm Mom's story about her premarital pregnancy and her fling with Albert. The last time I had seen him, at Father's funeral, he looked ready for the grave, hobbling about with a cane, face unshaven, smelling of decay. Once a tall man for his time at something over six feet, he had looked like me as a younger man, but at the funeral his cheeks were sunken and his eye sockets recessed. No one told me he had passed, but then no one would have.

I googled Frank Randle and was relieved not to find an obituary. There was a bio—Frank had been an underwriter at Colonial Life Insurance Company—but no hint of his current whereabouts. I doubted Frank was living on his own, but he could be in any number of "retirement" homes. Nonetheless, I googled "Senior Living in Columbia" and a list of twenty-one possibilities popped up on the screen. With no better idea, I pulled out my cell phone and began dialing. On the sixth try, Meadowlake Assisted Living, I struck pay dirt. Frank Randle was alive, but "he can't hear over the phone," the receptionist advised me. Not to worry, I said, I'm on my way to see him. "Oh, he'll like that," she said.

Maybe. Before I left I checked on Mom, who was still napping. Then I plugged the address of Meadowlake Assisted Living into Google Maps and began my quest for the truth about the dark past of Elaine Randle Marks and her ghostly son, Jack Randle Marks.

CHAPTER SEVENTEEN

The eighty-mile drive from Sacred Heart to Meadowlake, from one warehouse for the aged to another, took a little over an hour. The GPS sent me to the university district, where I found Meadowlake on leafy Pendleton Street across from The Inn at USC. I parked under willow trees, beside the white, multistory colonial that had once been the mansion of a wealthy merchant, and marched bravely through double front doors carved from oak. Unlike Sacred Heart, Meadowlake had a lobby and a receptionist's desk. I had to sign in. "I'm his nephew," I said.

The receptionist introduced herself as Clara, then said, "We knew you were coming so we moved him into the great hall, straight through the swinging doors." Clara pointed at the doors behind her station.

The swinging doors, easy for attendants to back through with a wheelchair or push through with a stretcher, were not original equipment. In a corruption of the ornate, nineteenth-century architecture, they had been hung in an arched entry to the original owner's ballroom, a spacious, airy room with a marble floor and frescoed ceiling. Inside, small round tables hosted games of checkers and chess while larger tables were used for card games. The tenants—they didn't look like patients—wore cardigans and summer dresses that bespoke their gentility and well-heeled heritage. If Sacred Heart cost seventy-five hundred dollars per month, this place had to cost twice that much. If Mom recovered, I would move her here to live out her life in comfort in her native state.

My uncle was easy to spot, sitting in a wheelchair along the far wall, gazing out a latticed window. A lap blanket in Gamecock garnet covered his legs, and a freshly ironed, button-up shirt matched a smart cardigan sweater. He was clean-shaven, and his silver thorns of hair had been neatly trimmed. Unlike his appearance at Father's funeral, now he looked like a man with a reason to live.

I walked into his vision and waited for him to acknowledge me. He gave me a slight nod. I slid a wing-backed chair in front of him and sat.

Before I could begin with pleasantries, he said, "I can't tell ya anything without Elaine's permission."

That implied he knew something I needed to elicit. "Your sister had a heart attack last Friday. She's in a rehab facility in Augusta. I thought you should know."

His lips moved as though he were chewing food rather than digesting information. "Will she make it?"

"We don't know yet. She needs surgery, but she's not strong enough."

He nodded his understanding. "We had our day, and now our time has come."

"She's made peace with it. Her affairs are in order, and we're all there to support her."

"Can you take me to her?"

"I'll see if it can be arranged."

"I'd be much obliged."

A waiter in a white tuxedo jacket and black bowtie appeared, and we ordered sweet tea. When he left, I began with the easy stuff. "As I organized her affairs, she told me about Albert." A small lie.

He nodded again, his eyes intent on my face. "I thought she might do that before she passed. Seems right for you to know."

If Mom's dalliance with Albert occurred when I was ten years old, I had no right or need to know the details. "Her memory is hazy. I think she might have a touch of Alzheimer's." A bigger lie. "She remembers, of course, that you introduced her to Albert. He was your friend, right?"

He nodded continuously for a minute, and I thought he might fall asleep. "We all met here at the university." He gazed out the window, recalling events from sixty years ago while I tried not to reveal my shock at learning that Mom had known Albert long before they had a "dalliance."

"Just blocks from where we sit," my uncle continued. "I met him first. We were ahead of Elaine in school, but when she got here, we became a threesome."

The waiter delivered our teas, and we sipped them as I considered how to smoke out the details around Mom's relationship with the mysterious Albert.

"She told me that she and Albert were just friends."

He grinned then. "Your mother is protecting her honor. Elaine was wild back then. Beautiful girl. Dated a lot of boys. She and Albert *were* just friends, but he wanted more. That's the way it always was between them."

"But they did get serious later, right?" I phrased that question so that "later" could be taken any way Uncle Frank wanted to take it.

"Sure. After Albert graduated, he hung around, took a construction job here instead of going back to Spartanburg, and she fell in love with him. After she graduated, she stayed here too instead of going back to Charleston. Then you happened."

What? I "happened" here in Columbia? When Mom fell in love with Frank's friend? How many lies had Mom told me this morning? I sipped tea to cover my shock, waited until I was sure my voice would sound calm. "Mom glossed over this part. Told me she was ostracized by her family, and later I was adopted by Joseph Marks. But I've searched birth records in Columbia and Charleston and can't find mine."

His hand shook as he moved the glass to his lips again. He took a sip of his drink and nodded some more. "Sure," he said, "she's embarrassed by this part. Your grandfather sent Elaine to Savannah, to a home for unwed mothers. Wanted her to give you up for adoption. That sounds harsh today, but it was routine back then. He wanted to protect the family honor—she was a Charleston debutante—and adoption was safer than an abortion in those days."

So the medical dangers of abortions saved my life. I vowed to check the Savannah records as soon as I left the senior living facility. With my handkerchief, I wiped spittle that snaked from the corner of Uncle Frank's mouth and ran down his chin. He thanked me.

"She didn't give me up for adoption. She married Joseph Marks three years later." Let him think I knew a lot.

"Elaine defied our father, had the baby—you—and our parents never spoke to her again. She moved to Augusta, with you, and that's where she met that carpetbagger, Joseph." He frowned. I got the feeling he wasn't a fan of Joseph Marks.

I went out on a limb. "She refused to explain why she and Albert didn't get married, why I wasn't raised by my real father."

He waved at me. "That wasn't her doing. Our father convinced Albert's parents to move him back home, and then Albert's parents made him enlist in the Navy. They were poor, his parents, and they couldn't afford to raise another child. Our father threatened them, and they gave in. Albert was still overseas when Elaine married Joseph Marks."

"But Albert didn't give up on Mom. Later he connected with her again, through you."

Frank jerked back in his wheelchair. "She told you that? She must want to cleanse her soul."

Uncle Frank thinks the extramarital affair is what Mom wants kept a secret. "She said she tried to divorce Joseph, but the Catholic Church stood in the way."

He waved again. "Now she's protecting your memory of Joseph. He fought her for custody of the other two—your half-brother and half-sister—and Elaine wouldn't abandon her kids. If it came out in court that she had an affair, she'd have lost them both."

So it was an affair. "Mom denies it was an affair that second time—called it a 'dalliance.'"

My uncle gave me a playful smile. "A mother's right to privacy, but I can tell ya they couldn't keep their hands off each other. Embarrassed me a bit." He winked.

I think I blushed. As an adolescent, I had been proud of my mother's beauty but had suppressed any thoughts of her sexuality. "Did they ever see each other again, when I was older?"

"Not that I know of, but Albert and I stayed close, and Elaine and I stayed close too. So they got their updates through me. For Albert, it was always about you: 'How's my son doing?'"

I thought I would lose control, but I clamped down on my heaving chest and blinked back tears. To remain calm, I took another sip of my sugary tea. "Mom said she wanted me to have a normal upbringing, without the stigma of adoption, but I wish that once I became an adult, she had told me the truth so I could have had a relationship with my biological father."

"He would have liked that, but your mother felt that she had made her bed and she would lie in it till the end. Now that Joseph is gone, I suspect the money has changed her mind."

"The money?"

He looked at me funny, wondered why I didn't know what he was talking about. "Albert's money."

It took me a minute to connect the dots, but once I did, Mom's cryptic references to *my* money became clear. "Oh yes. All she told me is that she fixed it. She didn't give me any other details."

He gave me an appreciative, knowing smile. "He often offered her money, but she never wanted anything to do with it while Joseph was alive. So Albert put her in his will. That way she couldn't refuse the money whether Joseph was alive or dead."

"We always had enough." I paused, thinking about the implications of money from Albert becoming a part of Mom's estate, an estate to which I had no claim. More to myself than to Uncle Frank, I mumbled, "Mom and I don't care about money."

His eyebrows rose to meet his furrowed forehead. "You didn't come to ask about the money?"

I shook my head. "No. I wanted to tell you about Mom and learn the truth about my father. Mom only gave me bits and pieces."

Another appreciative smile. "You are your mother's son. Same spunk, but it's hard to ignore a big pile of money."

He was right, of course. If a lot of my dad's money had become a part of the estate to which I had no claim, I would find the problem hard to ignore. "My father was rich?"

"Yes, Albert did very well in the construction business. Had his own company and developed multifamily housing all over the state. Everyone knew that except you, I guess. It's been like a parade, all the people coming over here to see him."

In the excitement, I forgot about the money and couldn't modulate my voice. I shouted, "He's here?"

"Upstairs." Uncle Frank pointed to the ceiling.

I had my hands on the armrests, about to lever myself out of the chair. "Mom told me he had passed."

The old man waved me back into my seat. "He's as good as gone. Albert had a catastrophic stroke about two months ago. He's strong as an ox, but he can't speak and the stroke affected his thinking too. He has lucid days and confused days."

I sank back into the chair. Sadness overwhelmed me—the first time I would meet my dad, he would be debilitated. At that moment, I remembered that Mom had written me about the family estate around the time of my dad's stroke. "Was Mom part of the parade that came to see him?"

"Sure, the money has drawn the moths to the flame." Shaking his head as he spoke slowly, thinking about each phrase before uttering it, he said, "Your sister brought her the first time." Pause. "Then Katie came back with a lawyer." He gave me a meaningful look and paused again. "Then your mother came with a different lawyer." He stopped and shook his head no. "Maybe your mother came first and your sister came second. I'm not sure." Pause. "But your sister came alone the last time. That seemed to settle it."

The estate problem Mom had written about wasn't her estate, it was Albert's. Mom said she fixed it, but Katie's been looking for the papers. They're all after Albert's money. "Can I see him?"

"You'll have to ask at the front desk. Tell them you're his son."

"Would you like to come with me?"

"No, Jack. I see him every day. This is your time."

I rose to leave and then remembered the most important item of all. "Mom never disclosed Albert's last name."

"Didn't want you to upset the apple cart. Czajka, C-Z-A-J-K-A."

I tried to mimic Uncle Frank's pronunciation, but it sounded like a baby's babble. I laughed out loud, a belly laugh. Couldn't stop myself.

Uncle Frank grinned. "That's right. Another reason my father opposed any thought of Elaine marrying the man."

I hugged my uncle hard and promised to stay in touch. He made me promise not to tell Mom anything he had told me.

*　*　*

The receptionist could not grant me access to Mr. Czajka as I had no proof of my relationship to him. When I pressed her, she summoned her supervisor, to whom I explained that I was his son and that my mother, who shared my last name, had visited my father recently. She cocked her head when she heard the story, but today broken homes are common, and she remembered Mom. She said, "Y'all are wearing out the road coming over here, aren't ya? Mr. Czajka has had more visitors in the last two months than most of our residents get in two years." Then she acquiesced.

A white-coated attendant, Luis, escorted me upstairs to a second floor filled with private and semiprivate rooms. Nurses hustled up and down the corridor administering to their tenants. When we reached a closed door at the far end of the hallway, the attendant rapped twice but didn't wait for a response. Albert couldn't speak.

Luis swung open the door to Albert Czajka's private room. He sat in a side chair in the splash of late afternoon sunlight that beamed through his window. He was a large man, not very tall but far broader and thicker than me, with a round head and Slavic features beneath a bald pate. I had inherited my height, facial features, hair, and eyes from my mother's side of the family, as first children often do. People seeing me with my father wouldn't guess the relationship.

Incongruously, my dad wore headphones attached to an iPod. He regarded me curiously as I eased toward him, and then his face suddenly illuminated, like a jack-o'-lantern the moment it's lit. He must have seen pictures of me, because I'm certain he recognized me. With one hand he motioned me closer, and I took two steps toward him. I smiled, and he returned it. Holding his other hand horizontally, parallel to the floor, he raised it like an elevator climbing upward, signaling that he thought I was tall. I made a motion as though I were shooting a basketball, and he smiled broadly.

Luis swooped in and removed Dad's forgotten headphones. "He's having a good day," Luis told me. "The music seems to help him organize his thoughts."

"What does he listen to?"

"B and B—Bach and Beethoven."

After nodding his thanks to the attendant, Dad motioned me even closer until I realized what he wanted. We hugged. I believe he'd have hung on forever if I hadn't separated from the ungainly pose. As Uncle Frank had promised, my dad was strong as an ox. Faces wet with tears of joy and redolent with warmth and love, we regarded each other as only long-lost fathers and sons can. All sorts of banalities presented themselves as possible things to say to him, but none of them seemed appropriate.

Discomfort and awkwardness had settled in when Dad signaled the attendant to hand him a pen and paper. The attendant fetched the instruments from Dad's writing table, and Dad wrote me a note. It said, "Now I can die in peace."

Reflexively, I reached for the pen and paper and then realized how stupid that was: Dad could hear. I said, "They tell me you're healthy and will live forever."

He gave me a small smile and tapped his skull a couple of times. Then he held a hand in front of him and wagged it back and forth, as though it were riding on waves.

I turned to Luis. "He's not in a wheelchair. Does that mean he can walk?"

"With assistance. His body is fine, but his brain forgets how to tell it to walk."

Back to Dad, I said, "Mom—Elaine—is in the hospital." I tapped my chest. "Heart."

Immediately, concern flooded his face. He wrote another note: "Will she be okay?"

"I think so. I want to take you over there. Uncle Frank too."

He grinned again, then looked at the attendant for permission. Luis shrugged, and I said, "I'll have to arrange it."

He wrote a note: "Please."

We continued our conversation for perhaps an hour. I did most of the "talking"—I didn't burden him with the need to write long notes in response—recounting my life, showing him pictures of Glenda and Jamie. He wanted the one of Jamie, so I pulled it out of the laminated sleeve in my wallet and placed it in his hand. He studied the photo of his granddaughter as though he could communicate with her through the picture.

He didn't bring up the money, and neither did I. I didn't want him to think I was only here because I was another moth drawn to the flame.

As the conversation wound down, he spread his arms and I read the signal. We hugged again, and when we parted I promised to return.

Chapter Eighteen

Flushed with excitement, I drove slowly and carefully until I reached the entrance to I-20 West at dusk. Then I grabbed my cell phone, intending to call Glenda and give her all the news, but Tim Rosenthal, my agent, interrupted my plans with a sudden call.

"Good news, buddy," he said. "I've landed you an interview at NPR Monday morning and a signing at A Cappella Books in the afternoon."

I didn't respond—I was thinking about my promise to Glenda to return home on Saturday. Tim added, "They're both in Atlanta, where you asked me to start your sales campaign. A Cappella Books is a famous indie bookstore. I'm still working on rescheduling the Florida gigs."

I blew exasperated air that made my lips flutter and blubber. "I promised Glenda I'd come home over the weekend."

"No way, buddy. You can't do that again, or it'll be a race to see who drops you first—your publisher or me."

Tim rambled on about his plans for my book launch in Florida and California while I considered the ramifications of blending my "Randle

Marks" life with my "Jack Czajka" life. After hemming and hawing for a few minutes, I agreed to do the Monday events. I could drive home on Tuesday and still have time to help Glenda prepare for our wedding. I wondered, however, when I could keep my promise to take Frank and Dad to Augusta. Had to be Saturday or Sunday. I imagined a sort of intervention for Mom, with two truth-tellers helping me shine a light on the last dark spaces of my hidden life.

After we disconnected, thirty miles rolled past while I rebuilt my excitement over meeting my dad. Then I called Glenda. She sounded soft and pleased to hear from me, so I began with the incredible tale of meeting my birth father.

"Are you okay with it?" she asked in disbelief.

"Yes, absolutely. It means that the mean-spirited man who neglected me was just a stepfather, a man with two blood kids he favored over me. It wasn't me he hated; it was the fact that I wasn't his, the fact that my mother had a child by another man."

"But your dad never tried to find you. If he's the kind of man you say he is, he should have tracked you down."

"Mom wouldn't let him, so Dad kept up with me through Uncle Frank."

"While your mother made you live her lie. She thought she had done something wrong, and she made you pay for it."

I hadn't thought of it that way. Instinct compelled me to defend my mother. "I'm sure Joseph Marks stopped her from connecting me with my dad. He probably knew about her affair since she asked for a divorce."

"At which point she had nothing to lose. She could have told you."

"I was only ten or twelve years old."

"I'm not going to argue about it, Randle, but I'd be pissed off at your mother and your real father. How do you know they aren't lying?"

The joy I had felt over dismissing Joseph Marks as a man who was nothing more than the father of my half siblings dissipated with the realization I had been duped. My parents had perpetrated the longest-running scam in the annals of parenthood. Billy and Katie must have known my true status—they would have seen the marriage certificate in the safe deposit box. And Katie had met my dad and launched a search for the mysterious "papers." Of course, I had been easy to scam, living far from the rest of Joseph Marks's real family. They had all been perfectly happy with my exile while they carried on as the Marks nuclear family unit. Now all the moths were fluttering around the flame of my dad's money.

While Glenda waited for me to re-engage, I carried on a self-deluding conversation in my head. I could walk away from the mess in Augusta, return to Florida and Glenda on Saturday, and let the chips fall where they may. That my reunion with my one true love paralleled my mother's attempt to reunite with Albert was not lost on me. The symmetry was satisfying; I would have the courage to consummate the reunion when my mother had not.

It was easy to fabricate many counterarguments. Could I walk away before I knew that Mom would be okay? No. Could I walk away before I knew that Albert's money followed the path of his wishes? No. Could I walk away before I exposed Billy's petty thefts and Katie's attempt at grand larceny? No. Could I leave before keeping my promise to Frank and Albert to bring them to Augusta? No. Could I abandon my life's work—my book—just as it reached fruition? No. And that's how I rationalized a decision to stay in Augusta until Tuesday. Never once did I admit that another moth had been drawn to the flame of "a big pile of money."

"Randle? Are you still there? I didn't mean to make you angry, but you aren't thinking clearly about the situation. Get a good night's sleep, and come home tomorrow."

I had to tell her then. I tried to explain my decision to Glenda, logically, but she wouldn't accept the idea that I, alone, could unravel the mysteries of the Marks family or even that the mysteries were worth unraveling.

"You know now that you aren't really a part of that family," she said. "Leave their business to them, and take care of your business down here."

"Katie should be here by Tuesday. We'll have time to prepare for the wedding." *And I'll have time to defeat her conspiracy to steal my dad's money.*

"Don't make me any more promises. You've got a key; just let yourself in whenever you get here."

I hadn't mentioned Dad's money because I had no idea how Mom had "fixed it." Nor did I know if Katie had managed to steal it. More importantly, I didn't want my free-spirited, once and future wife, or my straitlaced daughter, to think I had abandoned them simply to chase money. I didn't want to think that about myself either.

* * *

Dusk had yielded to total darkness before I reached Mom's house. Emotionally drained, I grabbed a beer from the refrigerator and sat in Mom's rocker to consider the key question: where would an elderly lady hide documents she *didn't* want found while she was alive, but *did* want found upon her death? Katie had searched the house, but, driven by manic energy, I retraced her steps. I even climbed into the attic and found it as empty of possessions as the garage had been. Mom had once stored keepsakes in the attic—old photo albums, musty report cards, 8mm home movies—but they were gone. *Katie?* It made me feel foolish to have thought my mother would climb the extension ladder to the attic to hide a new will.

Defeated and depressed, I dropped out of the attic onto the second-floor landing and retreated to my room. I stripped to nakedness and collapsed on top of my bedcovers. Staring at the time-stained ceiling, it all became clear: only a human being could control when or if the papers would be found. Mom would have given them to someone she trusted to act according to her wishes. Not her brother or my dad, who couldn't be counted upon to travel to Augusta or even to be alive when she passed. Not Billy or Katie, whom she was trying to outwit. Not a friend whom none of us knew. Had to be a relative—which left Brad, Nicki, and Trey. Brad was too close to Katie, of course, and Nicki was defiant and unpredictable, so my money was on Trey, the "straight"-and-narrow grandson. I would have to talk to him. And, with that decided, I fell into a ragged sleep.

Chapter Nineteen

On Friday morning, I overslept. As a result, I arrived at the rehab facility at eight-thirty to find Mom already in the gym. She wasn't having a good day. Monica and Rodney played good cop/bad cop. Monica berated her for her lack of effort, while Rodney encouraged her to try harder to complete the exercises. Mom responded with a stream of expletives any pissed-off sailor would have been proud to call his own. I didn't interfere.

"Why do I have to do this?" Mom asked. "Jesus is coming for me this weekend."

Monica and Rodney turned toward me simultaneously with a question on their faces. I motioned for them to continue their process. As Monica made Mom repeatedly push herself out of her chair and into a standing position—"We have to build strength in your legs, Elaine"— Rodney sauntered over to me.

"She doesn't eat well or sleep well, so she has no energy. You have to change that, or she'll never improve."

Medical caregivers adroitly shift responsibility to family members whenever patients progress slowly or are uncooperative. The tactic is taught in Medical Practice 101. Rodney's attitude annoyed me. "Don't let her take naps during the day so she sleeps better at night."

"This isn't a prison, Mr. Marks. Our guests have free will."

Is he making a sly reference to my past? "You can't have it both ways, Rodney. She's your patient, not mine."

My insolence surprised him. "Stick around for meals, and get her to eat."

"Serve her something worth eating."

He threw up his hands in frustration and turned away. To his back, I said, "Bring her out on the patio after you've cleaned her up. Don't let her nap."

He didn't acknowledge me, so I left the gym and walked into the cafeteria, poured a glass of orange juice, and found an empty table in the shade on the patio. Since Mom's discharge from the hospital, I'd been inundated with family dramas and had not read through her medical record for her last night and morning in Dr. Kaplan's care. I opened my iPad, accessed my email account, and downloaded her complete medical record. I paged past Friday, Saturday, Sunday, and Monday, all familiar entries but now officially recorded, until I found her last night in the hospital. I found a note to the overnight attending physician: "Station nurse in patient's room with crash cart. Closely monitor cardiac activity. Resuscitate with epinephrine in event of repeat seizure." The hospital staff didn't want her to die before they could discharge her. They obviously felt she was at extreme risk of another heart attack, and yet they kicked her out of the hospital the next morning.

There were no other entries Monday night into Tuesday morning until Mom threw her fit. Someone had noted that Mom "assaulted nursing staff and refused care." That entry was followed by the discharge order. "Patient discharged at patient's request. Transferred to Sacred

Heart Rehabilitation Center." Kaplan had abdicated all responsibility for her discharge by duping her into saying she wanted to get out of the hospital. He had not advised her of the risks and had not asked her to weigh the choices. The order also explained that Mom required a mitral valve repair "if/when patient attains strength to tolerate surgery. Patient susceptible to atrial fibrillation." Prescriptions for "continued courses of Coumadin and Lasix" completed the order.

One final note punctuated the medical record: "Family litigious. Do not readmit. Recommend alternate facility for future care." One scared, intimidated medical staff member had warned the next medical staffers to beware of Randle Marks. The one thing doctors fear more than failing to keep their patients alive is a malpractice lawsuit. Given a choice between saving a life and avoiding a lawsuit, many doctors will choose the latter. That's not the fault of the medical community; it's the environment created by lawyers, insurance companies, and our civil justice system. Ironically, the hospital's medical record could furnish me with the evidence to leverage the faulty civil court system and sue the pants off St. Thomas Aquinas Hospital.

Reading Mom's medical record sensitized me again to her precarious medical condition. How easy it had been to adjust to her new normal, confined to a wheelchair, confined to a rehab facility, because she had been able to think and talk and behave cantankerously. How easy it had been to delude ourselves into thinking her situation was temporary. Mom was fighting for her life, but routine exigencies allowed us to busy ourselves with trivial distractions. If we weren't delusional, we couldn't endure life on this planet.

One of those exigencies was my birth history. Knowing now that I had been born at a home for unwed mothers in Savannah, I searched for Chatham County birth records. I found my record and felt somewhat relieved that it reflected the date on which I had always celebrated my birthday. The mother was listed as Elaine May Randle of Charleston,

South Carolina. No father was listed. The child's name—my original name at birth—was simply listed as John Randle. I had another birth certificate, of course, and had used it to procure a passport. That birth certificate listed Elaine and Joseph Marks as the parents and conferred the name John Randle Marks on the little bastard.

* * *

Rodney rolled Mom next to my table, cutting my daydream short. He had nothing cheerful to say. He parked her, locked her brakes, and left us. Mom's features were drawn; she looked tired. I thought she had lost more weight.

"You didn't stay with me yesterday," Mom whined.

"You were napping, and I had an errand to run."

"I couldn't eat the food in the cafeteria. They pushed me into the break room so they could watch TV, and they left after only an hour. Then I was alone all evening."

I should have known I couldn't count on my brother. "I'll get you something today, but you have to promise to eat it."

She patted my hand in thanks, but I didn't allow her to enjoy the peaceful setting. "Today I'm going to unravel all our family secrets."

She gave me the small, knowing smile that the elderly use to signal they are about to impart wisdom that only comes with age. "The young overvalue the truth. When you're older, you'll learn when to ignore it."

"Maybe, but I want to know the truth about my past."

She patted my hand again. "I told you that story yesterday."

Should I get into it now or bring Frank and Albert over to join the intervention? I feared that a full-blown confrontation including my dad and my uncle might provoke a heart attack. I decided to see what new lies she had to tell before including my unimpeachable witnesses. That's how the cops do it, right?

"I found my birth certificate—the original one for Savannah."

Her eyes smoldered, and her eyebrows swam together under a brow furrowed like the rows in a cornfield. "You couldn't leave well enough alone."

"Why did you go to Savannah instead of a local hospital?"

She thought about that before answering, wondering how much I knew. She decided to play her story all the way to the end. "To save your father the embarrassment of a pregnant girlfriend on his arm everywhere he went. The home was a good place to get prenatal care in those days."

Lie number one. How many would follow? "That's not how Uncle Frank remembers it."

She looked frightened. "How would you know what Frank remembers?"

"I went to see him yesterday. At Meadowlake in Columbia."

Her hand covered her mouth, squelching a scream. "Oh my God, what have you done?"

"He says your parents sent you away to save *them* from the embarrassment of a pregnant debutante who had no husband."

One hand went to her hair, brushed it aside. The other went to her throat, as though it were vulnerable to attack. "My parents paid for me to go so I wouldn't have to be pregnant on my own in Augusta."

Lie number two. "As Uncle Frank remembers it, you were living in Columbia, with Albert, when you got pregnant. You moved to Augusta after I was born and met Joseph sometime after that."

She propped an elbow on the arm of the wheelchair so she could rest her head on her hand. The hand laid across her eyebrows and shielded her eyes. She didn't look up as she said, "Frank doesn't know what he doesn't know."

"Albert knows. I met him."

Her head popped up and her eyes leaked crystal tears that tumbled through her face powder like a mountain stream, creating dusty creeks in a craggy landscape. "Poor Albert, having you thrust upon him."

"No, Mom." I shook my head. "It was wonderful for both of us. We only wish it had happened years ago."

She held out a hand. "Can I have your handkerchief?"

I handed it to her. She pressed it gingerly to her eyes, blotted her cheeks, and manufactured a smile. She took a calming breath. "We couldn't get married, Jackie. We had no money, and neither my parents nor his would help us. Albert joined the Navy. I was supposed to give you up for adoption, but I couldn't do it. After you were born, I stayed away from South Carolina, made my own way in life."

"Because your parents disowned you. That's why we had no contact with your family."

She used my handkerchief to blot her eyes again. "Life is a series of choices, Jackie. I chose you over my parents."

Manipulating my emotions. I can do that too. "And you chose Joseph over Albert, even though Albert was my real father."

She choked back a sob. "I didn't know if Albert would take us both back. As fate had it, I fell in love with Joseph before poor Albert was discharged from the Navy."

"Poor Albert" wasn't present to fight for the woman he loved. "Albert never got over you. Still hasn't. You had an affair with him later, so maybe you never got over him either."

She relaxed. Turning on her seductive Southern charm, she said, "A woman can love two men, Jackie, but she can only make a life with one. I will always love Albert dearly, but your father gave all of us a normal family. Staying with him was better for my children."

I noticed that she hadn't disputed the term "affair." I noticed as well that she hadn't blamed the Catholic Church for limiting her choices. Instead, she took credit for keeping the family together. *Fine, let her have her dignity.* Uncle Frank's version of events also included a custody battle that Mom chose not to mention, and in that version Joseph Marks had been happy to relinquish custody of his bastard child.

"After you decided to stay with Joseph, you should have told me about my birth father. It would have been easier to understand Joseph's attitude toward me."

"Can you call him 'Father,' please?"

"No."

She sighed. "You were too young to understand."

"Then after I graduated college and made a life of my own."

"There was no need to embarrass your father. We had lost touch with Albert, and I didn't want to open old wounds."

Another lie. Uncle Frank was a continuous line of communication to Albert. "Then after Joseph passed. That would have been a good time."

She glared at me and growled. Having learned by watching Rodney lock and unlock her wheelchair many times, she unlocked it now and, mumbling loudly, rolled across the patio. Before she could reach the door and escape into the building, I raised my voice and said, "I know about the money."

She stopped. She tried to turn her chair around but couldn't figure out how to make it swivel. Over her shoulder, looking as angry as I'd ever seen her, she snarled, "I fixed it. Everyone will get what's fair."

She rolled through the door and out of sight. I didn't chase after her. I thought it best to allow her time to digest the fact that I had uncovered her dirty little secrets. Besides, I had more secrets to expose.

* * *

The drive to Milledgeville, ninety miles southwest of Augusta, took an hour and a half, time enough to consider and reconsider my mission many times. *Why bother with the Marks family mess?* I asked myself.

Because I want to know exactly how badly I've been screwed, I answered. *Self-delusion.* I want to know exactly how much to hate them.

Milledgeville had served as the capital of the new state of Georgia from the end of the Revolutionary War until Sherman's March to the Sea in 1863. The Yankee general didn't raze the entire town—many antebellum homes and commercial buildings survived the plunder—but he terrorized the politicians sufficiently to chase them northward, to Atlanta, where they labor to this day. That Southerners know this history and still agonize over it is the tragedy, and the fabric, of Southern culture.

Higher education and tourism now fund the lives of Milledgeville's twenty thousand inhabitants. Visitors tour antebellum homes, plantations, and the old governor's mansion before spending their money on relics and trinkets in the commercial district. As tempting as it was to lick an ice cream cone while strolling past the shops in this idyllic town, I focused on my mission. I found the huge, gorgeous campus of Georgia College and parked in front of the administration building.

School was in session, so the registrar's office was nearly deserted. An attractive young lady met me at the polished counter and smiled contentedly as I related my story: I was passing through on my way from our family home in Augusta to my residence in Florida, and I wanted to surprise my nephew, Joseph Marks III, but didn't know his dorm address. Could she help me locate him, please? She asked for my ID and, happy to see the name Marks on it, consulted her computer system.

"I'm sorry, sir, but Joseph isn't registered for this semester," she said with a frown.

"Oh, I should have asked his mother before stopping by. He did attend last semester and roomed with Raymond Morris, right?"

She glanced at her computer screen, then back at me. She decided I wasn't a suspicious character. "That's right."

"And Raymond is still in school. Joseph's mother told me he was in Milledgeville, so Raymond would know where I can find him."

I put the question mark in my eyes rather than at the end of my implied question. The nice young lady gave me a small smile, hit a couple of keystrokes, and said, "106 Adams."

I thanked her, grabbed a campus map off the counter, and left. I walked to the four-story dorm, past groups of students, some hurrying, some meandering, many of whom I'm sure thought I was a professor who'd lost his way. Several campus buildings sported Corinthian pillars, giving them an academic façade and a Southern ambiance.

Room 106 stood to the left of the main entrance, on the first floor, a convenience accorded to an upperclassman. Dorm life here was luxurious compared to my own experience forty years earlier. On the way to the room, I passed a communal space, a computer room, a kitchen, and a vending area. I found room 106 empty. I leaned against the wall, awkward and conspicuous in this youthful environment, until a passing student said, "They'll be back soon. Go on in, but leave the door open."

I nodded my thanks for the lesson in Millennial etiquette and went inside. The room consisted of built-in desks, bunkbeds, and a pair of locker-like closets. The clothes hanging in the closets were of two sizes and styles. There was also an en suite bath with shower. *Nice.* When the corridor quieted, I closed the door and searched the room. Quickly, I determined that the small space did not conceal Mom's papers.

I opened the door, took a seat on a desk chair, and waited uncomfortably. Intermittently, students passed by and glanced at me, but no one challenged me. To fit more perfectly into the milieu, I played a game on my smartphone.

Twenty minutes later, Raymond walked through the door with a question on his face: who had left his door open? Trey followed him into the room with a look of shock.

"Uncle Randle? Is Nana okay?"

"Better than ever. Very feisty." I stood and shook hands with both students.

Raymond dumped his books on the desk nearest the one window. Trey had no books. Raymond said, "Want some space? I can step out."

"That's not necessary," I said.

Trey took the other desk chair, and Raymond sat on the lower bunk. Instead of divulging anything I might not know, they waited for me to disclose the reason for my impromptu visit.

I went straight to the heart of the matter. "Your grandmother wants to direct the disbursement of a large sum of money. She's told me she 'fixed it,' but I'm worried about how she's done it."

I paused. Trey and Raymond exchanged knowing looks. They didn't say anything.

"I assume you know about this." Another knowing look. *I'm on the right trail.* "I want to make sure the money gets to the right people. The way she came into the money is complicated."

A questioned lingered on Trey's face. "Isn't it Grandfather's money?"

They know. "No, it's Nana's money from her side of the family. That's why it's complicated." Not a big lie.

The word "oh" seeped through Trey's pores and clouded his countenance.

"She's hidden the papers so no one can change what she wishes. There's probably a new will, but I'm not sure. Your Aunt Katie and I have searched for it, but we can't find it." All true, if misleading.

Raymond shrugged. "If she doesn't want you to find the papers, maybe you shouldn't look for them."

There it is. Raymond and Trey are moths too. "She may have promised some of it to you in return for holding the will."

Telepathic messages commuted between the lovers. I guessed at what they feared. "I promise not to change anything Nana wants to happen with the money. If the papers are in order, I'll leave them with you."

Trey gave Raymond a meaningful look, then said, "We don't have the papers, if that's what you're thinking."

I attempted a stern, parental look. "Maybe it's not a wad of documents, per se. It could be a thumb drive, a safe deposit key, or the name and number of someone who is holding the papers."

They shook their heads in unison.

"But you know about the money. Nana has promised it to you."

Raymond shrugged; Trey sighed. He said, "Yes, Nana has promised to pay for my sex change. She said I might have to wait a little while for all of it, but I could begin treatments now."

Holy shit. "Hormones?"

"To begin with."

"Has Nana given you money from her savings account? To get you started?"

"No," he said, shaking his head. "Wish she had, but I've had to come up with the money on my own."

Dead end. "Is that why you're not in school? Because you've begun the process?"

"No, I could still attend classes at this point, but I used the tuition and board money to pay for treatments. If my father finds out, he'll kill me."

"Where are you living?"

"Right here. They haven't assigned Raymond a new roommate because I dropped out after school started. So I'm squatting, and the other kids in the dorm don't know I shouldn't be here."

I pulled at my face, thinking. "If you don't mind me asking, how much will the whole process cost?"

He quoted an astounding number. "That's to go all the way, through all the surgeries and the psychological counseling. It will take years, and we'll have to live somewhere while Raymond finishes school."

"And you're going all the way?"

"We're committed," Raymond said.

"I want to be a woman, Uncle Randle, not a transvestite."

I nodded. The courage this path would require awed me.

When I didn't know what to say, Trey added, "I'm not gay, Uncle Randle. I'm a woman in love with a man."

"I'm not gay either," Raymond announced.

I slapped my knees with both hands. "I have to give Nana credit for wanting to help you through this . . . transformation. So, where would she hide papers while she is alive, but wants found if she should die?"

Trey shrugged. "She didn't tell me."

"What about your cousin, Nicki?"

"Maybe, she's far away. Nana promised her money too. Nicki has her own dreams."

"Nicki isn't as trustworthy as you are. She dances in a topless bar and uses drugs, right?"

Trey snickered. "She makes a ton of tax-free cash—more since she bought those big boobs—but she won't share her money with me. She doesn't trust Nana to give her money, so she's using her God-given talent to make her dreams come true."

Makes a certain kind of sense. "Is she clean?"

"She smokes some weed, but everybody does that," Raymond said.

I wasn't about to fly to Orlando to confront Nicki, so I asked Trey for her phone number. Then we hugged. "Let me know if you get kicked out of here so I can help."

* * *

Nicki finally answered the third time I rang her phone. Like her cousin, she assumed I had bad news about her grandmother. I assured her that Nana was fine. She apologized.

"I'm at work, and we're not allowed to carry our cells around with us."

G-strings don't have pockets. "I won't keep you, but I'm trying to find the paperwork that will transfer the money Nana promised you. Trey said you might have it."

"Is it real, the money?"

"It is, but it's complicated. I want to make sure Nana did it correctly."

"Well, I'm not counting on it. If it happens, great. If not, I can take care of myself."

I walked Nicki through the various ways in which Nana may have passed the documents. Nicki responded negatively to all of them.

"Uncle Randle, my Nana wouldn't trust me to fetch the evening newspaper. Thinks I'm doing something evil down here."

"She knows?"

"Everyone knows."

"Even your parents?"

"Of course. You figured it out, didn't you?"

"I suspected. Trey confirmed."

"What else did the little tattletale tell you?"

"That you have dreams and that's why you're chasing big money."

"True enough. I'd never achieve my dreams by working in a call center or typing memos for the boss, so—"

"Hey, it's your business, not mine. Can you tell me how much Nana promised you so I can get it right if I can find the papers?"

She gave me another astounding number, though not quite as large as Trey's. Nana was doling out the cash like it was Monopoly money. "That will buy a lot of dreams. I know Trey's; what are yours?"

She hesitated. "That's pretty personal, Uncle Randle. If I get the money, you'll know."

Garish movies about Nicki's profession and vulgar news reports about the stripper's lifestyle had me worried. Without becoming too intrusive, I inquired about her personal life and situation away from home. She said, "I have friends outside of the bar. I don't have a steady boyfriend, that's not safe in this business, but I do date occasionally— mature men with good jobs. No man is going to live off my hard work."

I took that to mean that she wasn't being pimped out, wasn't living with a drug dealer. Relieved, I told her to keep my number handy, and we disconnected.

Nicki is a lot like me, I thought. *She's independent, self-sufficient, able to thrive outside the family cocoon. Nana probably likes her more than Nicki knows.*

***

As the road to Augusta unwound beneath my wheels, I retraced the logic of the money and the papers, hoping for some euphoric epiphany. Mom had promised each of her grandchildren more money than her husband had left to her, so Mom was distributing Albert's money, not her own. For the briefest of moments, a neon sign flashed in my brain: *Am I in or out of my dad's will? If Albert left the money to Mom, her will, in the safe deposit box, would bequeath the money to Billy and Katie. So there have to be other papers that distributed Albert's money in a way being decided by Mom. "I fixed it," she had said. Katie knows there are other papers, and she's trying to find them to change them or hide them. She's been to see Albert with a lawyer. She's the enemy. So Mom's papers are in safe hands. But whose?*

I needed to obtain some kind of stability. I stopped at Mom's house and, using Joseph's ancient technology, I emailed the home for unwed mothers in Savannah and asked for a copy of my original birth certificate. I attached a copy of my driver's license, my adoptive birth certificate, Mom's marriage license, and my power of attorney to prove I was John Randle, the little bastard.

CHAPTER TWENTY

Late that Friday night, I reached the rehab facility to confront Mom yet again. As I walked through the front doors, Bonnie Mueller stepped out of the administrative offices and pointed to the private conference room on the other side of the vestibule. "You have a visitor," she said.

Acting nonchalant but feeling apprehensive, I thanked her and stepped into the conference room. Daniel Kaplan, dressed in a faded long-sleeved shirt, chinos, and sneakers, rose from his seat at the head of the table and stretched a welcoming hand toward me. Without his lab coat, ID badge, and stethoscope, Kaplan appeared smaller and lacked authoritative presence. I shook his hand and said, "Did you come to see Mom? Is something wrong?"

He motioned me into a seat and reclaimed his own. "No, I want to make you a deal." He offered a friendly smile that immediately set off warning bells in my brain.

"What kind of deal? Are you going to take Mom back to the hospital for proper preventive care?"

Kaplan's long face sagged under the weight of the message he planned to convey. Two documents lay in front of him. He nudged one toward me and picked the other off the table as though to read it. I got the hint. I picked up the document as he spoke.

"This is a nondisclosure agreement. In it, you promise not to disclose any part of the records you stole from the hospital." Kaplan looked at me. "You sent them to your own public email address, so there's no question of who stole the records."

The fact that someone had sent them to my address did not prove I had sent them, but still I said, "I don't care that you know. It doesn't change the facts in the record."

"You should care. If you don't sign the NDA, we'll prosecute."

I smirked as though to say, "You don't scare me." "That's it? I promise not to disclose the records and in return you give me nothing?"

"There's no medical reason to hospitalize your mother. But the contract is a bit more complicated. You should read it." He motioned to the NDA.

So I read it. By signing it, I agreed not to bring any claim or suit of malpractice against the hospital, and St. Thomas Aquinas Hospital was absolved of all liability pertaining to Mom's future disposition and health. In addition, I would promise to destroy or delete the records on all devices and in all media and would not disclose the contents of the record to any person not an employee or representative of the hospital. The second page was an affidavit attesting to the deletion. In return, the hospital would agree not to prosecute me for "unauthorized access to a protected computer system," which I assumed to be language straight out of the penal code. Essentially, I would admit guilt and surrender all rights by signing the document.

"You have to do better than this, Daniel."

"There's no reason for us to give you anything but your freedom from prosecution."

"And there's no reason for me to relieve you of your liability for the treatment of my mother."

Pointing a finger at me, he said, "You've committed a crime. There's no proof that we've done anything wrong."

"If that were true, you wouldn't be here. No, Daniel, we're going to play this like the Cold War." He looked confused. "Mutually assured destruction until Mom's condition is resolved. If she gets healthy, you're off the hook."

He leaned back in his chair and sighed in frustration. "I'm trying to do you a favor, and you're too pigheaded to accept it."

"I'm sorry you were chosen for this mission, Daniel. I thought you were one of the good guys."

He rose and started for the door. Before disappearing, he said, "Hell, no one else would even bother with you."

*　*　*

Residents hustled to the cafeteria as dinnertime neared, so I followed them into the boisterous room. Billy and Beth had staked out a table near the front windows, but Mom had not yet joined them. They didn't look pleased to see me as I took a seat without an invitation.

"Where's Mom?"

"Carol is trying to convince her to eat," Beth said. "She won't come out of her room if she knows you're here."

"I thought you were bringing meals in for her. She doesn't like the cafeteria food."

"We can't afford to feed her restaurant meals every night," Beth explained.

"She's really upset with you," Billy said. "You got her kicked out of the hospital, and now you're killing her with this exercise program."

If Billy thought Mom was upset about exercise, Mom hadn't told him what our conversation had really been about. "You want to stash her somewhere comfortable to wait for the next heart attack? Are you counting the days till you can abscond with the rest of her money?"

Billy turned red and tense, but Beth placed a soothing hand on his arm. "Go back to Florida, Jack. Mom doesn't want to see you anymore."

"She's not upset with me," I lied, as Carol, the nurse, walked up to our table.

Carol looked pained. "She's not going to eat in the cafeteria tonight. I'll make her a plate and take it to her."

"We'll keep her company in her room," Billy said.

"I don't think she wants company. She's going to eat with Maureen in the room."

"You've spoiled it for all of us, Jack," Billy said. He walked away, and Beth meekly followed him. Carol shrugged and headed to the serving line.

I left the building too but drove to a convenience store. I bought a quart of chocolate milk, two candy bars, and a pint of chocolate ice cream. I returned to the rehab center with the treats and asked Carol to deliver them to Mom and Maureen.

***

Back at the house, I went straight to Mom's closet and retrieved her pretty box of love letters. I took them into the parlor with a bottle of beer, and, sitting in Mom's rocker, read Albert's letters word for word, in chronological order. They were sweet and filled with lovers' clichés and became more insistent, more pleading over time. In the third to last letter, Albert had remarked, "You've fulfilled your bargain with him, now I hope you'll keep your promise to me." And, in the last letter, he wrote, "I will wait for you till my last day, and even if we never again share what we had together, you will have my legacy to remember me by. That will be my dying wish, and that will help me rest for eternity."

When I first stumbled upon the letters, I had thought them typical tokens of affection and an anguished record of unfulfilled love. Interpreting them now in the context of a shared child and a large estate, I saw them as proof of Mom's tortured life suspended between two men: one man who provided her with basic security and a mixed litter of children; and one man who offered her everlasting love and the gift of one treasured child.

Several conclusions bombarded me: Mom had fulfilled a bargain with Joseph Marks; Mom had failed to keep a promise to Albert; and Albert's reference to "what we had together" was surely a reference to me. However, the most revealing of Albert's phrases was "you will have my legacy to remember me by." He intended Mom to enjoy his wealth after he passed. I was certain. In turn, Mom wanted shares to go to Nicki and Trey. I had proof of that as well. What I didn't know was whether Mom had "fixed it" permanently, or Katie had undone her wishes.

Chapter Twenty-One

Saturday morning assailed me with the poison-tipped arrows of paranoia. I imagined myself in a battle with the Roman army, cowering under a shield as volley after volley of the deadly missiles darkened the sky above me. *Get rid of the medical records* ricocheted inside the barren cavern of my skull.

I sat at Joseph's desk and, using his decade-old printer, painstakingly printed Mom's medical records. Then I emailed the records to my former friend and attorney, Tony Zambrano, in St. Petersburg. I included a note that informed him the email was a client-attorney privileged communication and that explanations would be forthcoming. I hoped that would deter him from deleting it. With the unabridged medical records safely backed up, I deleted my email account, wiped my iPad's storage, and reset the device to factory settings. Good computer forensics people could restore the deleted files, but I doubted a local police department would have access to those talents, and I doubted the FBI would take an interest in my case.

I would drop the printed copy in Mom's safe deposit box on the way to the rehab facility that morning. Since the box was her property, a search warrant would be difficult to obtain as she wasn't the target of the investigation and was obviously incapacitated.

These defensive maneuvers seemed to be the product of an unstable mind, but I had a premonition the hospital had something to hide and wouldn't let the matter die.

The matter I wouldn't let die was the identity of the forger of Mom's savings account withdrawals. I compared the signatures on Mom's prescriptions for the painkillers Katie procured while in Augusta— presumably Katie's signature—to the signatures on the savings account withdrawals and found them to be different. However, each withdrawal from Mom's savings account preceded a prescription date by a day or two. Only one conclusion could logically be reached: Brad had forged the withdrawals to feed Katie's habit. The pills didn't cost a great deal, but the friendly dentist accepted bribes to write the scripts. To afford the bribes, Katie stole Mom's money, and now she wanted Albert's too.

***

Mom wasn't in the gym when I reached the rehab facility. That didn't surprise me. Rodney simply shook his head, and I headed for Mom's room. Bonnie Mueller caught sight of me as I passed the office and ambushed me.

"Your mother took two days to set a baseline, and now she's missed two days of physical therapy. She's three days off-pace."

"It's been less than a week. She's still adjusting. I'll see if I can get her going today."

I tried to move around Mueller, but she blocked my path in the hallway. "I can't report progress for Medicare payments. She should start two-a-day sessions on Monday."

I tried to appear menacing, and Mueller took an involuntary step backward. "The bureaucrats at Medicare aren't going to manage my mother's treatment, you are. You'll report progress just like you do for Maureen, my mother's roommate. Know what I mean?"

Mueller's eyes widened. She stiffened like a six-foot-tall two-by-twelve-inch board. "She has to do two-a-days starting Monday or we'll have to bill you directly." She did an about-face that would have made any Marine proud and marched back to the safety of her office.

I proceeded down the hallway and found Mom's occupancy slider set to red for privacy. Without knocking, I stepped through the door to find several nurses crowded around Maureen's bed. A couple of them stared at me in disbelief as one of them drew the covers over Maureen's naked body. They had been bathing her.

I said, "Good morning," and nodded as I pulled the privacy curtain across the room to separate that unpleasant visual from Mom and me. Mom sat propped up on her pillows but stared at the ceiling.

I sat on the edge of her bed and grabbed one hand. It was cold. "How are you doing, Mom?"

As though I had distracted her from some important thought, she slowly swiveled her face in my direction and said wistfully, "Not so good, Jackie. I don't feel right."

Is she conning me because she doesn't want to exercise? Maybe, but the words "I don't feel right" are often the first symptom of an impending heart attack. I laid a wrist across her forehead and found it to be cold as well. *Poor circulation?*

"Maybe we should get you up, get your blood flowing."

"No need for that, Jackie. Jesus is on His way for me."

Oh boy. "Do you still see Him? Here?"

"He's everywhere, Jackie. Like a spirit."

I stood. "I'm going to get a doctor, have him check you to see if you're okay."

"Can I go home to die, Jackie?"

"No, Mom, you need to be where the doctors can take care of you."

Lazily, she allowed her arms to flop onto the bed, frustrated that her caring son was so thickheaded. "You don't know what they do to you here. They come in the shower with me," she hissed.

"To make sure you don't fall."

"They pick me up off the pot and wipe my rear."

"They don't want you to get hurt, Mom."

She looked as though she might cry, so I walked out to the nurses' station and described Mom's lethargy and cold skin to an older woman who seemed to be in charge. She agreed to send the duty doctor.

Amazingly, it took him only minutes to get to Mom's room. He was old enough to be a resident at the rehab facility. I looked at his unruly gray hair and suspected he had retired from private practice and was moonlighting for a little extra cash. Better than being a greeter at a discount store. His name was Dr. Robinson.

The doctor checked Mom's vital signs—temperature and blood pressure normal, heart rate a bit slow, oxygenation a bit low—and asked her to describe her symptoms. Of course, she had none. He proclaimed her to be fine and left us.

"I have an idea, Mom. I'm going to go get Frank and bring him over here to visit with you. Would you like that?"

She managed a small smile, and the light of life crept back into her eyes. "Yes, it would be good to see him before I go."

I raised her bed into a semi-sitting position and turned her TV on. "Be back in a few hours, Mom. Try to eat something for lunch."

The fact that I intended to bring Albert as well as Frank and conduct an intervention gave me a brief pang of guilt, but I rationalized that I had no more chances to get to the bottom of the Marks-Czajka family mysteries before I would have to return to Florida on Tuesday.

* * *

Clara, the receptionist at Meadowlake, recognized me as I walked through the front doors. She left her counter to hold the community room door for me. "Mr. Randle is playing in a tournament today," she said with a grin.

I saw four tables arranged in the center of the room with four players at each table, and I understood: sixteen thriving retirees were playing a duplicate bridge competition. A few envious onlookers circled each table and kibitzed as the players energetically and gleefully tossed cards onto each trick. Frank noticed me and nodded but never lost his concentration—the tournament was serious business. Or maybe his partner was serious business. Bottle blonde and shapely, tastefully dressed and made up, the only woman at his table was at least ten years his junior.

"How much longer before the tournament is over," I asked a spectator.

"This is the last game of this rubber," he said. "There's one more rubber after that."

As the cards were being dealt once more, I caught Frank's eye and pointed to the ceiling, to the second floor where my dad would be in his room. He nodded yes, and I gave him a thumbs-up sign for luck with the cards and his partner.

Back at Clara's counter I asked to see my dad, and Clara requested I sign the visitors' register. The facility restricted access to residents' rooms on the upper floors. As I signed in, I realized Mom and Katie would have had to sign in as well.

"Do you have logs of visitors by resident?" I asked Clara.

"Yes, on the computer. The handwritten log is reentered each day into each resident's account."

I gave her my most trust-inspiring smile and said, "Can you look up my dad's record and tell me when my mother has been here? Elaine Marks? She came with my sister, Katie van Kamp, a few months ago."

Clara decided the request was innocent enough and pulled up Albert's account. The visits happened in this sequence: Mom and Katie; then, within a week of the first visit, Katie visited with someone named Charles Butler; and, two weeks later, Mom came back with someone named Robert Taylor; and last, another week later, Katie came alone. I assumed that Butler and Taylor were lawyers. The letter Mom sent me in prison would fit into the timeline between her visit and Katie's visit with Butler, the attorney. After seeing Albert the first time, Mom had wanted my help with the estate, but after Katie's first visit, she had taken matters into her own hands, with help from Taylor, and she had "fixed it." But then Katie had one last, ominous bite of the apple. When I received Mom's letter in prison, Mom had been willing to share information with me, but after Katie's surreptitious visit, Mom kept her machinations a secret. What had she done that she didn't want me to know? Had she cut me out of Albert's will too?

Luis, Dad's attendant, emerged from the elevator with a grin and extended a hand. I shook it. "Albert will be happy to see you," he said. "He's not having a good day."

"Maybe I can brighten his day. I want to take him to Augusta to see my mother. She's bedridden."

Luis's smile became a frown. "No can do, *señor*. Mr. Albert cannot leave without me, and I cannot leave today. We only go to doctors' appointments."

Fatigue engulfed me. At every turn, I seemed to encounter rules and bureaucrats with whom I had to battle for common decency. Clara, anticipating an argument, walked around her counter and leaned against it with her arms crossed over her chest.

I had no energy for another fight. "Can we arrange it in advance, for a day when you can come along with him? I don't know how long my mother will be with us."

Clara looked sympathetic. "We do that sometimes. He has to be transported in our van, and there's an additional charge for long-distance travel."

"No problem," I said. "Can we do it this coming Tuesday?" Scheduling Albert's trip to see Mom on Tuesday would mean delaying my return to Florida until Wednesday. That meant disappointing Glenda once more. *What a mess.*

"I'll make a note of it and ask the center head when she's in the office on Monday." Clara walked back around her counter and wrote on a pad of paper.

"What about my uncle?" I asked.

Clara looked up with a question on her face.

"Can I take him to Augusta today?"

"Yes, if Mr. Randle wants to go, you can take him. You have to get him back here no later than seven p.m."

"Thanks. I'll visit with my dad while Uncle Frank finishes the bridge tournament, then I'll take him to see his sick sister."

Clara knew I was tugging at her institutional heartstrings, but she took it well with a tight smile and a wave of her hand.

Luis and I rode the elevator to the second floor. We dodged carts and patients shuffling along with their intravenous drips hanging from three-wheeled poles and made our way down the busy corridor to Dad's room. Luis swung the door open for me, and I walked into the overheated space. As before, Dad sat in his easy chair next to the window with his headphones over his ears. His eyes were closed. He may have been napping or just enjoying the classical music, but he neither heard us nor sensed us.

I approached him and saw that the book open on his lap was a compilation of Shakespeare's plays. He had been reading *Macbeth*. *There's more to this man than building condos,* I thought. The quote that came to my mind was, "False face must hide what the false heart doth know."

I bent to kiss his bald pate, and that roused him. His head jerked around, and his eyes fell on my face. First there was confusion, then a hint of recognition. I smiled at him, but his eyes clouded over quickly and he became catatonic.

His headphones had been knocked askew, but he made no attempt to right them. I removed them gently and laid them upon his open book. I sank to a catcher's squat beside his chair and said, "It's Jack, Dad. I came back to see you."

He did not respond.

"Told you it's a bad day," Luis said. "Maybe tomorrow he'll be better."

With a sigh, I rose and kissed Dad's cheek. I took Luis by the arm and led him away from Dad. "Luis, do you remember when my mother and my sister came to visit him?"

"Sure, many times."

"I mean the first time, when they came together."

"*Sí.*"

"How was my dad at that time? Did he know them, talk to them?"

"Oh yes, he write many notes."

"And then my sister came with another man."

Luis nodded.

"Did he write notes that time too?"

"No," Luis said, and paused, thoughtful. "He was confused, but he signed the papers."

Ah, yes, the papers. "And then my mother came back with a different man."

"He signed the papers then too, but I don't think he knew what they wanted."

Crap! I took a deep breath and let it out slowly. "My sister came back again, right?"

Luis grinned. "He no want to see her. I tell her he sick."

Good! "And she left without seeing him?"

He shook his head slowly, left and right. "She not happy."

Relieved for the first time in days, I clapped Luis on the shoulder. "You're a good man, Luis. I appreciate what you do for my dad."

With one backward glance at my mother's one true love, I left the room to fetch my uncle.

***

Infatuation is cute when it blossoms in the very young or in the very old. Uncle Frank and his blonde partner made a cute pairing, like Riesling and strawberry shortcake, as they chatted at their bridge table. The tournament had ended and the old folks had dispersed, but Frank was holding court, and the object of his intentions listened raptly. I stood away from his table and waited for him to notice me. He did, then waved me over and introduced me to Miriam. On closer inspection, I decided Miriam was closer to Frank's age than I had guessed. Obviously, she had been the subject of some very good cosmetic work.

"We placed second," Frank said.

"Congratulations," I said. Then, looking at Miriam, I said, "If you have plans today, I'll go back to Augusta. But I hoped I could take my uncle over there to see his sister. She's convinced her passing is imminent."

Miriam's lipsticked mouth formed an "O." A look of concern, tinged with a border of irritation, descended on Frank's face.

"Will he be back for dinner?" Miriam asked.

"Maybe. He has to be back by seven p.m. but you may have eaten by then."

Miriam rose, then nuzzled my uncle's cheek. "I'll wait and save a seat for you."

Resigned to his afternoon away from Miriam, Frank drove his motorized wheelchair like a Formula One racer, through the doors into the lobby—a hearty wave for Clara at the front desk—through the front doors and down the ramp that desecrated the formal staircase. At my white Bronco, he surprised me with his ability to stand and lever himself into the front seat unaided while I loaded his chair into the truck's cavernous backend. Then we were off on our road trip.

Immediately, Frank confessed his unease about visiting his ailing sister. "We all know we'll reach the end eventually, but that doesn't make it any easier when you have to face it. Every time we lose someone at Meadowlake, it's a reminder that our turn is coming. It's like we're standing in formation and God is pacing back and forth in front of us, deciding whom to call next."

"I know your time with Miriam is precious, Frank, but your sister needs a kick in the pants. The doctor says she's able to do the rehab but she refuses, keeps saying Jesus is coming soon to get her."

"Depression. Easy to fall into, and sometimes you can't get back out of it."

Remembering an idea I had the first time I came to see my uncle, I said, "Maybe I should move her to Meadowlake. She could enjoy your company, see Albert, and have a social life there. She hates rehab, so maybe I shouldn't push her through it."

He gave me a one-shouldered shrug. "I'll ask her. We all have to decide for ourselves how much longer to fight for breath and when to let go."

"And meeting someone like Miriam might encourage a man to stay here for a while longer?"

He smiled, and we fell into silence for ten miles before I said, "Do you know how I came to be named John?"

He grunted and gave me a querulous look, so I explained. "Mom told me I was named after Joseph—John was his middle name—but I was at least eighteen months old before she met him."

A dreamy look appeared on his craggy face. Remembering a time seventy years ago, he said, "Your mother's favorite grandparent was our mother's father, John Wesley Clark. I believe you were named in his honor, but that didn't change our parents' mind about you."

I made a mental note to google my great-grandfather, John Wesley Clark. I wanted to fill in the blank spaces in my heritage, but of more pressing concern were the blank spaces in Mom's recent past. Running out of time before we would reach Augusta, I asked him to describe Mom's reunion with Albert, after his stroke.

Frank appeared happy to be distracted from thoughts about his sister's current condition because he rambled on for miles. I rarely interrupted. Most of what he told me, I already knew: Albert had suffered a stroke that left him speechless but able to hear and communicate by writing notes; Frank had informed Mom and asked her to come see her former boyfriend; Katie had been visiting Mom (scoring pills from the friendly dentist, no doubt) so she drove Mom from Augusta; Mom wore a summer dress and was all "dolled up"; the five of them—Albert, Mom, Katie, Frank, and Luis—visited in Albert's room; the encounter was emotional and tearful. The shocking revelation: after catching up for a while, Mom sat in Albert's lap, hugged his neck, whispered in his ear, and kissed his cheek. Frank said the display of affection had embarrassed him, but he had been happy for his sister and his friend.

Before they separated, Albert excitedly told Mom (in a note) that he had kept the promise he had made when their affair ended—he had left his estate to her and their son, Jack.

"That's why you thought I came the first time to talk about the money," I said. "But I never knew he was my father, never knew he was worth a lot of money."

"Your mother didn't know he was rich until that day. She was flustered, said he should share it with his family or donate it to charity. He said he wanted to keep his promise so he could rest easy for eternity. Your mother said she never wanted you to know about Albert, and Albert said, 'You have to tell him, for my sake.' So your mother asked if she could change the will, divide the money among deserving people on her side of the family, and he agreed to let her do it. He said, 'Bring it when you're ready, and I'll sign it. But don't wait too long.' That ended the discussion. Albert was satisfied that he had kept his promise, and your mother was satisfied that she could control how the money would be divided. She left then, and she took all of Albert's notes, as a memento, I guess."

That's why Mom could promise large sums of money to Nicki and Trey. I tried not to wonder who else was in my dad's will. "Mom did come back with a new will." It was more a statement than a question.

"Your sister came first, and she had a lawyer with her. Met with Albert alone, except for Luis."

"So you don't know if Albert signed a new will?"

"Luis said he did sign it. Your sister told Albert she brought it for your mother."

"I doubt that because Mom came back later, right? With a different lawyer?"

"Yeah, nice fellow. Asked Albert a lot of questions to see if he was able to think straight. Albert didn't do too well with the answers, but he knew he was signing a will and he knew he had already signed one for your sister, so they went ahead with it. Luis and I were witnesses."

"Did Luis witness my sister's version?"

Frank chuckled. "No, Luis said he wasn't authorized, so they corralled a couple of nurses."

"He's a good man. Did Katie know that Mom had undone her will? Is that why she came back one more time?"

"I don't know for certain, but I don't know why else she would have come."

"Did you see my sister when she came back the last time?"

"No, she didn't ask for me either."

Frank had been unsure of the sequence of the visits when first we spoke of them, but now his version of events matched exactly the visitors' log. As I replayed what Luis and Frank had told me about Mom's and Katie's visits to Albert, the struggle over Albert's money congealed like Jell-O. It appeared solid at first glance, but the slightest probing caused it to shimmy and shake precariously. Mom brought Albert's notes back to Augusta, but since I couldn't find them in the house, I assumed that Katie had stolen them. If I were her, I'd have destroyed them and written a new will for Albert's signature on the next visit. Katie may not have known about Mom's subsequent visit, but if she didn't, why did she try to see Albert one last time? If she didn't know, why did she search the house for the "papers" that Mom had hidden? I bet that the last version of the will Albert signed was Mom's version and that it "fixed" the money problem. My money was on Mom.

As we approached the Sacred Heart rehab facility, I finally asked the question that had begged for release all the way from Columbia: "Just how much money are we talking about, Frank?"

"More than four million smackeroos, as I understand it."

I kept the Bronco on the highway, but just barely.

CHAPTER TWENTY-TWO

Two Richmond County police cruisers squatted in the parking lot and sent a tremor of fear through my loins. *Someone needed resuscitation,* I thought first. *No, the fire department takes those calls. Someone has died.*

I unloaded Frank's wheelchair while he slid out of the passenger seat and steadied himself with a hand on the Bronco. When I had the wheelchair in position, he aimed his backside between the arms of the chair and let himself fall onto the seat with a grunt.

"When I was a kid that was fun, but now it hurts," he said.

I punched the big metal button to activate the automatic front doors of the facility, and Frank cruised through the small lobby and into the main corridor. Asking him to follow me, I walked through the cafeteria and made a visual sweep of the room. Mom wasn't eating or sitting at any of the tables. The contrast between Sacred Heart and Meadowlake suddenly crystalized for me. At Meadowlake, well-dressed and well-heeled "residents" engaged in games and social activities and generally exhibited an air of happiness. At Sacred Heart, infirm and fragile "patients" camped morosely in rooms that were too similar to hospital waiting rooms to inspire happiness. At Meadowlake, uniformed waiters served iced tea garnished with lemon. At Sacred Heart, the patients crept behind their aluminum walkers to a cafeteria line where they served themselves. Patients here were cheaply attired and less well-kept than the residents at Meadowlake, and I wondered, not for the first time, whether the correlation between wealth and health was accidental or a cause-and-effect relationship. I vowed to move Mom to Columbia as soon as possible. It would serve Billy and Katie right if she lived long enough to spend the rest of her money on uniformed waiters.

We had no choice but to see if Mom was in her room, so we motored through the TV room into Mom's hallway. As we approached her closed door, two cops, a uniformed sergeant and a patrolman, exited her room and slouched against the wall. *Mom is the one who died!* I froze, and the patrolman noticed my apprehension. He stiffened, elbowed the sergeant, then pointed at me. The sergeant stiffened as well.

Frank stopped ahead of me and rotated. "Which room is it, Jack?"

"The one they came out of," I said, pointing to the cops.

The cops looked confused and so did Frank, but for different reasons. When I didn't move, the sergeant edged in my direction. "Are you Randle Marks?" he asked.

I nodded, and with that the patrolman moved to my side with surprising agility and quickness. He reached for the handcuffs hanging from his thick black belt, but the sergeant waved a dismissive hand and the patrolman quashed his urge to put his hands on me. Frank watched and listened with increasing dread as the sergeant said, "We need to take you downtown for questioning. We have a search warrant for your computer and your cell phone." He held out a hand for the electronic devices and swept his other arm down the hallway like a maître d' ushering a special guest to a special table at a special restaurant.

Relief washed over me. Mom wasn't dead. Daniel had simply escalated our little spat.

"Am I under arrest?"

"Not yet."

I handed over my innocent electronics. "My uncle"—I pointed to Frank—"needs to get into my mother's room for his visit."

"I'll open the door for him," the sergeant said, and he did.

"Don't worry, Frank. I'll be back to take you home."

Frank shook his head in disgust, reversed his course, and rolled into Mom's room. From inside, I heard little gasps and the sounds of a joyful reunion. Then the mood was spoiled, not by the police, but by Billy, who stepped into the hallway and, with a broad smile, said, "Once a jailbird, always a jailbird."

Beth peeked around the doorjamb, so I moderated my response. "Do Mom a favor and let her have some private time with her brother."

Billy sneered. "Don't waste your one phone call on us. We don't answer calls from jail."

Before I could fire a smart retort at Billy, the sergeant became impatient, took my elbow, and led me to the front entrance. To the chagrin of the patrolman, who had wanted the honor of conveying the prisoner, the sergeant put me in the back of his cruiser. On the way downtown, he remarked that I was his first detention for stealing computer data. "Had to look it up. Title 16-9-90, the Computer Systems Protection Act. You one o' them hackers?"

"I accessed my mother's medical records on the hospital computer."

"That's called computer invasion of privacy. Weird, huh?"

"What's weird is that they won't let you look at your own records. They're worried about a lawsuit, so they pressed charges."

That shut him up until we arrived at the intimidating, sickly gray jailhouse. Cells were stacked eight stories high behind a two-story administration building with a long, single-story appendage for receiving and admitting. At one end of the low building, a fenced and gated cage reminded me of a drive-in service bay at an auto dealership—it acted as the secure onloading/offloading point for prisoners. Once our cruiser was locked in the secure area, the sergeant opened my door for me. Other than making me walk in front of him into the reception area, he didn't exert any security precautions. I found that odd until I saw Daniel standing at the booking desk.

"You getting booked for some dastardly crime, Daniel?"

"Please don't make me do this, Randle. I brought the NDA for you to sign, if you've come to your senses."

"And you'll give me a ride back to Sacred Heart if I sign it?"

A small smile. "Sure."

"Not going to do it, Daniel. St. Thomas wouldn't go to all this trouble if you weren't hiding something in Mom's medical records."

"Be sensible. You committed a crime, and we're giving you an easy way out. Your mother is no longer in our care, and under the law, we have a right to protect our records."

"Did your lawyers make you memorize that speech?" I turned to the booking sergeant and said, "Book me, Danno."

Apparently the sergeant was too young to remember *Hawaii Five-O* because he said, "My name's Michael, but it's sergeant to you."

He handed my iPad and cell phone to a plainclothes cop who had been loitering behind the desk sergeant. The plainclothes cop looked like a Marine drill sergeant—square head, square brush-cut hair, square jaw, square shoulders, but with a lopsided, sneering smile. He flashed a folded sheet of paper at me. "Search warrant. What are your passwords?"

"The devices aren't password protected. Don't ogle my wife's pictures."

There was no need to explain that Glenda had once been my wife and would be my wife once again. He leered at the iPad, gave me a little sneer, and disappeared.

Daniel shook his head in wonderment and shuffled toward the door. To his back I said, "You know I'll figure it out, Daniel."

As I had seen him do once before, he waved goodbye without turning around.

The jail staff gave me the deluxe treatment—no fingerprinting or mug shot—and placed me in a holding cell by myself. I didn't have to change into the attractive orange jumpsuit. The jailer told me someone would be around to take me to an interrogation room, so I stood at the bars, waiting and watching the hallway for that someone. After fifteen minutes, I sat on the bunkbed. After thirty minutes, I stretched out flat. A metal rack served as a bed with a paper-thin synthetic mat for a mattress. The hard surface was uncomfortable, but lying down and waiting was easier than standing and waiting. After about an hour, a different jailer walked past, and I flagged him down and asked to make my one authorized phone call. He said that I hadn't been booked, so I wasn't owed a call.

Obviously they were sweating me, wanting me to give in to Daniel and St. Thomas hospital's lawyers. As I sweated, they searched my devices for the medical records I had allegedly stolen. Without those records, I doubted they would have sufficient evidence to arraign me. At least not today.

Thirty minutes later, the plainclothes cop appeared at my cell. "I need your email account information."

"I don't have one."

"You sent the data you stole from the hospital to your email account."

"Someone sent it, probably a disgruntled hospital employee."

The cop's eyebrows flickered like a failing fluorescent lightbulb. "What did you do with the records?"

"I can't answer that question without my lawyer present. Which reminds me that I want to make a phone call."

"You'll get one after we book you."

The cop disappeared, and I went back to sweating. More than an hour passed before a jailer unlocked my cell. "Am I finally getting a phone call?"

"Follow me," was all he said.

He led me back to reception, where the plainclothes cop waited with my iPad and cell phone. "We're requesting a search warrant for your email account," he said. "When we get it, you'll get another ride downtown."

"Right now I'll take a ride uptown, back to Sacred Heart."

"Sorry, all our limos are busy."

The desk sergeant snickered. The plainclothes cop handed me a Post-it note and waved his hand, shooing me toward the door. I looked at the note before moving. It said, "Call me when you're ready to get out of trouble" and listed a phone number I assumed was Daniel's.

As I walked out the front doors, the plainclothes cop said, "Your wife is hot. Play it right, and you'll get to see her again."

Loud enough for him to hear, I muttered one word, "Pervert."

That annoyed him. Pointing a long, strong finger at me, he said, "Tell your brother to stay away from that bookie, or he'll be your cellmate."

The detective walked away as I tried to digest what he had said. "What?"

He disappeared through a door without answering me. With no other choice, I exited through a walking gate to a long driveway and onto a deserted stretch of Fourth Street. There was no taxi rank waiting to take released prisoners back to freedom. More than a little irritated, I ordered an Uber, and five minutes later I was on my way to Sacred Heart.

***

Mom's room door was still closed, but I barged through it to find Billy sitting at her bedside. He jumped to his feet as though he had been doing something shameful.

"Where's Frank?"

"I didn't think you'd get out of jail, so Beth took him back to Columbia."

"Did you give them time to visit or just rush him away?"

"Mom's worn out."

Mom lay on the bed with her eyes closed, but at Billy's comment she said, "Can I go home to die, Jackie?"

I sat on the edge of her bed and held her hand. She opened her sad eyes and said, "I think Jesus is coming tomorrow."

"Sunday is His day off, Mom. But I have a better idea. We're going to move you to Columbia, to be in the same home with Frank and Albert. Would you like that?"

The smallest of smiles, a mere tug at the corners of her mouth, grew on her face. "Thank you. I can die there."

Billy grabbed my arm and pulled me a few feet away from Mom's bed. "Medicare isn't going to pay for that," he hissed.

"Medicare isn't going to pay for this place either, because Mom won't exercise. She has plenty of money to live in comfort. We can always sell the house if she needs more."

Billy recoiled. I calculated that the money I now held for Mom would pay for twelve to eighteen months at Meadowlake. After that, money from Albert could fund a lifetime. Although I had hoped Mom would exercise at Sacred Heart and get strong enough to withstand surgery, now I was more realistic about her future. If she moved to a comfortable environment, like Meadowlake, with family and social activities, her attitude toward regaining her health might improve. That was one of the advantages the wealthy class had over the middle class.

I don't think Billy shared my outlook. He gave my arm a tight squeeze and a tug.

"We should vote on it, as a family."

So the two money-grubbers can vote me down? I don't think so. Obviously Billy doesn't want to reveal that he's already stolen Mom's house. "Sure, Billy, and Mom gets a vote too. We'll do it in person when your sister gets here. Meanwhile, I'll schedule Mom's move for Tuesday."

Billy dropped his hands and left the room. I sat on Mom's bed again and told her I had to go to Atlanta for book events. So I wouldn't see her on Sunday, but I'd be back on Monday.

"I'll ask Jesus if He can wait for you," she said.

***

I drove through a fast food restaurant pick-up line and bought a hamburger and fries. I was eating at Mom's kitchen table when Glenda called.

Before I could update her, she said, "Have you heard from Jamie? Carrie's parole has been granted."

Instead of telling her about my battle with St. Thomas Aquinas Hospital, about Trey's and Nicki's plans, about Katie's problem, about Albert's money, and about my visits with Frank and Dad, I said, "These things take time, Glenda. It could be a month before the bureaucrats process the paperwork."

"I need you, Randle. Come home now."

"I can't. I'm going to Atlanta tomorrow for my interviews and signings on Monday. Then I'll move Mom to Columbia on Tuesday, and I'll come home on Wednesday. In the meantime, lock the doors and set the alarm. Keep the backyard lights burning all night. Her daddy will bring her by boat, not by car. Keep the Berretta loaded and cocked on the nightstand."

I heard a sound like an angry cat being strangled. "I don't want to be this kind of wife, Randle, but you need to make a choice: it's me or your mother."

"Glenda, it's not that complicated. If you see Carrie, just shoot her."

In the old days, I'd have been assaulted by a loud bang as Glenda smashed the receiver onto the cradle. Now I heard only silence as she pushed the "End" button on her smartphone.

CHAPTER TWENTY-THREE

The drive from Augusta to Atlanta is uphill, from what was in prehistoric times oceanfront property, to what is now the nation's second-highest large city at approximately one thousand feet above sea level. The sprawling metropolis is a patchwork of discreet, cloistered neighborhoods, crouched on a plateau beneath the foothills of the Appalachian and Blue Ridge mountains.

The drive from Augusta to Atlanta is also a transition from the Old South to what is euphemistically called the New South, although there's little Southern culture and charm left in cosmopolitan Atlanta. In the 1970s, the city's commercial foundation exploded with success and attracted white-collar workers from Los Angeles, Dallas, and Chicago by the planeload. These "immigrants" landed the best jobs, earned most of the local wages, voted their Republican sensibilities, and reshaped the political and economic demographics forever. Atlanta accommodated the influx of college-educated talent with unprecedented suburban sprawl that stretches nearly seventy miles from Canton in the north to Peachtree City in the south and seventy-five miles east to west from Covington to Villa Rica. Atlanta's infamous traffic jams can make one of these edge-to-edge journeys take a longer time than a flight from there to New York City.

During the housing booms of the 1990s and 2000s, suburban sprawl was followed by urban flight, and Atlanta's suburbs became as racially integrated and culturally homogenized as any in the country. Today, Millennials born in the city have no accents and wouldn't know how to spell, much less say, "y'all" or "fixin'." More than one hundred years after the War of Northern Aggression, Margaret Mitchell's city is truly gone with the wind.

What remains of the original city, the turf inside the circular Perimeter Highway, are minority districts resting cheek-by-jowl beside leafy enclaves inhabited by old-money denizens. The Vinings section of Northwest Atlanta is one such enclave.

Early Sunday afternoon, I wound my way through the clogged and twisted streets of Vinings to the Freedom's Path drug and alcohol rehabilitation center. It was not lost on me that for more than a week I had spent my days in hospitals, rehab centers, and old folks' homes, places that ordinary Americans visit rarely and never enthusiastically. Freedom's Path did not inspire joyous anticipation for my visit. A converted motel built in the days when I-285 was the boundary between city and country, and when travelers rested near the highway before continuing pilgrimages from Canada to winter in Florida, it squatted just inside the Perimeter and mostly out of sight of the well-heeled Vinings residents. Two stories of rooms formed an L shape, with offices, communal rooms, and therapy rooms forming the short side of the L.

I parked in a visitor's space in front of the office and walked into a reception area that smelled of desperation. A woman who may well have been a former patient waited for me at the counter.

"I'm here to see my sister, Katie van Kamp. First name Katherine, maiden name Marks." I slipped my driver's license out of my wallet to prove my relationship to the patient.

The woman frowned and shook her head as though she couldn't quite remember something, then tapped on her computer keyboard. "She's no longer here."

"Her recovery period has already ended?"

She frowned some more, this time with a tinge of sadness. "She disappeared last Wednesday, skipped out on her bill. Later her husband called to say she was taking a break and would come back soon." She gave me the look you give people when you're wondering if they'll buy that bridge.

"How long was she supposed to stay here?"

"Six weeks, but she left in less than two. Usually if we can keep them for two weeks, they stay for the whole program. The first two weeks are all about physical withdrawal."

"So she's still physically hooked?"

"I can't give you any medical information, but this was her third time here, and she's never made it through the first two weeks. She hasn't hit rock bottom yet, so she isn't ready to bounce up."

"Maybe you should keep her under lock and key."

"Oh, we're not a prison, sir."

"But you should be. She committed a crime, and she's sick but not in jail and she's not in here either."

The woman didn't like my attitude. "We're here to help when people want help, sir." She gave me a foul look and wandered away to a back room. So I left.

As I walked back to my car, I summarized what I knew about my sister: Katie refused to come to Augusta; Katie wasn't in rehab; Katie had stolen Mom's savings; Katie was trying to steal Albert's money; Katie wanted Mom dead so she could afford a life of drug abuse. I had to find her.

I knew the way to Katie's house, four exits to the east on I-285 and half a mile north of the Perimeter on Riverside Drive. Her and her husband Brad's home was on the left, shielded from prying eyes by hundred-year-old oaks and magnolias, in a neighborhood of slightly newer money than the neighborhoods inside the Perimeter. A long driveway descended from the roadway before rising to an elevation a hundred yards from the street. Built in the 1970s of small bricks painted a dull white and trimmed with black shutters under a black tile roof, the single-story home was as wide as a strip mall. Otherwise the façade was unpretentious, which is how the old-money people in the South prefer their homes to look. Of course, Brad and Katie were not heirs to old money; they were interlopers, social climbers clinging precariously to the lower branches of Atlanta's social tree.

A large black Lexus SUV posed in front of the three-car garage, so I assumed someone was home to receive me. Brad answered the door in shorts, a T-shirt, and flip-flops. Tousled brown hair capped an aristocratic face and the thick chest and heavily muscled shoulders of a former swimmer at Vanderbilt. Our common experience as college athletes had produced a tenuous bond between weak allies in the internecine battles within the Marks clan. Like me, Katie and Brad kept their distance from the Church of Marks.

"Randle?" Brad was genuinely surprised.

"I need to speak with Katie."

"She's in rehab."

"I went there first, Brad." I opened the glass storm door, but Brad grabbed the inside handle and we staged a tug-of-war.

"She won't let you see her."

"I know she's a mess. It doesn't matter."

"She sleeps when she's high."

"I have time to wait." I yanked the door out of his hand and got my left foot past his left foot, a basketball move, and bumped his chest with mine as I slid into the foyer. The master suite was off to the left, and I beat him through the doorway to find the king-sized canopy bed unmade and unoccupied. A quick look in the bathroom was also unproductive.

"Where is she?"

"On the couch in the family room, but please don't go back there." Brad looked pitiful.

"Okay, let's sit down and chat until she wakes up." I headed past him and around the corner into the formal living room. It was empty except for one folding chair.

"Where can we sit and talk?" I asked.

"Let's go out on the patio. Would you like coffee or tea? Orange juice?"

"Tea."

I walked through the living room and out French doors to the backyard patio. A glass-topped table suitable for a large family dinner sat beside a pool with no water in it. I waited for Brad to return with two iced teas before taking a seat. "You don't swim anymore?"

Brad regarded me carefully before he said, "Can't afford to keep the pumps running, so I drained it."

"What happened to the living room furniture?"

"Sold on eBay. All the jewelry too. We needed the cash."

"All because of her habit?"

He snorted. He was beyond help. "There are worse consequences to our sad story. She lost her job six months ago, and her car has been repossessed. We've missed two mortgage payments, and it's only a matter of time before we lose the house. I can't leave her alone, so I can't go to the office. Soon I'll be fired too."

"Brad, you stole fifty thousand dollars from Mom. Doesn't that keep you afloat?"

"We didn't steal it." Indignant now. "Billy gave us the passbook so we could pay our bills. He said it was an advance on our share of Mom's estate and that Mom didn't need it now."

Now? They'd siphoned the money off over a period of a year. "But you made the withdrawals, right?

He sneered. "Oh yeah. Billy wanted to keep his hands clean."

"And you didn't pay your bills with it, so what did you do with it?"

"Pills," he said as though that should have been obvious.

"The pills are cheap."

He looked at me as though I were ignorant of the ways of the drug world. "We pay the dentist a premium for the risk he's taking in writing the prescriptions."

A premium? A bribe. "So you paid fifty thousand dollars for what might have cost five thousand dollars on the street."

"And we're not in jail. We used a dealer in Smyrna for a while, but he got arrested. I'm not crawling around downtown Atlanta looking for her fix, Randle."

"Is it all gone, the fifty thousand dollars?"

"The last of it will either pay for her rehab or pay for one more fix."

"So you need fresh cash to live this way?" I swept my arm to encompass the untended backyard, pool, and patio.

"It takes two incomes to afford this place. We'll be downsized soon."

"But Katie had a plan to get more money."

"Huh? She can't work in her condition."

"Not work, more theft. She wanted to steal my inheritance from my real father."

Brad acted as though he were totally confused by that. Even after I explained Albert and his money, Brad claimed to have known none of it.

"Katie didn't tell you she took Mom to Columbia?"

"Sure, to see her brother, Katie's uncle."

"No, to see my dad, my mother's lover before Joseph Marks. And then she went back with a lawyer, to see if she could steal my inheritance to fund her habit and your lifestyle."

"I promise you, Randle, I knew nothing about it."

I turned nasty. "Get her ass out here, Brad, so we can both learn what she's done with my dad's will."

Reluctantly, he got to his feet and staggered away. Shortly, I heard loud voices, a scream, something striking a wall. I rose from the table, but I didn't intend to lend assistance. I loped through the vacant living room and back into the master suite. In the bathroom, I opened cabinets and drawers until I found what I was seeking—a prescription pill bottle of hydrocodone, the powerful painkiller, prescribed by Dr. Burton to my mother and filled by a pharmacy in Augusta. The bottle held seven pills. I poured six of them onto the counter, resealed the bottle, stuffed it into my pocket, and headed back through the living room. Brad and Katie continued to shout at each other, so I walked down a narrow hallway to the family room.

They were shocked to see me. Brad had lifted Katie from behind with his arms around her waist, ready to drag her out of the room, but now he dropped her. Dressed only in a filthy wife-beater T-shirt and panties, my diminutive, dishwater-blonde sister looked as though she had just climbed out of a dumpster. She was six years younger than me, but her face looked ten years older than mine. And the room could have used a visit from those people who clean up after floods or fires. Dirty dishes, rotting containers of take-out food, and pillows and blankets were strewn everywhere. The carpet was stained beyond salvaging.

"Get out of here!" Katie screamed.

"We need to talk," I said calmly.

She picked up a heavy bronze swimming trophy off a side table and threw it. It crashed through a glass-topped table beside me. While Brad and I were stunned and frozen in place, she darted out the sliding glass door and ran into the trees behind the house. I thought he'd chase after her, but he didn't.

"She'll be back when she needs another pill," he said.

"How the hell did this happen, Brad?"

He blubbered incoherently for a bit before gathering his thoughts and telling me the truth. "She had oral surgery and Burton, my classmate, prescribed Percocet, but she needed a refill to get through it and he gave it to her. That was the beginning. Then she sprained her knee playing tennis, and the orthopedist wouldn't give her a strong enough painkiller, so she went back to Burton and he gave her Vicodin. Then we were off to the races. Now she takes hydrocodone."

He shrugged and waved a hand as though saying it could happen to anyone.

I pitied him. "I suppose I should thank you for sticking it out with her."

His head fell into his hands, and he sobbed. "I'm no saint, Jack. I intended to leave her—I can't live like this—but then your mother had her heart attack and Katie agreed to rehab, so I'm still here."

"Well, I appreciate it. I have business in Atlanta tomorrow, so I'm spending the night. If she's able to have a rational conversation, call me and I'll come back over."

I left him to his misery and headed for Midtown. Clearly, Katie was on the precipice of heroin addiction. Having graduated to hydrocodone, one of the last rungs on the ladder before street drugs, and since the Van Kamps were broke, thieving or whoring to score heroin would be her only choice now. If Katie's current condition wasn't rock bottom, I shuddered to think what rock bottom would be. I was conflicted: should I help my sister through her addiction, or should I punish her for trying to steal my dad's money?

***

That night, I stayed at the W Atlanta on 14ᵗʰ Street, from which the local NPR station, WABE, would be a short jaunt up Piedmont Avenue in the morning. After walking a couple of blocks to Mi Cocina for dinner, I sat in the hotel bar nursing a beer and preparing for my interview by making notes on my iPad. My concentration wavered. My priorities were constantly shifting. After the interview, I'd have to arrange with Meadowlake for Mom's transport to Columbia. Meadowlake would have to do it for me, and I couldn't go along to get her settled. Maybe Beth could accompany her. I'd have to say goodbye to Mom temporarily at Sacred Heart so I could fix my Carrie problem. And, before leaving for Florida, I would have to ruin Brad's life to save my sister.

CHAPTER TWENTY-FOUR

I mistook the ringing for my wake-up call and slapped at the house phone on the night table. The receiver fell to the floor, but the insistent screeching did not stop. Irritated, I flipped the light switch and saw "4:00 a.m." on the bedside clock. My cell phone, plugged into its charger on the other side of the room, was ringing. *Not a good omen.*

I made my groggy way across the dark room and focused on the caller ID screen—Beth. A really bad omen.

She choked out the words between sobs and gasps for air. "They want the family to come right away."

"What's wrong?"

"Her heart and lungs, Randle. They're shutting down."

The doctor said she was fine on Saturday, just cranky and uncooperative. *I think Jesus is coming tomorrow.*

"Sacred Heart or St. Thomas?"

"Augusta Regional, downtown. They knew St. Thomas didn't want her."

"I'm in Atlanta, Beth. It will take me at least two hours to get there."

"Hurry, Randle."

I brushed my teeth with shaking hands, splashed cold water on my face, and pulled a ballcap over my bedhead. Without stopping to check out, I carried my bag to the carpark and headed for Augusta.

At least there was no traffic at that hour. But, unfortunately, I was isolated with my thoughts too. Daniel had been right: Mom could die at any moment. The thought that she might die before I could see her tormented me. I was ashamed of myself for the selfish desire to see her before she passed, so I altered my thinking and tried to boost my morale and hers too through some sort of telepathy. She had survived a heart attack and a medley of associated ills, and she could survive this. Right? *Hang in there, Mom. Don't leave me.*

I drove as fast as I dared while avoiding a traffic stop. Then I realized that a speeding ticket was the least of my concerns, and I increased my pace. I wanted a distraction, but neither music nor talk radio seemed appropriate. *Talk radio!* I called WABE and canceled my interview due to a family emergency.

Then I was alone with my thoughts again. Unbidden, sad times came to mind first, and I fought the memories off and tried to remember the good times. The memory that popped into my jangled brain was neither particularly good nor especially bad, but it reflected the characters of my mother and stepfather quite accurately. It took place ten years ago, before Glenda and I divorced, before Carrie and I married, before Joseph died, and before Carrie tried to kill me. Joseph and Mom made their one and only trip to Florida to vacation with Glenda, Jamie, and me. The entire week consisted of Joseph's complaints and Mom's aloofness. The Mexican food was too spicy for Joseph, and the Chinese restaurant was too dirty for Mom. The stores where Glenda shopped didn't carry the goods Mom wanted to buy. When we went fishing, Joseph didn't catch anything worth photographing.

On their last night in Florida, we went to a rib shack so Joseph could have a meal that suited his palette. While waiting for a table, we had a drink in the bar. My beer was served in a tall schooner engraved with the restaurant logo.

"I really like that glass," Mom said.

"It's yours," I said. "I'll steal it for you."

Mom had gushed and tittered while Joseph scowled but held his tongue. When we were led to our table, I hid the schooner under my light winter jacket. Our table was in a corner, and Mom and I had the seats next to each other along the adjoining walls, out of sight of other diners. While Glenda and Joseph perused the menu, Mom tried in vain to stuff the tall schooner into her purse, but it wouldn't fit. Mom chuckled as she struggled with the schooner, but Joseph turned ugly.

"Stop that," he said between clenched teeth. "You're not going to steal a damn glass."

"I'll just hide it under my jacket when we leave," I told Mom.

"You will not do that while I'm with you," Joseph said.

We put the glass on the floor and ordered dinner, including another beer for me. Like the first beer, the second was served in one of the distinctive schooners. We ate in relative peace—Joseph loved the ribs—until the waitress brought our check.

"Do you sell these schooners?" I asked her, pointing at the one on the table in front of me.

"No," she replied, "but you can have one." She grabbed my empty glass and said, "Let me get you a clean one."

When she left with my credit card, Joseph said, "See? All you had to do was ask. You don't have to behave like a criminal."

Mom and I were suitably abashed until the waitress returned with my charge slip and a clean, frosted schooner. Setting it on the table, she said, "Just hide it under your jacket and walk out in a group. No one will notice." She winked at me.

I gave her a tip large enough to cover the cost of the glass in case she was caught. Then I hid the clean schooner and the first schooner under my jacket and walked out as though I owned the place. Joseph trailed behind, pretending he wasn't a part of our group. Mom then had a matching pair of the schooners, and she was overjoyed. Southern women like their men to be brave and willing to do risky things for them. I doubted that either devoted-but-reticent Albert or Mr. Goody-Two-Shoes Marks were the loves of Mom's life, and I doubted that Mom had ever met and experienced her soulmate. *It's tragic how we waste our short time on earth.*

That thought brought me back to the present and to the question of how much time Mom had left. I wound my way from I-20 to the center of Augusta and to Augusta Regional hospital in the city's medical complexes on the north side of the business district. The original local hospital looked grim and foreboding in the faint morning light. I really did not want my mother to die in this place.

I consulted with the receptionist, then took a broad wooden staircase to a second-floor ward that had no medical title. As I hurried down the hallway, I felt "out of my body," as if I were watching this ominous tableau from some high vantage point, waiting to see how I would react to the crisis. I couldn't feel my arms and legs, but they obeyed nonetheless.

Mom's room had no sophisticated equipment of any kind, no hoists, no cables, no tubes or sensors or monitors. Just a bed and chairs. It was a room in which people die. I stopped as I entered and absorbed the scene. Mom lay perfectly still on her bed, her hair matted with sweat; tears streamed down Beth's plain face; Billy looked taciturn. In the corner, Trey sat in a chair with his head in his hands. Raymond had a hand on his back. A large black man in nursing scrubs stood to my left with his arms folded, discreetly giving the family space.

"Is she—"

Billy shook his head no.

The nurse said, "We've been waiting for you so we can administer her cocktail."

"Her what?"

"Her comfort cocktail, drugs that will ease her pain and the discomfort of dyspnea."

I must have looked confused, because the nurse explained the cocktail in a surprisingly gentle voice: "Morphine for pain and benzodiazepine to reduce the anxiety she feels because she can't breathe. The drugs will suppress her resistance to dying."

Daniel's words came echoing back to me: *Desperate measures just prolong the inevitable.* "Put her on a ventilator. Right now!"

"I signed the DNR," Billy said.

"You couldn't wait for her to die naturally? You must really need her money."

Billy's nostrils flared. "I called our priest too, for last rites."

"And you think that legalizes her murder?"

Billy started around the bed, but Beth caught his arm and stopped him.

I turned to leave the room. To the nurse, I said, "I'm going to get a doctor. We're not giving up on her."

Like a linebacker sliding into a hole in the line to tackle a running back, the nurse blocked my path and we bumped chests. I had three inches on him, but he had fifty pounds on me. He motioned for me to follow him into the hallway.

"It's too late to help her, Mr. Marks. She had an A-fib episode yesterday evening, and her heart stopped functioning so her lungs have filled with fluid. We've given her drugs to dry up the fluid, but there's too much of it and her heart is too weak to counteract it. If we don't give her the cocktail soon, she'll drown. That's a terrifying way to die."

The nurse must have had a lot of experience on this ward—the death ward—because he handled me as adroitly as any professional salesperson selling a used car. Would you like the red one or the blue one, sir? Would you like your mother to suffer or to pass peacefully?

"Will she lose consciousness, her cognitive abilities?"

"Not immediately."

"I can have a few minutes with her?"

"You need to be quick."

I made a gesture that meant "Do what you have to do," and the nurse moved to Mom's bedside and gave her an injection. I followed hesitantly. We suffer with our loved ones as we witness their fight for survival. We mourn for the loss of their love and warm presence. We share their fear of what lies beyond because, if we're honest with ourselves, no matter the degree of our faith in the hereafter, we simply don't know for certain what we'll find "on the other side." But, most of all, as I stood over Mom, I feared my own mortality, my own time in the bed with family gathered around me. *What will I be thinking when I'm where Mom is now? What will I say to my loved ones?*

Mom recognized me and tried to smile, but her struggle for breath tore her lips away from her teeth and contorted her face into a grotesque mask. She wasn't "doll face" anymore. She was white as a Colorado ski slope, and her chest heaved like an avalanche, but her breathing was shallow and rapid. I bent to kiss her cheek. It was cool and felt like vinyl, not the supple skin of a healthy human.

One word at a time, between gasps for breath, she said, "Jesus. Waited. For. You." Clearly in pain, she gathered her strength before continuing, "No. Regrets. Not. Afraid. To. Die."

I grabbed her hand and kissed her bony knuckles. I thought that on my dying bed I wouldn't regret things I had done, but I might regret things I hadn't done. "What do you want me to do for you?"

"Let. Me. Go."

I teared up then. I couldn't help it. "I'll take care of Dad—Albert—and Frank too. Thank you for letting me meet them."

Her eyes clouded over. She grimaced. I thought she was about to take her last journey, but she was straining to speak. "Jamie."

"Sure, Mom. I'll tell her. And Glenda. I'll take care of them."

She grabbed my wrist with surprising strength and desperation. "Ask. Jamie."

All the air in her lungs escaped with a whoosh, and she moaned. I thought she had passed, but her chest rose and she sucked air before gurgling and gagging. When she caught her breath, her hand dropped away and she said, "Go."

There are many reasons to fear death, but in the end what we fear the most is that death will rob us of our dignity. We all suffer the indignity of a barbaric ending that belies our claim to be an advanced civilization.

Before I could obey my mother and leave the room, Billy leaned in and, too loudly, said, "If you see Father, go with him."

Then I couldn't leave the room. *No*, I thought, *you should wait at the gates for Albert and guide him to your final resting place together.*

I bent low and whispered in Mom's ear, "I'll see you in heaven, but send me a sign. I want to know."

Fear flamed in her eyes, and she gripped my hand tightly. To say goodbye or to hold onto this world? She nodded, then stiffened, and her chest expanded and crashed once, then again, like a building collapsing, and she made a choking sound. I recoiled involuntarily and watched, aghast, as she shivered and then fell still. With that, her eyes turned opaque and her face stiffened into a rigid mask of anguish.

Trey wailed. The nurse eased past me and used his stethoscope to confirm Mom's passing. When he nodded, I turned and ran into the hallway, too shocked to cry, too affected and disgusted by the raw violence of the event to absorb the loss of my mother. In front of my eyes, Mom's soul had been ripped from the earth. I felt as though I had witnessed a vicious mugging and could no longer pretend that the streets aren't dangerous. No longer could I relegate death to the unvisited realms of my consciousness. No longer could I treat it as a story told by strangers about others. No longer could I deny that we are all as perishable as raw fruit. Death is the fairest of all events we experience. Whether we are good or evil, wealthy or poor, smart or ignorant, it waits for us.

I remembered a rare visit to Katie's place in Atlanta when we were caught in a freak winter ice storm. As we traveled secondary roads in the suburbs to reach her house, we came to a stop sign at the top of a hill and waited our turn behind a long line of slow-moving cars. When we were close to the front of the rank, we watched as each car eased away from the intersection and slid down the icy road, accelerating and swerving as it lost control of its destiny. At the bottom, each car smashed into those that had preceded it, and yet the next car in line repeated the same improbable attempt to avoid a collision. Life is like that; we all know the end but we all ease away from the stop sign at our birth and slide down the perilous hill of life toward our inevitable collision with death.

I choked back foul bile and leaned against a wall to catch my breath. *What kind of a God does that to His children?* The nurse caught up with me and grabbed my arm. "I'm sorry you had to see that. She wanted to say goodbye and then pass in private. I should have gotten you out of there."

"Is it always like that? That … that *brutal?*"

"We didn't get the cocktail in her soon enough to make it easy. Sorry."

"It's my fault. She told me not to go to Atlanta."

He nodded sympathetically. "I have to find a doctor to pronounce her and sign a death certificate. Then we'll need instructions on where to take her."

"Now? Today?"

"Yes," he said apologetically. "We can't keep her here."

Trey and Raymond, with his arm around my nephew, walked out of Mom's room. Then Trey leaned a forearm on the wall and rested his head there. I walked over to him and put my hand on his shoulder. I murmured clichés, but he was inconsolable.

I moved farther down the hallway and called Glenda to tell her the news. She and Mom had never been great friends, but Glenda was saddened and sympathetic. I wanted her to run to the airport and fly to Augusta immediately, but she demurred, said she couldn't leave her shop on short notice. She asked about funeral arrangements. Of course, I had no idea when the funeral would take place. After I begged a little, Glenda agreed to fly up the next day if I'd make the airline reservation. She was out of money.

Then I called Jamie and woke her. She had worked the night shift and would have to do it again that night before she could get time off, but she agreed to fly up with her mother if I would buy the ticket. She had no money either.

So I called Delta and made Glenda and Jamie a flight reservation at a sympathy fare. They would arrive midafternoon the next day. In my disturbed state, I had forgotten to ask my daughter why her grandmother's last words were, "Ask. Jamie."

As I spoke to my family, I watched the doctor come and go. Then the priest came, and soon he departed as well. Billy, Beth, and the nurse joined Trey and Raymond in the hallway, so I hustled in their direction to join them. Before I could get there, my agent, Tim, rang me.

"Where the hell are you?"

"At a hospital in Augusta. My mother died about thirty minutes ago."

That drained the anger out of Tim's voice, but after offering his condolences he reverted to business demeanor. "Your publisher has dropped you. You're not reliable, and you've cost them a ton of money.

They want their advance back as well, and they'll sue you if you don't pay it within thirty days."

The advance is long gone. "It's a family emergency, Tim. Don't they have a heart?"

"Frankly, they regret doing the book deal in the first place. There's no buzz in the marketplace for a book. While you were in prison, the research institutes to whom you gave free patent licenses have made a lot of progress, and your theories are now old hat."

This was exactly the argument I had made during the mediation of my divorce settlement with Carrie. She had wanted a share of my patent royalties, and I had argued they'd be obsolete within a couple of years. It hadn't taken even that long. I had donated the free licenses to the institutes and universities partly out of an altruistic desire to further medicine through the application of advanced analytics, and mostly to keep the money out of the hands of my ex-wife and my former employer. When I was convicted, the company I had helped found fired me and revoked my stock options. But with free patent licenses in the marketplace, that company had collapsed.

"Can you get me a job with one of the research facilities? A consulting gig? That might create buzz, and I can update the book."

"Already tried that. The institutes have done just fine without you, and your rep isn't the best."

"Then another publisher?"

"It's not worth trying, Randle, so I've got to drop you too. Can't make any money off you, mate."

I shouted a two-word expletive at him and hung up. My "family" heard it and turned toward me with horrified looks. I walked up to them as though nothing had happened and said, "What do we do now?"

"It's all arranged," Billy said. "Mom will be taken to Weber and Franklin Funeral Home today, and the funeral will be at the home on

Wednesday afternoon. Our priest will preside, and then Mom will be buried next to Father. The plot is paid for."

"Mom didn't want a priest, she wanted a Baptist minister. And she wanted to be buried in her family plot in Charleston, where her brother will be buried." All lies. I had no idea what Mom wanted but couldn't help myself. I had to strike at someone.

Billy just shook his head and started away. Beth and Trey and Raymond tagged along.

"Where are you going?" I asked.

"To the funeral home to finish the arrangements," Trey said over his left shoulder. They kept walking.

"Would you like to see your mother one more time?" the nurse said.

"No, I don't want to remember her death pose. Maybe I'll look at her at the funeral home, but I wouldn't bet on it."

CHAPTER TWENTY-FIVE

A trancelike shroud had dropped over me, and I couldn't think for myself. I followed Billy's car to the funeral home and trailed after the grieving family into a large room where food was often served after the funeral ceremony. We sat around a cafeteria table answering questions for the servile, annoyingly ingratiating funeral director. I had nothing to contribute, but I had nowhere else to be, so I listened as the funeral director proceeded down his checklist.

Casket open or closed? Open. Viewing Tuesday evening or Wednesday morning? Wednesday morning. Flowers? Of course. From which florist, and where should they be placed? From Beckman's and on either end of the casket. Do we have photos that can be made into a collage to be displayed in the home's foyer? Yes, Beth will deliver them tomorrow. Agenda for the ceremony? The priest will conduct a standard ceremony. Accompany the casket to the gravesite? No, we don't do that. Ready to choose a casket? Yes.

It bothered me that we had to endure this mundane questioning after Mom had just died. Her passing became a business transaction that distracted us from the monumental grief welling up in our chests. Perhaps that's its purpose.

We traipsed behind the salesman into a showroom with a dozen caskets on display. They ranged from cheap models that wouldn't survive an exhumation to elaborately padded models that would ensure Mom's comfort for eternity. Billy chose a mid-priced model, although I have no idea what criteria, other than price, he might have applied to the decision.

Then the preparations were complete. Trey hugged me, and Raymond shook my hand while Billy and Beth ignored me and walked away. "We have to get Nana's things at Sacred Heart and then stop by the bank to empty the safe deposit box," Trey said.

"Has Katie been notified?"

"Dad spoke to Uncle Brad. They'll be here tomorrow. They'll want to stay with you at Nana's house."

"Okay, see you Wednesday I guess."

In the parking lot, I leaned against my Bronco, and for the first time in thirty years I craved a cigarette. The urge to race Billy to the safe deposit box came and went quickly—I knew what was in that will, and it had nothing to do with me. I could get the paper copy of Mom's medical records from them later.

Now my last mooring line had been severed, and I was adrift on the open sea. At first I was fearful, but it occurred to me that I was suddenly free of Joseph's despicable family. Mom had been our last connection, and she was gone. Then I thought of Dad. I still had Dad, and he was now my mooring line.

I called Meadowlake and asked Clara to relay the bad news to Dad and Frank. I also asked if she could arrange for them to be driven in the

Meadowlake van to the funeral on Wednesday. She agreed to make the arrangements and offered her condolences.

Then I called Daniel, hoping to wriggle out of that problem. "I'm sure you know the cops didn't find anything and had no grounds to charge me."

"You destroyed evidence—another crime, I believe—and they have a search warrant for your deleted email account and should have the contents in a day or two."

I had assumed St. Thomas hospital would cave in after nothing was found on my cell phone and iPad. I was wrong, so I had to fight back. "The situation has changed, Daniel. My mother passed away an hour ago. Her lungs filled with fluid overnight, and she basically drowned this morning."

"I'm sorry to hear that, Randle, but I predicted it."

"Which is exactly why you should have kept her in the hospital and nursed her back to health. You knew this would happen, and you turned your back on her. The rehab facility had no idea she was failing until it was too late this morning."

"Which is exactly why St. Thomas has no liability. She wasn't in our care."

The hospital administration's thought process became clear: *we screwed up; he's got the records to prove it; get her out of here; make sure she dies somewhere else.* "Let me make you a different deal, Daniel: walk me through Mom's records and point out all the places where you messed up. If you fix the problems, I'll sign the NDA and promise not to sue."

Daniel actually considered it, but after two minutes, he said, "I'll have to consult with our lawyers, and that will take time. I can't stop the cops from picking you up again as soon as they find our records in your email account, and it won't be a walk in the park this time."

Of course, I knew that possession of Mom's records didn't prove I had stolen them, but I did not want to fight the issue while incarcerated.

"Ask them for a small mercy, Daniel. Mom's funeral is on Thursday. If we don't have a deal by then, I'll turn myself in after she's buried."

"I'll tell them, but cops have their own agendas."

Don't I know it.

***

I had begun to sweat in the Augusta heat, so I climbed into the Bronco and started the engine and the air conditioner before calling Tony Zambrano.

"He says he's not your lawyer," Melissa said.

"Tell him he's in possession of evidence in a criminal case. I emailed it to him."

Melissa was away from her phone for a full five minutes. "He's not your lawyer, Mr. Marks, and he's upset about being dragged into this. He wants to know where to send your email so he can get it out of his hands."

Everyone wants to be absolved. "Ask him to have Fred review it with a doctor he trusts. A cardiac surgeon would be best." Fred was Tony's investigator and another former friend of mine.

Melissa put me on hold again. "He says he'll have Fred report to you directly and bill you directly. He says you should hire an attorney in Georgia."

I thanked Melissa and asked her to thank Tony. She said that Tony preferred I not call again.

***

I called the cops then and asked how to report a crime and turn over evidence. The operator directed me to the Richmond County Sheriff's Office on Walton Way, just down the street from the county jail, and advised me to ask for the detective on duty. "Do you know how to find us?" she asked.

"Yes, ma'am. I'm familiar with the area."

The Sheriff's Office was hopping with business, and I had to wait in a queue for a parking spot. Inside the glass-and-steel, modernistic but minimalistic center, thirty people sat on cheap metal chairs in front of a glass-enclosed set of offices. The glass was thick and obviously bulletproof. The window attendant had me sign in and take a seat.

I had plenty of time to reconsider what I was about to do, and more than once I stood to leave only to sit again and wait for my turn. *I have to help Katie.* That's self-delusion. *I want to keep her from stealing my inheritance.* That's despicable but honest. *I want to do both.* Rationalize if you must.

After about an hour, I was called and led around the side of the enclosure to a tiny room with half a table and two metal chairs. I was told to wait.

The experience was not a lot different from a doctor's office appointment: sit in the waiting room; get called to an examination room; wait a while longer. I took the seat on the far side of the table, against the wall—the usual location for the suspect—and noted the camera snuggled in a corner near the ceiling recording my presence. Another fifteen minutes passed before the detective entered the room. He was the same guy who had examined my cell phone and iPad at the county jail. Almost as tall as me, about the same age as me, not as trim as me, wearing a cheap sports coat and wrinkled trousers, the detective could have been an actor in a TV police drama.

He was shocked to see me. "I'm Detective Sergeant Rodgers. You can't turn yourself in until we get an arrest warrant."

That implied that Daniel had already contacted the authorities and that they would wait for my surrender. *Good.* "I'm not here for that problem. I'm here to report a different crime, a serious crime, and I'm going to hand over evidence of it."

I placed the three prescription bags, the receipts, and the pill bottle on the table. The detective sat and appraised the evidence as though it were a rare species of insect, looking at it from one angle and then from another, but he did not touch it. He leaned back and said, "Tell me your story."

I explained my sister's pill addiction and her relationship to the dentist, Dr. Burton. "There was no hydrocodone in my mother's system when she was admitted to St. Thomas Aquinas Hospital. My sister's husband forged my mother's signature on savings withdrawals to pay the dentist for the pills—over fifty thousand dollars in less than a year. You should be able to trace the money from my mother's account to my brother-in-law to the dentist. My sister and her husband will be here tomorrow, at my mother's house, to attend the funeral on Thursday. You can arrest them then."

Rodgers's right eyebrow took a quick trip up his forehead. *Civilians always tell the cops how to do their job.* "The prescription bags came from your mother's house?"

"Yes, I found them in Katie's—my sister's—bedroom."

"Uh-huh, but she doesn't live there anymore. Any guest could have stayed in that room. And you took the pill bottle from her home in Atlanta?"

"Yes. When you test the pill in the bottle, I'm sure you'll find that it is hydrocodone or OxyContin."

Rodgers shook his head dismissively. "There's no chain of evidence, no proof that your sister ever had the pill bottle or the prescriptions in her possession. And now your fingerprints are all over the stuff."

I leaned back in my chair, depressed by my lack of foresight. I should have reported my suspicions and let the cops search the two houses. Grasping at straws, I said, "Wouldn't my sister have signed for the narcotics at the pharmacy?"

He shrugged. "Maybe. But that doesn't prove she took the pills."

"My brother-in-law admitted that Burton wrote the prescriptions for my sister, detective." *And I want my sister in jail so she can't steal my inheritance.*

"Hearsay. By the time this gets to trial, he'll change his mind."

"The dentist is a bad guy!" I said as I slapped the table.

The detective had witnessed far more violent reactions in this interview room. Calmly he said, "Prescription pill addiction often begins with a dentist. Some of them are bad guys, and some of them are just trying to help their patients, and sometimes the patients don't follow instructions and they become addicted."

"You need to investigate this guy, see if he's supplying other people as well as my sister."

He tried to be patient with me. "You can make a citizen's report if you want." He took forms from his clipboard and pushed them toward me. "I can have my supervisor review it and see if there's probable cause for a search warrant, but I wouldn't get my hopes up."

"What about a warrant for my sister's house? See if there are other pill bottles there."

"You'd have to make a report in Atlanta."

I sighed. "Okay. Let me fill this out. My sister needs help, detective." *After she goes to jail.*

"She should go to rehab."

"She tried three times, and it doesn't work."

"Maybe the fourth time will be the charm." He rose, prepared to leave, but said, "I'm sorry to hear about your mother. We won't bother you until after the funeral, but then we'll want to see you. The hospital has a real hard-on for you."

"They screwed something up, and they're desperate to avoid a lawsuit."

He gave me a slight nod. "Drop the forms in the box at the window on your way out. They'll give you an evidence bag for the rest of this stuff."

He stood to leave, but I quickly asked, "Are you going to arrest my brother?"

Hands on his hips, his face scrunched up in a shrug, he said, "His problem is the bookie. Your brother will get his legs broken long before we get around to arresting him." He left me to think about that.

It took twenty minutes to fill out the forms, but I understood, while converting my suspicions to writing, how flimsy my story would sound to a detective. The only potential misstep by the dentist was the fact that my mother wasn't his patient. He had illegally prescribed a controlled substance.

* * *

Drained of all energy by the day's events, I returned to my mother's house, a house owned by Billy. *And doesn't that fact further complicate the connection between my "evidence" and a crime?* While Billy and Beth, Katie and Brad, and their children could console one another on this dreadful day, I had to mourn in private. I sat in Mom's rocker and drank beer while my mind wandered from memories of my childhood to my impending arrest, to my destitute financial condition, to Carrie's release from prison, to my lack of a publisher, to my tentative hold on Dad's inheritance, to my sister's addiction and my failure to help her, and back to Mom again. Self-pity is an ugly emotion, but I rode that horse for hours before passing out.

Chapter Twenty-six

awoke dehydrated and famished. Emotionally I was crushed, but I pushed that depressing weight aside to address my physical needs. First, I needed hydration. I drank three eight-ounce glasses of tap water, and my hangover eased. Then I searched for something to eat. The pantry contained nothing enticing, and the refrigerator held nothing edible, so I opened the freezer drawer. Staring me in the face: expired packets of meat, a chilling bottle of vodka, and a tub of ice cream. Hoping to find frozen waffles or breakfast sausage hiding beneath the refuse of an old lady's life, I pushed the meat and vodka aside and lifted the tub. It was light as air. *What the hell, Mom? Dementia?* I shook the tub and heard a rattle. *Frozen chunks of freezer-burn ice?* I pried the lid off and discovered a wad of yellow Post-it notes. Within seconds, I confirmed they were my dad's side of his conversation with Mom in their first meeting.

I forgot about eating. I dumped the yellow notes onto the kitchen table and began to sort them into stacks: one for the social chitchat and one for the discussion of the will. Like a kid saving the best Halloween candy for last, I pushed the money discussion to the side and flipped through the lovers' conversation.

I found: **You're still beautiful**, and imagined that as Albert's opening line.

Later I found: **Joseph is gone. Aren't you lonely?**

Still later: **How's my boy?**

And then: **When does he get out?** which I took to be a reference to my prison release date.

And the inevitable: **Have you told him?**

The desperation mounted with: **Do we have to keep the secret? Joseph is gone.**

It was impossible to discern when Mom sat on Albert's lap, but he wrote a note while she was aboard: **Light as a feather, but you feel good.**

I imagined the transition to the discussion of the will was: **I've never gotten over you.**

There were more sweet nothings, mixed with all the questions you ask someone you haven't seen in more than forty years. Before delving into the financial discussion, I rose from the table and paced around the kitchen, imagining the scene in Albert's room. That visit must have been intoxicating and yet bittersweet. The two of them had wasted their lives apart. Nothing could possibly be more piercing, more debilitating, more draining than regret.

I parsed the remaining notes while standing, unable to contain myself. The conversation seemed to begin with: **You kept your bargain and I kept my promise.**

The next note read: **Jack's not in Joseph's will.**

Another note read: **All to my son.**

If Katie hadn't already known the secret, she certainly knew at that point that she and I did not share a father.

And if she wasn't shocked by that revelation, she certainly must have been by the next one: **About 3 million.**

Mom and Albert had argued then, and Albert turned insistent: **It's Jack's** and **You can share some of it** and **Let me rest easy in my grave.**

Mom must have negotiated then, because one note simply read: **OK** and another said **Change it, and I'll sign.**

The penultimate note was an admonition: **Most for Jack.**

And the parting shot was: **You should hurry.**

I paced again. Either Frank was wrong about Albert's net worth or Albert had lost track of it. But what's a mere million dollars when you're fighting with your sister for your real father's money? A draconian scene of a probate court session came to mind: my mother and I arguing one side, Billy and Katie arguing the other. The notes weren't dated, but Mom's visits to Albert were recorded in Meadowlake's register. The notes represented only one side of the conversation, but clearly Albert intended to leave his wealth to me whereas my mother had wanted me to share it.

And Katie wanted to steal it. She would have worried that Albert's robust body could outlive both his ruined brain and our declining mother. In that case, Albert's money would become mine. Katie couldn't allow that. If Albert passed before Mom, Mom would get the money and her will would govern the disbursement upon her passing. But Katie knew that Mom wanted to prepare a new version of Albert's will, and she couldn't trust Mom to leave her some of the money. Therefore, Katie's version of Albert's will would cover both scenarios.

The money wasn't the issue, I told myself in Mom's kitchen, but maybe I was deluding myself. I couldn't deny that the money would be a welcome windfall—after all, I was a convicted felon trying to figure out how to find work, and I needed to repay my publisher, pay my credit card debts, and feed my family. Then I chided myself for these impure thoughts: my dad was still alive and strong as an ox. He needed a good financial advisor to take care of the money.

Mom had done a fine job of hiding the notes, so I scrabbled through the rest of the freezer contents and tore open packages of spoiling food, but I found neither Albert's original will nor a will representing Mom's wishes. I assumed Katie had found and destroyed Albert's will. It was also safe to assume that Brad and Katie would stay with me at Mom's house.

Although Katie hadn't found Albert's notes during her previous visits, I couldn't risk another search by my devious sister. I replaced the notes in the ice cream tub and retrieved Albert's love letters from Mom's closet. Then I walked around the side of the house to the crawl space door and unlatched it. It was raining. With the ice cream tub and love letters in hand, I crawled again to my hiding place and set the precious possessions on top of the financial records. With the valuables safely hidden, I backed out into the rain and allowed the downpour to rinse the red Georgia clay from my body as it cleansed my soul.

* * *

Showered and fully dressed, I sat in the dim drawing room with the blinds closed against the intense sunlight, waiting to ambush my sister and her husband. Mom's house had become a museum devoid of her spirit, which had injected life into the stale, decaying spaces. Brad and Katie did not show up. After two and a half hours, the time it would have taken them to make a leisurely trip from Atlanta, I concluded they had chosen to stay in a hotel rather than share Mom's house with me and my family. I was about to leave for the airport to meet Glenda and Jamie when Nicki called.

"Can you meet Trey and me at Mahoney's for a drink?"

I told my niece that I had to pick Glenda and Jamie up at the airport.

"Great, bring them along," she said.

"An Irish wake?"

"Sort of. We can toast her life. You know how she enjoyed her one drink per day."

True enough. Mom lived in anticipation of one cocktail each evening before dinner, but since she hadn't been eating lately, I doubted she had maintained the ritual. "Are your parents coming too?"

"I haven't talked to them."

"What about your aunt and uncle?"

"No way, Uncle Randle. They're pissed about the charges at the rehab home. Sacred Heart refuses to bill Medicare because Nana never made progress in the exercise program. They said to tell you they do everything by the book and to come pay in cash."

My threat to expose them hasn't had the impact I had hoped for. "Tell your uncle to take it out of the money he'll make on the house he stole."

Nicki was nonplussed momentarily. Not sure she understood the reference I had made to Mom's house, I added, "And bring Mom's medical records that were stored in the safe deposit box."

She said she would and agreed to meet in an hour at the popular after-work saloon downtown.

***

The Augusta Regional Airport is a shining example of what is good about air travel in the US. Although the terminal building is small, it is roomy and airy. Although it is modern, the architecture is traditional Southern—red brick with columns at the main entrance, a tall, ornate clock in the atrium, comfortably appointed waiting areas, and a garden courtyard. Unlike larger airports, one does not get the impression that the airlines are merely herding cattle through Augusta. Of course, the primary impetus behind the polished look of the airport is that each spring thousands of millionaires and business tycoons arrive at the terminal to attend the Masters Golf Tournament.

I sat in an area that could have been an upscale living room and became increasingly nervous. My quick trip to see my mother had stretched into eleven days away from my family, during which time I had created a trash pile of bad news to impart when they arrived. Our reunion would be sad and depressing enough without the fact that I had discovered the secret of my birth, had lost my publishing contract, and would be arrested on Thursday. I wondered which of those debacles would irritate Glenda the most.

As though upon a silent signal, a crowd began to assemble around the arriving passengers' entryway. I joined them. Passengers streamed into the terminal to squeals of joy and passionate kisses. Kids jumped into grandparents' arms, and small family units broke away to squeeze through the crowd and out the main doors.

Finally, I spotted Glenda and Jamie among the largest group to emerge. As they searched the shifting crowd for a familiar face, they looked as nervous and disoriented as I felt. I waved and pointed toward a quiet area away from the doors. They moved in that direction as I pushed my way through the bedlam. Glenda had her wild red hair pinned down on the sides, but she was still as easy to spot as a sea buoy as she bobbed along above the shorter passengers. She wore a trademark floor-length skirt and a summer blouse in forest green to match her eyes. Fit, athletic, and tall, our twenty-eight-year-old tomboy possessed all the physical gifts to be a good cop, but she was also plagued with the cop's uneasiness about the touchy-feely stuff, so she lagged behind her mother, pulling a roll-aboard suitcase. Today she wore sneakers, jeans, and a concert T-shirt, but her badge and service weapon were clipped to her belt.

As I moved, my eyes watered embarrassingly. In a quiet oasis, Glenda walked straight into my arms and hugged me warmly. She whispered sympathies in my ear, and the moisture in my eyes turned to leaking teardrops. Leaning back in my arms, she daubed my eyes with a Kleenex. Her eyes were as round and hard and impenetrable as polished emeralds, the color so deep and consistent that the pupils were indistinguishable from the irises. The eyes were level and equally spaced above a nose as straight and narrow as a contractor's rule, with small nostrils leading directly to pronounced vertical ridges that drew her upper lip into a wave with two sharp crests. It was a face so perfectly symmetrical, so classically formed, that it was uninteresting at first glance, but eternally magnetic upon further examination. She was my "doll face."

"It's okay," she said. "You have me."

Then it was Jamie's turn to hug me and tell me how sad it was that Nana had passed.

Expecting to drive home after the funeral on Wednesday, the two of them had stuffed funeral clothes, shoes, and makeup into the single roll-aboard so we didn't have to wait for checked luggage. I grabbed the handle and led them to the Bronco in the parking lot.

As we walked, I said, "We're going to meet Nicki and Trey for a drink on the way to Mom's house."

Jamie and Glenda groaned in unison. "Do we have to, Randle? I'm tired, and Jamie hasn't slept."

"There's nothing to eat at the house," I said, "so we can grab something at the bar."

They groaned again but accepted the arrangement. Then I used the short drive to the bar to bring them up to date. I started with the hospital/police problem. It alarmed Glenda.

"What are we going to do?"

"Well, I'm not turning myself in. We're leaving for Florida immediately after the funeral. When I get Fred's report, I'll sue the hospital."

"You'll be a fugitive," my cop daughter said. "You'll violate your parole."

"The hospital will cave in."

Jamie said, "Florida isn't a safe place to go. Carrie left you a present on the front porch."

Alarmed that someone had been on the property while Glenda was in the house, I said, "What kind of present?"

"A vase of dead roses," Jamie said. "Just sitting there in front of the door when I came to get Mom today. The card said, 'See you soon.'"

"I didn't notice it when I got home from work last night," Glenda said. "I park in the garage now and don't come through the front door, so I don't know when it was delivered."

"Well, not in broad daylight," Jamie said.

A cold shiver shook me. "She can't be out of jail yet, so someone did it for her—her daddy or her no-good son."

"In the middle of the night," Jamie said. "Surprised they didn't ring the doorbell."

Glenda said, "We have to sell the beach house, find someplace safer. When you travel to book shows and signings, I'm not staying there alone just waiting to be attacked by a madwoman."

That opened another can of worms. I disclosed my loss of the book contract and said, "I'll shop the book around, find another publisher, get a consulting gig with one of the research institutes." All lies.

"We'll be eating dog food if you don't find something quick."

Fortunately, we reached the bar before I had to explain why my mother wanted to give my rightful inheritance away.

***

Government employees celebrating another lazy day of work for Uncle Sam packed the bar, so we took a table in the quieter part of the restaurant. Moments later, Nicki and Trey appeared. Nicki wore cutoff jeans and a modest cotton top. Trey wore shorts and a long-sleeved shirt, designed to be worn untucked per the Millennial style, with the sleeves rolled up to his elbows.

After hugs all around, Nicki said, "We should have Nana's favorite drink—CC&7."

So Nicki ordered five Canadian Club whiskeys with 7-Up soda. I didn't object to Glenda having a drink. It was her first in years. We toasted Nana, told funny stories about her, and pretended to have a good time, but soon we ran out of tall tales and sober, sad looks descended on our faces. There was no escaping that we had gathered to attend a funeral.

After a silent lull, Nicki broached the topic that had really brought us together for a drink. "I don't want to sound crass, but when do we read Nana's will?"

Missing the point, I said, "Whenever your uncle gets around to it. He's the executor."

Nicki and Trey exchanged wary looks.

"And how long does it take to hand out the money?" Nicki asked.

I get it. "Your mother and Uncle Billy will split the proceeds of Nana's will. None of us"—

I spread my hands to encompass the table—"are heirs to Nana's estate."

Shock replaced sorrow on Nicki's and Trey's faces.

"Nana promised," Trey said with a whimper. "You were looking for the papers."

"I wasn't looking for Nana's will; I was looking for Albert Czajka's will." I explained that Nana's money was in fact their grandfather's money and that there wasn't enough of it to make their dreams come true. Nana had promised them money from my real dad, who was still alive in Columbia. Then I told them about the fight over my dad's conflicting wills.

I ended by saying, "So you see, I'm not sure when or if any of us"—I swept my hand around the table again—"will get any of that money either."

"That bitch!" Nicki said, meaning her mother. "She'll never give me a penny."

"That's our money," Glenda said.

"Nana promised," Trey wailed.

"Nana was our last hope to learn the truth about the wills, and now she's gone," I said.

"We need the damned money, Randle," my future wife said.

She was right, of course, we needed money. I let them express their emotions—anger, hostility, despondency—without interruption for at least five minutes, but I also kept an eye on my daughter. Despite the uproar, she was strangely silent and stiff. She had the look of a woman who had something on her mind but couldn't bring herself to say it.

I held up a hand to stop the chatter, and everyone ceased talking. To Nicki, I said, "Did you bring Mom's medical records?"

Nicki hesitated, and Trey answered for her. "Dad threw them away, said they don't matter now that Nana's gone. He said your desire to keep them was morbid."

I pretended to shrug it off, although my brother's action could send me to jail again. Now I was totally dependent on Tony and Fred to help their former friend.

To Nicki again, I said, "Are your parents with Billy and Beth?"

Trey and Nicki shook their heads. "They aren't coming until tomorrow," Nicki said.

My sister was probably trying to make herself presentable. She'd want to appear sober at the funeral. "When they get here, we're going to have an intervention."

Everyone agreed with that plan. "Then I'm going to South Carolina to have my dad sign one more will." Everyone agreed with that plan too.

Nicki ordered a second round of drinks, but I discreetly placed a hand over Glenda's empty glass. She slumped in her chair but didn't voice her displeasure. We had two secrets, Glenda and I: one was her struggle with alcoholism, and the other was that I had divorced and abandoned her in her time of need.

***

We ate dinner, but the specter of a funeral and a confrontation tomorrow put a damper on our enthusiasm for food. During the drive home, Glenda berated me for not sharing all my dark secrets, but before we reached the house she decided that most of my troubles were the result of my own faulty actions, so she berated me for that. The discord worsened when we turned into Mom's driveway and found a plain beige sedan waiting for us. Detective Rodgers was leaning against his car.

"Who's that?" Glenda asked.

"A cop," Jamie offered. Apparently, just like dogs, cops recognize their own species on sight.

"Is he going to arrest you?" Glenda said.

"Not today," I said. "He's doing me a favor."

"Great! More intrigue," she responded.

Neither Glenda nor Jamie moved to exit the Bronco, so I said, "Just take your things inside, and I'll be along in a minute." I handed Glenda the house key and told her the passcode.

"Can I help, Dad?"

"No, Jamie. I've got this one."

They looked skeptical, but they climbed out, grabbed the roll-aboard suitcase, and hurried past the detective as though he might bite.

The detective watched them appreciatively. "Your wife's even better in person, and your daughter's not bad either. Cop?"

How do they do that? "You can offend me on Thursday when I turn myself in, but today you should treat me like an innocent citizen."

He gave me a wise-assed smile. "Sure."

"Are you just making sure I'm still in town? Going to turn up at the funeral, take pictures like the RICO cops do at Mafia funerals?"

He canted his head as though he hadn't thought about shadowing me. "Not a bad idea," he said, "but today I have news for you. We did some checking. If money passed from your mother to your sister to the dentist, it was all in cash. There's no banking transaction trail. The dentist hasn't bought a new car, hasn't taken a trip to Hawaii, hasn't made any investments."

"Smart guy. Went to Vanderbilt."

The cop shrugged. I doubted he could find Vanderbilt with a smartphone and Google Maps.

"We had the pill in the bottle analyzed. It's not hydrocodone. It's fentanyl, the strongest of all prescription painkillers."

"How do fentanyl pills get into a hydrocodone bottle?"

He shrugged again. "A pharmacist could have intentionally mislabeled a bottle, but I doubt it. The controls on pharmacies are pretty tight. Your sister was probably hiding the pills from her husband, dumped a fentanyl prescription into an old hydrocodone bottle. We're checking prescriptions at the pharmacy to see if the dentist wrote a fentanyl script for your mother."

I inhaled and exhaled, digesting the information. "So, my sister has graduated to fentanyl, and next she'll graduate to heroin."

"You don't 'graduate' to heroin. In terms of potency, it's the other way around—fentanyl is fifty times as potent as heroin, but the high doesn't last long and it's an expensive habit. Addicts default to heroin because it's cheap and easy to find. Four out of five heroin addicts start with opioids, and then you get the overdoses because heroin's not as powerful."

"My sister will come into some money, through my mother's will, so she won't be looking for heroin for a while. Can you set up a sting operation? Catch the dentist supplying her with fentanyl? Send them both to jail?"

"Oh. A sting? I love stings." The cop being facetious. "Should have mentioned that your mother was a patient of his. He did a root canal about a year ago. Great excuse to write prescriptions for painkillers. But he won't be writing any prescriptions for your mother anymore, will he?"

CHAPTER TWENTY-SEVEN

We moped around all evening, tried the television but found nothing uplifting or entertaining. What little conversation that did transpire was always about the money, and Jamie became especially morose.

"You okay?" I asked her.

"Yeah, just don't like funerals."

Can't blame her for that.

A little later, Raymond pulled up in Mom's old car. He had dropped Trey at Billy's house, but Billy wouldn't let Raymond stay there. Raymond thought Billy was suspicious of their romantic relationship. We told Raymond to take my old room and Glenda and I would use the master bedroom.

My cell phone rang as we headed to our respective bedrooms. It was a 727 area code—Pinellas County, St. Petersburg, Florida. I wondered if our beach house had been burgled, but the voice on the phone was a deep bass I recognized from my preincarceration days. *Thank God!*

"Have you read your email?" Fred the investigator said.

"I deleted my account because the hospital records were in it."

"Open a new one. I have the report from my doctor friend, and you'll want to read it. The hospital made several mistakes in caring for your mother, and the doctor will testify to that. He's a paid witness, but he's pretty objective for one of those scumbags."

Jamie wasn't willing to lend me her account—"I'm a cop, Dad"— and Glenda wasn't pleased by the idea of getting involved, but she relented and Fred resent the report to her account. While we waited for it, Fred and I reminisced and promised to rekindle our friendship when I returned to Florida. He was the first of the old gang to show any desire to be friends with a convicted felon.

When the report appeared in Glenda's inbox, Fred walked me through it.

"It all starts with your mother's primary care physician, Dr. Fowler. He didn't take her water gain seriously, just prescribed a diuretic, and didn't take the dermatitis seriously enough either, just gave her a topical antibiotic. The water retention signaled imminent heart problems, and the infectious material from the dermatitis became a dangerous complication."

"The dermatitis material exacerbated the mitral valve malfunction?"

"Probable but unprovable."

"So I sue him too, because the more defendants the merrier?"

"That's the way it's done in the land of the free, my friend. Had he recognized the impending problems, she might have had surgery to correct that faulty mitral valve before she became too weak to have surgery."

I remembered what a claims adjuster once told me after a car accident: "One mistake rarely creates an accident; usually two mistakes, one by each driver, cause an unavoidable situation, and that division of responsibility makes the life of a claims adjuster difficult."

"Does he have a history?"

"Oh yeah, three malpractice suits in the last five years. One more and he won't be able to find insurance."

"All settled out of court?"

"Of course."

"You know, we give star ratings on the Internet to everything from books to sunglasses to blog posts but not to medical practitioners. Doctors should be required to have social media pages with reviews and 'likes' and 'dislikes' so we know how good or bad they are."

"If you talk about your doctor on social media, you'll never find another one willing to treat you. They're like weathermen, exempt from performance measurements."

At the moment, I was more concerned about the hospital because they were the people trying to throw me in jail.

"Okay, I sue him and his dog as well as the hospital. Maybe the heart attack was preventable, but I'm guessing that's hard to prove in court."

"Yes, especially since your mother never filled the prescriptions he wrote for her."

I already knew those medicines weren't among the bottles on her vanity, but I wondered anew why she hadn't filled the prescriptions. "Then they'll claim that Mom was complicit in her own death: her health had been skidding downhill, and she never threw on the brakes."

I stopped to think, and Fred let that alarming information sink in. To get us back on track, I said, "So she has her heart attack and then what?"

"When your mother first admitted to the emergency room, the initial prognosis was that death was imminent and unpreventable. Because the first responders didn't find her until hours after her heart attack, they didn't believe they could save her. They shunted your mother aside to deal with a serious auto wreck—four people critically injured—

and they didn't get back to her for several more hours. When they did she was still alive—tough old bird—so they gave her a drug to regulate her heartbeat, but it was too late. Her heart muscle had been severely damaged, like a car engine running on seven cylinders instead of eight."

Same analogy Daniel had used. "So, that's it? They forgot about her, and that caused her death?"

"They didn't forget her, they deprioritized her. The car crash victims were young and could be saved. Your mother was old and terminal. Created a snowball effect. The on-call cardiologist up and left after he dealt with the car wreck, and no one called him back because your mother was expected to die at any moment. The surgeon finally saw her at about six a.m."

"Metzger."

"Yeah. Unpleasant, but good at what he does. He told you the truth about her prognosis once he got involved."

"The damage was already done."

"Sure. They gave your mother a drug to regulate her heartbeat, but the drug they used for the A-fib counteracts blood thinners, so she didn't get one of those until Metzger took over. By then the infectious material on her valve had traveled to her brain, triggered three small strokes, and blinded her."

"But they cured her blindness, and the strokes didn't cause her death."

"True, but if they had regulated her heartbeat at the time of admission, she'd have gotten the blood thinner by the time they actually discovered her, and she wouldn't have suffered the strokes."

"But the strokes didn't kill her."

Fred huffed down the line, frustrated with me for not letting him tell the story the way he wanted to tell it. "No, but it influenced their thinking the next morning. They didn't know the source of the strokes, and they knew the heart muscle was severely damaged so they chose not to operate, didn't even give you the option. Metzger said to me, 'No one has ever died on my operating table, and that woman was not going to be the first.' She was in such bad shape overall that they still expected her to die at any moment. Metzger and Kaplan told you the truth—her problems would cause her death eventually, and it was too late to prevent it."

"Was that before or after the B strep infection?"

"Before. She improved somewhat, but then the B strep weakened her again."

"But they told me to nurse her back to strength so she could endure surgery. They cured her dermatitis."

"Eyewash. They suspected you were snooping on them, and they wanted you to believe they were doing their best for your mother. You saved her life by threatening them, but only temporarily."

"They agreed that a rehab facility was best, so she could gain strength. They encouraged me to get her into Sacred Heart. They found the bed."

"More eyewash. Once fluid started building in her lungs, she was a goner. As soon as the fluid temporarily receded, they got her out of the hospital so she could die somewhere else. They knew the fluid would come back, but they just prescribed Lasix for her legs. If they had told Sacred Heart that she couldn't rehab, Sacred Heart wouldn't have taken her."

"I had the Sacred Heart doctor examine her before I left for Atlanta, and he said she was fine."

"The doc at rehab is a retired old guy who doesn't have all his marbles."

"They made her go through all that exercise stuff for nothing."

"This is where your case is weak, Randle. They'll claim she didn't do the exercises so she didn't give herself a chance."

"But she shouldn't have been there. They should have kept her in the hospital."

"They could have delayed her passing, my friend, but it was too late to save her. The best option would have been hospice, but you wouldn't allow that."

Fred's judgment that I had caused my mother undue discomfort scratched a hole in my heart. Mentally replaying the entire chain of events, I said, "Does the medical record actually say they deprioritized her in the emergency room?"

"No, but each interaction a doctor had with your mother was time-stamped, and the gaps are obvious. The notes on file are in doctor-speak, but my medical expert can interpret them for a jury."

And the hospital lawyers can find their own experts to interpret them differently. "Do I have a case or not, Fred?"

"Oh yeah, you have a case. The kind that never goes to trial. Both sides are shaky, so you'll file a suit and they'll make you a deal and no one will ever hear about your mother's case."

"You don't know me as well as you think you do, Fred."

He grunted. He knew me very well. "There's another odd notation in your mother's record: the toxicology report on the six pill bottles you gave them. They were filled with over-the-counter cold and allergy pills. All different kinds."

"What? They weren't the meds on the labels?"

"Nope. Maybe she was crazier than you thought."

I didn't think Mom was crazy. There had to be a logical explanation.

***

When everyone had gone to bed, I crawled under the house and retrieved Mom's financial records and love letters and my dad's handwritten notes. I put all of it in the back of the Bronco so it would be with us when we made our escape.

***

In the morning, we dressed in funeral attire and packed our bags so we could flee the state immediately after the funeral. Under a low, forbidding sky, we loaded the bags into the Bronco and drove to the funeral home, where we found the parking lot overflowing with cars. Initially, the turnout for Mom's service pleased me, but then I realized the home had booked funerals back to back and that Mom would have to wait her turn to be memorialized. We parked in the back of the building and walked around it to enter through the front doors.

In the lobby, a small group of people clustered around an easel on a tripod. Frank and Miriam had been delivered by the Meadowlake van, but I didn't see my dad.

"Where's my dad?" I asked Frank.

"Wouldn't let him travel. Too risky," Frank responded.

Dammit! The man even missed the funeral of his one true love. "I'll take you back home and see him then."

I turned to the rest of the mourners. Billy, Beth, and Nicki adopted solemn poses beside the easel; Raymond and Trey stood shoulder to shoulder to one side; two elderly women, members of the church Mom rarely attended, clutched small purses as though they might be snatched; Bonnie Mueller, from Sacred Heart, offered condolences; and a well-dressed man of advanced years introduced himself as Mom's primary care doctor—Dr. Warren Fowler.

After politely shaking hands and accepting sympathies, I stepped in front of Billy and said, "Where are Mom's friends?"

Beth answered for him. "They've all died or moved to Florida."

A pang of regret stabbed my heart; I should have moved Mom to Florida years ago to live a more socially active life. I had been selfish.

"Where are Brad and Katie?"

Beth answered again. "Katie stole the car this morning and ran off without saying where she was going. Brad didn't have any way to get here."

"I'm worried about my parents," Nicki said.

"You should drive back through Atlanta. Check on them on your way to Florida," I told her.

"She's in trouble, isn't she?" Nicki said, meaning her mother.

"Yeah. Her pill supply has been cut off, so she's looking for a fix."

Nicki and Beth stared at me in disbelief, so I turned back to the easel and examined the photos Beth had chosen to depict Mom's life. More or less in chronological order from upper left to lower right, the photos traced her time on earth from her wedding with Joseph through motherhood, birthdays, anniversaries, vacations, graduations, and finally, grandmotherhood. In one photo, Mom was at bat in a neighborhood softball game, and I was poised beside her to run the bases. When no one was paying attention to me, I unpinned the photo and slipped it into my jacket pocket.

Beth had done a nice job of erecting a record of supposed success and happiness, but I now knew better. We take the pictures, save the pictures, and post the pictures online to delude ourselves into believing our time on earth had meaning, that we were happy, that we wouldn't be forgotten. But the pictures can't capture our true emotions. Photos tell lies because everyone smiles for the camera.

I paused for a long time to examine a photo of the five of us at a time when I was perhaps twelve years old and my siblings were about six and four years old. We had our arms around one another and smiled dutifully for the camera, but I knew now that it had been taken at a tumultuous time, the time when my mother ended her affair with Albert and chose—no, was forced—to remain married to Joseph. Leaning closer, I searched for signs of discord and surrender, but the photo revealed no genuine feelings.

Behind me, the mourners from the preceding funeral filed out of the chapel, laughing and socializing as though they were leaving a play or a concert. Their tensions had been released; today wasn't their turn to be relegated to "the undiscovered country." After those mourners had departed, the funeral director waved us into the chapel. Pews in a dozen rows occupied most of the space in front of a nondenominational pulpit and grotto. As we entered haltingly, attendants rolled Mom's casket into the room and positioned it in the grotto. They removed the flowers from the preceding funeral and placed Mom's bouquets at either end of her casket. Then they raised and propped up the forward half of it. The attendants kept the assembly line moving. After they retired back stage, the funeral director lined us up to walk past Mom, as though in a military review. A priest appeared and stood at the foot of the casket, murmuring comforting words to each of us as we approached our turn to view the remains.

When I reached him, he introduced himself as Father Morrison, the parish priest, and shook my hand.

"Did you know my mother well?"

"No," he admitted. "I don't believe I ever met her."

I tried to hide my disgust by thanking him for officiating and shuffled along until I reached Mom's side. She looked like the woman I had first discovered in the hospital and not at all like my mother. Billy had rushed this process so the embalmers had not colored her hair or restored her "doll face." I did not want to remember my mother this way. My stomach retched and reeled, but I forced myself to kiss the dead body's cold forehead. Then I took a seat between Glenda and Jamie in the front row.

The service was short and devoid of any personalization. The priest uttered a litany of clichés about death as part of life, read passages from the Bible, and was about to wrap it up without once saying anything specific about my mother's life or her worth as a former member of the human race. Hot anger rose from my chest and spread through my neck and across my cheeks.

"Father, if you don't mind, I'd like to say a few words."

The priest seemed surprised, needed time to find the right response, but I didn't give him any. I rose from my seat and walked behind the pulpit, easing him to the side. He stood very close, practically touching elbows, reluctant to surrender his position of authority as though the pulpit were his throne. Then I delivered an impromptu, rambling, stumbling, cliché-riddled eulogy—she was warm, devoted, funny, feisty, beautiful, individualistic—that was no more genuine than the priest's hollow tribute. That disgusted me.

I scanned the small gathering of mourners and saw nothing but dry eyes. I couldn't let this be Mom's farewell. While the funeral parlor staff grew impatient—they had a schedule to keep—and the mourners grew uncomfortable at hearing the truth, I retold Mom's courageous story. I talked about her decision to defy her parents, her decision to keep a baby born out of wedlock, her decision to start a life as an unwed single mother, her decision to spurn her lover in favor of an abusive husband to keep her children together. I talked of the sacrifices that weren't captured by the pictures in the vestibule.

The small gathering sobbed in unison. That had been my intention.

"Would anyone else like to say a few words?"

I saw looks of fear and shaking heads. I gave Billy a questioning look, and he used his hands to mimic an umpire signaling that the runner was safe.

Ignoring his signal, I said, "My brother, Billy, would like to say a few words."

Beth urged Billy to his feet, and I nudged the priest away from the pulpit so Billy had a crutch for his shaky knees. To my amazement, Billy delivered a poignant eulogy between gut-wrenching sobs. At the end, he turned to Mom's casket and said, "I'm sorry, Mom, I could have been a better son."

When he turned around again he nearly collapsed. I grabbed one arm and Trey grabbed the other. We guided him back to his seat where he bowed his head.

I nodded to the priest and resumed my seat. Mom had gotten the respectful farewell she deserved. The priest had the last word. He asked us to line up again to say our final goodbyes. I couldn't do that. Without drawing too much attention, I slipped out of the chapel and the building's front doors. The skies had descended, crushing the earth and pummeling the ground with torrential rain. Under the portico, a long, shiny hearse, glimmering with rain droplets, waited with its rear cargo door agape. Two men in black suits and small chauffeur hats, with their hands clasped in front of their genitals, stood at parade rest beside the hearse. Just another day at the office for these people whose business would never run dry of customers.

When their wives asked that evening how their days had been, they would reply, "Same old, same old."

Dr. Fowler was the next person to escape the gruesome scene inside the funeral parlor. He nodded to me and unfurled a large black umbrella.

"Just a moment, doctor," I said, and he waited for me to approach with a question on his face.

I sidled up to him so the hearse drivers couldn't hear me. "You killed that woman in there."

Shock and displeasure exploded on his face. He attempted to move away from the crazy man who was accosting him, but I grabbed the umbrella handle and held him in place.

"If you had diagnosed her mitral valve problem and not allowed the dermatitis material to trigger her heart attack, she'd still be with us today."

"Let me go," he growled and jerked the umbrella out of my hand. I didn't stop him, but as he hurried away I yelled, "Tell your attorneys and insurance company to watch for the lawsuit, doctor. I'm going to make you pay for your mistakes!"

Through the rain, I could barely see him as he trotted toward his car, and I almost didn't notice, across the road in a used boat dealer's parking lot, a nondescript beige sedan with two males in the front seat. Detective Rodgers, or two of his men, watched and waited like hunters in a deer blind. Would they allow me to keep my word, or would they simply arrest me on the spot?

Not wanting to find out, I retreated into the building, found Glenda and Jamie, then corralled my uncle and his girlfriend. I was about to shepherd them through a door marked "Employees Only" when Billy grabbed my elbow and spun me around.

"You owe me $300 for the motel room you didn't use and $1750 for Mom's stay at Sacred Heart. Medicare won't pay for your bad decision."

"Take it out of the inheritance you stole."

An evil grin formed on his face. "It's Father's money. We're reading the will this afternoon, and you won't need to be there."

I tried for an evil grin of my own and reached toward Glenda. Out of her rather large purse, she pulled a sealed yellow envelope and handed it to me. "You'll need this at the reading," I said as I passed it to Billy. "Let the lawyer open it. You don't want to faint in front of the ladies."

Billy turned the envelope over and back with a look of confusion. Inside that envelope were the durable power of attorney that named me as Mom's financial guardian and the bank statements showing that her remaining monetary assets—one hundred fifty thousand dollars—were safely stored in an account in my name.

Billy started to tear the envelope open, but we had no time to wait for a reaction. Like a sheepdog, I herded my family through the employees-only door and into the secret recesses of the funeral home. "Hurry!"

"Are you afraid of Billy?" Glenda said.

"Keep moving."

We darted through private offices and wandered through disgusting embalming rooms and past startled employees until we found an emergency exit to the rear parking lot. As we crashed through that door, the alarm sounded and the downpour drenched us. We hustled to the Bronco, where the others climbed aboard gasping for breath and uttering profanities. The rain soaked me to the skin as I loaded Frank's wheelchair through the swinging rear gate.

In the driver's seat at last, I said, "Buckle up tight."

"What's going on?" Miriam said meekly.

The only paved way out of the parking lot was around the front of the building, so I drove the Bronco over the curb, up and down a grassy knoll, and into a weed-infested field that separated the funeral home from a strip mall on the next street. As we careened through ruts and swerved around rocks, my passengers were thrown side to side and catapulted into the air, straining ten-year-old seatbelts. Glenda yipped and Miriam yelped and Frank grunted and the Bronco protested with tortured screeches as the suspension bottomed out repeatedly.

"Jamie, unmarked cruiser in the boatyard. Are they coming?"

Jamie swiveled around in the third row of seats and looked through the back window. "They're moving, but they're taking the street."

Over hillocks like a boat on rough seas, we reached the back of the mall, then dashed between stores while canted precariously at a forty-five-degree angle, carving ruts into a steep embankment, until we found an opening in the mall parking lanes and bounced over the curb and onto parking lot pavement. My passengers simultaneously issued heavy sighs as I roared down the line of cars to a red light guarding the entrance to the main thoroughfare.

"Where are they?"

"Turning the corner two blocks behind us," Jamie said.

I whipped around the waiting cars into the oncoming traffic lane and ran the red light with tires squealing. I turned left and headed for the expressway entrance two hundred yards ahead, smashing the accelerator into the floorboard.

"Lights and siren now," Jamie advised. "They're hemmed in by traffic."

I accelerated and took the eastbound ramp onto I-20. The South Carolina border was less than five miles ahead, but we needed to get there before the cops could set up a roadblock.

I needn't have worried. "They went west," Jamie said.

I exhaled and eased off the accelerator. "They think we're heading to Florida."

The questions came all at once then, from Frank and Miriam and Glenda. Wet, bruised, and shaken, they demanded an explanation. As we crossed the Savannah River into South Carolina, I calmly narrated the circumstances that had led to a police chase. None of them was mollified, and I faced another volley of simultaneous questions.

"Are you crazy?" Glenda asked.

"Will they arrest all of us?" Miriam wondered. I wondered if she might find that exciting.

My passengers, loved ones, seemed to feel I should have cooperated with the cops, but my instincts argued otherwise. We had only reached Aiken, South Carolina, when my cell phone rang, silencing the furor in the Bronco.

Detective Rodgers. "Where are you?"

"Tomorrow, sergeant."

"I want you downtown right now!"

"Not today. I'll keep my word; you need to keep yours."

He barely hesitated. "We found the medical records in your email account."

"Then you must have found the independent analysis of the records too."

A longer hesitation. Shaky ground. "We only had a warrant for your mother's records."

"Come on, sergeant. You ran your dirty little fingers through all of my emails."

Another hesitation. "We looked for corroborating evidence of the record theft. The email you refer to isn't relevant to our investigation."

"Give the report to Dr. Kaplan and let him decide if it's relevant."

No hesitation. "That would violate police procedure, Mr. Marks."

"It's exculpatory, sergeant. You have a duty to find the truth, not follow some convoluted rules written by the idiots we elect to the legislature."

"Exculpatory," he said as though thinking out loud. "Big word for an ex-con." I heard him take a deep breath. "If you don't show up tomorrow, I'll issue a BOLO and you'll be behind bars before you ever reach the Florida border. You follow?"

I assured him I did. I was well-intentioned, but for some reason things rarely go as I plan them.

Twenty miles later, my phone rang again. Glenda picked it off the console, read the caller ID screen, and said, "Billy."

"You talk to him. Tell him we'll divvy up the spoils tomorrow."

Glenda listened and held the phone away from her ear as Billy spewed venom down the line. After Billy exhausted his emotion, Glenda said, "We'll be back tomorrow. I'm sure we can work everything out."

She was well-intentioned, but for some reason things rarely go as she plans them either.

Chapter Twenty-Eight

Jamie guided Frank's wheelchair up the ramp, and Glenda and Miriam clutched my arms as we ascended the steps to the front entrance of Meadowlake. Frank suggested we have lunch before visiting Albert, but I told him to start without me. I wanted to commiserate with my dad and evaluate the possibility of revising his will. Glenda and Jamie excitedly opted for meeting Albert as well, so my uncle shrugged and whooshed away with Miriam trailing. "We'll be in the great hall when you come down," she said over her shoulder.

The three of us walked up to the receptionist's counter. "We're here to see Albert Czajka," I said.

Clara, the nice lady behind the desk, froze. Her face contorted, deformed first by sadness and then by something more like fear. "Let me get my supervisor," she said as she hurried through a hidden door in the blank wall behind the counter.

We all traded questioning looks, but in less than a minute a well-kempt woman of about fifty emerged from behind the wall. "I'm Mrs. Donnelly," she said. "Will you follow me, please?"

She didn't wait for questions, simply turned and walked back through the wall, expecting us to follow. The blood in my veins turned into an icy stream, and my legs became rubbery. Giving me questioning looks, Glenda and Jamie preceded me through the door that Clara held for us. Mrs. Donnelly, ten yards ahead of us, stepped briskly down a narrow hallway and disappeared into a room on our right. Fearing the worst, we followed her into a windowless room with a couch facing two easy chairs. Mrs. Donnelly took a chair. We huddled on the couch.

"I'm so glad you came, as we didn't have your contact information. We tried"—she referred to a piece of paper—"Jamie Marks but got no answer. So we were waiting for Mr. Randle to return from Augusta. We thought he would have your contact information."

Jamie blushed. "I switched my phone off for the funeral."

I wondered why in the world Meadowlake would have Jamie's number, but my discomfort with our little soiree outweighed my curiosity about Jamie's connection.

"What's going on?" I said.

"Clara tells me that you are Mr. Czajka's son. He listed John Marks on his admittance form."

I hesitated because I had no official record of the relationship, had never made the claim in a public setting. Glenda nudged me, and I said, "That's right. He and my mother never married, but I am his son."

Mrs. Donnelly was clearly uncomfortable. "Do you happen to have, ah, your father's will?"

My brain operated at the speed of a man sloshing through wet concrete. Why did she need my father's will? Glenda came to the rescue. Ironically, many wills had been sworn, but we possessed none of them, so she lied. "We don't have it with us," she said. "We came straight from his mother's funeral."

Mrs. Donnelly leaned back in her chair and looked at me. "Oh, you poor man." She took a moment to think. "I suppose," she said slowly, "we can sort that out tomorrow. The hospital wants to see you as soon as possible. You can bring the will when you meet with the judge, Colby Flood."

Although I remained seated, I felt like I had fallen over a waterfall only to be battered by rocks in the rapids below.

Glenda said, "We aren't following you. Is Mr. Czajka in the hospital?"

Mrs. Donnelly covered her mouth with her hands and rocked back in her chair. "Oh my. I thought you were here because you had gotten word. Mr. Czajka suffered another stroke this morning, and he's on life support. The hospital needs a decision about how to proceed."

My lifeless body slammed into a boulder and slid down its face to submerge in a frigid, dark, undulating pool. Glenda wrapped an arm around me and cradled my head on her chest. Jamie took my hand and squeezed.

"I'm so sorry," Mrs. Donnelly said. "The judge would have acted in your father's stead, but since we had heard of your relationship, the judge deferred to you."

"There's no one else?" I stammered.

Mrs. Donnelly shook her head. Had I been thinking clearly, I could have predicted what was to happen, but I was not thinking clearly. I wasn't thinking at all.

Glenda managed the situation. "Which hospital is Mr. Czajka in, and how do I find it?"

Mrs. Donnelly explained that my dad was at Good Samaritan Hospital, a place normally reserved for indigents. She gave Glenda directions.

Jamie drove while Glenda held me close in the second row of seats. When Mom died, I wanted to lash out at someone, punish them for the needless death, extract a measure of revenge. This time differed; God was taking my dad from me, and I felt only crushing sadness and regret for a life apart.

Jamie dropped us at the emergency room entrance, and we wandered down depressing corridors until someone directed us to the family counseling offices. The offices were institutional green with frosted glass windows and tin desks. We could have been transported to 1950s America or present-day Russia.

A meek little woman with straight black hair and glasses invited us into her office. It was easy to imagine her wearing a nun's habit. Her name was Barbara Williamson.

"Doctor Maxwell will join us shortly," she said. Then she shuffled some papers and tried not to make eye contact. Five minutes later, a baldheaded man wearing a lab coat and sneakers cracked the door open and entered after Ms. Williamson gratefully waved him in. The doctor perched one cheek of his buttocks on the corner of the desk. The Beatles song about "Maxwell's silver hammer" trundled through my sick brain.

"Your father," he said, "has suffered a massive stroke and is comatose. He has no living will, but since he has next of kin—you—we put him on life support. We're breathing for him."

As had been the case since learning of Dad's condition, my vocal chords refused to respond.

Glenda took charge. "What are his chances?"

Maxwell shook his head as though it were a nonsensical question. "We're breathing for him. There's insufficient brain activity to sustain life without mechanical assistance."

Maxwell's silver hammer came down upon my head. Glenda patted my shoulder.

"Can we see him?" she asked.

"Of course," Maxwell said. "He's in ICU." Maxwell nodded to Williamson, some sort of private code.

The doctor did not accompany us to the ICU. Williamson led the way and carried a clipboard.

The ICU reminded me of the one in St. Petersburg, the one in which I eluded death after getting shot. Unlike Mom's "death room," Albert's critical care alcove was a maze of tubes, monitors, cords, and *Star Wars*-like technology. The big man lay deathly still, eyes closed, face obscured by an oxygen mask, his chest rising and falling in rhythm with beeps from the machine that kept him alive. Four plastic, crinkled extension hoses were connected to various parts of his inert body.

Pointing to each one, the nurse said, "Fluids in and fluids out, medications and nutrition."

"And the ventilator, of course," Williamson said. "His brain no longer controls his bodily functions."

The monitor above and beside the bed measured heart rate, oxygenation, and respiratory rate. The inert body was functioning smoothly, like a car engine on the mechanic's rack. At the very top of the screen, however, a line traveled flat from left to right, interrupted infrequently by tiny spikes.

"Don't those little blips indicate there's still brain activity?"

"There's hope?" Glenda asked.

"No," the nurse said. "That's just the amygdala, the lizard brain stem. It's not a cognitive response."

"You should make a decision as soon as possible," Williamson said.

I frowned at her. "What decision?"

"Whether to keep him on life support, or—"

"Whoa! Why me?"

"You're next of kin."

"He can't decide for himself, and he left no medical directive," the nurse said.

I turned to Glenda and Jamie, standing behind me. They wrung their hands, fear painted on their faces. "I can't decide whether a man lives or dies," I protested.

"Technically, he's already dead," the nurse said. "Without the ventilator, he'd stop breathing."

"It's incredibly expensive to keep him on life support," Williamson said. "The emotional toll it takes on the family is more painful than death."

I slithered between the rolling carts and the machines and took Dad's left hand in mine. It was warm, unlike the cold hands of my dying mother. This man's body was alive. "I read a report on the Internet that people sometimes wake up years later."

From the doorway, Dr. Maxwell said, "One in a million. One in ten million." He had eavesdropped on our conversation.

"But you don't know," I said to him. "You can't predict."

He crossed his arms, gave me a lecture. "As Nurse Adams said, he's technically dead already. When brain functions cease, the patient is dead."

I looked at the monitor again. The intermittent blips of primitive brain stem activity were smaller, and the gaps between blips had grown longer. The lizard brain was slowing down.

"He's already gone, Dad," Jamie said. "You're not deciding to let him die; you're deciding not to make his remains stay in this state." She motioned to the bed, the machines, and the room.

"She understands," Maxwell said. His little silver hammer struck me again.

"Do you need some time alone?" Williamson asked.

"To get comfortable with what you want me to do? No, I'll never get comfortable with sending him away forever."

That left her speechless. She didn't know whether to offer me her clipboard or leave the room. So she chose to stand motionless and helpless beside Glenda. I didn't mind inflicting a bit of my pain on the social worker.

I looked at Dad then and realized I had never seen him in motion, had never heard his voice or his laugh, knew little about him except his preferences in reading material and music. But I had his letters to Mom and his notes from his meeting with her, and I had seen his genuine joy at meeting me. On the flimsiest evidence, I imagined him to be cultured and learned and devoted and kind and a darned good businessman. I was proud of him. I kissed his bald pate and gently rubbed his head. *All these years I had a real father, but when I finally met him, all I did was pull the plug.*

I had tortured Mom with senseless attempts to extend her life, and I couldn't do that to Dad. One last glimpse of the monitor revealed no blips interrupting the flat line. I turned back to Williamson and said, "Where do I sign?"

She relaxed—her shoulders sagged, her countenance cleared. Out of the corner of my eye, I saw Maxwell give Nurse Adams a thumbs-up before he slipped away. Albert Czajka was merely one more carcass ready for disposal.

Williamson approached me with her clipboard and tried to hand me a pen. "Not in here," I said, and I swept my arms to indicate we should all leave. Nurse Adams moved swiftly toward the control panel, and I yelled, "Wait! I'm not going to witness another death."

Adams stopped and nodded respectfully. She said, "You won't see it. It may take six or even eight hours to happen."

"Oh my God!"

"Don't worry," she said softly, "he won't experience any distress or pain."

"Sure. You'll give him the 'comfort cocktail.'" I pushed everyone out of the ICU and into a hallway where I scribbled a signature on the DNR.

"You'll have to make arrangements," Williamson said.

Here we go again. "I have to consult with my uncle at Meadowlake. He was Dad's best friend, so he'll know what to do."

"If we don't hear from you, we'll have to send him to the city morgue."

"Do what you have to do, Ms. Williamson, but please don't bother us today."

***

At Meadowlake, we told Frank and Miriam that Albert was gone. Miriam gave me a warm hug, and the overly sweet smell of an elderly woman exuded from her hair and her dress. Albert's passing did not surprise Uncle Frank. He said that Albert had been in rapid decline, had lost all ability to communicate since I had first met him, had stopped walking around the building for exercise.

"Albert took the news of Elaine's death very hard. He shivered so badly I thought he was having a seizure. Probably the stroke coming."

When I asked about funeral arrangements, Frank said, "He wants to be cremated. We always hold a memorial service here when we lose a community member. Miriam and I can organize it for tomorrow."

"I'll help," Glenda said.

"Good." I was very appreciative that others could take control. "I want to go to his room and see what keepsakes I might want."

Glenda, Miriam, and Frank went off to arrange things, and I headed toward the receptionist's counter, but Jamie stopped me. "There's one other thing I have to tell you, Dad."

I wrapped her in a bear hug and said, "Thank you, sweetie, but let me take care of my dad's things first."

I disengaged and asked Clara if I could sign in and go up to Dad's room to collect keepsakes. Surprisingly, she said I couldn't until Judge Flood finalized the disposition of Albert's assets.

"Who is this Judge Flood?"

"He's the executor of Mr. Czajka's estate. He manages the affairs of many of our residents."

Oh crap. Depending upon which will is validated, I could end up without any of Dad's things. "When will the judge decide?"

"Mrs. Donnelly has scheduled the meeting for tomorrow afternoon. That way everything is cleared up without delay."

And the Meadowlake bill will be the senior debt. I didn't argue with Clara, didn't blame her for the haste with which Meadowlake wanted to dispose of dead residents. I agreed to meet the judge in the community conference room Thursday afternoon.

"Can we talk now?" Jamie said.

"Sure, sweetie, while we wait for your mother." I led her into the great hall, where we ordered iced tea, but quickly the hall became a poor place to hold a private conversation. One by one, residents approached us and offered their condolences. Their expressions of sympathy comforted me, and they were cathartic for the residents too. They knew they were on the short list to leave this world. They knew that Meadowlake was one of God's many waiting rooms. But today was their day to mourn rather than be mourned, and they were grateful for the reprieve.

As we graciously accepted the condolences, I saw the elevator doors open and Luis emerged. When he noticed me, he stuck his foot between the doors to hold them open and peeked around the corner at the receptionist's counter. Then he waved at me, inviting me to join him in the elevator. I excused myself and told Jamie to wait.

I squeezed past Luis and into the car, and Luis let the doors close. "Albert wants you to have some things," he said.

In Albert's room—the bed neatly made, flat surfaces dusted, headphones and iPod stacked on top of Shakespeare's plays—Luis opened a drawer of the wall cabinet and extracted two sheaves of paper. I took them in my hands. In my left were Mom's letters to Albert, and in my right was a document labeled "Last Will and Testament."

"Can I look through this?" I asked Luis, meaning the will.

"Nobody come now," he said.

I sat at Dad's table and removed the paper clip. The document was old and faded, dated forty-six years ago, when I was twelve years old. I assumed the date corresponded to the end of my mother's affair with Albert. Paging through it, I found it quite simple: everything Albert had owned and everything he might own upon his death was bequeathed to "Elaine (*née* Randle) Marks of Augusta, Georgia." The contingent beneficiary was listed as, "My son, John Randle Marks, a minor child, no Social Security number, also the son of Elaine (*née* Randle) Marks of Augusta, Georgia." Upon the passing of my mother, I had become the sole heir to my real father's estate according to this will.

That we found no other wills was not proof that they didn't exist. Katie may have filed a copy of the will she had coerced Albert to sign with some court or with Judge Flood. Then there was Mom's version that we had never found, perhaps because Katie had found it and destroyed it. And what if Albert had sworn another will in the forty-odd years since this old one had been sworn?

"Are you sure there were no children?" I asked Luis.

"No *bambinos, señor*."

"A wife?"

"No wife."

"Any other relatives that you know of?"

Luis shrugged in an exaggerated manner. "Nobody come see him."

After a sigh, I nodded. I added the book of plays, the headphones, and iPod to my stacks of paper, and we left the room. Luis said I shouldn't carry Albert's things past the reception desk, so he led me down a back stairwell and out a side door to the parking lot, where I deposited my treasures in the Bronco.

Since Katie had gone missing and since I had Albert's original will, there was some chance that I would inherit everything. It wasn't that I wanted the money, I told myself, it was that I didn't want Katie to steal it. I carried Albert's original will back into the building and asked Clara to give it to Mrs. Donnelly so she could give it to Judge Flood. That would make Mrs. Donnelly feel better about my relationship to Albert.

Uncle Frank told us the memorial service would start at ten Thursday morning and would be followed by lunch in the great room. I called the Inn at USC, directly across from Meadowlake, and reserved two rooms for the night. Glenda and Jamie, still dressed in funeral clothes, wanted to find a shopping mall so they could buy a change of underwear and fresh blouses. I convinced them to have dinner first and drop me at the house, as I was in no mood for shopping. We drove to the Blue Marlin restaurant, near the student hangouts on Gervais Street, and we all ordered shrimp and grits for dinner.

As we waited for our food, Glenda and Jamie chatted and I surfed the Web. Feeling queasy about my decision to "pull the plug" on my dad, I googled "Definition of Death" and found the "Uniform Determination of Death Act." It listed two proofs of death: 1) the irreversible cessation of circulatory and respiratory functions; or 2) the irreversible cessation of *all functions of the entire brain, including the brain stem.*

"Oh my God," I said. "I killed my dad."

"What?" Jamie said.

"Settle down, Randle. You did no such thing," Glenda said.

I read the act to them and expected outrage but instead received complacent shrugs and soothing assurances that I had done nothing wrong by terminating my dad's life.

Jamie said, "They were breathing for him, Dad, pushing air in and out of his lungs. He wasn't doing that for himself."

"The doctor decided the situation was irreversible," Glenda said.

"How can anyone but God decide that these conditions are irreversible?" I asked.

Glenda balled up her napkin and threw it onto the table. "This is your biggest problem, Randle. You don't trust anyone but yourself."

"I'm usually right," I said.

Her eyes shone like red-hot fireplace embers stoked by a winter chimney draft. "You pretend to be aloof, blasé, and cavalier. You have a glib answer for every question. You want people to think you are unaffected by human travails, that you can make any situation turn out in your favor. But you're afraid of yourself, Randle. Afraid you might have emotions. Afraid you might be as human as the rest of us."

At that moment, I hated my once and future wife. Hated her for forcing me to feel her probing that was like an ice pick thrust into my chest. I wanted to stop her before the probe could reach that secret pebble of nuclear energy that fueled my being. I had emotions, but I turned them off to deny Joseph any satisfaction from his abuse. Now I didn't know how to turn them on again.

"If we're honest with ourselves, we're all afraid of who we might really be," I said pedantically.

Glenda snuffled and sneered. "Let's get out of here. We need to get you away from this mess and back to our lives in Florida."

I slid to the end of the booth, preparing to leave, when Jamie stopped us.

"There's one more thing, Dad, that I've been trying to tell you all day."

I stopped moving and so did Glenda.

"I have a package of documents that Nana asked me to hold for her."

She paused. Glenda and I waited silently for her to continue. My skin tingled. Mom had said, "Ask Jamie," and I had forgotten those last words as we dealt with one Randle-Marks-inspired crisis after another.

"There's a letter that Nana wrote to me and a sealed envelope for you in the outer pocket of our suitcase."

It annoyed me that I had forgotten to follow up on Mom's request. "Why didn't you give it to me yesterday, when you got here?"

"Nana made me promise to wait until she had been buried. We've been sort of busy since then."

CHAPTER TWENTY-NINE

They dropped me at the hotel with the letter and the envelope, and I registered for our rooms. The Inn at USC has a lobby bar that serves drinks on the veranda facing Meadowlake, so I ordered a CC&7 and took a rocking chair away from two small but boisterous groups of traveling businessmen. Before opening the envelope, I read Mom's accompanying letter to Jamie.

Dearest Jamie,

I'm so happy we've reconnected after all this time, and I sincerely regret not reaching out to you sooner. We waste our lives over family squabbles. When your father gets home, please encourage him to bring his whole family to Augusta to spend time with me.

In the meantime, please keep the enclosed documents in a safe place and do not tell anyone, not even your mother, that you are holding them for me. Please keep the envelope sealed. I'm sure, as a policewoman, that you are discreet.

I have added you to dear Albert Czajka's notification list. As I told you, he is in medical distress and I'm not sure how long we'll have him with us. Albert has asked that I submit these documents to Judge Colby Flood in Columbia when he passes, but my own health is faltering so I can't be sure I'll be around to do it. He could hang on for years in his current state, but I doubt I'll be here that long. I've been feeling very unwell lately. You are my backup plan. Ha, ha!

As we discussed, if Mr. Czajka precedes me in death, please deliver or mail the envelope back to me. I will give your father the details as he will want to come to the funeral. In the event of my passing first, give the envelope to your father. He'll know what to do.

Please do me one last favor. If I die before Albert, please wait until I've been buried before you share this envelope with your father. Let everyone say nice things about me before your father reads the letter in the envelope. Please?

I so hope I can last long enough to see you and your father again. If not, keep me in your prayers and know that I will watch over you and keep you safe in your perilous occupation.

Love always,

Nana

So Nana outsmarted Katie by hiding Albert's last will with the least likely person in the family, a person who would have no contact with Katie. Jamie and Katie hadn't been on speaking terms since Jamie was fourteen or fifteen and a defiant, rebellious child. Jamie had spent a week in Atlanta with her aunt, and it had not gone well. Jamie and Nicki had found temporary boyfriends, and they had repeatedly snuck out of

Katie's house at night for mischievous rendezvous. Whether Nicki or Jamie was the instigator was never clear, but Jamie got the blame.

The waiter delivered my drink, and I gulped half of it before ripping the envelope open. Why would Mom want to be buried before I read the documents? I pulled a longer letter out of the envelope and began to read.

My dear Jackie,

If you are reading this letter it means that I've passed on to my final reward, as they say, and I never had a chance to tell you these things in person. If Jamie followed my instructions—she's a nice and dutiful young lady, so I assume she did—you've held my funeral (I hope someone had something nice to say), and now I lie beside my husband. Once upon a time I wished for a different end, but this is as it should be. As Joseph always told me, I made my bed and now I must lie in it.

To rest easy, I must tell you a story, the story of a carefree, rebellious young woman who chafed at the rules and morals and ideas of my Southern debutante upbringing and made decisions I learned not to regret but often reconsidered. How different life would have been had I made different choices!

Like other women of my class and generation, I was expected to attend the College of Charleston, meet a boy from a respectable family, and produce the next generation of fine Southern ladies and gentlemen. As you know, I did not follow that traditional path.

I insisted upon following my brother, Frank, to Columbia, to the University of South Carolina, and he was asked to look after me. There the academic freedoms, the intellectual flexibility, the enormity of the big city, and the mix of people and cultures were exhilarating and intoxicating for a sheltered young woman, and I wanted to experience all of it.

Sometime during my first year, when Frank was a junior, I met a boy named Albert Czajka. He was Frank's best friend, and we quickly became a threesome. Sometimes Frank would include a date, and we would appear to be double-dating couples. That was not quite the truth. Albert and I became best friends, but we weren't romantic for the longest time. In fact, I occasionally dated other boys although I didn't meet anyone who swept me off my feet.

Albert was dismayed by my flirtations, but he never faltered in his devotion to me. He followed me around like a puppy dog, doing me favors and running errands for me. I may have taken advantage of my position as a genteel Southern belle, but I assure you that Albert didn't mind.

When Frank graduated, he took a position in Columbia, but we didn't see him as often and Albert and I were usually a couple. On more than one occasion, I gave in to his advances, but that didn't mean I wanted to marry the man. I should have mentioned that there was sexual freedom on the campus in the big city as well as academic freedom!

Albert was adamant that we were meant to be together, wanted to marry me, but I still had wild oats to sow! When he graduated, he took a job in Columbia, and we lived together in his apartment during my senior year. Now I hope you are sitting down as I tell you this part.

I was sitting down but becoming more nervous with every line I read. I swallowed the rest of my drink and ordered a refill. Then I continued reading.

Shortly after I graduated, I became pregnant, and the situation became a mess. My parents were outraged and embarrassed. Please don't stop reading or tear this letter to pieces. There's so much more!

How much more can there be? First, she let me live my entire life believing that an abusive man was my father, then she wanted to die before revealing the truth. Glenda had been right: my mother had made me live her lie. And I had to "pull the plug" on the poor sap who could never convince my mother to marry him. I respected Mom's courage—I wouldn't be alive without it—but her decision to keep it a secret had altered my life dramatically. I resisted the urge to chug my drink. I resisted the urge to scream. I resisted the urge to shred the letter. I decided to read the rest, to see how Mom justified her behavior.

Your grandmother immediately sent me to a home for unwed mothers in Savannah where I was to hide, have the baby, and give it up for adoption. Your grandfather dealt with Albert's parents. They agreed that Albert would enlist in the Navy and would never contact me again.

Neither Albert nor I were good at following the rules. You get that from me, so don't turn up your nose at that news! I carried you to term, but when you were born I did not give you up. You were mine, and I wanted nothing more than to be your mother. So I took you to Augusta and got a job and thumbed my nose at my family. In revenge, they disowned me and told me never to bring "the little bastard" to Charleston.

If you did it for me, Mom, why in the world didn't you tell me? The tears began then, and I constantly swiped them with my jacket sleeve.

The others on the porch may not have noticed if Glenda hadn't opened the squeaking screen door to the hotel lobby.

"We've checked in, but we can't check out. The credit cards are officially maxed out," she said, and she showed me two plastic room keys.

I was reminded of the song "Hotel California." "I'll be up after I read the rest of this," I said.

I reached for a key, but Glenda noticed the tears and eased into the rocker beside me. She patted my arm and said she'd stay with me until I was ready to go inside. I handed her Mom's letter to Jamie and picked up where I had left off with Mom's letter to me.

A couple of years later, I fell in love with Joseph. Yes, I did love him, differently than Albert, but it was a form of love nonetheless. He was the black sheep of his family, and I was the black sheep of mine, and that formed a bond between us. It pains me to think of it now, but at the time it was us against the world, and that's why you never had close grandparents on either side of the family.

Joseph wasn't as doting as Albert, but we forged a union and committed ourselves to a future together. In fact, we made a bargain. By now I'm sure you know that you are not an heir to Joseph and Elaine Marks. Joseph agreed to adopt you if I agreed to leave you out of his will. We agreed we would have children together, and we did just that.

Joseph gave you a family to belong to with a brother and a sister. He held our family together and gave you a normal life, and all I had to do to be part of it was to keep your beginnings a secret. Sometimes that was easy, but sometimes it was very hard. You made it difficult because you were so different from your brother and sister. You were more like me, but you were also more like the man who was your real father.

Joseph was cruel, Mom. You can give him credit for playing a role in a traditional family unit, but you cannot convince me he was a good father to me.

Many years later, when you were eleven or twelve, Albert found me because Frank gave my whereabouts away. Things were difficult in the Marks household, both for me and for you. Anyway, Albert and I became lovers again. Maybe I wanted the excitement I had felt in Columbia. Maybe I wondered if Albert wouldn't have been a better father to you.

For months, I agonized over whether to leave Joseph and Billy and Katie for Albert. Frank might say it was the Catholic Church that stood in the way. Frank might say it was the loss of the Marks children that convinced me to stay with Joseph. I let Frank believe those things. The truth is that I didn't want to deceive Albert again. I wasn't at all sure I loved him the way a wife should love her husband. He's a big teddy bear of a man, rough and tough on the outside and pure mush inside. I wasn't sure I could deal with his sticky-sweet devotion to me. I'm not that good a person.

So I cut it off and decided to live the lie I had been living with Joseph. In a few years, you'd be off to college and then off on your own and that wasn't long to wait for your freedom. I know you struggled to earn Father's respect, but what you never understood was that he struggled to earn yours. I hope those years were bearable for you.

They weren't, Mom. You know they weren't. You know I am who I am because of how I was raised.

Glenda had finished the letter to Jamie, so I handed her the pages I had already read of Mom's letter to me. Then I resumed reading her confession.

The secrets could have been buried with me, but you would have wondered why you weren't mentioned in my will and I hadn't thought of a good explanation for that. I thought I had a few years to work that out, but it appears that won't be possible.

Lately my health has begun to fail. I take the pills Billy gets for me, but now they make me feel bad. I'm never hungry, and so I'm growing weak. Billy promises to take me to doctor's appointments, but then something comes up and he can't do it. I know I'm going to die soon. He's letting me die.

You also know that Billy and Katie did not turn out like you. You were always like me, and they were more like their father. You ran away and built your life in other places. I wish you had moved me to Florida, but you had your own problems, so I understand.

I'll have to live with my selfishness, and that won't be easy.

Now there is a new complication, so I have to tell you more about this man, Albert Czajka. A couple of months ago, Albert suffered a major stroke and moved into the same home where Frank lives. Frank asked me to please come see him, and Katie drove me to Columbia. She was visiting because she is having an affair with a dentist here in Augusta.

I was surprised to learn that Albert had become a multimillionaire, and he wanted to leave all his money to you. He had made his will when we broke up, back when you were twelve or thirteen. I urged him to leave the money to his relatives, but he said there were none. Finally, I got him to agree to change his will and leave money to several people of my choosing, including you.

I wrote to you while you were in prison because I wanted you to know about the will and help me with the details. But your sister, Katie, saw a chance to steal the money and she got to Albert first, made him sign a will that I'm sure would leave her some, or all, of his money. Apparently, Albert thought I had asked Katie to deliver it for me.

To protect my interests, and yours, I had my lawyer draw up another will to replace Katie's will. Katie searched my house and went back to Columbia to search Albert's room, but I outsmarted her. I sent it to your Jamie, and it is in the envelope attached to this letter.

In my version of the will, Albert's money is divided among Trey and Nicki and Jamie so they can make their dreams come true. Please believe me on this and don't pry unnecessarily into their lives.

Jamie has a dream too? I finished my drink and ordered yet a third. Maybe if I was drunk, the letter would be easier to digest.

So now you have choices, and I hope you do better with them than I've done with mine: you can keep all the money for yourself, or you can file my version of the will. The first choice might seem a just reward for your painful upbringing, but it would defile my memory and deprive my grandchildren of their dreams. It might also leave the money in your sister's hands, and that would be feeding the thief.

Actually, there was a third choice: I could divide the money according to my sense of justice.

> For me the man who was your real father is a pleasant memory I have taken with me to my grave. For you, I hope he is not an unpleasant one. You are not defined by your biological father. You are not defined by your name. You are defined by what you do as a mature man. The choice you make in this matter will define who you are.
>
> Perhaps I should feel shame for all the times I was unfaithful to Albert and to your stepfather, but I don't. I lived a wonderful life full of love and adventure. But now I want you to pray for me, Jackie. I am only 80% certain there is a God to judge me and only 50% sure He will welcome me to paradise.
>
> Your loving mother

I couldn't erase the thought from my fevered brain that Mom could have told me the truth while she was alive, which would have saved me much anguish. Maybe that's what she intended when she wrote to me while I was in prison. Maybe that's what she intended before she fell sick.

> As we discussed, if Mr. Czajka precedes me in death, please deliver or mail the envelope back to me. I will give your father the details as he will want to come to the funeral.

Maybe she'd have come clean if Katie hadn't tried to hijack the estate. *Maybe I should give Mom a pass and say a prayer for her tortured soul.*

I handed Glenda the last of Mom's letter. My brain was a-swirl in a bath of alcohol, but the other groups had retired. We were alone on the veranda, so I read the last document before attempting to stand and walk to our room.

The will was dated just two months ago and had been witnessed by Luis Rodriguez and Frank Randle. Albert's signature was an illegible scrawl, like the "X" used by illiterates.

After some legal boilerplate, the will listed detailed assets of various kinds totaling about three million dollars. The beneficiary page was also a detailed list of people and institutions and amounts totaling to Albert's entire estate.

As Mom had promised, Nicki and Trey received large bequests, one quarter of Albert's net worth for each. A smaller bequest was allocated to Jamie Marks in the amount of one-eighth of Albert's assets. Another eighth went to the University of South Carolina in Albert's and Mom's names. I didn't think it was enough money to get their names on a building, but it would probably merit a plaque somewhere on campus.

The last quarter was bequeathed to me. Albert had asked that I receive the lion's share of his wealth, but Mom had contravened his wishes and distributed the wealth according to her own sense of fairness. Whether Albert had been convinced of this division or simply appended his signature where and when asked, I had no idea.

Glenda muttered something unintelligible as she finished Mom's letter. I handed her the will and chugged the rest of my third drink.

After she perused the will, Glenda said, "That woman lied all the way to her grave. Over and over, she deceived you."

I pointed to her letter. "In the end, she told the truth."

Glenda collapsed in a fit of derisive laughter. "How do you know that this story isn't another lie? Why would you believe anything that woman said?"

"She's the only mother I'll ever have. I think she would have told me in person, but Katie tried to steal the money."

"Yes! Your money. *Our* money." She shook the will at me. "Now she's twisting your arm to give it away. Albert wanted you to have it, and we need it."

"He never even knew me."

"Don't be an idiot. He didn't know these other people either." She shook the will at me again. "What are you going to do?"

"Sleep on it," I mumbled.

Glenda grunted her disapproval but rose to her feet and told me to get up. Acting as a crutch, Glenda guided me through the lobby and into the elevator. Together, we staggered down the hallway to our room. I threw my suit jacket into a corner and flopped onto the bed. When the bed stopped whirling, I fell asleep in my clothes.

Chapter Thirty

Glenda roughly shook me awake. "Give me your clothes so I can press them."

She sounded angry, so I pushed myself to my feet and began to strip. The room rocked and the floor rippled as though we were in an earthquake. My mouth was dry and my head pounded in the aftermath of three CC&7 cocktails in honor of the only mother I'd ever have, but I managed to disrobe. A hot shower chased the demons from my brain, but when Glenda asked what I was going to do, I admitted that I had no idea.

Glenda grunted and growled and sat on the bed as I dressed. Despite her ministrations, my funeral suit still looked as though I had found it at a Goodwill store, and despite the hot shower, my joints ached and my lungs throbbed with each breath. After I dressed, we zipped up the suitcase and met Jamie in the lobby. We didn't check out as we had no money to pay for our rooms. We acted as though we'd be back and walked across the street to Meadowlake.

The great room overflowed with residents dressed in their Sunday best and sipping coffee or orange juice. The conversations hummed along at a discreet murmur. We wound our way through the crowd until we found Frank and Miriam standing near the serving tables.

I took my uncle by the arm and led him away from the women. "Where is Albert?"

Frank recoiled and gave me a look that clearly meant I must be stupid. He pointed to a rostrum and table at the far end of the room. A pewter-colored urn sat in the center of the table.

"That was fast," was all I could think to say.

A man of the cloth, denomination unknown, stepped to the rostrum and the residents took seats in an orderly fashion. We sat near the back of the room. The minister then proceeded in much the same way the priest had done at my mom's service: he delivered a combination of Bible verses and banalities. When he finished, he said, "Mr. Marks, if you'd join me, please?"

That was unexpected; I had not prepared to participate. I looked at my uncle and said, "Shouldn't you do this? You knew him better."

He shook his head. "No, Jack, this is all for you." He swept his hand to encompass the room full of mourners.

Unsteadily, I rose to my feet and zigzagged between tables until I reached the minister. He picked the urn off the table and presented it to me with a flourish and a few solemn words as though presenting me with a trophy. I clutched the urn like a mother cradles her newborn child. Then the minister asked me to deliver the eulogy.

I turned to the crowd and froze. What could I say about a man I never knew? After a couple of moments and feeling faint, I realized that only my uncle knew Albert well so I made up Albert's life story for the rest of the mourners. I talked about his business success, his devotion to me and my mother, and his love of classical music and classic literature. I threw in a passage about the charities he supported and the civic groups to which he belonged. My uncle chuckled. I struggled to maintain a straight face.

I thanked everyone for coming to the service and turned to place the urn back on the table, but the minister stopped me. He shoved the urn securely into my arms and said, "Maybe there's a place he might want his ashes spread?"

Maybe. How should I know? Embarrassed, I walked back to the table with Albert Czajka's remains. I thought that an apt metaphor for the upcoming meeting with the judge.

Servers pushed food carts into the room, and the residents abandoned their orderliness to race for a place in line. Men elbowed others out of the way as did brazen old ladies. We waited until the line dissipated.

I couldn't eat and had nothing to say, so Uncle Frank regaled the table with true stories of Albert's life. My dad had been a loner, single-minded in his commitment to his work; a determined, even ruthless competitor in a rough business field. He did not join any civic organizations. His only personal interests were my mother and me. That made me sad. Mom had strung him along, and he had never recovered.

After lunch, most of the residents dispersed and we were left to wait for Judge Flood to arrive. Frank continued to carry the conversation—Jamie found him charming—so I drank fluids in the hope of easing my headache.

At one point, Glenda leaned close and whispered, "Know what you're going to do?"

I nodded. "I'm going to take all the money. Mom manipulated Dad during his whole life, but I'm not going to let her control him from the grave. He wanted me to have it, and I'm going to take it."

She smiled. "Cool. We'll be able to pay the hotel."

Judge Flood arrived thirty minutes late but did not apologize. We were shepherded into the community conference room and joined by Mrs. Donnelly, Uncle Frank, and Luis Rodriguez. The judge looked askance at my witnesses but didn't question their presence. Jamie, Glenda, and I sat on one side of the table with me closest to the judge at the head of the table. I guessed that Judge Flood's days on the bench were long past and that the title "judge" was now honorary. He still possessed an air of authority and a full head of slicked-back silver hair, but his cheeks were fleshy and drooping, his hands pocked by liver spots. Silver reading glasses rested low on his nose.

Mrs. Donnelly introduced the judge as executor of Albert's estate and took the seat at the foot of the table. Luis and Frank sat in chairs along the wall.

After we were seated, the judge said, "Where's the other couple?"

What other couple?

"They're in the parking lot," Mrs. Donnelly said.

A cold shiver traversed my spine and wrapped around to clench my chest. I imagined some long-lost relative walking through the door to sweep away all the money I had only decided to claim an hour ago. Then the door opened, and my sister and Brad walked into the room. Katie's left arm was in a sling, her left foot wore a walking boot, and she had a garishly blackened left eye. She looked like she had been in a barroom brawl with someone who threw right-handed punches. They nodded at us and then took seats across from us.

For lack of a gavel, the judge slapped the table once with his open hand and we all came to attention.

"As executor of the estate of Albert Czajka, I am authorized today to adjudicate the disposition of Mr. Czajka's worldly assets with a current value of"—he referred to a sheet of paper—"$2,704,918. That's after all debts have been paid but before taxes. After taxes, I estimate the value of his assets to be $1.65 million."

He looked at all of us as the number sank in. Albert's wealth seemed to have shrunk. The idea of hiring a financial auditor crossed my mind. No one commented; everyone waited for the final act in this drama.

He announced that one very old will had been filed for his consideration and then asked if there were any more recent wills to consider. The judge looked directly at Katie, so he obviously had been tipped off to the presence of another will. Just as obviously, Katie intended to steal Albert's money.

"There's a new will," Brad said as he passed a document to the judge. "I'll have to speak for my wife as she can't talk."

I noticed then the slight bruising along Katie's jawline and the rigid set of her mouth. She wasn't being insolent or subservient by not speaking for herself; her jaw was wired shut.

The judge said, "For the record, Mr. Van Kamp, please describe the circumstances under which this will was prepared and executed."

"My wife's mother had the will prepared, judge, and she asked my wife to bring it here for Mr. Czajka's signature. He was pleased to do as Mrs. Marks requested. We were afraid that other wills might turn up, so we held onto this copy until today."

"That's a lie!" I shouted. "They're trying to steal my dad's money."

"Behave yourself, Mr. Marks," the judge said. "You'll get your chance to speak."

The judge accepted the will, paged through it, stopped to examine Albert's signature, the witness signatures, and the notary stamp. "This seems to be in order," he said.

"Is it my turn now?" I asked.

The judge glared at me. "No, it is not, Mr. Marks. Let's review the bequests."

The judge turned pages until he found the beneficiary page. "The primary beneficiary is Mrs. Elaine Randle Marks of Augusta, Georgia. She is bequeathed 100 percent of the estate." He paused.

Had Mom outlived Albert, which must have seemed likely at the time, she would have inherited the estate as the judge had just stated, and on her passing, her will in the safe deposit box would have split my dad's assets between Katie and Billy. Smart, except that Dad had outlived Mom by two days.

The judge looked at me. "I understand that Mrs. Marks is deceased."

"Yes," I said. "This past Monday."

"Do you have a death certificate?"

"I do." I pulled it out of Glenda's purse and gave it to the judge.

"Excellent. Then let's proceed to the contingent beneficiaries." The judge turned the page and read, "The contingent beneficiaries are Mrs. Marks's children, John Marks, William Marks, and Katherine Marks, in equal parts.'" The judge laid the will on the table and removed his readers. "This seems to be in order."

The way the contingent beneficiaries were named was also smart; the equal division would have convinced my dad that Katie was doing this version on Mom's behalf and that Mom wanted all three of her children to benefit.

Glenda leaned close and whispered, "That works for us, Randle. It's enough."

Sure, more than half a million dollars. Katie's willingness to play it smart rather than succumb to uncontrollable greed impressed me, but I wasn't willing to allow her to steal anything. I reached for Mom's version in Glenda's carryall bag and she resisted, swept it away from me. I gave her a stern look and reached again. She relented, and I handed Mom's version of Dad's will to the judge.

"As you can see, Judge Flood, there is a later version of Mr. Czajka's will that more accurately reflects his wishes immediately preceding his . . . demise."

Katie and Brad didn't react. That baffled me. *They should be shocked and scared.* The judge nodded and turned to the signature page. Then he consulted a notepad covered in scribbles.

He removed his reading glasses and said, "I cannot validate this will because it was signed a week after Mr. Czajka was declared incompetent, and I was named executor of his estate. After that, I would have had to sign any legal documents for him."

The floor opened beneath me, and my heart dropped through the hole. Katie and Brad hadn't reacted to the presence of Mom's will because Katie had learned on her last visit to Albert that he had been declared incompetent before signing Mom's version of the will.

Glenda clutched my arm and whispered, "It's okay. Let Billy and Katie take care of their own kids. We can give Jamie some of our money."

Billy and Katie's kids will never see a penny. The money will buy pills and pay off Brad's and Katie's debts. Billy isn't about to fund a sex change for Trey. I snatched her bag before she could secure it and removed Dad's notes from his meeting with Mom and Katie. I tossed them at the judge. "These notes, that Mr. Rodriguez and Mr. Randle can attest were written by Mr. Czajka, clearly indicate his wishes in this matter."

Reluctantly, the judge paged through the Post-it notes. He pursed his lips. "These notes constitute what we call a holographic will, a handwritten will. South Carolina does not recognize holographic wills. The notes also indicate a willingness to consider a new, properly executed will." He tapped Katie's version with one fat finger.

I pulled Mom's letter to me out of Glenda's bag and handed it to the judge. "Okay," I said, my patience being tested, "this letter clearly indicates the wishes of the beneficiary, my mother, in the event of her passing before Mr. Czajka."

Again reluctantly, the judge perused the letter. He sighed. "This letter was written long before the new wills were sworn. Perhaps Mr. Czajka—or your mother—changed their minds." He shrugged.

I jumped to my feet and pointed an accusing finger at my sister. "You orchestrated this incompetency trick so you could steal the poor man's money."

Brad and Katie leaned away from the table. Katie shook her head. At the far end of the table, Mrs. Donnelly spoke up. "We arranged the competency hearing, Mr. Marks. Your father wasn't paying his bills, no longer knew how to manage his everyday expenses."

"So you couldn't wait for the poor man to die either. Disgusting."

She merely shrugged. "It's routine, Mr. Marks."

Routine, yes. Routine for Meadowlake to want its money and routine for the judge to get another client.

"I think we're done here," the judge said.

"No, we're not," I said. To Mrs. Donnelly, I asked, "How many payments to you and others had my father missed before the competency hearing?"

"Two months' worth," Mrs. Donnelly answered. That had to be the truth because it could be checked.

"So, my dad didn't suddenly and conveniently become incompetent on the day of the hearing. That thing"—I pointed to Katie's will—"was signed only a week before the hearing. My dad had been mentally debilitated since he suffered the stroke."

"He have good days and bad days," Luis chimed in.

"And which was it on the day he signed this will, Luis?" I asked.

"Very bad day. He no understand."

"There you go."

"Take a seat, Mr. Marks," the judge said. I did. When order had been restored, the judge said to Brad, "Is your mother's lawyer present?"

"No, sir," Brad said. "He isn't a member of the South Carolina bar. He prepared this will under the laws of Georgia. He said you would recognize a will from Georgia."

"We recognize Georgia wills, but that's not the point. It's up to the lawyer to affirm the testator's state of mind."

"He didn't think he had to be here," Brad said.

The judge leaned back in his chair. "Can you produce the witnesses?" he asked.

"They no longer work here," Mrs. Donnelly said.

"Filipinos," Luis said with a hint of derision. *"Deportado."*

"Deported?" The judge's eyebrows rose.

"Sí. Visa expirar."

I jumped to my feet again. "They overstayed their visas and got deported? Doesn't say much for the employment practices at Meadowlake." Mrs. Donnelly looked away. To the judge, I said, "Under Georgia law, witnesses have to be 'credible and reliable.' Is it the same for South Carolina law?"

"Yes, Mr. Marks, but let me interpret the law." To Luis, he said, "Were you present for the signatures?"

"Sí, señor."

"Are you a legal immigrant?"

"Sí, I have green card."

"Did the witnesses see Mr. Czajka sign the will? Did they know what they were witnessing?"

"No. Señor Albert make his mark and they want me to sign, but I wouldn't do it. This not what Señor Albert want. He want his son to have the money. So they look for nurses to sign."

The judge dropped his glasses on his notepad. "I can see why your lawyer didn't want to be present," he said to Brad. "Foreigners can witness a will if they know what they are witnessing, but they must be present at the reading if the will is contested."

The judge looked at Brad through his eyebrows. Brad sat frozen and silent. The judge nodded to signal the finality of his ruling. He picked up Albert's old original will, hefted it, testing its validity by its weight, then paged through it.

After a long pause, he said to all of us, "I can't authenticate this version because it is dated after the competency hearing." He touched the version that Mom thought had fixed everything. "And I can't authenticate this version"—he touched Katie's copy—"because the witnesses aren't credible, reliable, or available." He paused to let that sink in. "I declare both of these wills invalid due to an inability to establish testator's state of mind. Therefore, I have no choice but to declare the older original will to be Albert Czajka's last will and testament. Since we've established that Mrs. Marks is deceased, 100 percent of Mr. Czajka's estate is bequeathed to Mr. John Randle Marks."

Stunned silence. After several dozen heartbeats, Glenda sighed loudly. Katie cried, but since she couldn't move her mouth her wailing came out as a muffled series of grunts and convulsions and rocking shoulders.

I didn't wait for anyone to change their minds. I rose and shook the judge's hand. He maintained his grasp and said, "I feel okay about this, the notes and your mother's letter . . ." He let his comment trail off, hoping for encouragement.

I wondered if the judge felt okay about the judgment, because he and Mrs. Donnelly had skimmed the missing two hundred thousand dollars off the top, but I decided this wasn't the moment to question them. The sale had been made, and it was time for the salesman to get the hell out of the negotiating room. "I feel good about it too." He nodded and let my hand go. I felt good that none of the money was in the hands of my brother or sister.

Glenda elbowed me and, with a big smile, whispered, "We won. Now we can have a good life."

We began to file out of the room. Katie remained seated, tears dripping from pink-rimmed eyes, but Brad leapt in front of me and said, "Can we talk? Somewhere private?"

Whether he wanted to escape my family or his wife, I didn't know, but I reluctantly agreed and led him down the hallway and out the side door to the employees' parking lot.

As soon as we were alone, he said, "We need some money, Randle. We need it bad."

I could have predicted the wolves would be at my door if I inherited the money. "What happened to her?" I jerked a thumb back toward the conference room, meaning Katie.

"That's the thing, Randle. She ran off to get a fix, and she overdosed. Then she tried to drive—to a hospital or home, I don't know—and she got into an accident. Caused it."

"So you need a new car?"

He huffed and spun in a circle. "No, Randle. She T-boned a small foreign compact with our big SUV. The guy in the other car died. Katie killed the man."

The destructive force of drug abuse had found its way into my own family. "That's terrible, Brad, but it was an accident, no?"

Manic energy contorted his face and distorted his voice. "That's just it. She was driving under the influence and speeding, so they've charged her with vehicular homicide."

All sorts of responses came to mind, but I decided to be cruel to the guy who tried to hijack my dad's money. "Maybe she'll dry out in prison. Might be good for her." I tried to walk away.

"Randle, please!" He gripped my shoulders and shook me. "It wasn't her fault. Some street pusher sold her heroin laced with Carfentanil. That's what they're using now to cut the heroin."

"You mean fentanyl? That's what was in her pill bottle, by the way."

"No, Carfentanil, an elephant tranquilizer one hundred thousand times more powerful than morphine."

I shook his hands off my shoulders. "So, you need money for lawyers?"

"Sure, but it's worse than that. The dead guy's family has threatened a lawsuit. They want a quarter of a million dollars to drop the suit."

"You tried to steal a lot more than that."

He ran his hands through his hair, then squeezed his head between them. "I know," he said. "I know. She said it had to seem logical to Czajka, how the money was split. I'm sorry, Randle."

"If Albert had passed before Mom, as your wife expected, I'd have been cut out of his will entirely."

Brad put his palms together, like a sinner in church. "Please, Randle," he wailed.

I felt sorry for my brother-in-law. Being married to an addict had to be hell on earth, but I wasn't sure I could find the same sympathy for my sister. She hadn't expected me to be here, out of prison, to contest her theft.

"Here's what you do, Brad. Bring your wife and your daughter, Billy, Beth, and Trey to Mom's house tomorrow morning. We'll sort it out there once and for all."

Brad collapsed onto my chest and hugged me tight. "Thank you, Randle. Thank you, thank you, thank you."

I pushed him away. "No promises, but I'll think about it."

"She looks up to you, Randle. She really does, when she's sober."

Chapter Thirty-one

"Are we going to spread your dad's ashes before we leave town?" Glenda said.

"No, we're taking them with us."

"I'm not going to live with that urn on the mantel, Randle."

"You won't have to."

Jamie offered to drive. That allowed me to sit in the second row and contemplate the distribution of two inheritances. I wanted to respect my mother's wishes, but I also wanted to use the money to wipe the slate clean, to bring my involvement with the Marks family to a guilt-free conclusion. I was mentally subdividing three and a half million dollars when my cell phone rang. Daniel.

"Are you already in Florida?"

"No." I thought about how to answer without triggering an ambush. "I'm in Columbia. My . . . dad died, and today is his memorial service."

"You've had a tough week, Randle, but I can make it better. Come back through Augusta on your way home so we can settle our dispute."

"So you can have me arrested if arm-twisting doesn't convince me? I'm not that stupid, Daniel."

He cleared his throat, a delaying tactic. "I can't keep doing this, Randle, so this has to be my best and final offer."

"I'm listening."

"Good. We've changed our tracking system in the ER, ensuring that all patients are logged in at the time of triage and then tracked with reminders during their stay there. It's a new piece of software so we aren't dependent upon humans to remember patients."

More eyewash. They didn't lose track of Mom, they deprioritized her. "Keep going."

"We've put a letter of reprimand in Dr. Harrison's file."

"Send me a copy."

"Okay. Are we good with this?"

"I hope you're not done."

Daniel observed a moment of silence. "There's one more step we could take, but we don't really want to if we don't have to."

"What?"

He cleared his throat. "We could fire the nurse who decided not to call the cardiologist back to the hospital."

"Do it."

He sighed. "None of this can go into the settlement agreement itself. We can't admit any responsibility for your mother's death."

"You didn't warn Sacred Heart about the fluid in her lungs."

"There wasn't any when we transferred her."

"But you knew it would return."

"If your mother gained strength the fluid wouldn't return."

I exhaled in frustration. "Okay, Daniel, why didn't you tell me about the lab report on her pill bottles?"

He was ready for the question. "Didn't seem relevant. We thought perhaps she stored antihistamines in her prescription bottles for easy access. Or maybe you gave us the wrong bottles and she had another set containing her medications."

"Did you test for antihistamines?"

"Not until we found them in the bottles."

"And by then they were out of her system?"

"Yes. If she ever took them."

"What if she had been taking them, thinking they were her prescription meds?"

Daniel explained the terrifying repercussions, and with that new knowledge, I formed a strategy for handling my dad's money.

"So, that's it? St. Thomas is relieved of responsibility?"

"Dr. Fowler, too. He has decided to retire immediately, and he hopes you won't sue him. He did everything right, Randle. He prescribed the right drugs and expected your mother to return for a follow-up to see if the drugs were working."

Power over people is a terrible thing: It encourages cruel behavior. "I'll think about it."

"One last thing: You have to take the money. The money cements the deal legally because you receive something in kind. It's the same as when you give your car to someone but you have to make a sale for a dollar."

Take the money, I thought. Punish them and make Glenda happy. Ask for more money, I thought. Mom's life is worth more. No, don't take the money. It's a bribe, blood money like Judas' thirty pieces of silver.

"Are you still there, Randle? I can't ask for more money."

I had an epiphany. "I can't accept two hundred fifty thousand dollars, Daniel. Give me fifty thousand dollars, and we've got a deal."

Daniel chuckled. "They'll think I'm a negotiating genius."

The fifty thousand dollars had a special meaning for me: It represented one third of Mom's brokerage account, the one third that should have come to one of hers and Joseph's three children—me. Since

I now had the money that was rightfully mine, I could redistribute Dad's and Mom's estates in a way that would put my past behind me forever.

* * *

Detective Rodgers was surprised to hear from me. "I thought you made a deal with the hospital."

"We did. I need your help with a different problem. And a favor."

I explained the situation and the favor, and the detective agreed to help.

* * *

"I want to go to the cemetery. I want to see Mom."

Jamie and Glenda complained that they were tired, but I insisted and Jamie dutifully drove us through the stone arch entrance. We traveled in circles for a while until we spotted a freshly dug grave, it's mound of covering earth not yet sunken to ground level. I carried my dad's ashes with me to the gravesite. Jamie and Glenda stood ten yards away, assuming I wanted a private moment with my mother; but this was Dad's moment, not Mom's.

I knelt beside Mom's grave and dug a hole in the soft mound with my hands. Then I poured Dad's ashes into the hole and covered it again with loose dirt.

"That's all I can do for you, Dad. You couldn't be with her in life, but now you'll be with her in eternity."

There was one more thing to do. On the drive from Columbia to Augusta, I had concluded that Joseph Marks had indeed held his dysfunctional family together. Nuclear family is the popular term, and that's what we were—electrons and protons and neutrons held together in an atom that none of us had the strength to escape. When Joseph's uniting force was removed, the atom imploded.

During the drive, I also rationalized Joseph's behavior toward me. I wasn't his son: I was an unwelcome appendage to his real family, the product of a fetid bargain with the devil. Before Mom's affair with Albert, Joseph tolerated the appendage, but after her affair, he couldn't control his contempt for me. That's why he didn't come to my Little League Baseball games—Mom had her affair while I was playing catcher, and Joseph punished me for her indiscretions.

I stood and walked around to Joseph's grave. I removed his Rolex from my wrist and laid it on his headstone. After his retirement ceremony, he had handed it to me and said, "You wear it. You're the one who's happy being a catcher, but I'm not."

The pinstripe-suited men who had spoken at his ceremony commended Joseph for his diligence in keeping the pumps humming, the steam flowing, and the generators producing the electricity that was the ultimate product of the nuclear energy facility. Except for the reactor itself, the mechanical processes that produce electricity in nuclear plants are the same as the those in coal-fired plants and Joseph had cared for those mechanisms. He had played catcher on his team of engineers.

I had worn the watch not to admit that I would always be a catcher, but to remind myself to be a better father and husband than Joseph. I was still working on it.

"I don't need this anymore, Joseph. I don't have to compete with you anymore. I've come to terms with your behavior. Your abuse wasn't justifiable, but I do understand it."

***

We drove to Mom's house. Raymond made scrambled eggs. We went to bed early. Tomorrow promised to be another long day.

Chapter Thirty-Two

While the women dressed, I carried my coffee into the backyard. The early morning weather was mild, a hint that moderate fall temperatures would soon eclipse the oppressive heat of summer. Today would be the last day I would ever be in this house, would ever be in this town. Nostalgically, I circled the house. It was in good shape and would fetch a good price. As I examined the roof, as solid as ever, a strange cloud formation hovered in the sky. The jet stream in eastern Georgia follows a very predictable pattern from west to east and then bounces to the northeast to travel up the Atlantic coast. The clouds always travel that path and often have wisps torn from their edges indicating their speed and consistent direction of travel.

Now, directly above the peak of the house's roof, a connected formation followed that path from west to northeast, but another connected row of clouds moving from northwest to southeast bisected that formation. The clouds formed a huge white cross.

It simply wasn't possible for the jet stream to blow in two opposing directions at the same time on a clear, windless day.

I marveled at the unusual formation for a few minutes, sipping coffee, waiting to see how the clouds might separate or join to travel the usual route. They held steady, right above the house. Suddenly, I realized why the weather and wind patterns were not behaving in contravention to physics: Mom was sending me the sign I had asked her to send.

Mom is okay "on the other side." No, there's more to it. Mom is urging me to follow her directions. Even from the other side, she is manipulating me. That's Mom: manipulative and well-intentioned at the same time.

"Don't worry, Mom, I'll do the right thing."

"What did you say?"

I didn't realize Glenda had walked up behind me.

"Talking to Mom," I said. "She sent me a sign." I pointed to the sky, but the clouds were gone.

Glenda looked up and said, "Hunh?"

"I guess they're over here," I said as I moved around the house searching for the odd formation.

Glenda followed, looking at the empty sky with a question on her face. "You're scaring me, Randle. Are you okay?"

I stopped walking, stopped searching. The clouds were only meant for me. "I'm fine. Everything will be fine."

"You've decided to keep the money, right?"

I hated doing it, but I had to lie. "Sure."

"If we're keeping the money, why don't we just leave?"

"There are loose ends to tie up, Glenda."

She shook her head in disgust.

***

As we waited for my family to arrive, I opened the front door to chase the musty smell from the drawing room. On the doorstep lay a pile of mail that had apparently become too bulky for the mailbox at the street. Distracted by everything going on, I had not thought to check Mom's mail. I carried the bundle into Joseph's office and quickly sorted the wheat from the chaff. Most of it was junk, but a few envelopes held bills we would have to settle for Mom. At the bottom lay a large, thick brown envelope from the home for unwed mothers. *My original birth certificate!*

Inside, I found not only my birth certificate but also Mom's entire file. It held a registration form, invoices paid by my grandfather, Stephen Randle, as well as medical records and test results—John Randle had entered the world without material defect. One test, however, made me sink into Joseph's chair and sigh. It was a paternity test of the kind used in the 1960s—an HLA test of white blood cells—and it concluded that Albert Czajka could be excluded as the father of "the little bastard" with 80 percent probability. Eighty percent was the maximum probability in those days. The test was as certain as it could be that Albert Czajka had not fathered John Randle. One of the last lines in Mom's letter came to mind: "Perhaps I should feel shame for all the times I was unfaithful to Albert . . ."

Uncle Frank had told me that Mom had dated other boys while she was friends with Albert, but now I guessed she had been unfaithful while she and Albert were living together!

Thoughts raced through my mind like billboards zipping by on a highway:

Mom knew Albert wasn't my father, and yet she had allowed him to believe it.

Mom knew Albert wasn't my father, and yet she had allowed me to believe it.

"For me the man who was your real father is a pleasant memory I have taken with me to my grave."

Mom knew Albert wasn't my father, and yet she had tried to hijack his estate.

Mom knew Albert wasn't my father, and yet she had urged me to hijack his estate.

She was the only mother I would ever have, but her secret changed my thinking for the last time.

❦ ❦ ❦

Brad, Katie, and Nicki arrived first, and I asked them to sit in the drawing room with Jamie. Brad had to help Katie walk. Her eyes were glazed by painkillers, her legs and arms akimbo. Not a good start to recovery. Nicki wore the insolent look of a child forced to accompany parents to a parent-teacher conference.

Raymond and I carried chairs from the dining room and formed a circle. Glenda served orange juice and coffee as Jamie and Nicki chatted like long-lost friends. Brad and Katie and I were nervous. This family gathering in the Church of Marks felt like a forlorn support group meeting in a church basement.

When Billy, Beth, and Trey arrived, I shooed them toward the drawing room but made sure the back door was unlatched. I closed the door between the drawing room and the kitchen, and no one questioned the odd action.

Trey took the seat between Raymond and Jamie. Beth sat obediently in the chair closest to me with her hands folded in her lap, but Billy, on her other side, refused to sit. "It's not right that you're in charge, Jack. You have no right to all this money. You're just an illegitimate bastard."

"That's a compliment in this family, Billy." I stood in the middle of the floor as though I were the master of ceremonies about to command tricks from circus animals. "The fates have intervened, and I am in charge."

Billy edged forward, deciding whether to attack me. It was too soon for that, so I waved him back and calmed him by saying, "Don't worry, everyone will get a piece of the pie, but I'll decide this morning how three and a half million should be shared by my loving family. Actually, Albert's money will shrink to about 1.65 million—round numbers— after taxes."

Everyone waited. Even Billy held his tongue. Reluctantly, he sat down.

"I've come to know that several people have good uses for this money, and we're going to let those people describe their . . . dreams, so we can all feel good about the decisions I make."

Trey shifted nervously in his chair. Nicki gave me a flat, defiant stare.

"Let's start with Trey."

Trey shook his head and looked to Raymond for support.

"Okay, then we'll start with Nicki."

She jumped to her feet. "No way, Uncle Randle. I'm not playing this parlor game."

I was squeezed in a vise, trying to exercise power over people who hadn't willingly ceded it to me. My daughter saved me.

"I'll go first," Jamie said. She stood next to her uncle Billy, and said, "I don't want to be a cop for the rest of my life. I want to become a nurse, a pediatric nurse. I don't have the money for school and I can't stop working to go to school, so it's just impossible. But Nana said I would get some money."

Beth said, "That's a wonderful dream, Jamie."

The fact that Jamie wanted to be a nurse came as a complete surprise to me. She had never mentioned it. I felt shame for not having been close enough to her to know. I said, "I'm going to give Jamie two hundred fifty thousand dollars so she can quit work and go to school full time." I wrote a note on my sheaf of papers.

Jamie sat down again, and several people congratulated her. Glenda gave me a questioning look. I had promised to keep all the money.

"Who's next?"

I could smell the fear now, like nervous perspiration and foul breath. To Brad, I said, "If you want to fix your problems, you have to tell your story."

Visibly shaking, Brad stood. Looking directly at his daughter, he said, "Your mother is addicted to painkillers. She's run us into debt, and we're going to lose our home."

Nicki covered her mouth, choked back a sob.

Bravely, Brad continued, "She was being supplied by her dentist, but Randle found out and scared the dentist away. He's moved out of state, and we don't know where he's gone so we don't have an author."

Brad saw questioning looks from all around the circle, so he explained. "'Author' is urban slang for a doctor who writes illegal prescriptions."

The questioning looks were replaced by amazed expressions. We would never have guessed that our upscale sister and brother-in-law would know urban drug slang.

Brad gave me a hopeless look, and I signaled him to continue. In his whiney, spoiled frat-boy voice, he spoke directly to his daughter. "She looked for a dealer on the street and bought what she thought was heroin, but it was cut with Carfentanil, a powerful drug used to anesthetize large animals. She overdosed, got into a car wreck, and killed a man. She's been charged with vehicular homicide, and we're being sued by the dead man's family."

The room filled with gasps.

"I helped you. I gave you Mom's savings account," Billy said.

"You enabled your sister's drug habit," I said. "You could have signed the checks, but you made Brad forge them. Did you want to keep your hands clean, or did you want something to hold over Brad's head?"

Billy turned red, and Beth tried to comfort him but he slapped her hands away.

Getting back to his story, Brad said, "The dead man's family wants two hundred fifty thousand dollars to drop the lawsuit, and there will be legal costs."

"Right," I said. "So, I'm going to give you three hundred thousand dollars to pay off the family and your lawyers."

I wrote another note as some people made surprised sounds and others sounds of relief.

"Thanks, Randle, but we have bills too," Brad said.

"Katie is beneficiary to Mom's annuity. That's enough," I replied.

"We need money for criminal lawyers, to keep Katie out of jail," Brad pleaded.

I turned to face Brad to my left. "Sorry, but that's not going to be possible. I've spoken to the police, and they've agreed to reduce Katie's charges to vehicular manslaughter in return for a guilty plea. As a condition of getting money today, Katie will spend a year in prison."

Katie broke down and leaned into Brad, sobbing through her wired jaw.

"That should be enough time for her to kick her addiction," I added.

Brad looked confused, not sure if he should be happy with the deal.

"As another condition, Brad, you must agree not to divorce my sister. You must stay by her side and nurse her back to health."

Katie swiveled in her chair to see Brad's face. Fear lit up her eyes. I doubt she knew Brad's plan to divorce her.

Embarrassed into action, Brad put his arm around Katie and said, "Of course I'll stand by her. She's my wife."

I wasn't sure about Brad's sincerity, but I decided against revealing Mom's suspicions that Katie had had an affair with the dentist. Mom could have been wrong. Maybe the dentist had extorted sex as part of the drug payments.

"Who's next?"

Heads swiveled, each person hoping someone else would stand and testify. Glenda glared at me. Finally, Raymond rose. He took Trey's hand and pulled him to his feet.

"I'll speak for us," Raymond said.

Billy jumped up. "I don't have to listen to this crap." He tried to leave the room, but Raymond slid in his way and Jamie grabbed an arm and jerked him back into his seat.

Composed, Raymond announced, "Trey and I are in love. Trey is transsexual, a woman in a man's body. He needs hormones and counseling and several surgeries. Then we'll get married."

Raymond stared down the room. No one said a word.

"I knew about Trey's dream, and Mom approved of it," I said. "So I've allocated three hundred thousand dollars to make the dream come true."

Trey smiled. Raymond nodded at me. Mom had promised them the money; I was just facilitating.

"You have to go next, Nicki," I said.

"You can tell us," Brad said.

"You can tell us," Beth echoed.

Glenda shook her head in disbelief.

Nicki leaned forward in her chair as though she were about to rise, then she leaned back again. She looked at each of us in turn and sighed. Slowly, she rose.

"Alright. Fine. You want to know my business? Two years ago I had a baby, a little boy named Ethan. His father is a married man from Atlanta who was in town on business. I met him at the restaurant where

I worked at the time, and we had a one-night stand. When I told him I was pregnant, he wanted me to have an abortion, but I wouldn't do it. He wanted me to give the baby up for adoption, but I wouldn't do it. After I had Ethan, I started dancing to make enough money to support him. Ethan's father went to court and asked the court to declare me unfit because I dance in a gentleman's club. Now Child Protective Services is harassing me, but I have no other way to pay for childcare and support my baby. I've been saving my money so I can quit and move us into a better apartment, but I could lose Ethan before that happens."

She waited for a reaction. No one spoke. "I couldn't stay long while Nana was in the hospital because I had to get home to Ethan."

Several people nodded their understanding but no one spoke.

"So there," Nicki said, and took her seat.

It dawned on me that in Nicki's story, I was witnessing a reprise of my mother's situation, fifty-eight years and two generations later.

I said, "Thanks, Nicki. I know that was hard." To the rest of the room, I said, "Nicki needs money in the bank to support Ethan, money for school so she can get a better job, money so she can stop dancing. I'm going to give her two hundred fifty thousand dollars."

Murmurs. The money was going fast. I avoided eye contact with Glenda but as I looked at the others I saw sympathetic faces. When I looked at Brad, I caught his eye and gave him a nod and the look that means, "Well, say something."

"I want to meet my grandson," Brad said.

I nodded at him again, and said, "Some of you know that I was born out of wedlock, that like Nicki, Mom was forced to make difficult decisions. She went to a home for unwed mothers in Savannah and had me there. I'm grateful to that institution, so I'm going to donate two hundred fifty thousand dollars to it."

Whispers. Glenda cocked her head, formed the obvious question on her face: "Is the rest ours?"

I couldn't look her in the eye. To the crowd, I said, "Mom also wanted to donate money to the University of South Carolina in her name and Albert's name. I'm going to honor her wish with a donation of two hundred fifty thousand dollars."

More whispers. Directly across the circle from me I saw Glenda had bowed her head and covered her face with her hands. I'm sure she thought me an idiot for not keeping more of Albert's money for us. Only fifty thousand dollars remained.

"And, finally, Luis Rodriguez, Albert's caregiver, will get the last fifty thousand dollars."

Glenda couldn't stand it any longer. She rose and headed for the door to the kitchen. I couldn't let her go out there.

"There's more to discuss, sweetie," I said to her. "Please sit back down."

Glenda hesitated with her back to me, then with her jaw clenched, she returned to her seat. Before I could resume the proceedings, Billy stood.

"This is just like when we were kids. You always favored Katie over me. What do we get?" Billy said, indicating Beth and himself.

"Albert's money is spoken for, but we're going to talk about Mom's money."

"There's nothing to talk about. "We"—he pointed back and forth to Brad and himself—"have a deal. Give the money back, Jack."

Beth drew her husband back into his chair. I ignored him.

To the family, I said, "Katie never told Billy she was trying to steal Albert's money and would cut him in on an equal share, so Billy thought the only money he could steal was Mom's money. Mom's will divided her assets equally between Billy and Katie, but Billy stole from his sister before Mom ever got sick. He gave Mom's car to Trey and signed Mom's house over to Beth."

Katie jerked back in her seat, and Brad said, "What the hell?"

"Billy is joint owner of Mom's checking account, and he was stealing from that account as well. There's not much left, but he can have it."

Group dynamics kicked in, and my family became a mob.

"I get the investment account," Billy said.

Ignoring him, I said, "When he was sure Mom wouldn't live much longer, he took out a two-hundred-fifty-thousand-dollar insurance policy and named himself the sole beneficiary."

Brad jumped to his feet and yelled, "You son of a bitch! You said half was ours!"

"Sit down, Brad, there's more to tell."

Red in the face, Brad sat and I resumed my summation for the "jury." "Billy let Brad have the savings account and in return he was to get the entire stock investment account, about one hundred fifty thousand dollars. Tell me, Beth, why does your husband need that money so badly?"

"Shut up," Billy yelled at his wife.

Beth stood and started away from Billy's seat, but he grabbed her arm and stopped her. She looked at him for a minute before deciding how she wanted to live the rest of her life. Then she tore her arm away and walked behind me, hiding from Billy.

"Gambling," she said to the room. "Gambling on sports. He owes his bookie one hundred thousand dollars."

"He used Mom's monthly income checks to place his bets," I told the crowd, "but he just kept losing."

Jeering from several people. Nicki stood and pointed a finger at Billy, yelled an epithet. Raymond wrapped an arm around Trey to comfort him and maybe to protect him. Jamie was rigid, on guard in case Billy became violent, but he was frozen in his seat.

I shushed everyone. "He gets nothing!" I said, pointing to the heavens and shouting like a fire-and-brimstone preacher in his Sunday pulpit. "Mom's investment money and life insurance goes to Beth."

Pointing to her, cowering behind me, I paused for dramatic effect before lowering my voice and saying, "After she divorces Billy."

Billy scoffed. "She's not going to divorce me."

"When she learns what you've done, I think she will. I know you didn't fill Mom's prescriptions for her dermatitis and water retention. That weakened her so she couldn't have surgery."

Billy made a face. "Beth was supposed to take care of that."

"I know you didn't keep her follow-up appointments with Dr. Fowler. Surgery could have repaired her faulty valve when she was still strong."

He shrugged. "I forgot."

Like a prosecutor harassing a suspect on the witness stand, I surveyed my jury and let my eyes ask if they believed the witness. The jury had doubts.

"The hospital tested the drugs in Mom's pill bottles and found they were all antihistamines, six brands to make them look like assorted medications. Of course, Mom wouldn't know the difference, would trust that her son was giving her the right medicines."

"Mom was losing her mind. Dementia," Billy said unconvincingly to the jury.

"Mom left me a letter." I held it up for everyone to see, as though it was being entered into evidence at trial. "In the letter, she says, 'I take the pills Billy gets for me, but now they make me feel bad. I'm never hungry, and so I'm growing weak.'" I let that sink in a minute before continuing. "Most people don't know that you can overdose on antihistamines. Dr. Kaplan told me that young, healthy people just feel like crap when they do it by accident, but old, weak people with heart trouble can suffer a heart attack when they do it by mistake." Turning to the witness on the stand, I asked, "How did you know that, Billy? Did you google *how to poison your mother?* Will we find the search on your computer?"

Billy spoke directly to the jury. "Do you believe this bullshit? He's trying to frame me so he can keep the money."

The jury sat in shocked silence, knowing where my line of questioning was headed.

I waved the letter at them again. "Mom goes on to say, 'Billy promises to take me to doctor's appointments, but then something comes up and he can't do it. I know I'm going to die soon. He's letting me die.'" Pointing an accusing finger at my brother, I said, "You weren't 'letting' her die, you were intentionally causing her death. First you kept her from having surgery while she was strong, then you weakened her by not filling her prescriptions, and then you replaced her medicines with antihistamines so she would overdose. You triggered her heart attack with the cold remedies."

Shifting nervously, Billy gave the room a cocky grin. "You can't prove a thing."

My voice rising, I said, "You destroyed her medical records to cover your tracks, but I have an electronic copy."

Finally, a desperate, worried look descended on Billy's square face. "This is ridiculous. You can't pin this on me."

"You didn't want me to stay here because you didn't want me to discover that you murdered your own mother," I shouted, "and now you'll be arrested!"

That was the cue for the cops, hiding in the kitchen, to storm into our makeshift courtroom. They yelled for everyone to get down on the floor and my family dove for cover. Before the cops could maneuver through the circle of chairs and prone bodies, Billy jumped to his feet and pulled Joseph's military-issue Colt .45 from his jacket pocket. As he swung it toward me, family members screamed and I dove headlong to my right. Jamie reacted to her training and made a rolling tackle into the back of Billy's legs. He folded up like a quarterback being sacked from the blindside, but on his way to the floor he fired a shot at me. Fortunately, the gun was aimed high over my head.

Billy and I crashed to Mom's hardwood floor simultaneously, our heads not six feet apart. His gun smacked the floor, and it skittered toward me.

Our eyes locked onto the weapon that lay between us. "I need that money, Jack!" he said.

Billy reached for the gun, but Jamie climbed up his back and pulled his upper arm away. I grabbed the huge weapon and pointed it at Billy's ugly face.

"She had her life, now I need mine!" Billy shouted. An evil snarl appeared on his face, daring me to pull the trigger. I could probably have gotten away with it but I hesitated, inhibited by some ancient moral code embedded in my psyche.

One uniformed cop snatched the gun from my hand as another rolled Jamie off Billy and roughly handcuffed my brother behind his back. They pulled Billy to his feet by yanking on the handcuffs, and I did a pushup to get unsteadily to my feet. Without warning, two screams erupted—Nicki and Glenda—and two more cops hustled past me. I turned to see the cops bent over Beth, who was lying beneath them, shockingly inert amidst the chaos.

Detective Rodgers stepped over Trey and Raymond, who were obediently prone on the floor, and joined me at Beth's side. Her eyes stared vacantly at the ceiling. A wound in her chest gurgled blood as her chest rose and fell spasmodically.

"It's a sucking chest wound," Rodgers said. "Cover it and put pressure on it. Call 9-1-1."

He broke away then to confront Billy. I watched as he said, "You're under arrest for the murder of Elaine Marks. If that woman dies, it will be two counts." He pointed to Beth. Horror clouded Billy's eyes as he stared at his immobile wife. He lunged toward her, but the uniformed cops restrained him. The detective read Billy his Miranda rights, but I doubt he heard a word of it as he wailed incessantly. Then the cops dragged him away. I would never see my brother again.

We heard the sirens then, but they were too late for Beth. Her chest no longer rose and fell. Her dull eyes appeared as lifeless as the button eyes on a rag doll. Poor Beth. She had finally defied her abusive husband and had paid for her defiance with her life. No, that too simply dismissed my role in her murder. I had intentionally provoked Billy, and she had trusted me to protect her. She sought shelter behind me, and I had instinctively saved my own life at the cost of hers. I had judged and punished and rewarded as though I were sitting on God's throne, and I had caused Beth's death.

Glenda must have known what I was thinking. She slid an arm through mine and, looking down at Beth, said, "She should have left him years ago. She shouldn't have been here today."

CHAPTER THIRTY-THREE

The cops took all of us to the station, where we endured hours of questioning. Detective Rodgers was particularly upset that I had made his team wait in the kitchen while I accused my brother of murdering my mother.

Glenda was upset that I hadn't shared my plan with her. "I could have been in the way of that bullet, Randle!"

Jamie was upset that Detective Rodgers had agreed to a dangerous plan that violated police procedure. "You should have turned over the evidence, and he should have conducted a proper investigation. The evidence always identifies the perpetrator." I was happy, then, that Jamie would give up her shield to become a nurse. She was far too naïve to be a good cop.

When the police released us, it was too late to drive to Florida but Brad and Katie left for their home in Atlanta. I doubted I would ever see my sister again. Trey and Raymond went to Billy's house. They would have to bury Beth before going back to Milledgeville. The rest of us spent the night at a cheap motel on the Bobby Jones Expressway. We couldn't stay at Mom's house—it was a crime scene.

In the morning, we said our goodbyes to Nicki and headed for our different Florida destinations. Jamie and I shared the driving of the Bronco. Each of us retreated into our own cocoons to replay events, forecast our futures, and battle recriminations. Billy's last words cycled over and over in my head: "She had her life, she had her life, she had her life . . ." Many young people believe that an eighty-year-old person has breathed all the air, has consumed all the government benefits, has experienced all the goodness of life in America that they are due or have a right to expect, so the eighty-year-old carcass should be thrown onto the scrap heap. Unlike Asian and Native American cultures, the Judeo-Christian culture is a morally bankrupt wasteland when it comes to end-of-life rituals. Then I thought of Beth, the sweetest and purest of us all, and I said a prayer for her. I said a prayer for myself too.

Somewhere around Lake City, while Jamie was napping, Glenda hissed, "You lied to me. You never intended to keep the money."

I knew I'd have to face her wrath somewhere along the line. I was ready with stock answers. "Albert's money wasn't ours. We got our pound of flesh from the hospital."

"You paid your family off. Why did you do that?"

"It's a Catholic tradition. In the Middle Ages, bishops and popes routinely sold absolutions, tickets to heaven. Now I have mine." I told myself for the umpteenth time that I had been correct in my judgments: Billy was a despicable clone of Joseph; Katie was a spoiled, entitled child who would need care the rest of her life; and Mom was a manipulative liar, but the only mother I would ever have.

I don't think Glenda would have agreed with that rationalization. She grunted, disgusted by my flippant attitude. "You humiliated them for your own purposes, to trap Billy like you trapped Carrie."

"Confession is good for the soul. They're all free of their secrets now."

"And what are you free from?"

It took me a minute to decide which answer to give her. The obvious answer would have been this: free of the guilt for hating my family, my childhood. The less obvious answer was more honest. When I couldn't get Joseph's attention in any natural father-son way, I had competed with him to see which of us was the better man.

"I no longer have to prove myself better than my father, because I don't have one. Never had one."

"So that's why the stunt with the watch in the graveyard?" She wasn't whispering any longer. "We don't get to choose our parents. It's the luck of the draw, and you could have done far worse. Your parents gave you the tools to be a success, and you should be thankful."

Anger came unbidden. "I didn't need tools, Glenda. I needed warmth and caring. Nurturing, dammit!"

Glenda didn't hesitate. I think she had rehearsed this conversation. "It's not your fault that you had the childhood you experienced, so it's time to get over it, Randle. Your compulsion to replace your father with some mythical ideal is just a deception to cover the fact that you've been searching for yourself."

Blood drained from my head and puddled at my feet and left me shivering as though the Florida sunshine had instantly become an Alaskan snowstorm. Glenda was right, of course, but she was also wrong. I knew where to look for myself but had used my childhood and the search for a birth father as an excuse for whom I had become. I hadn't been searching for myself; I had been running away from myself. Glenda stared at me impassively, certain she had hit the proverbial nail on the head. Contrary to the John Donne poem, we are all islands and it can never be any other way—we come into this world alone and we leave it alone. The bell doesn't toll for the dead, it tolls for the living.

Regrettably, I didn't feel free to share that dismal philosophy with Glenda. When I didn't respond, Glenda slumped in her seat and closed her eyes. The last hundred fifty miles of the drive passed in silence.

***

We dropped Jamie off at her apartment in Tampa and made our way across the causeway to St. Petersburg and then to Dolphin Beach. Our house looked abandoned. In just a week, the combination of Florida sunshine and daily thunderstorms had produced tall weeds that choked every flower bed. The outdoor lights in the back of the house were burned out. The interior smelled musty and stale. Thankfully, the security system had not been breached.

***

Over the next few weeks, we tied up our loose ends. Glenda sold her business to her assistant manager, just a transfer of the lease on the storefront and the sale of an eclectic inventory for a few thousand dollars. We hung a for sale sign on the *Wahine II* but didn't receive a single fair offer. Apparently, bloodstains and bullet holes diminish a boat's value. We couldn't afford the slip fees at the marina, so we gave the boat away for little more than salvage rights.

I also put the beach house up for sale and while my emotional attachment to the place will take some time to distill into a fond memory, I understand the importance of cutting all ties to Dolphin Beach so we can start a new life.

I made two trips to Atlanta for interviews and finally won a position as Chief Data Scientist for Global Business Services Inc. (GBS for short), an Indian-American company that performs outsourcing services for insurance companies. After I repaid the advance on my book, the publisher consented to keep it on the list and in the distribution system. GBS execs were impressed with my status as an author and overly swayed by the technology the book described. The book may sell a few copies, and I won't have to share the royalties with an avaricious agent.

Meanwhile, Glenda and I intend to move back to Atlanta immediately after our wedding. We hope to find a place in our old neighborhood in Duluth, where our married life began so many years ago. We expect it to be nostalgic and romantic. We plan to make new memories. We plan and plan and plan, like kids who naively believe they can mold their futures, kids who don't yet know that life is chaotic, unpredictable, and largely uncontrollable.

Jamie has resigned from the police force and applied for admission to several good nursing schools in the Atlanta area. As we look for a house, Jamie will look for an apartment.

On a mild, sunlit afternoon, I took all of Mom's letters to Albert and his letters to her and sat beside the pool with a cigar and a snifter of port. Glenda, worried about my obsession with all things "Mom," tempted me to skinny dip, but I ignored her. I put the letters in order so I could read them as they had been written, and the pattern quickly became clear: Albert chased and Mom backpedaled. His letters, the ones I had read in her bedroom, were ardent; hers, which I hadn't read before, were distant, cool, cautionary. The chronologically ordered letters placed the "affair" in context, and I saw my mother's indiscretions in a different light. She had not been sorely tempted to leave Joseph. She had a fling with a man she had cared about for years. In the end, she couldn't maintain the deception that he was my father and she ended the affair. She never told Albert about the paternity test. I was pleased then that his money had been spent for good purposes, and I was happy that I hadn't taken any of it.

No one ever inquired about Mom's one-hundred-fifty-thousand-dollar investment funds, stored in one of my accounts. All the living members of the family had received their payoffs, and none of them were bold enough to seek more. The money gathered dust as time dimmed our collective memories of that last fateful day in Augusta, so I decided that Glenda and I deserved to keep it. That made Glenda happy. We'll use the money to make a down payment on our new home and seed a retirement fund. How ironic that the child who was written out of the will walked away with the biggest piece of the pie.

Once we had Mom's money in our hands, I called Daniel Kaplan and offered him a new deal. If St. Thomas Aquinas Hospital would publicly announce our settlement and their remedial fixes, I would donate the fifty thousand dollars they paid me, in Mom's name, to fund further emergency room improvements. Initially, Daniel wasn't interested, but someone higher up the chain of command found the money irresistible. Their insurance company had paid me the settlement for our dispute, so the donation was found money. They accepted it, and soon St. Thomas will have the most highly automated emergency room in the county.

Trey inherited Mom's house, of course. At my suggestion, he had it bulldozed and sold the land. There is no evidence that the Church of Marks ever stood on that plot, no evidence that a troubled family was raised in that neighborhood of brotherly Christian love.

Eventually, my troubled siblings had their day in court. The police did not charge Billy with Mom's murder. Although they traced his purchases of antihistamines, they couldn't prove he had put the pills in Mom's bottles. Had he kept his cool that last day, he'd have gotten away with Mom's murder.

As it turned out, the cops didn't charge him with Beth's murder either. They charged him with voluntary manslaughter for her death and with assault with a deadly weapon against me. He'll serve five to six years in the state penitentiary. Of course, he'll never get another government job.

Katie is also in prison, and that makes it a clean sweep—all three of Joseph and Elaine's children have been convicted of crimes.

Carrie remained my last loose end in Florida. On two occasions, she floated down my inlet in her father's Boston Whaler. The first time I waived and she gave me a one-finger salute. The second time I flashed my Glock and she showed me a small chrome-plated pistol.

Chapter Thirty-four

O n our wedding day, the sun targeted Treasure Island Beach with a laser beam of intense heat and light, even at ten a.m. On the sand behind the Bilmar Beach Hotel and Sloppy Joe's restaurant, Glenda had commissioned an artist to construct statues of a bride and groom, like you would find on top of a wedding cake. Between the sand sculptures a white, flower-bedecked arch stood waiting for the blissful couple to share their vows. I stood in the shadows of the restaurant veranda, sipped a Bloody Mary, and watched as guests arrived to sit on folding chairs.

Most of the guests were Glenda's store employees and their spouses, but Jamie also arrived with her former boyfriend, Officer Riordan. Riordan had saved my leg, and probably my life, with an expertly applied tourniquet after I'd been shot on my boat. Glenda's mother, Ruth, quite active in her seventies, arrived with the minister and two of my former friends: Fred, the investigator, and Marty Weinstein, the psychiatrist. I said a silent thank you to my bride for arranging that. Thinking back on my previous wedding days, I realized that neither Katie nor Billy had attended any of my marriage ceremonies. Mom—and Joseph—had been present for my first marriage to Glenda, and Mom was sorely missed at this one.

Glenda and I had spent the night in separate rooms at the Bilmar, in homage to the ancient tradition of not seeing the bride in her gown until she walked down the aisle. Somewhere in the hotel, she awaited a signal to emerge. With everyone seated and the minister sweating under the arch, the ceremony began.

I walked down the sand aisle and shook hands with our guests, then took my place beside the minister, a woman Glenda had found online. When I turned to face the crowd, I realized we were facing East and that the morning sun beamed down from above the roof of the restaurant. I squinted but could barely see our guests and couldn't see into the shadows of the restaurant at all, so I was surprised when Glenda appeared, adorned in a white knee-length dress, arm in arm with a man. She gracefully descended the stairs from the restaurant, onto the beach, before I could identify her escort as Tony Zambrano, once my best friend and lawyer. I smiled like a little kid on Christmas as he delivered my bride to our makeshift altar. He shook my hand as I thanked him, and then Glenda and I turned north and south to face each other. She looked as radiant and happy as I'd ever seen her. In that moment, I knew we were doing the right thing.

The ceremony was short and nonreligious. Glenda had composed the vows, which contained no reference to obedience, but we both had trouble with the phrase "for richer or poorer." When I stumbled over it, the crowd snickered. When Glenda faltered, the crowd cheered. Our kiss was long and deep, giving the guests plenty of photo opportunities. Then we marched back down the aisle as everyone tossed bird seed at us.

The reception would be held at Sloppy Joe's, where we had rented the entire space. After the party, Glenda, Jamie, and I would drive to Atlanta. That was the plan.

As we entered the shadows of the restaurant, two people became visible at the top of the stairs: a tall, dark man stood to one side, and a short, voluptuous woman in a bikini stood directly in our path, her fleshy thighs spread in a confrontational pose. I recognized the man from the photos Carrie had hung in our house in place of mine: Dr. Richard Puralto.

We stopped at the bottom of the stairs and Carrie said, "Congratulations. Try and try again, right? Like the little engine that could."

I didn't respond, just stared at my ex-con ex-wife. Our guests had gathered around us now at the bottom of the restaurant stairs. No one laughed, but several people shifted uncomfortably on the sand.

Relishing her time in the spotlight, Carrie said, "I heard about your mother. Please accept my sympathies."

"Let's not make a scene," I said. "Move aside so we can pass."

"Oh, I'm not done. Am I, dear?" She looked at the tall, dark man she had conned into taking my place. Her boyfriend was still as a statue. Our guests remained silent and still as well.

At some unspoken signal, Fred and Officer Riordan pushed their way to the front. They began to ascend the stairs, but Carrie held her ground.

"Billy told me how you stole his money, just like you stole mine," Carrie said, pointing a red-tipped finger.

As though they had choreographed the scene beforehand, Fred and Riordan each grabbed one of Carrie's arms and lifted her off the floor, her feet kicking, one sandal flying down the steps at us. They carried her to the disabled ramp on the side of the veranda and gave her a shove. She didn't lose her balance entirely, but she stumbled to the bottom, to the sand beside the hotel swimming pool.

"I'll sue you. I want my money, you bastard!" she yelled at me.

A cold shiver raced up my spine and stunned my brain, the sensation you get when you drink a frozen Margarita too fast. Fortunately, we had a plan for this contingency.

The crowd urged us forward. If the boyfriend thought he could win Carrie's heart, if he thought she had a heart, he should have defended her honor at this point, should have taken a swing at Fred or Riordan. He didn't. He eased past my two centurions to join his girlfriend in disgrace.

As we ascended the stairs, Glenda picked up Carrie's sandal. When we reached the top, she hurled it at my ex-wife. Carrie dodged to the left and the missile struck Puralto in the chest, leaving a sandy imprint on his black silk shirt. "Next time bring a gun," Glenda said with a smug smile. "I'll have mine." Before Carrie could react, the crowd pushed us through the doors and into the restaurant.

Glenda and I joined Tony, Jamie, and Glenda's mother at the head table. Tony rapped a fork against his water glass to quiet the crowd and toasted us as though he had been my best man. Glenda and I took the obligatory first turn on the dance floor. Lines formed at the buffet tables. The cocktails flowed, the dance floor filled, and the noise level rose appropriately. All the while, Fred kept a lookout from a window facing the beach. Soon, he waived me over and Tony and Glenda joined us. Carrie was camped on the sand as her boyfriend stood over her, gesticulating and pointing. She yelled something at him, her teeth bared like a cornered Pit Bull. He jerked back, as though struck, then strode away purposefully, toward the condominiums where we knew he lived with his mistress.

That relationship won't last, I thought. Despite the allure of the doctor's money, Carrie won't tolerate his cowardice.

From her vantage point, Carrie had a good view of the hotel parking lot, where our getaway car waited for us. However, she'd be expecting us to leave in the old white Bronco that Fred had bought from me, not in our new crimson Acadia. Only Jamie knew our destination. Everyone else thought we were going to the Tampa airport to fly to a honeymoon resort.

We drank champagne. Glenda and I danced as though no one were watching. The celebration became boisterous.

During a band break, Tony leaned close and said, "I'll prepare a protective order against both Carrie and her doctor friend. When the beach house sells, give me your new address and I'll file the order with the court."

A pang of guilt shot through my stomach. Just as I reunited with old friends, just as I accepted favors from them, I would deceive them again. My new life would have an empty hole where their friendship should have fit, but I couldn't trust the "law" to protect us. We would never disclose our new address to Carrie via a court document.

So, I lied yet again. "Will do, Tony. We'll have to change our phone numbers as well, so notify me by email, the one we use for privileged communications, if she files a lawsuit."

After three hours of socializing, Fred brought our car around to the restaurant's front entrance, out of view of the beach, and we snuck away without saying goodbye. We wondered how long Carrie would wait for us to emerge from the party. We wondered if she'd tail the white Bronco all the way to Fred's house. We wondered if she'd keep a vigil on the inlet behind our beach house. I didn't worry about Carrie tracking us. Not only was our destination a secret but also our names.

She won't find John Randle Marks listed in any phone book. She won't find his address or phone number through any online search engine. That person no longer exists. I've changed my name legally to John (no middle name) Randle. Glenda and I are Mr. and Mrs. John Randle now. John Randle has always been my name; the name on my original birth certificate, the birth certificate that listed no father. Joseph and Elaine Marks changed my name to hide their secrets, but now the only secrets belong to us. Going forward, the people I meet can call me Jack or Randle, or Mr. Randle, or even Jackie. I know who I am.

~ The End ~

About the Author

Mike Nemeth is a retired Information Technology executive living in the Atlanta suburbs with his wife, Angie, and their rescue dog, Sophie. His previous works include the Amazon Bestselling crime thriller, *Defiled*, and groundbreaking books about college basketball—*128 Billion to 1*—and college football—*Lies, Damned Lies and Statistics*.

Morgan James
Speakers Group

We connect Morgan James published authors with live and online events and audiences who will benefit from their expertise.

Morgan James makes all of our titles available through the Library for All Charity Organization.

www.LibraryForAll.org

CPSIA information can be obtained
at www.ICGtesting.com
Printed in the USA
FSHW01n1953181018
53136FS

9 781683 506973